# The Bride Stripped Bare

Rob Bliss

## Also Available from Necro Publications:

# CUT

Dear Diary,

I am a star. I've finally found the yellow brick road to fame. I could teach anyone. As long as they are willing to die for it.

---

A bomb goes off in Buffalo, N.Y. That same day FBI agent, Daryll Peltier, receives the first of many correspondences from a serial killer calling themselves, Sam-I-Am.

The gruesome torture and murders of the killer's victims are filmed and broadcast on live television. Creating a puzzling masterpiece of blood and torture which the FBI can't unravel.

Daryll and her partner, Frank Zepano, began a hunt for the killer across the continental United States and into the Caribbean. The hunt involves cryptic messages, a strange and powerful cult, an unstoppable nano virus, the International Space Station, a trailer park psychic, a tabloid newspaper journalist, a computer hacker, the Oscars...and a body count of one victim per state.

# The Bride Stripped Bare

NECRO PUBLICATIONS
- 2019 -

FIRST EDITION TRADE PAPERBACK

THE BRIDE STRIPPED BARE © 2019 by Rob Bliss
Cover art © 2019 by Stefan Gesell

This edition 2019 © Necro Publications

ISBN: 978-1-944703-71-4
LCCN: 2019940622

Book design & typesetting:
David G. Barnett
www.fatcatgraphicdesign.com

Assistant editors:
Amanda Baird-Schmidt

Necro Publications
necropublications.com

All rights reserved. No part of this book may be reproduced or transmitted in any form or by any means, electronic or mechanical, including photocopy, recording, or any information storage and retrieval system, without permission in writing from the author, or his agent, except by a reviewer who may quote brief passages in a critical article or review to be printed in a magazine or newspaper, or electronically transmitted on radio or television.

All persons in this book are fictitious, and any resemblance that may seem to exist to actual persons living or dead is purely coincidental. This is a work of fiction.

Printed in the United States of America

10 9 8 7 6 5 4 3 2 1

*For Psycho - a Touring Iguana*

# THE BRIDE STRIPPED BARE

# PART
# - 1 -

# Chapter 1

I got an email out of the blue from my old buddy, Gord, telling me he was getting married. I hadn't heard from him for about five years, didn't think he would still have my email. We were still friends, didn't hate each other, just drifted apart. I had finished my Masters and became an English professor for a small college no one had ever heard of, and which paid shit. But it was better than working at a real job.

Gord was blue collar, an auto mechanic, drank a two-four every weekend and a six-pack every night after work. I drank wine and sometimes liked it. He and I were poles apart, but that wouldn't come between us. Friends were friends, no matter how far apart they were in character.

Or where they lived, for that matter. Gord had moved across the country to Washington State. Said he loved the redwoods, the Douglas Firs, that he had started hiking and camping. Back and forth emails told me how much he had changed.

And, goddamn, he was getting married! Thought he always liked girls too much to settle for just one. One email said the bride-to-be was amazing, gorgeous, great in bed, "fucking rich, too, buddy," and the two of them had too many things in common to count. He attached a few pictures of them somewhere tropical. Laughing, swimming, sitting by the pool, standing arm in arm on a beach, sunset behind them.

# THE BRIDE STRIPPED BARE

Tourist photos, romantic and sappy. Had they already gone on their honeymoon? I wondered.

She *was* hot, I'll give him that. She looked like a 1920s flapper with black hair cut into a bob, with a skinny body, hint of ribs, even a string of small pearls wrapped three times around her slender neck, hanging down between her ample breasts. D cup, minimum. She must've been a bit of a freak. Who wears pearls with a bikini? A Wicked Weasel at that. Heavenly camel toe and not a trace of razor burn.

Gord was sending this to me to make me jealous. And I was. Lucky bastard. I had the pick of some of the ugliest women, students and teachers, at a third-rate college. The kind losers went out with…like me.

I'll admit, I *was* jealous of Gord's life in more ways than one. I was an egghead who had spent his life reading boring books, giving boring lectures, talking to boring people, having boring sex. Gord made more money than me, didn't take his job home, relaxed on weekends instead of marking papers, went to bars, and slept with women who had never heard of Franz Kafka. I slept with women who looked like Franz Kafka.

I was happy for Gord to be getting married, and happy for myself to go on vacation, away from my East Coast, buttoned-down, cardigan life. I couldn't wait to get on a plane to see my old best friend and his new bride-to-be.

They looked so happy in the photographs.

Her name was Venus Baer.

# Chapter 2

He paid for my flight—or, he said, his fiancée did. Venus had money, he repeated—her own and that of her family. Old money, but the Baer family weren't blue bloods. A large family that went back, possibly, to the Mayflower. Gord hadn't met them all, doubted he ever would, since they were spread far and wide. They had lived in the same area of the Northwest, close to the Canadian border, for generations. Some had crossed the border and were now Canadian.

He reserved a flight for me as soon as I said I had booked vacation time, then sent me another email confirming my flight details. Said I could stay at his place to save on a hotel. He picked me up at the airport in his pickup truck and I could easily tell that time had taken its toll on him. Less hair, bit more of a waistline, a few wrinkles. To be honest, I wondered what a gorgeous girl like Venus was doing with him. It wasn't his paycheck she was after if she was richer than him. Then I stopped my silent trashing of my friend, and we caught up on old times.

We headed to his one-bedroom apartment, where I would be sleeping on the couch. I considered getting a motel. At least he was clean, and it didn't look like I would stick to anything; he confessed that he had started cleaning—and bathing—more often since he had met Venus. He threw out old clothing that had holes in it instead of waiting until the holes expanded to reveal too much skin. His bathroom was

# THE BRIDE STRIPPED BARE

spotless, and I didn't mind having a shower in it. I thought to myself: God, what the hell's my problem? Am I glad to see Gord or not? Was *I* such a neat freak? Why was I criticizing him so much in my head?

I sat on the couch and cracked open the first Pabst Blue Ribbon (Gord never changed his beer brand after all these years), and when the alcohol hit me, I realized why I was being such an anal-retentive dick.

The jealousy rearing its head again. Gord had it all. He was successful, doing what he loved, and now he had an incredible girl to marry him; I did a job I hated, loved no one I fucked, felt as though I had made all the wrong decisions, and Gord had made all the right ones. The beer was relaxing me, so I decided not to be such a snobbish prick, and relaxed. I congratulated Gord on all his success and his love life.

He told me how they met.

"You know how much I've always loved horror shit, right? Movies, books, comics—you name it. That wasn't just when we were kids. Hell, I still re-read all my Brian Lumley and Clive Barker, even my Anne Rice. I never could get into the smarter stuff you liked." He said 'smarter,' it seemed, instead of 'boring.' "But remember that time we had a zombie movie marathon in my basement? Me, you, Josh and Rick...what'd we watch, like, five zombie movies in a row? And that was in the '80s. I didn't know they made that many back then."

We chatted about all the movies we had rented—when you still could *rent* movies—which seemed to correspond to Gord's personality phases. When he had a vampire phase, we watched every vampire movie we could get our hands on. *The Lost Boys* and *After Dark* being two we watched again and again.

Gord even became a Goth for a year or two. Had a black cape, wore black eyeliner and lipstick. I could barely look at him without laughing. I knew why he was doing it. He was going to some school to

# ROB BLISS

upgrade his high school diploma in the hopes of getting into college. Which he did, taking auto mechanics. At this school, he met a cute Goth girl with big tits. Very big. So he changed his appearance for her, went to Goth nightclubs, even took photos of himself and the girlfriend (what was her name again?) which he showed to me. Well, he showed me the ones where they both still had their clothes on. I didn't want to see my friend's dick as he growled at the camera with bloody plastic fangs in his mouth.

He had many phases, to put it mildly—Goth, prep, punk, metalhead—but he gave up each one when some girl broke his heart. All phases were centered around a girl.

Hell, I couldn't blame him. All guys did crazy shit for pussy.

I watched him go from phase to phase just as I had watched all those movies with him. It was entertainment to me, which wouldn't jeopardize our friendship. It never did. Still, I didn't read any of the novels he had on his bookshelf; I tried, but I just couldn't take seriously the world of vampires, werewolves, shape-shifters, zombies, and everything in between. There was no way in hell I could read 300 pages or more about that shit without wanting to toss the book out the window.

I wanted to be a serious writer, so I felt I needed to read serious literature. Essentially, a snob.

I guess that was why it came as a big surprise to Gord when I told him, in one of my emails, that I had read all five beginning books of Lumley's *Necroscope* series and had finished Clive Barker's *Weaveworld* and his *Books of Blood*. And I confessed that I could read H. P. Lovecraft every day for the rest of my life.

Gord howled and laughed when I reminded him of the email. We clanked bottles in celebration.

"You're changing into me!" he laughed, then asked, "Explain this email—I thought it was a typo or something…what the hell made you come over to the dark side?"

# THE BRIDE STRIPPED BARE

I explained. The 'literature' I had been trying to write wasn't getting published. That's why I had to get a job as a teacher. My career as a full-time writer wasn't happening. So I fell back on the age-old rule: if something isn't working, change it. I still wanted to write, I just had to change the *type* of writing I would do.

I recalled his library of horror from when we were in our teens and twenties, so I went to the library and started reading the novels Gord had loved, and which I had intentionally ignored.

We toasted again, and he showed me his expanded horror collection. Battered copies of writers I had only discovered in the last year. He asked me if I had written anything yet, he'd love to read it.

"Just a few stories, published online," I said, suddenly shy. "But I've got a few ideas for novels. Teaching takes up too much time."

"Well, hell!" he smacked my arm. "Get writing! I want an autographed copy of your first book."

His excitement—and the fact that his horror obsession hadn't changed—fueled me on. I felt like grabbing a pen and some paper and start scribbling a horror novel right there. The beer hit me harder than I thought. He slapped a hand around my shoulders, and I felt time reverse—like we were seventeen again.

"Let's watch 'Evil Dead'!" I yelled, my beer frothing over as I speared my arms to the ceiling.

He laughed and tried to reign me in. I had completely forgotten where I was and why I was there.

Gord was getting married. He had grown up, and I was, once again, trying to deny my age, wanting to go back to our collective youth. He must've seen the sorrow in my changed disposition, so like a good friend, he cheered me up.

"Wanna see some pictures of her?"

"I saw the ones you attached to the email," I said, half-slurring my words.

# ROB BLISS

He winked. "That was nothing."

Firing up his laptop, we sat down, guzzled beer, and he opened a folder of pictures of him and Venus.

Naked Venus.

Porn shots. Shots of her sucking his dick (was he waiting all these years to show me a picture of his dick?), of getting fucked in every position, of her posing like a porn star. One of them on a beach, like in the email.

"Dude, she's hot!" I said before a small belch escaped. "You don't mind showing her to me naked?"

"Fuck no—I'm bragging! I get to fuck *this*!"

I raised my beer. "Yes, you do. Where's this beach?"

He smacked himself on the forehead and barked out a laugh. "Holy fuck me—I forgot to tell you. All the horror shit. Yeah, I went to a horror convention in Los Angeles. That's where Venus and I met. It was a four-day convention, so I got a motel. Met her on the first day, we hit it off, went for dinner and drinks that night. I told her everything. I mean *everything*. I knew it was a cliché, but I seriously bared my soul to her. She did the same to me. We have so fucking much in common, it's freaky. Way more than you and I ever had, no offense. I never met a woman who was like my twin. So, we fucked like psycho rabbits that night—the shit she does in the bedroom! Goddamn! Everything—she does *everything*! And a few things more. I swear, we're *perfect* together, it's eerie."

I was in awe, still jealous, wished I could meet *my* female twin. I sat behind the laptop as Gord went to answer a knock on the door. Didn't even realize, in my increasing drunken stupor, that I was gazing at a photo of Venus with her legs spread wide, pouring what looked like a margarita—with umbrella and pineapple wedge—down between her naked breasts, a cherry held between her teeth. My mind instead focused on my self-pity.

# THE BRIDE STRIPPED BARE

That is, until the girl in the photo came to life. Standing on the other side of the laptop, with clothes on, smirking down at me from between her perfect breasts, was Venus.

Her hair was dyed white—platinum blonde actually, with a metallic sheen to it, somehow—ruby lips, and a black mole at the corner of her mouth. She wore a low-cut tight t-shirt on which a reproduction of The Dead Kennedy's album "Give Me Convenience or Give Me Death" was warped by the curve of her breasts.

Tight jeans rode low on her hips, two lacy strings of her pink thong rose out of the denim and rested on her hipbones. Camel toe, again. I was easily mesmerized by a stunning girl, especially when drunk and stupid.

Venus saw my tranced gaze as it roved up and down her body and giggled to herself and to Gord. His arm was around her hip. Venus snapped me out of my libidinous hypnotism by leaning down and kissing my forehead.

"He's cute," she told Gord.

She smelled like cinnamon candy hearts. Gord smacked her ass and pulled her down to sit on his lap beside me on the couch. His hands came up from either side of Venus' ribcage and tucked under her breasts. Venus moaned and arched her neck back as Gord kneaded her tits. He peered at me and winked.

"She likes you, buddy—you're in."

I crossed my legs, feeling an erection growing that I couldn't keep down. I slapped the laptop closed. "In what?" I asked.

"The club," Gord said, planting a kiss on Venus' neck under her ear. "The Venus Club."

She giggled as she looked at me, with the seductive gaze of a vamp. She spread her legs open and scratched red fingernails up the inside of her thighs.

"I hear you like horror. Only bad boys like horror. And bad girls, of course." She licked the tip of her tongue along the upper row of her perfect teeth, staring deep into my eyes. "You wanna be in my club, Chris?" she asked.

I chuckled uncomfortably, took a swig of beer, tried to remain nonchalant. "I dunno. What do I gotta do?"

She moaned and pressed back hard against Gord, who pressed his hands harder against her breasts.

"Worship me," she cooed, her throat expanding, a red flush forming on her cheeks. I was sure I was hallucinating. My libido fogging my vision, and my mind. "Worship me, just like my Gordy does."

Venus turned her head and played tongue-tag with Gord for a few seconds. I felt like a third wheel. It's always kind of hot, but also kind of uncomfortable, when your buddy makes out with his girl right in front of you. Makes you wish you had a girl too. He had done it before with old girlfriends; I may have done it too, when he had nobody.

I took a swig, slapped my knee, and stood while they weren't looking. Perused Gord's stacks of DVDs and books. Hoped that walking around—with my back to them both—would help my erection go down. Tried to block out the smacking lips of the lovers on the couch.

Gord liked the same movies, as always. Lots of horror, grindhouse, blaxploitation, and Kung Fu flicks from the Seventies and Eighties. I stared at the titles, many of them I knew well, and my eyes blurred as I realized that I didn't like my friend's fiancée.

Sure, I liked her body, but not so much her personality. The Venus Club? *Worship me*? What the hell were they talking about? Part of me said they were just being a cutesy, annoying couple who still adored each other since they hadn't known each other for that long. And that's what the other part of me picked up on. Gord had done this before—changed his life for a girl. And he was doing it again, it looked like.

So what? I had learned back when he was a Goth, that if I told him what I really thought, he'd hate me. Maybe he gets married, it lasts six months, he calls me up drunk and asks if he can come out East to visit

# THE BRIDE STRIPPED BARE

and tells me how she broke his heart. Maybe that'll happen, but I sure as hell wasn't going to join The Venus Club.

I had been suckered in by girls like that too, but not as bad as Gord had.

"Look—he's feeling shy," Gord said to my back.

I turned around—my erection gone—and saw Venus lying flat along the sofa, her legs across Gord's lap. He slipped out from under her and strolled to me.

"We're not watching any movies, buddy. We're getting seriously pissed drunk at my bachelor party."

# Chapter 3

Venus left and I headed out with Gord since he had a few things to do in preparation for his wedding. We drove around the town where he now lived, popping into stores, everyone wishing him congratulations. A *very* small town, lots of rednecks and people who looked as they had been in one place too long, never straying far from home. Inbreeders? Was that the word I was looking for?

Back in his truck, I asked, "Do you know *everybody* in town?"

"Pretty much," he laughed. "Small towns are all just one big family. You'll see them all again tonight. The bachelor party might be bigger than the wedding."

"Are your folks in town yet? Your brother and sister? I haven't seen them in years."

"Nah, they're coming last minute. Venus is putting them up at her place with her folks. They got a big mansion. Family with family, that sort of thing. You're not family, so you'll have to stay with me. Took time for my brother and sister to book vacations from their jobs. I guess my quick engagement took everybody by surprise."

"It did to me, too," I said as we passed beyond the town sign, 'Red Wood,' then down a rural highway. "I was surprised you still had my email."

"Hell, I wouldn't forget my best bud. You and me are more brothers than me and my brother. Hate that fucker, but I like you."

# THE BRIDE STRIPPED BARE

His brother, Kevin, was ten years older than him, and his sister, Elizabeth, was five years younger than Gord. I had a huge crush on Elizabeth and was always kind of terrified of Kevin. He was big—big-boned, a bit chunky—didn't look anything like Gord. Looked more like David Berkowitz. Used to be a bouncer at a few shitty bars and strip clubs where we used to live when we were teens. Gord said that Kevin was still doing the same kind of work. He had been diagnosed bi-polar, manic-depressive, possibly even a little touch of schizophrenia when he was a kid. He had been on a ton of medication since puberty. Kevin sometimes talked slower than most people, and I'd catch him staring at nothing for a long time.

I'm glad I had never gotten on his bad side when I was a kid. He was the kind of guy who seemed like he could kill you without thinking—literally kill, and do hard time, and be happy in jail as long as he had a good supply of cigarettes.

Elizabeth was the opposite. Petite, not an ounce of fat, cute as a button, incredibly blue eyes, and a band of freckles across her nose. Dark brown hair which she eventually dyed blonde when she was about sixteen, and kept it dyed. She could put you in your place with a glare and a few choice words, but she didn't go out of her way to pick a fight.

She broke my heart by not liking me as much as I liked her. And I was older. She was too young. For a year, she drank like an alcoholic—around the time she first dyed her hair. But after that she found a guy—blue collar, tool and die—whom she liked enough to get married to, even though the family didn't see anything special about him. Ugly, ten years older, but he had a steady job. They tried to have kids, but it didn't work out. I never knew all of the details, but she may have been barren. His name was Mike, if I remember correctly, and Gord hated him. Last I heard, Elizabeth and Mike split up, and she was single again. Gord confirmed their separation as we drove out of the town and into the countryside.

Gord's mom and dad, Don and Pam, were in their late sixties, long retired, happy that their middle child was getting married and would hopefully be providing grandkids.

"I don't know," Gord said. "We'll see about that. I've never been big on kids, but maybe one or two for Venus. She wants them."

I watched the forests and the farm fields pass by, thinking about what he'd said. He'd have kids—for *her*. Venus controlled him absolutely, called the shots. Gord had always hated the idea of having kids—with anyone, no matter how hot she was, or how much she controlled him—so he had really changed his tune with Venus.

I said nothing and watched the scenery. We left the highway and went down back roads, from asphalt to gravel to dirt. Trees hedged in the road, the forest thick and dark, even in the afternoon. Crumbling farm houses and ramshackle log cabins, the occasional truck on blocks tucked back into the trees, driveways of dirt and mud.

The truck bounced along a rutted dirt road that wound into forest for miles, lakes and streams and marshes popping up on either side, nature wild with little evidence of human beings. Though once I saw a gutted truck from the 1940s sitting across a stream, water flowing through its busted windows. I wondered who had driven it into the bush, tried to cross the stream, and gave up. Abandoned it to time and the wilderness.

We drove for a long time, bouncing in our seats, having to slow down for some of the bigger ruts and potholes. Eventually, we arrived at a house made imperfectly of boards nailed together, opaque plastic sheets for windows, a weed-penetrated porch stretching around three sides of the house. The lawn—if you could call it that—was just churned up mud and grass, tree branches fallen and left to lie, and covered with battered and broken cars and trucks, two snowmobiles and an ATV, even an old farm plow, now an antique, half-sunken into the soil.

Gord pulled up and we got out. An incredible silence surrounded us, felt like cotton stuffed into my ears. I followed Gord up to the broken

# THE BRIDE STRIPPED BARE

steps of the porch and saw that some of the vehicles were riddled with bullet holes. I swallowed a lump.

Gord opened a door covered with plastic sheet and called before he stepped inside.

"Paco? It's me, Gord."

He waited for a response, not stepping further into the house. I peered around his shoulder but could see nothing but a mass of junk. Then I felt cold steel at the base of my skull. I froze, heart hammering, had to pee. My voice croaked out, "Gord?"

He turned around to see what was behind me.

"Paco, hey—it's okay, he's with me."

"I don't like strangers in my forest," a voice with a Spanish accent said close to my back. My hands had instinctively raised in the air, began to shake. I didn't dare move until, at least, the gun barrels lifted off the back of my neck. I watched Gord to see his facial expressions—like looking in a mirror to see if I was about to die without being able to look directly at my killer.

"I know, man, but it's cool," Gord said, looking over my head. "He's my best man. You're not going to ruin my wedding, are you? Venus will be so pissed; she won't dance the lambada with you."

A chuckle sounded behind me, and the steel left my skin. Gord saw the fear in my eyes. I heard steps squeak rotted boards behind me.

"It's okay," Gord said to me, "you can turn around."

Hands still raised, I turned slowly on a pivot, both feet still balanced on the porch stair, to look at the man who had wanted to kill me.

A tattoo of a rooster covered his left jugular and a flying serpent covered the right pulsing vein. Black hair, probably cut by himself with rusty scissors, a thick moustache stained yellow by tobacco, a tan face. His big belly half-hung out of his stained and ripped Harley Davidson t-shirt, jeans spattered with holes and grease stains. He held the double-barrel shotgun against his shoulder like a soldier about to march.

"Hi," I said through barely-moving lips. "I'm Chris."

"Don't talk to me—*ever*—you hear me?" were Paco's first words to me. I expected something a little more civil, but he had the gun, so he could say anything he wanted. "You fuck with me—I don't care if you're Gord's best man—I'll blow your balls off, rip out your eyes, and switch them. Got it?"

I barely nodded; my tongue made of sandpaper. "Got it."

Paco looked over my head at Gord. "Why'd you bring him here? Now he knows where I live."

I listened to Gord's voice while watching Paco's face to see if he was about to change his mind about killing me.

"Venus gives him the okay."

I thought that was odd. Venus knew Paco? Paco would obey the word of Venus?

"Yeah, well, she didn't tell me this *cabrón* was okay," Paco hissed.

Gord tried to calm the man with the shotgun. "Paco, dude, she's about to get married. You know girls. She'll spend days picking out the right nail polish—never mind styling her hair, finding the right shoes, and then the wedding dress. She's a little busy. Can we do this or not?"

Paco looked at me, lowered the gun barrels to angle at my eyes, glared at me with his lips twitching under his moustache.

"He stays here."

"No, he comes in," Gord replied.

"*In* my fucking house? He's got eyes to see."

"He's cool. I told you…what he sees, smells, hears—he forgets and doesn't *ever* tell. Right, Chris?"

I felt Gord's hand on my shoulder but kept my eyes on Paco and his gun. "I can stay here, I don't mind."

The gun barrels were two inches from my chin. "That's not the right answer, *bendejo!*"

# THE BRIDE STRIPPED BARE

"Paco—don't worry about him!" Gord came to my defense. "I can vouch for him and Venus can vouch for him. She said he comes in. He's not fucking up anything. Want me to call her?"

"No reception out here in the Nowhere," Paco said. "You know that. I don't exist, right?"

A silence held, and I tried not to show how much I was shaking inside. I felt as frozen as the Tinman in Oz, not daring to move, watching Paco until he lowered the gun and stepped away.

"I'll meet you inside," Paco said as he kept his eyes on me and walked backwards toward the corner of the house.

"Is the shit off?" Gord called before Paco rounded the corner.

"Gimme five minutes."

He disappeared around the side of the house, and I slowly lowered my hands. Heard Gord chuckle as I turned around.

"Did you piss yourself?"

"Not sure," I said, my voice cracking. I felt numb from the neck down.

"Sorry. I guess I should've warned you, my bad. He's just got to turn off a few…let's say, security devices, before we can go in. Or we won't be going very far."

"How do you know him?" I asked in a whisper, glancing through the screen door, afraid that Paco would somehow overhear and find an insult where there was none.

"Venus," he said, looking at me with hard eyes, a strange glint in them. One-word answer: his eyes told me not to ask for more details.

I didn't. My legs were still rubbery, felt as though I was standing on a plank about to drop into a sea of sharks. Looked around at the property, the mess of machinery, but I didn't want to look around too much. Paco obviously didn't like people to see—or to remember what they saw—while over for a friendly visit.

"Okay," a voice called from within the house.

"We're clear," Gord said, pulling open the battered and torn screen door.

I followed closely, didn't want to lag too far behind—might seem suspicious. I didn't *obviously* look around, but it was hard not to see what Paco's house contained.

A lot of garbage, metal and plastic, bags of dried food and camping gear, which made me think he was a survivalist. So deep into the boonies, I wouldn't put it passed him. He had tools of every kind, for automotive, carpentry and electrical—a jack of all trades with his toolbox spread across the floor and piled on the furniture. Gord and I had to step carefully over the junk to get through the room. Paco waited for us in the doorway of the next room, shotgun still in his hands, but pointed up, leaning against one shoulder.

"Watch where you're going—don't break anything—you'll pay for it with your blood, fucker."

Paco was a great tour guide. I didn't want to touch anything, not because he commanded me not to, but because it was all filth. But I made sure to keep away any look of disgust from my face. And watched my step.

The next room was, apparently, the kitchen. Dishes and glasses, food-encrusted pots and pans piled over all counters, cans and jars and boxes of food sometimes inside doorless cupboards, sometimes left where they were last touched, cockroaches skittering away. But at least there was enough of a cleared space across the floor so that Gord and I could follow our host down a flight of wooden, creaking steps to a poorly-lit basement.

This was my vacation?

Bulbs on wires lit our way. It smelled of mildew and some kind of animal shit. The air was cold. As we reached the bottom of the stairs, I could smell turpentine and windshield-washer fluid, gasoline and oil, and other acidic smells which I couldn't place.

We passed a closed door papered with pages ripped from 1970s porn magazines. Other doors were closed, some open but too dark to

# THE BRIDE STRIPPED BARE

see what was inside (I consciously didn't take a good look); and still other doors which were closed, but with holes the size of boots kicked through and the spray of shotgun pellets peppering them.

Paco liked to have a lot of fun in his basement.

We wandered through a bit of a warren, heading down another short flight of concrete steps, to get to the best-looking room in the house.

All concrete, like a bomb shelter, but missing were the food and supplies, seemingly kept upstairs. This room was organized, with things in their places on the walls and floor, yellow paint outlining each object or groups of objects.

And tons of guns. Rocket launchers, grenades, smoke grenades, machetes, trip mines, boxes labelled "C4", machine guns sitting on the floor on tripods, and a hundred other weapons I couldn't name.

Paco stopped the tour, glanced at Gord, but stared at me.

"Now you see this," his moustache twitched to me, "now you don't. *Comprendé?*"

I nodded and swallowed, forcing myself not to look anymore at what the room contained in all of its corners, even strapped to the ceiling. "I see nothing," I choked out.

The room was about the size, length and height, of two handball courts. The three of us walked in a straight line to a small alcove at one end. Turned a short corner and came to a steel door. With a punch pad.

"Don't fucking look at me," Paco said, his usually polite self.

I looked away as he punched in a code and the steel door opened. *James fucking Bond*, I thought. Paco took his survivalism very seriously. We stepped through the door, which led to a flight of steel mesh stairs. Paco clicked a switch on the wall and a wire of strung lights pinned to the ceiling came on. On either side of us were stone walls with bore marks gouged deep into the rock. Were we inside a mountain? The staircase went down about thirty feet, and just off to the left at the bottom were shipping pallets wrapped in plastic stacked three high and four deep, each pallet about ten feet tall.

Stacked on the pallets were sandbags. What looked like sandbags, anyway.

Until Paco and Gord approached the closest pallet for a better inspection.

"Don't fucking move from there," Paco told me.

I didn't move and used only my eyes to watch what they did.

Paco pulled out a switchblade and made a slit in the plastic wrap. Pulled out a sandbag, stuck the knife into it, lifted the blade up to Gord's nose.

Gord snorted some of whatever was on the knife. Then Paco snorted the remainder.

I gazed up and across the towering pallets. Thought: goddamn, that's a lot of cocaine. Next thought: I didn't know Gord did coke. A lot of thoughts went through my head as I stood like a statue and watched my best friend and his asshole buddy enjoy the quality of the drug.

Then Gord said, "Chris, you gotta try this, it's too damn good!"

I found my voice enough to say, "No, thanks, I'm fine."

Paco, of course, glared at me and tightened his grip on the gun. "I don't trust no one who doesn't do what everybody's doing. The man told you to get over here."

The gun waved me over. Gord held the switchblade with a mound of powder on the tip about the circumferance of a penny. I stared at it, looked at Gord's bobbing head and wide smile, avoided Paco's face completely, though I felt the barrels close to my ear.

Leaned in, pressed one nostril closed, snorted. An electric bullet shot up my nose and shattered against my brain. I backed away and sniffed repeatedly, squeezed my nostrils a few times, blinked like a blind toad, and shook the quake out of my head.

# THE BRIDE STRIPPED BARE

The guys laughed as they watched my struggle, then had themselves a bit more of a switchblade tip each. Paco put the knife in his pocket and started lugging down sandbags, stacking them onto Gord's outstretched arms.

"Hey, coke boy," Paco called. "You don't get the prize without working for it. Get back here."

He loaded up my arms too, then took a couple bags himself—what little he could carry with a grasp still on the gun. We all formed a line, heading back through the cave tunnel toward the stairs. But Gord stopped before the stairs, took a right, and vanished into a dark alcove. I stopped, not knowing where to go, Paco behind me.

"Hang on," Gord's voice echoed back. "Where's the fucking light, Paco?"

"You're too fucking coked up—it's right over your head, reach up."

A bulb clicked on. Gord stood on the base of a small wooden elevator that sat in a shaft of stone. A control panel of buttons hung from a cable over the frame of the elevator, linked to a small grey electrical box.

The bulb dangled from a wire stretched across the open top frame of the elevator, dangling and swaying. Gord tucked his bags of coke into a corner of the elevator, stacking them neatly, then stepped out.

"Fill 'er up, buddy," he said, slapping me on the back.

I lined my bags next to his, and stepped out, following him back to the cavern. I wanted to ask a thousand questions, but not while on Paco's property. So I kept quiet and followed Gord's lead. Once the elevator was filled, Paco stayed below to work the buttons while Gord and I went back up to the main house, and outside. Gord was speed-walking. I followed closely as we headed behind the house to an outhouse tucked a little ways into the trees. The shithouse's door was boarded shut. With two hands, Gord heaved and tipped it over onto its back, the base of the entire outhouse on hinges, to reveal the mouth of the stone shaft beneath.

"Okay, let 'er up," Gord called, voice echoing down to Paco.

Once the elevator rose to ground level, Gord and I carried all of the bags in several trips from the outhouse, traversing the junkyard lawn, and stacked the bags into the back of his truck. He took out a folded tarp first and set it aside.

"So, Gordy…" I began to say.

"Not yet. Okay? Wait until we're on the road."

I shut up and we kept filling the truck. Paco never came up from underground. Once the elevator was empty, Gord called down the shaft, and we returned to the cave to meet the elevator below. We filled it up again. Continued doing this until Gord's truck was full. Paco rose up with the elevator on the last trip. Gord slammed the tailgate closed and I helped him tie the tarp across the bed.

Gord said to Paco, "Thank you, my friend. I'll see you at the wedding. Wear a tux."

Paco, gun still in hand, said, "Fuck your tux."

They did a secret handshake of some kind. I stood still, not daring to put out my hand, but thinking that if I didn't, that too would offend Paco.

His eyes bulged at me. "Well, get in the fucking truck and piss off, asshole."

Great guy, that Paco.

I stepped up into the passenger seat and tightened my seat belt. Looking nowhere, my face taut until we were bouncing down the rutted road, then off it to smooth, level dirt.

"So, Gord…" I repeated.

He laughed. "Remember, you didn't see nothing."

"Okay." I glanced over my shoulder through the back windshield, the tarp rippling in the wind, dust smoking behind the truck. "So…you like coke, hunh?"

Gord laughed, punched my arm. "Dude, this is my wedding. The greatest party of my life. No way in hell I'm going to be sober for it.

# THE BRIDE STRIPPED BARE

Nobody else is either. Everybody's getting stoned. That means you too. How're you feeling, buddy?"

I noticed that I had a hand gripped on the door handle. "I feel pretty fucked up."

"You ever done coke?"

"Uh, yeah, once in my second year of college," I admitted. "Guy I knew had some. But it was just a thin line. Not a fucking switchblade." I started licking my gums compulsively, my entire mouth feeling like rubber. Gord laughed.

"You're my best man. I will not let you have a shitty time! No watching movies. We *are* the movie, motherfucker!"

I was jittery and paranoid for the whole ride back, my nose felt thick, and I was twitchy as hell. Then absolute panic hit.

"Fuck, Gord—we got a truck full of coke! What if we get stopped?"

He blew a raspberry. "Don't worry about it. We're in the boonies. I've got connections everywhere. It's good to know—and definitely to be marrying—Venus. I told you, buddy, she doesn't just rock my world—she's a fucking earthquake! A tsunami! No one fucks with her or anyone who knows her. Hell, if some hick cop I don't know tries to stop me, I'll either throw him a bag of coke and invite him to the party…or I'll blow his fucking head off!"

He reached under his seat and pulled out a .357 Magnum. His window was rolled down, so he shot a thin tree and blew its trunk half away.

Then he raised the barrel pointed up and blew a hole in his truck roof.

I screamed, ducked, covered my head, and convulsed in my seat. Realized that it was not a good idea to be in a truck with a coked-up driver with a massive gun in hand, laughing like the devil at nothing.

"It's okay, Venus'll buy me another one!"

# Chapter 4

Incredibly, we made it safely back to Gord's apartment, parked the truck in his parking space at the back of the building, barely hidden from neighbors. We got out of the truck and my head was twisting in every direction, paranoid and coked up.

"Uh, Gord…is the, uh…" I muttered, pointing at the tarp.

"Oh yeah, thanks, almost forgot." Gord dipped a hand under the tarp, pulled out a bag, held it like a football.

"Uh…no, I meant, is it safe here?" I asked, eyes flicking across every window I could see, looking for eyes looking back at us.

"Oh yeah, it's fine, no one will take it. You want to unload it, 'cuz I don't. We'll have people from the wedding do that."

I followed him into the apartment, still trying to fathom how no one would steal even one sandbag from the truck. Was a small town really that trustworthy?

He dropped the coke bag onto his coffee table.

"Help yourself. Got plenty more where that came from, as you saw," he laughed, heading into the kitchen.

I stared at the sandbag. My mind spun, thinking a thousand paranoid thoughts. I kept rubbing my face and scratching my neck and didn't realize I was doing it.

Gord came back in with a tall bottle of Jack Daniels and two glasses.

# THE BRIDE STRIPPED BARE

"Drink," he said as he sat on the sofa and poured. "I don't want you sober or not stoned the whole time you're here. Got it?"

I couldn't sit down. Gulped the Jack where I stood to swish out my numb mouth, barely feeling the burn. Then I started to pace.

"Shit, Gord, what about your parents?"

"What about them? If they wanna get high, that's cool."

"No, I mean...I'm coked up. So are you. And I think it's obvious."

He laughed and patted the sofa cushion beside him. I sat, hands squeezing my empty glass. Gord scooted closer to me on the couch, put a tight arm around my shoulders, said with mock seriousness. "Shit, you're right. What will mommy and daddy think? Maybe I should put some coke in dad's Harvey Wallbanger and in mom's Singapore Sling at the reception."

"I'm serious. Are you gonna be stoned during the ceremony?"

"I better be."

"What about Venus?"

"She better be, too. Hell, the priest better be, or we'll get one who knows how to party."

He took his arm from around me, so I stood and kept pacing, glancing out windows, trying to see the truck, waiting for a ton of cop cars to pull up.

"Stop goddamn worrying about everything, Chris. You're being a pussy. No offense, but I think that college has shrivelled up your balls. I'm gonna help you grow a pair over the next few days. You're gonna be a dangerous motherfucker, baby! We all are!"

He howled, then brought out two large pieces of mirror and a pack of razor blades from a drawer in the coffee table. Opened the sandbag and started portioning out thick lines for both of us on each mirror.

"Oh, fuck no, man," I sputtered. "I'm already gone. I'm gonna O.D. if I keep going."

"Oh shit, right, you're a newbie. Let me get you something."

He did a quick line, then stomped into his bedroom. Came back with a large oval black pill, something a horse would chew.

"Pop it in, let Jack wash it down. It'll help you keep up."

"What is it?"

Gord refilled my drink. "It's a drug condom. It'll keep you safe while you get fucked. Trust me."

I trusted him after staring at the pill for about two minutes. Put it on the back of my tongue, washed it down, felt it slither down my throat then sit like lead in my stomach. Then I felt almost sober. The effect of the coke had almost washed away.

"Do more coke," he instructed.

For some reason, I did. I wanted to. Bigger and bigger lines, cutting them myself. Felt a buzz each time, but not as much as I should have felt. My head felt clear. I could concentrate and focus, was calm, my hands steady, and my mouth felt normal.

"I think it's working," I said.

"Good for what ails you, son. God, what time is it? Fuck. I think we're gonna be late for my bachelor party."

"Where is it? A strip club or something?"

He laughed and slapped my back. "Or something." He stood and searched around for his cell phone, found it under a couch cushion. I snorted more coke and felt alert and happy. Felt alive. "Shit," he said, "had it on vibrate." Pacing, he checked through his text messages, then made a call. Said into the phone, "Hey, fucker, I had it on vibrate. We're here, me and Chris. Chris. My best man. Yeah, he's cool—his face is in the snow right now and he's got a Black Betty bouncing in his belly. Hell yeah! You picking us up? Okay, get here when you get here." He dropped back onto the couch, put the cell face-up on the coffee table, and cut another thick line.

"Where're we going?" I asked, waiting for him to fill his nose.

# THE BRIDE STRIPPED BARE

He squeezed his nostrils a few times and sniffed compulsively. "The brother of the bride is coming to get us. Poppy. He's fucking awesome, you're gonna love him, dude. We are gonna have a fucking blast!"

I looked at the split-open sandbag. "Do we bring this?"

He howled out a laugh, looking at my face, tears breaking from his eyes. Grabbed my head and shook it. "You're getting into it, ain't ya? Hot damn—atta boy! Have some more. Don't worry, Poppy's catering tonight's party. Our stash is for the wedding."

"Where's it going to be?"

"Venus' place, the big-ass mansion."

I glanced around at his apartment. "Why do you live here—no offense—when your fiancée lives in a mansion?"

"Her idea, a family tradition or something. We can't live together until we're hitched. Hell, I've spent half of my life in shithole apartments. If this is the last one I'm ever in before I move into a mansion, I'll keep with my bride's traditions, no problem."

All of the other questions I once thought to ask were now gone. I could only think about the coke and the party coming up. Nothing else was important. I wondered for a second why anything other than coke and partying was ever important. Gord had broken me of my bookworm, geeky self, and my balls were finally growing.

«««—»»»

Poppy was about five feet tall, had straight black hair down to his ribs, wore a long black trench coat that draped just above his red Doc Martin boots. He wore circular blue sunglasses, which he never took off, night or day, I would eventually learn. They had rubber or leather shades on either side that sealed to his temples, so I couldn't even see his eyes looking at them from the sides. His fingers were heavy with thick rings, pewter and silver and gold, some with jewels—skulls and devil's heads. He clasped my hand and one-arm hugged me, called me brother, was the opposite of Paco.

Before we headed out, we sat at the coffee table and Poppy filled his nose, asked me how my flight was, asked Gord about the wedding supplies.

"Truck's full."

"Fucking sweet," Poppy said, nodding. "I'm stocked too. Fuckin' Paco."

Gord chuckled. "Fuckin' Paco."

"You don't like him?" I asked Poppy.

"Fuck no. He's just the supply for our demand. Fucker needs an attitude adjustment. He holds his goddamn shotgun like it's his dick. Compensating for what he doesn't have."

We laughed. I was glad I wasn't alone in hating Paco. Poppy was on my side. I needed to stick close to him in case Paco was ever again in my vicinity.

"Is he going to be at the bachelor party?"

"He better not," Poppy said.

"He might be," Gord added.

"I'll shove that gun up his ass," Poppy said, forming a white line on Gord's mirror, "but I think he'd like it."

I looked at Poppy's glasses…opaque blue. Couldn't see even a hint of his eyes through them. I wondered if he was partially blind, but I didn't ask. He didn't move like a blind man.

"So, what's happening at the party?" I asked.

"What usually happens at a bachelor party," Gord laughed, smacking my forehead. "Booze and pussy!"

"And more!" Poppy cheered.

"Oh, hell ya, a lot more!" Gord winked at me.

"We going to a strip club?" I asked again.

# THE BRIDE STRIPPED BARE

Poppy and Gord laughed, high-fived each other. Poppy clicked open a jeweled skull ring, a hollow cup. He dug it into the coke, filled it, snapped it shut.

"A *kind* of strip club," Gord vaguely explained.

"Don't worry, my new brother," Poppy said to me after he licked clean the jewel of his ring. "You will not be disappointed tonight, that I assure you."

For the next fifteen minutes we all snorted and drank, and I wished I had a pop-up ring like Poppy's, and I told him so. He and Gord laughed, with me and at me. I had snorted more coke since we had gotten back to Gord's apartment than I had in a lifetime, and I felt very, very good.

Then we all got into Poppy's black, jacked-up truck with the tinted windows. He cranked hardcore Norwegian death metal—some band named 'Gorgoroth'—as we drove through the sleepy streets of the quaint little town.

# Chapter 5

I don't remember how far out of town we went, or how long it took, but we eventually pulled into a roadhouse that was surrounded by swamp. I had no idea there was swamp land in Washington State, but the mosquitoes that attacked my face and neck and hands proved we were back in nature.

Inhaling the thick stench of swamp gas, I followed Gord and Poppy up the porch steps of the roadhouse. Laughter and screams and blaring music poured from the walls. All of the windows were bricked or boarded up, and the only sign, reading simply "Roadhouse" in hackneyed smears of flaking paint, hung above the porch.

Poppy opened the door and noise crashed over us. We passed two bouncers, each with a large amount of metal piercing their tattooed faces. They slapped Gord on the back to congratulate him on getting married. Multicolored lights shot around the dark room, showing flashes of flesh—semi-naked and naked women dancing on tables as men howled up at them. The men looked like a cross between a motorcycle gang and survivors of the Apocalypse.

Beards cinched by rows of elastic bands, pierced ears punctured by wooden and steel dowels, tribal tattoos on faces and bald heads, a man with a golden metal ring tight around his neck, muscle shirts, and a helluva lot of leather.

# THE BRIDE STRIPPED BARE

I followed in the slow slipstream of Gord, who could barely take a step through the crowd without being hugged, slapped, given a shooter, a beer, a pill of some kind. Girls flocked to his side to kiss his cheek and let him put his hand on their asses and elsewhere. I saw it all from the back. Gord was finally able to breathe once we reached a horseshoe-shaped booth against a wall deep in the room.

A mounted grizzly head hung over the booth, and Gord took his seat beneath it. Poppy was on his left and I sat on his right. We never paid for a drink, or anything else, all night.

Must've been the cocaine—the Black Betty wearing away—but I remember the night only in flashes. Too drugged up to recall all the people I met or how they may have been important to Gord. He introduced me as an old friend and his best man, and I was lavished with attention almost as much as he was. I felt like royalty, though many of the people I met scared the hell out of me. Others *tempted* the hell out of me. I recall a man with two thick purple scars up either nostril which I couldn't take my eyes off of. I blinked and he was gone. In his place was a gorgeous black girl wearing a glittering gold bra. She lifted it up to her neck and I saw a superfluous nipple beside her right nipple. Whether she pulled my head down or I dived in, I don't know, but I sucked on the third nipple. It fed me milk that tasted of salt and iron. The liquid may have been blood, actually. There were a lot of flashing lights dyeing the color of everything and everyone. The girl happily said "Thanks, baby, you can suck mama's nipple any time." I *do* remember that. And I somewhat recall that, at one point, a drop of milk glittering with gold flakes hung from the nipple and I was about to suck it off, but then a strobe light blinded me, and the drop fell. I saw it hit the back of my hand and turn into an anemone. I yelled and snapped it off.

I doubted whether or not that black horse pill was saving me or making things worse.

I *think*, but can't be sure, that at one point during the night, with Gord lost in the crowd, I had my pants pulled to my knees and at least one girl under the table. I stretched my arms along the cushioned leather back of the booth and felt like a king. I don't remember if I ejaculated or not, but it felt great and lasted for hours. I was getting a secret blow-job in a crowded room! (Well, maybe not so secret.) My drab college life was far behind me.

During the whole time, I was fed more drinks and coke and pills and weed, and who knows what else. I sucked Jell-O shooters from many pairs of amazing breasts and out of vaginas. Girls, some wearing leather bondage gear, sat on the table in front of me with their legs spread, a tiny plastic cup with green gelatin nestled between their labia. A gathering crowd watched me and cheered, and I had no idea who anyone was, not even the girls.

I didn't remember moving from the booth for much of the night, except twice. I have vague memories of being in two other places that night, though I didn't know how I got to either one. And one of the places, I think, I left and returned to.

The first was a bedroom with walls made of mirror, in the middle of which sat a retro '60s circular bed, draped in red satin sheets, that revolved as I lay on it. Me and three girls, that is. A white girl, a black girl (not the same previous one), and an Asian girl. We were all naked. Girls with me, girls with each other.

In that place, my penis rose and never went down. In fact, oddly, it felt at least twelve inches long. That couldn't be real. I remember fucking all three girls for hours, shooting my load, then kept fucking them and I was never tired. Nor were they.

Then the next scene I remember had the four of us outside in the swamp. The girls were dressed in bikinis, each holding a shotgun, and I had a four-foot-long machete in my hand.

# THE BRIDE STRIPPED BARE

A skinny man in a suit and tie, collar open, with a pencil-thin moustache and a black eye, was pinned against a tree, lengths of rope tied around his waist, sweating and crying and begging for his life. The girls held their guns on him, screaming at him not to make a move, to hold still while I killed him. Then the girls—all who were calling me Daddy—told me to give it to the man, torture him, hack him to pieces, do anything I wanted. He was a present for me. He wept and pleaded for mercy.

I swung the machete. He put up his arms instinctively to block the blow, and both of his arms flew off, between wrists and elbows. The Asian girl caught a piece of one arm in mid-air and used it as a club to smack the man in his face. He didn't react to the blow, too busy screaming as blood gushed from his arm stumps. The girl then rubbed his dead hands between her legs.

While he stared in horror at his life pouring out, I stuck the tip of the machete against his trachea, pushed and twisted, reached fingers in, and pulled out a piece of his throat. I was going for his voicebox to shut him up. His screams turned to gurgles and whistles. The girls hooted and laughed, and I stared at the wedge of bloody flesh and the little bones I held in my hand. Then I put a two-handed grip on the blade and swung it like a baseball bat. His screams cut off as his head flew into the white girl's arms.

The girls all howled with laughter, and each took turns kissing the dead man's lips while fury consumed me, and I hacked and hacked at his lifeless body on the ground.

We all cheered, hearts pumping adrenaline, sweat covering my face, blood on us all. The Asian girl threw the arm on the corpse, looked deeply into my eyes, and whispered, "My husband." I smiled and nodded.

The victim's head stayed with us as we headed out of the woods.

The next scene was back in the bedroom. The girls and I naked again, the severed head propped up on a pillow. I was as hard as iron again, so we all fucked.

Each girl used the head obscenely, putting its mouth between their legs, then the black girl lined the thing up with its mouth open. She grabbed a heavy glass ashtray filled with old joints and smashed it against the head's mouth, and all its teeth dribbling down the chin.

I fucked the toothless mouth of the decapitated head as the girls urged me on, two of them caressing my body as the Asian girl held the head stable to bear the brunt of my thrusts.

I shot semen across its tongue to the back of its throat. Then the girls all sucked my cream from the dead mouth and caressed me with their hands and lips as I rested from the greatest orgasm of my life.

They then plucked out the dead man's eyes and told me they were delicacies, as sweet as grapes. I believed them and ate the eyes.

I recalled one of them saying, "Welcome to the family" before the rest of the night erased itself from memory.

# Chapter 6

I woke on Gord's couch, clothes on but stained with lipstick, alcohol, blood, cocaine, not remembering all that had happened the night before, or how I got back to the apartment. My head felt fine, no migraine, but my muscles were burning sore. I sat up on the couch and saw the slit sandbag of coke still on the coffee table. Part of me wanted to start a coke high again, but I knew that wouldn't be a good idea.

I headed to the kitchen and drank a glass of water. Peeked into Gord's room, hearing his snores. He was sprawled on his bed naked, the sheet covering his crotch, thankfully. I closed his door quietly and stepped outside to get some fresh air.

I was in a small town, so I walked the main street, going nowhere, just needing to move my muscles and let the scenes of the night come back to me. Took me a while to piece things together, wondering what was true and what false, doubting everything—the girls, the man, the machete in my hand. It had to have been a drug-induced hallucination. How many drugs had I been given? It was how I explained it to myself, so I didn't worry about it anymore.

As I strolled, feeling the sun on my face, people passed, smiled and waved at me, saying hello, very friendly. They all seemed to know me, but I knew none of them.

Then a short, old man with a cane and straw hat stopped and said, with a smile and a wink, "That was a helluva party last night."

My eyebrows wrinkled as I peered down at him, stooped over, a bit of a hunchback. "You were there?"

"Oh sure, wouldn't miss it for the world."

I may have hallucinated, but I was pretty sure there were no old men at the roadhouse. He was about to keep walking, but I stopped him. "Did you see me?"

He chuckled and false teeth rattled in his mouth. "Of course. You're Chris, the best man, and one of the star attractions."

"Uh…no offense, but I don't remember seeing anyone over the age of, let's say, fifty or sixty. And you don't look like a motorcycle gang member."

He snorted and rested a shaky, liver-spotted hand on my shoulder, patting me as if I was his grandson. "Looks can be deceiving. You're in Red Wood now."

A weak smile formed on my lips as I stared into his rheumatic eyes. He patted me a few more times, then kept walking, cane tip tapping the sidewalk as his feet shuffled him away.

I turned, stuffed hands into my pockets, then I heard the old man call at my back, "Cut that fucker's head off good."

I spun to see him stopped, looking at me. He winked and tipped his hat, kept walking. I stood frozen for a while, before I turned and continued down the sidewalk.

I passed through the center of town, a gas station on either side of the main intersection, but no one seemed to work at either of them or were stopped for gas. A small town, I guessed, looked deserted, not due to anything strange, but because the handful of people who lived there were all elsewhere, probably at home, asleep, watching TV or movies, feeding livestock or cooking pies to cool on the windowsill.

I came to a small bridge which spanned a creek. To either side, lining the water, was a park. I strolled away from the street across the grass. Feeling calmed by the sound of the trickling water, I watched

# THE BRIDE STRIPPED BARE

minnows in the shallows, the water pristine and clear, straight from some distant mountain in the Rockies, colored pebbles on the banks. I walked and plopped stones into the water, glancing around the small parklands for a place to sit. I needed to get my head straight from the nightmare flashes of the night, and from what I thought I heard the old man say. There was no way he could've been at the roadhouse—the noise, the lights, the naked skin, the smoke in the air alone would've killed him.

He must've been joking—hazing the new guy. Of course, he would know who I was—it was a small town and Gord was popular. And Gord was popular because Venus was popular. I wondered what she and her bridesmaids did the night before. If there was an all-girl roadhouse with male strippers. And was she sleeping off her exhaustion too?

Would that day still be the day of the wedding, or would it have to be cancelled due to excessive…excess.

I rounded a bend in the stream and rose over a small hill. A gazebo was just ahead, standing near the stream. My legs were still aching, so I hoped the gazebo had benches lining the interior.

(Had I run a marathon last night? No. I had fucked three hot girls multiple times. The ache centered above my legs, met at my pelvis—definitely an ache from vigorous sex.)

As I approached the gazebo, I saw that at least one person, maybe two, were already in it. The locals were friendly enough, so I figured I wouldn't be a snob. Before I could climb the stairs up into the structure, I saw the faces of three sweet old ladies smiling back at me. They sat around a wrought iron circular table on wrought iron chairs, sipping tea, with a teapot steaming in the centre of the table.

One lady was white, one was black, and the third was Asian.

"Hello, Chris," they said in unison. "Thanks for the good hard fuck."

# ROB BLISS

<<<—>>>

I awoke on Gord's sofa—again—squeezed into a ball, with Gord sitting by my feet in his underwear, white powder rimming his nostrils and a razor blade in his hand hovering over a mirror.

"Want some?" he offered.

I shook my head, cleared my eyes from the latest dream (one of the most vivid dreams I'd ever had), and sat up. Saw that I was dressed in the clothes I had worn in the dream, and began wondering again if it was real or not.

"How can you do that so early?" I asked Gord as he rubbed residue coke off his fingers onto his gums.

"I told you, buddy, I'm staying high for the whole wedding…probably the honeymoon too."

I yawned and rubbed the heels of my palms into my eyes. "I never asked—where are you going for your honeymoon?"

"Haven't decided."

"Haven't decided? It starts tomorrow, doesn't it?"

"What I mean is, we might hold off for a month or two."

"Oh, okay."

"One day at a time, my friend." Gord slapped my foot, smiled. "You look like hell—I guess I did my job." He laughed.

Groaning, I said, "That was a good party, I'll give you that. I can barely remember half of it."

"Well, don't go to sleep on me yet, we gotta try on tuxedos today."

A shot of fear went through me. "Oh God, isn't it a little late? We should've done that when I arrived. God, where's my head, I totally forgot we gotta dress for a wedding—you especially."

He laughed. "Well then move, son—get in the shower. Hose yourself down."

# THE BRIDE STRIPPED BARE

I did, and an hour later he and I went to a small shop above a closed-down toy store facing the main street. Gord had stuffed himself with coke and a few strange pills before we left. In the truck, there were three bags of coke under our seats, but the rest of it had vanished from the back, presumably removed to be delivered to the wedding—not stolen, or so he said. He nestled one bag beside his thigh as he drove, poked a hole in it, snorted it off his finger. I said I had had enough, thanks.

"You'll want some later, don't worry. Help yourself, you don't need my permission to have fun. Plenty for everybody," he said as we drove slowly down main street.

I squinted at the sunlight coming through the hole he had shot through his roof, then looked away, feeling a pain in my temples. "I had no idea you'd become such a coke addict," I said bluntly.

"Oh hell, it's no big deal. We're in the boonies—gotta have fun. You only live so long."

He clicked his tongue with that last line, sounded like he expected to die at any moment. That was when I thought that maybe he had an incurable disease which he was keeping secret. Things started making sense. He was dying and he wanted to get a rush marriage before he was gone, and he wanted to go out with a bang. Why not do as many drugs as possible—he'll be dead soon anyway?

It made sense and was horrible. I said nothing. I felt sad as we got out of the truck. The ground-floor store front was a boarded-up door with a rusted lock, peeling green paint, and two large windows fogged by mildew and grime from many decades. Wooden soldiers, a hobby horse, building blocks for the kids, all bearing price tags from fifty years ago, were covered in dust, dead flies and spiders.

We entered through a door inset beside the locked door. Climbed worn wooden steps to an upper floor, a heavy smell of wood dust and mildew in the air of the narrow staircase. At the top of the stairs was a single door down a short hardwood hall.

Gord knocked and twisted a creaking glass doorknob. We were in a tailor's shop. Open closets of suits and costumes, mannequins standing naked, wooden heads hearing wigs and old hats. Looked like it belonged to the London of Dickens. Heavy black drapes on the windows blocked out the view of the street, a few antique lamps scattered around illuminated the room with dull yellow and orange light. In one corner stood a full-length oval mirror on a wooden stand.

A thin old man in a black suit emerged from a doorway of black crystal beads, and greeted Gord morosely. "Hello, my friend. Congratulations on your approaching nuptials."

He looked more like a coroner than a tailor, though a measuring tape hung around his neck. His hands were skeletons covered in skin, fingers long and narrow, knuckles like vertebrae, fingernails pointed and yellow. He smelled old.

"Thanks, Gorman," Gord said, then patted my shoulder. "This is Chris, my best man. We're here to look pretty."

A flicker of a smile twitched on Gorman's lipless grey mouth. "Pretty. Interesting choice of words. I have your uniforms already prepared."

He disappeared back through the beads, and I whispered to Gord, "Uniforms?"

He whispered back, with a dismissive wave of his hand, "That's just what he calls our tuxes."

I could hear Gorman's slow shoes tap as he stepped and creaked the wood of whatever back room he was wandering around in. The sound faded, became distant, as though the backroom was immense, stretching far behind the limits of the small store on main street.

Then the sound of steel wheels creaked, rolling across floorboards, until the tailor pushed out two half-mannequins on rolling stands, each dressed in shirts and vests and jackets that looked from the court of Louis XIV.

# THE BRIDE STRIPPED BARE

I thought it was a joke, but Gord smiled proudly and headed to one of the mannequins.

"Oh, they're beauts, Gor!"

The tailor helped Gord change from his modern wardrobe into an ancient one. Gord did up the hook and eye clasps of the vest while looking at himself in the oval mirror.

"Goddamn! Whaddaya think, Chris?"

"Of course, there is an appropriate shirt to accompany the outer wear," Gorman added as he adjusted the vest on Gord's shoulders, then retrieved the jacket off the mannequin.

You never know what you're going to be asked to wear when you're in someone's wedding. I tried to be nice.

"Incredible," I said, looking at my 'uniform' still hanging on its mannequin. "Like something out of a movie."

Gorman caught my eye—the man did not smile.

"Shall I help you get dressed, sir?"

"Oh…uh, yeah, I guess so," I stammered as I stood, arms limp at my sides to let the tailor do what he did best. "I wouldn't know the first thing about putting one of these things on."

As the tailor slipped the vest on me, I wondered two things: where were the pants and shoes that went with this *uniform,* and how could Gorman know what size I was? Well, maybe he had an expert tailor's eye and could accurately guess from just a photograph. That must've been it.

Gord and I were soon dressed as though we were about to hear Bach in person play a harpsichord. The vest and jacket were woven with golden thread on a black background, depicting strange mosaics of animals and people and monsters in the ornate tapestry. The fabric was a little stiff, but I could move my arms easily. Didn't feel like I was wearing cardboard, but I assumed that both pieces could stand up on their own if I stood them on the floor. They must've been old, but didn't smell of dust and age, and the cloth was pristine. The gold and black both shined.

Gorman brushed us off and adjusted the jackets across our shoulders and the vests around our midsections.

"Whaddaya think?" Gord asked me again.

I remained polite. "Yeah, wow, this is wild—I guess this is going to be one fancy wedding."

Gord laughed. "Fancy's not the word for it. Right, Gor?"

The tailor gave his Mona Lisa smile again as his dark eyes looked at me. "Your best man is skilled in his choice of words."

Gorman gave me the creeps—up my spine and down the backs of my legs. I expected to hear funeral music play from the depths of the room through the beads.

I swallowed a lump of fear and asked Gord, "Are there pants that go with this?"

Felt Gorman's eyes on me, saw his smile, knew he was, again, thinking about my choice of words. Maybe there were no pants that went with the uniform. Then I recalled a few books I had read and period-piece movies I'd seen. I was pretty sure that nylons and buckle shoes went with this type of *costume* (a better word).

Shit. Nylons? I could *not* see Gord wearing those. I hoped to hell Venus wasn't behind this bizarre costume for her fiancé and his best man. Gord was too pussy-whipped to argue. It was getting harder and harder to figure out my old friend. Coke? Nylons? Five years and new scenery can really change a man.

"Not to worry," Gord said, "those come later." He started taking off his jacket, Gorman helping. "These will be delivered?"

"Yes, sir," the tailor said, "I will be available to assist in your dressing this evening."

Gord started unhooking the vest, smiling and dancing with joy where he stood, as Gorman put the jacket back on the mannequin. "At the Swamp Hotel, you mean?"

# THE BRIDE STRIPPED BARE

Gorman's hands froze. He looked at Gord, glanced at me, cleared his throat. "Yes, sir."

The tailor held his stare, and I saw a slight look of fear cross Gord's face. His Adam's apple jumped. Gorman's hands didn't move off the shoulders of the mannequin, and his eyes didn't blink. I watched them both, as though there was some unspoken Mexican stand-off happening in front of me.

Gord shook his head slightly and said in a choked, hushed voice. "I wasn't sure."

Dust motes held in mid-air as the two stared at each other. I glanced down and saw Gord slowly clenching his hands.

"Are you *sure* now, sir?" Gorman asked slowly, shadows filling his eyes.

Gord's jaw muscles clenched and he swallowed a few times in rapid succession. He was terrified. I was confused. I assumed for half a second that he was having some kind of reaction to the cocaine.

"I'm...yeah... I'm sure," he mumbled.

The tailor straightened the shoulders of the jacket on the mannequin, looking away from Gord. The stand-off was over, and it didn't look as though Gord had won. He quickly, but carefully, undid the hooks of the vest, handed it to the tailor without looking at him.

And then another very strange thing happened. Gorman looked at me, lifting his chin, and smiled. Showed black teeth, smiled with his eyes as well, and looked like everybody's favorite grandpa instead of Death warmed-over. Except, that was, for the black teeth.

I was in shock and my head lurched back an inch.

"Would you like assistance in removing your uniform, sir?"

I glanced from Gorman to Gord, but my friend wasn't looking up. His fingers paused on the hooks; ears trained on the tailor's voice—the change of tone from morose to friendly—kept his eyes always on the floor. A whimper escaped from the back of Gord's throat, which he quickly covered up with a cough.

The stand-off hadn't ended, it had just changed gears. But I still couldn't tell what it was about.

Gorman helped me with the jacket and vest first, putting both of them back on a mannequin, before he took Gord's vest. Gord held it in two hands patiently, like a schoolboy waiting to be sentenced to detention. A thin film of sweat shone under the yellow light on his forehead. I gave him a questioning look, but he wouldn't meet my eyes. Just held the vest until Gorman was ready to take it from him.

We left, me lagging behind Gord as he hammered feet down the dusty hardwood stairs, saying nothing, beelining for the door.

I turned to thank Gorman, who bowed and smiled. Smugly. He had won something and was smiling at his victory. Stood between the two mannequins, a skeletal hand on either of their shoulders.

The tailor smiled his black teeth. His eyes twinkled at me as he pushed one of the mannequins over, let it crash to the floor. The mannequin holding Gord's uniform.

Then, still smiling his immense horse teeth, he put an arm around my mannequin, and brushed an invisible flake off the jacket which I would be wearing for the wedding.

«««—»»»

Gord had punched his way through the tailor's street-level door and was gone. I caught up to him as he sat in the truck, hands clenched on the steering wheel, foot revving the gas. As soon as I got in—before I had finished closing the passenger door—he squealed the tires and shot off, smoking rubber down the main street.

I held onto the dash with one hand, working to get the seatbelt on with the other.

"Whoah, Gord—what the fuck!"

# THE BRIDE STRIPPED BARE

I looked over and saw his face streaming tears. He couldn't hold the wheel straight, wiping tears away, the truck slewing across the lane divider. Almost hit a pickup with hay bales in the back.

"Gord, what's going on? You're gonna get us killed!"

"Fuck man—I'm already dead!" he stammered out. I thought he was about to reveal that he *was* dying of cancer. Something back at the tailor's had maybe triggered his sorrow. But I was wrong. "I fucked up—but I didn't know! How the hell was I supposed to know?" He banged his palms on the wheel and yelled at the windshield.

"Know what?" I asked. "Goddamnit, Gordy, there's some weird shit going on with you since I got here. You gotta start telling me! What's with the coke—what was that party last night—I had some fucked-up dreams!" My face burned with anger as I stared at the road ahead, watching to see if Gord was about to kill us. I glanced at the speedometer and he was doing close to sixty-five. I didn't know what the speed limit was, but it wasn't that.

"I can't tell you now," he said, smearing the heel of his palm under his eyes. "I think I said too much already. Fuck, I don't know. I gotta make a call. They gotta understand it was a mistake—a tiny little nothing mistake!"

"What'd you say? You mean back at the tailors? I didn't hear anything." I swallowed from fear; my hand clutched onto the door handle. Looked at the speedometer again, felt the truck slow. "What did you say? The 'Swamp Hotel'—was that it?"

He looked at me in anguish and muttered, "Aw fuck, I'm dead. You *did* hear it. Fuck it, I'm calling."

I kept asking what 'Swamp Hotel' meant, but he wasn't answering. Pulled to the side of the road, tires grinding gravel, trees on either side—it didn't take long to get us back into the wilderness. I could see a mountain range in the distance and wondered if that was the Rockies.

Gord pinned the truck in park, killed the engine, and dug a cellphone from a pocket in the visor over his head. His hands shook and the odd tear fell, which he blinked away, trying to read the screen of the phone. He scrolled through phone numbers until he got to one. Took deep breaths before punching a key to dial the number. One hand gripped the steering wheel as he held the phone to his ear, waiting for the line to pick up. I watched his fear increase as he spoke.

"It's me. Look—I didn't know, okay? I figured he's already called you since this town is so…close-knitted. It was a *small* mistake—it's nothing, not a big goddamn deal!" His eyes flickered over to me for a second. "Yeah, he was there. But he doesn't know. The wedding's tonight—in just a matter of hours. *Hours!*" He paused and listened. I listened too but couldn't hear even the tiniest metallic echo of the voice coming through the phone. Gord's head sagged forward to touch the steering wheel, eyes closed, before he interrupted the person he was listening to. "Okay, okay, fine—then let me go. I'll leave today—we're gone and never coming back, I swear. Tell my folks it's off, I left, they'll ask their questions, but then they'll go too. I won't say a goddamn word. I'll go to another country. I'll get off the continent—whatever you need. She can have him, have anyone and everyone—I don't care." His head leaned back against the headrest and he didn't blink as he stared at the ceiling of the cab. I stared at the road ahead. No cars passed. The road was abandoned, only we were on it. Gord's jaw tightened and his voice dropped. "Then, you know what, I'm saving myself. I'm not going to lay down and take this shit. It was a fucking tiny mistake—you're not giving me a shred of mercy. So I'll get it for myself. Any of your boys get in my way and I swear I will fucking kill them and take them to hell with me!"

He rolled down his window and tossed the phone onto the road, swearing under his breath. Gripped the wheel, cranked the engine to life, and spat gravel off his tires. The engine revved up high, the speedometer needle jerked, and I held on.

# THE BRIDE STRIPPED BARE

"I'm sorry, Chris, for bringing you into this shit."

"Gord, you gotta tell me what's going on!" I yelled at him.

He shook his head. "If I say any more, who knows what they'll do. I just wanna get out of this backwater shithole—alive!"

"Where are we going? Back to your place?"

"Hell no! They're probably already there. I don't know where to go so I'll just keep driving until I think of something. And pray to goddamn God."

"Who're you running from? Paco?"

A simple question. All I could think of since, of all the people I'd met since I arrived, Paco was the scariest, meanest, rudest piece of shit ever. I could see *him* wanting to hunt down and kill Gord…and me.

Gord stared at me as though a slow light was trying to shine in his brain. "Paco?" he repeated softly.

"Yeah. Did you forget to pay for the coke or something?"

His head swiveled slowly to gaze through the back windshield, and a smile bloomed on his lips.

"Fucking Paco!" he yelled and laughed, banging the heel of his palm on the wheel.

"It *was* him, wasn't it? Shit. I don't know why you'd get mixed up with that unstable fuck. Is he gonna kill you?"

Gord flinched, a crease slicing between his eyebrows, looking at me like I just grew a horn out of my forehead. "What? No, Paco's okay. I mean, yeah, he's a fucking psychopath, but he really has nothing to do with these people."

"What *people*?"

He waved away the question. "Never mind." He glanced behind him again, then scanned the left side of the road, rubbing his chin. "There should be a lake around here. Miser's Pond. We can go around the south end of it and double back. It's the long way around, but it'll get us to Paco without getting us nailed."

I glared at him. "You *want* to go to Paco?"

"No, Chris, calm down." He reached under his seat and pulled up one of the cocaine sandbags, tossed it onto my lap. "Here, keep it, snort the whole bag. Relax."

I clutched the bag in my fist and shook it at him. Could barely speak in coherent sentences. "Relax? With coke? Are you fucking… Paco!" I rolled down my window and tossed the bag. Felt sorry for whatever animal would eventually stumble across it.

"Hey! That was good shit!" Gord said, but not angrily.

"Gordy—what the goddamn hell is going on?" I spat out, leaning over to stare at the side of his face. Hoping my bulging eyes would make him confess.

But it just made him chuckle.

"Okay, sit back. I can tell you about Paco. He's *just* a drug runner."

"*Just?*"

"Hear me out. He operates a tunnel that goes from here to Canada. That's the tunnel we were in. Now do you get why he was so suspicious of you? He's suspicious of everybody for a year or two, then he calms down…a bit. He's the contact for Mexican druglords to ship Columbian coke to Canada and to get Canadian weed down here. B.C. Gold—it's some seriously good shit. You had some last night."

Flashes erupted through my memory of the party, and then of Paco's place. The psychotic bastard was starting to make sense. Looks were deceiving. On the exterior, his place was a dump, but underground he had a sophisticated operation going on. No wonder there were *pallets* of sandbags—not just a pile or two. And the arsenal he kept was now justified in my mind as belonging to a major drug-runner, not a survivalist nut-job.

Suspicious of everybody for a year or two! Made sense. And it also made sense why Gord and I loaded the coke into the truck while Paco stayed underground. Just in case the operation got busted (cop helicopters

# THE BRIDE STRIPPED BARE

dropping out of the sky?), then only Gord and I would get nailed while Paco locked himself behind his computerized, punch-pad subterranean doors and made his escape to Canada.

"Motherfuckin' Paco," I mumbled.

"Yup. He controls that tunnel. We just gotta convince him to let us through it. I was thinking about going to the airport and flying out of here. But my passport and all my I.D. are at the apartment, including my fucking bank card and credit cards. Shit. Gonna take a while to replace all that, then I can fly far away. I'll hold up in Canada until then."

I threw up my hands. "Shit, man, mine is too! Who's at your place? How am I going to get home?"

"Neither of us can worry about that right now, you gotta trust me. We just get to Paco's, go through the tunnel, get to Canada. That's the only plan right now. Once we're out of this country, we can figure out the small stuff."

"My passport! My ticket home! That's *small* stuff?"

"Chris," he said calmly. "Trust me. I'm getting us out of this."

And that was when the police siren blared behind us.

# Chapter 7

Simultaneously, Gord and I twisted in our seats to look through the back windshield. A single cop in a single cruiser, red and blues spinning. I glanced at the road behind the cop, which wound in a gentle arc and vanished in the trees. No one else in sight on the road, either behind us or in front.

"Where the hell did he come from?" I yelled.

"Probably out of the forest," Gord said, matter-of-factly, not a hint of sarcasm in his tone. Glanced repeatedly in the rearview mirror. "There's only one, so that's good. We got a bit of a headstart. And I think that's the start of Miser's Pond right there."

I looked where he was pointing. A marsh at the side of the road, the trees thinned, stumps broken and chewed, standing like pillars to a lost civilization in the shallow water. Sunlight was reflecting orange off the flat surface of the mirror-still water. I shook my head and looked at the green digital clock on the truck's dashboard, reading 12:42. According to the position of the sun in the sky, it should've been about five or six o'clock. The sun was going down and it was verging on twilight. (I'm such a geek, I know.)

"Is your clock broken?" I asked, then glanced at the cop behind us. "And why aren't you pulling over?"

"Sorta, and I'm waiting to make my move. Got a plan that might work."

# THE BRIDE STRIPPED BARE

The truck started to slow and Gord edged to the side of the road, only half of the truck on gravel, half on asphalt. Gord kept his eyes on the rearview and side mirrors, one arm hanging out his open window, one hand on the wheel, his left foot easing pressure down on the brake pedal.

His right foot free, he twisted it, hooked it beneath his seat, used his shoe toe to shuffle out the .357 Magnum. I had forgotten about that secret piece of weaponry. He also inadvertantly nudged out another bag of coke. I'd forgotten about that, too. We were fucked.

I glared down at the floorboards and asked Gord from between unmoving lips, "What the fuck are you doing, Gordy? You are not seriously going to kill a cop, right?"

"Just do what I tell you when I tell you." His foot pushed the gun across the floorboard to my side. "Try to pick it up without looking like you're picking it up. Take your shoes and socks off if you have to."

I was aiding and abetting, and I knew it. Sweat poured into my eyebrows. I could fry and die for this. I didn't know what Gord had planned (well, I could guess), but I knew cops didn't like it when you had bigger firepower in your vehicle than they had on their hips. I was going to die in a cop shoot-out. I would die in a matter of seconds. But I tried to block out the fear and concentrate on doing what Gord had said, since I had no plan to get out of such a mess, and he seemed to have one. I had to help him out. I really wished I had snorted half of that bag of coke I'd thrown away.

I slipped off my shoes and used my toes to slip off both socks, glancing in the side mirror at the cop. Wasn't easy, but I managed to lift the gun high enough to get it in my hand. Put it delicately on the seat between me and Gord.

Between clenched teeth, I said, "Okay, now what?"

"Got your seatbelt on?"

"Yep."

"Hold on tight, duck low when I say to duck."

My heart was hammering, and I felt a strong urge to piss. My back was stiff, pressed hard against the seat, though I glanced with my eyes only—didn't dare move my neck—over at Gord, waiting to see his next move so I would know more.

My sockless toes were scrunched in and freezing cold, almost numb. Gord took his hand off the wheel, foot hard on the brake, softly clicked the transmission into reverse and held it there. Put his hand back on the wheel while his other hand slowly picked up the gun. Cocked it and raised the barrel to just under the line of the windshield. His eyes stayed on the rearview, watching the cop get out of his car, hoist his pants up, tilt his hat back, adjust his mirrored sunglasses, and sidle towards us.

"He's going for his gun," Gord said quietly. "As soon as he does, you get on the floor. Got it?"

"Yep," was all I could mutter.

His feet flashed from brake to gas and he yelled, "Hit the deck!"

I dropped to the floorboards and curled into a ball, hands covering my head. The truck sped backwards and Gord fired a stream of bullets over my seat, through the passenger window. Cop bullets shot into the truck from outside. The windshield shattered. Brakes squealed, Gord's foot on the pedal, and he fired more rounds through the shattered glass. He jammed the truck into park and leapt out of the vehicle.

I rose off the floor, glass sliding off me, and peered over the dash. Bullets had punched the clock and radio and Gord's door. There were a few bullets in the cop car.

And at least one in the cop.

I peered over the ledge of the smashed windshield to see Gord checking out the cop on the ground, blood splashed across the lawman's face and chest. Swore under my breath and quickly got my socks and shoes back on, figuring I'd have to run for my life at some point. Peered back over the dashboard to see that Gord had the cop's gun in

# THE BRIDE STRIPPED BARE

hand as he wrenched open the door of the cruiser. He searched the interior, grabbing a shotgun, which he brought to me, tossing it through my window.

"They don't teach you how to shoot in that college, do they?" he chuckled. "Time to learn."

I left the gun where it lay on the bench seat, edged myself up off the floorboard, and watched him go back to the cruiser. He stretched the handset of the radio up to his mouth and yelled into it.

"I got one of yours, fuckers! I told you I ain't goin' down!"

A radio voice called back, asking who it was, but Gord was back in the truck. Slammed the door, tucked the cop's handgun under his thigh, and started to drive.

He twisted the wheel so that we intentionally ran over the cop's body. He laughed and howled like a wolf as he hit the gas and we raced down the road.

I held on, saying nothing, afraid to even look at Gord. A lake spread out beside us—a lot bigger than a pond—and the truck followed its banks until it narrowed. We got off the highway and onto a dirt road, bouncing across ruts and grass and twigs, the lake still in view out Gord's window.

I didn't know what to say. My best friend had just killed a cop. We were on the run from at least two forces—the law, and whoever scared Gord in the first place. I thought about my life, and figured that being a boring teacher at a boring college really wasn't so bad.

"So, *do* you know how to use a shotgun?" Gord finally asked.

"Nope," I said. "I've seen them in movies, but I've never even held one."

"Well, what are you waiting for? Pick it up and get a feel for it."

I glanced at the seat beside my hip, saw part of the stock and the barrel jutting out, wondered how such a relatively small piece of metal and wood could cause so much carnage. I was afraid of it. I picked it up like I was handling a snake, thinking its barrels would double-back on me and strike. I aimed the barrels out my side window, cradled its body in two hands, finger nowhere near the trigger.

"Go on, fire it! Watch the kick-back."

At Gord's urging, I leaned the barrels on the window edge, my hands shaking too much to aim the weapon properly. Had to look down to see where the trigger was, my hands too cold and numb to feel the details of the gun's design. I squeezed the trigger and the thing came to sudden life. Roared out its rage as it fired into a passing bush. It punched my bicep and ribs and fell to the floorboard.

Gord laughed as my ears rang from the blast.

"You've got too much college in you!" he said. "Just leave it on the seat—barrel pointing at your door, not at me…and hope we don't need to use it."

I delicately lifted it off the floor and laid it behind my ass along the seat. I kept shifting and looking at the gun, hated to have it even touch me. Gord laughed, then slid the weapon out from behind me, lined it behind our headrests. I didn't feel any better having the serpent resting behind my head, but if it wasn't touching me, then I could ignore its existence.

I dared to ask another question. "So…what if we die today?"

He snorted a laugh. "Don't worry about it. If you're dead, you're dead. Nothing you can do about it."

That didn't relax me. I told myself that, yes, death was death, but it was the trail leading up to it that scared the shit out of me. Was that where we were going? To our deaths via back roads around a lake?

I tried another question. "So, do you think Paco's going to welcome us with open arms?"

Smiling, Gord said, "I don't know what he's going to do. Probably freak out a bit."

"A bit?"

# THE BRIDE STRIPPED BARE

"Or a lot. I'll tell him, I dunno, that some punk tried to steal some of my stash, so I had a shootout with him. That'll explain the windshield and bullet holes."

I looked at the hole piercing the radio, put my finger through it. Wondered what time it really was. Couldn't see the sun behind tall trees, and the forest was too dark once were we inside it, but I figured it was still twilight, soon to be night.

"And then what?" I asked. "You buy more drugs? Or tell him you just want to go for a walk through his tunnel? He seems like the paranoid type. Think he'll be suspicious?"

Gord bit his lip and nodded ahead at the road as it disappeared around a bend in the trees. "Yeah he will. That's what I'm trying to figure out. How do we get around *him?* He's like an ogre guarding a cave of gold." He looked over at me, and I didn't like the look in his eyes. "We might have to kill the ogre."

I took a deep breath through my nostrils, felt a wave of pure stress shiver my body, pressed two hands against my head and tried to squeeze away the tension I felt.

I couldn't take it anymore, so I yelled.

"What the fuck, Gordy! You tell me right now what the fuck is going on! Who are you? What have you gotten yourself into since you moved out here? Why are you even messing around with this shit?"

My voice rang, then cut off, and it was suddenly too silent. I shook, shifted in my seat, couldn't get comfortable. I looked at him, then looked away, saw that he was thinking, choosing what to reveal to me. I wondered if, by telling me, he would put himself further at risk with some unknown person—and, if that was the case, it only proved further that he was into some bad shit.

"Okay. I'll tell you." He inhaled deeply, then started patting his jacket. Then added, "Wish I had a fucking smoke."

Another new thing: I didn't know he smoked. Cigarettes, that is. Instead, he reached down to lift the sandbag of coke that had fallen during our cop-killing.

I sighed in exasperation. "Ah, fuck, Gord, haven't you had enough of that shit?"

"Hell no," he said, trying to punch a hole with his finger through the bag. Some of the powder went up his nose, a lot more on his lap and the seat. "Now's the best time for it. Gives me quick reflexes, good hand-to-eye coordination. If I'm going out, I'm going high. Say the word and I'll give you some—but I ain't giving it to you so you can throw it out the window."

He shoved another pinch up both nostrils, then popped the glove box and stuffed it in beside a couple boxes of shotgun ammo.

I breathed like a pregnant woman in lamaze class. I wanted to snort and *eat* the coke bags. Part of me wanted the coke, but only to see if it would lessen my stress. I knew it would probably increase it instead. And I wanted to be sober when Gord confessed.

"Don't evade the issue," I demanded. "Start talking."

After he was through sniffing and squeezing his nostrils, he said, "Okay. I'd say don't repeat what I'm gonna tell you, but it may not matter at this point. Venus is an awesome girl—I gotta say that. But, like I told you, she comes from a *big* family. Huge. They're all over this part of the world—and beyond. I don't know exactly how far they're spread out. And they're powerful. That cop I killed was probably an uncle or a cousin. They're in the police, the government, the courts…in the public works—even the sidewalk sweepers are related to Venus. They're *everywhere*."

He licked his gums and was a little twitchy, eyes flashing from the road to me to his hands on the wheel.

He continued. "With me marrying into that large and powerful of a family, I would have access to that power."

# THE BRIDE STRIPPED BARE

"Is Paco in the whole thing?"

"No, like I said, he works for others. But I wouldn't be surprised if the family gets a cut of his profits, and they keep him secret and protected. They probably own the land he's on. They control all of the law around here. That's how we can all get tons of shit from him. But you saw how paranoid he is—comes with the business. I can vouch for you, but he's still gonna be a prick."

Wheels turned in my head. Sounded as though Gord lusted for Venus *and* for the power she could give him...that was the whole thing in a nutshell? There were still too many questions.

"Is it her family who wants you dead? Because of whatever you said to the tailor?"

He sighed, body sagging where he sat, as he tried to muster courage to tell me the next part of his confession.

"It's a little more complicated than that. They're a weird family. And I don't just mean strange personalities and habits. There's that too. Let's put it this way: I saw one of them—a niece about nineteen or so—with a tail."

I stared at him, eyes bulging, not sure whether I should laugh or vomit. "I've heard about those. A vestigial tail, it's called. An evolutionary leftover from when we were monkeys."

He was shaking his head. "Not that. Not a little nubbin...a piece of flesh-covered spine. I mean, a *tail*. About three feet long with all the colors of a bruise—black, red, purple, yellow—all blending into one another. And she could flick it. Snapped it in my face while she giggled—had about three teeth in her head. Speaking of which, her head looked like a lump of dough with thumb marks pressed into either temple. Fucking ugly bitch, let me tell you."

I felt a wad of bile nestle at the back of my throat picturing this person. Wondered if she was at the party. Hoped to God I didn't stick my dick in her.

"You think there's a lot of inbreeding in this family?"

"I'd put money on it. They keep the freaks mostly out of view. I met that girl—that *thing*—about six months after Venus and I hooked up. She had introduced me to her immediate family—they all seemed pretty normal at first, kind of eccentric—but then we headed out to a party in a shack in the woods—I forget where it was, I was so drunk and stoned—and that's where I met some of the lesser-seen members."

Things were piecing together, and I still saw Gord's old weakness playing a part. Giving in to a gorgeous girl, not caring about how strange she, or her family, might be, as long as she had nice cleavage.

"It sounds like Venus has kept you doped up pretty good." I looked at his flared nostrils and the powder still on his pants. "She's controlling you with dope."

He only shrugged. "Maybe. You know me, buddy—I like a party. And she's one helluva party girl. So what if her family's a little fucked up? Whose isn't? All that she offers is huge compared to what weirdness I'd have to tolerate. It looks—looked—like a great deal, and I'd come out on top."

"Looked?" I questioned, watching the change in his opinion about his golden ticket. "What happened back at the tailors? Is he family too?"

Gord nodded. "Yeah. He's Venus' father. Everyone in town is related. That's why I can have a ton of coke in the back of my truck and not worry about it getting stolen or have a cop bust me for it. It's for the party—a thief would be stealing the party's hors d'eouvres—plus the thief would be on the invitation list."

"That's fucked up," I mumbled. "So what exactly happened at the tailors? Venus' father is…one creepy freak, to put it mildly."

His mouth tightened as he slowly shook his head. "I can't tell you about that. It might be nothing, anyway. As long as we can get away from here. I'd rather say nothing so you can always say you never knew. Just in case."

# THE BRIDE STRIPPED BARE

"What 'in case'?"

He stared at me, serious, scared. "In case we don't get away."

The light coming through the trees was dying. Gord turned on his headlights. One came on, the other was probably shot out. The road was still hell, parts of it overgrown with grass, just a trail of two dug-in wheel ruts. We were off-roading basically, still going around the lake which appeared from time to time through gaps where the trees thinned. Every time we saw water, Gord looked at it as though he was expecting something to come across it toward us. He was more paranoid with the single headlight on. Marking our passage, in case anyone was looking for us. Which, of course, they could be, especially with a cop lying dead on the highway, his body half-pulp, tire tracks across his face.

The bush suddenly opened up into a bit of a clearing and what looked like a tall slope of earth. But at the top of the slope I could see stars. When you're on drugs—still have them in your system, which I must have had from the night before—time does strange things. A minute can feel like an hour, and hours can go by when you think it's only been a couple of minutes.

We drove clear of the bush and Gord stopped. Let the truck idle as he hung his head out the window, staring in every direction, listening. Even told me to stop breathing for a minute. I did, listened, and heard only crickets and a small breeze through tree branches.

"Okay," he whispered. "I'm going up there to look around. It's the road we need to take to get to Paco's. If the coast is clear, you get behind the wheel, put the pedal to the metal, and get the truck up that rise. As fast as you can. Back up a bit and take a run at it if you need to, but I want the truck up there in one shot. Got it?"

I nodded. Gord opened his door slowly, trying to keep its metal creak quiet, left it open. Walking softly, glancing in every direction as he listened, he stepped to the hill. Scanned its top as he took a gun out of his jacket. The .357, it looked like. Checked the rounds, but there couldn't have been any bullets left in it. He tossed it into a thick clump of grass, no sound. Took out the cop's gun, checked the clip, put it back in. Climbed the hill with gun in hand.

I shifted over the seat and got behind the wheel. The engine was still running. One hand on the wheel, one on the stick, ready to jam it into drive. Waiting. Too many thoughts in my head telling me that I was becoming crazy. But once you were inside madness, I figured there was nothing to do but ride it to the end. I might die, but I'd go down fighting—I wouldn't get killed by some backwoods, inbreeding family while slinking away, betraying my friend.

Holding my breath, I watched Gord crest the hill and scan the area. Slowly, he stood up and paced at the side of the road, peering into the dark. Nothing drew his attention down either direction of the road, so I assumed no traffic was approaching, no distant headlights to be afraid of. He crossed to the other side of the road, I guessed, since he disappeared from my view. Checking out the opposite ditch most likely.

I waited, prayed that he reappeared quickly. Twisted my hands on the wheel, eyes unblinking. I was awake. Very awake, from fear and stress. I looked between my legs at the floorboard, coke dusted everywhere, the gas and brake coated, the poked-open bag spilling its wealth. I reached down and brought the sandbag to my lap. Jabbed a finger in and coated my nose. If I was about to die, die stoned. Gord had a point.

As I sniffed and squeezed my nostrils, a series of gunshots echoed from the road.

I convulsed at the blast, the bag jerking out of my hands to thump beside me. I smacked it onto the dashboard, held from rolling out down the truck's hood by a strip of ragged glass. Panic filled my veins, but I was able to use the panic to act. Slammed the truck into drive and stomped on the gas. As I did, Gord appeared on the road, waving me up. The driver's door slammed as the truck lurched forward, wheels

# THE BRIDE STRIPPED BARE

spinning, the rear end slewing, but my foot didn't leave the gas pedal. The steering wheel wrenched in my hands as the tires bounced over rocks and ruts, smoke billowing out behind me as the engine churned and tail pipe rattled. The coke bag rolled off the dashboard and landed back on the seat beside me. Looked like a sign that I should do more coke. In thirty seconds, I was up the slope and my front tires were on the gravel edge of the road. The center of balance tipped over and the truck was on a flat surface again.

I braked only long enough for Gord to get in the passenger side. He yelled, "Go! Go!," pointing down one direction, but I was able to glance for a few seconds at the other side of the road.

Two hillbillies were scrambling up from the ditch. The fatter one dressed in torn jeans, rubber boots, no shirt to cover his pot belly. Bald, with blood washed over one eye, and spurts of blood jetting out of his head over an ear. He carried a long shotgun which he tried to aim at us, but he lost his footing on the gravel. The skinnier one was in overalls and steeltoe workboots, also with a shotgun, but he couldn't aim—had it tucked under his good arm, the other limb dangling at his side, dripping blood from the shoulder down.

They swore and hollered as they skittered to the center of the road, the bald bleeder firing at us, the skinny one trying as best he could to aim and fire his weapon.

Gord and I ducked when we heard a ricochete off the truck's tailgate. I swerved across the lanes and soon put enough distance between us and the hillbillies. The road curved and the enemy vanished from the rearview mirror.

Gord got off the floor (his turn to curl and hide) and looked out the back.

"Hell, that was some fun, hunh?" He laughed, but I couldn't express any emotion except panic and shock.

"Who were they? Family?"

"Probably. Gorman must have half the town looking for us, checking all the roads, and where the road ends. Put those two boys there to wait for us."

"Do they have a vehicle?"

"Didn't see one, but that won't matter. They'll report back and say where they saw us, what direction we're headed in. The grapevine, cell phones, and CB radios can move quicker than we can. But we're coming up to the road to Paco's—the back-way in. I doubt they'll head down it to get us. They'll take their time, think they'll hedge us in, do a slow squeeze."

"You think they'll figure we're gonna try for the tunnel?"

"Maybe, maybe not. Remember all those guns and bazookas Paco has? They might think we'll try a stand-off. We gotta get some of that hardware anyway." He checked the cop's gun. Empty. He threw it out the window, took the shotgun from behind the headrests, checked the rounds. Popping the glove box, he tossed out another bag of coke and pulled out boxes of shotgun ammo, reloaded as the truck bumped and threw shotgun shells everywhere. "We better get there soon. If more family members show up, a little shotgun ain't gonna kill them all."

Gord saw the split open coke bag on the seat between us, winked at me, figuring I'd finally given into temptation. Which I had, of course. He snorted, then offered me the bag. I dug two fingers through the hole, widening it, shoved my powdery fingers up both nostrils. Wind whipped through the cab and puffed coke into the air. We were heading to Paco, who seemed to have an unlimited supply of good shit.

And the Black Betty must have still been working in my system, because I wasn't feeling it like I should have. Which meant, of course, that I needed to snort more and more just to feel a little happiness. Goddamn cocaine…created by God to turn people into devils.

I stepped on the gas, saw nothing but black road ahead, stars littering the sky. The shotgun stood obscenely upright between Gord's knees

# THE BRIDE STRIPPED BARE

as he bowed his head like a praying priest and stuffed more coke into his nose. He offered some to me, but I tried to be a good boy and reigned in my urges, kept my hands on the wheel and concentrated on driving.

"The dirt road to Paco's is coming up on your left."

And just as Gord pointed through the shattered windshield, wind battering our faces, I thought I saw a star that had fallen to Earth. Then two stars appeared low on the road. My addled brain finally clicked in that two headlights were heading towards us.

"Shit," Gord said, taking up the shotgun and aiming it through the windshield. "Just keep it steady, eyes wide…your job is to get us onto the dirt road. I'll take care of the shooting."

He was stating the obvious, but I needed to hear it. My arms started shaking and I couldn't stop swallowing, neck tight, mouth dry. In my head I started a mantra: "oh fuck oh fuck oh fuck" as the vehicle closed in. I slid my ass down in the seat and must've looked like a little old man barely seeing above the wheel. I was preparing to duck and drive blind.

The vehicle—a Jeep jacked up on thick tires—rushed up on the opposite side of the road. Gord got off the first shot—the gun blasting me to deafness—and hit a man standing up in the back of the Jeep, aiming something at us. He flew backwards like an airborne crucifix and then folded up and tumbled on the asphalt.

Gord was a good shot, thank God. I had stayed low but sat up again when the Jeep passed. Looked behind me to see it smoke its tires to do a one-eighty and head after us. I stepped on the gas.

"It's right there," Gord said, pointing at a dirt road that was almost invisible. Just dust and dry, rutted mud that descended from the road and wound into dense trees. I cranked the wheel as Gord scrambled a hand around the floorboard and dash and seat, collecting shotgun shells, then he shifted his ass and aimed the gun through the back.

He loaded and shot, but since there was a limited number of shells, he didn't fire too randomly. Plus, when the truck was on dirt, bouncing and skidding, and the Jeep behind us doing the same, it was tough for Gord to get off any decent shots.

In the rearview, I saw a driver and a passenger—the passenger with a revolver aiming from his side window, firing wildly. Bullets hit the truck or deflected off into the forest. Gord and I kept low. I was basically driving by aiming the truck's single headlight between stands of trees. If there was something on the road, I would've hit it. At least the top of my head was below the line of the back window. Though the wind howled into the cab, I thought I heard the hiss of a bullet or two just over my scalp. I scootched a little lower.

Gord fired shells, then ducked down to reload, hand scrambling in the dark cab. "Fuck yeah! Got a headlight and his windshield! Glass in the face, you fuckers!"

I didn't hear any more bullets for a few moments and Gord looked over at me. "The driver's blind—think he got a piece of glass in the eye—but he doesn't have the gun. I got an idea. When I say so, hit the brakes and brace for impact."

My left foot was hard against the floorboard, already braced, and my head and neck were pinned against the seat, so I wasn't worried about whiplash. Gord edged higher up the seat, exposing himself, the gun holding as steady as possible in his hands.

"Come on, fuckhead—that all you got?" he yelled, then ducked down as a few bullets came in response. He whooped and laughed, looked at me. "They're weak—hit the brakes!"

I did. Gord had both legs bent, feet on the glovebox to brace himself, shoulders against the seat. The impact jolted us, but not as hard as it could've—the Jeep's speed was too low with the driver probably trying to pick glass out of his face.

In a flash, Gord stretched half his body through the rear windshield and started firing off shells, reloading, firing again until he couldn't find anymore shells littering the cab. The last headlight behind me had

# THE BRIDE STRIPPED BARE

snapped off with a crash of glass. Then Gord got out of the truck. I sat up to watch him rush to the Jeep's passenger side, wrench the door open, gun barrels aimed inside, though the gun was empty.

The passenger fell out when the door opened. "Chris, they're dead," he called. "Come here."

I put the truck in park, raced to the driver's side of the Jeep. Face covered in splashes of blood, shards of glass protruding from skin, buckshot shearing away a good chunk of the right hemisphere of the brain…I could still make out that it was a woman. Once beautiful, in fact. I stared at her, chin sagged to her collarbone, arms limp at her sides, a rake of blood pouring down her shirt, over her heavy breasts, pooling on the seat between her cut-off denim shorts.

I felt sick, puked a small puddle onto the ground.

Gord tossed the shotgun aside and rifled through the Jeep, the glove compartment and under the seats, and through the pockets of the dead passenger on the ground. The search gave him a revolver. Found a box of bullets in the glovebox, but there were no other weapons. The man who was blown off the back had taken his weapon with him. I checked under the woman's seat without looking at her. Trying not to get her blood on me, but that was impossible.

"Turn off the ignition, throw the keys into the bush. This thing will help block the road just in case more are on their way. We got lucky twice—third time's the charm. Let's get the fuck to Paco."

I threw the keys into dark trees and Gord and I headed down the road. Leaving behind another scene of death. My mind couldn't process all I had done or seen in the last few hours. So I told myself to stop thinking—just act. Thinking too much got you into trouble—acting kept you alive.

# Chapter 8

Paco's house at night was more ominous than in daylight. No lights on inside or outside, which made it look more abandoned and derelict. Like a lonely house where a killer once lived just before he shot his whole family then turned the gun on himself. Or a serial killer's humble abode, where every pebble and leaf on the lawn, and every nail holding the clapboards together, had a spot of someone's blood on it and would tell a hellish story if any of it could talk.

Gord told me to pull into the driveway, but not right up to the house. Kill the remaining headlight fast. Stop and wait and listen and watch. Just because it didn't look like anyone was home didn't mean Paco wasn't watching us, about to creep up behind us and press a cold barrel behind one of our ears. Been there.

I whispered as quietly as I could, keeping my lips from moving. "I'm following your lead. You tell me what to do, I do it. But please don't get me killed. If you can help it."

"I'll try" was the response, not encouraging. "We don't go in the front, don't knock on the door—Paco wouldn't answer anyway. Safe bet that the place is locked up, all booby traps in place, and he won't be happy to see us."

Gord had the revolver in hand, re-loaded, the box of bullets sitting on the seat between us. He shoved the gun down the back of his pants, flipped his shirt over its bulge.

# THE BRIDE STRIPPED BARE

"He can only shoot one of us at a time."

"You really know how to make me feel better, Gord, you fuck," I whispered.

"Just stating facts."

"He has an arsenal. Automatic fire can kill two birds with some pretty quick stones. And we can't fly away."

"We're not going to give him that chance," Gord vowed.

"You have a gun, I don't. What do you think the chances are of me wrestling *any* gun out of his hands—and living—after he kills you?"

"Not good." At least Gord was honest, the bastard.

"I hate you, Gord."

"I love you, Chris."

I followed his lead and squeaked open my door as quietly as possible. But with the kind of silence only heard—felt—in the depths of a dark forest, a squeak sounds like a banshee wail. I winced with every inch that the door opened. Like pulling off a bandage, I chose to just push the door open in one shot. If the sound woke up the ogre, so be it.

Leaving our doors open, Gord and I stepped to the front of the truck. I followed behind as we made our way over and through the labyrinth of litter on the lawn. Slow steps, like walking across a minefield, feeling with the soles of our shoes where we were stepping before putting weight down on each foot. This wasn't a comedy, so thankfully we didn't kick a hubcap and send it rattling into a pyramid of scrap metal, bringing it crashing down.

I had a feeling I knew where Gord was leading me before we got there. And I was right. The outhouse. He motioned for me to get on one side, he on the other, then we slowly tilted it backwards on its hinges and let it rest on soft weeds. A hole faced us that was so black it was two-dimensional. Like looking at the portal into another dimension. Paco's dimension.

Gord stepped to my side, pulled my shirt to draw me a little way from the hole—as though it were able to hear us.

He whispered, "You lower me down. It's not too far a drop. I won't break my legs, but I'll make a helluva noise once I land on the elevator platform at the bottom. Might wake our friend—wherever he is—might start him shooting. If he kills me, you gotta figure out what to do on your own. Kill Paco then try for the tunnel—do *not* go back to town."

All the air left my lungs. "I fucking hate you. Don't you dare die. I've still got too many questions."

He smiled in the darkness, hissed a laugh, and gave me a quick one-armed hug. Then he knelt down at the edge of the hole and listened. I knelt beside him. I had never seen anything darker than that hole, I felt that if I put my hand in, the darkness would consume my flesh, crawl up my arm, devour me.

Gord and I kept silent, though our shoes scraped dirt, making me even more nervous. I regretted doing that coke, but regrets never kept anyone alive, so I told my mind to shut the hell up.

Dipping his legs into the blackness, Gord sat on the edge of the hole. I tried to figure out the best way to hold his weight, lower him down, but not go down myself. I lay on my stomach and felt around with my feet for something to hook my toes around. A tree root arched out of the earth for my left foot, and a half-buried piece of metal was enough of a sturdy post for my right foot to hook around. Gord shifted his sitting position, grabbed my hands, and slipped his ass off the ground. Soil and stones fell and clattered on the wooden elevator platform. We both winced, held silent for a moment, waited for Paco. But he never arrived. So, I lowered Gord deeper into the hole.

I could only see his hands clasping mine, the rest of him swallowed by blackness. Then his fingers loosened, and his grip left my wrists.

I opened my hands and it seemed to take hours of freefall before Gord landed on the plank of the elevator. The hollow boom of his boots

# THE BRIDE STRIPPED BARE

on wood echoed up the shaft. We both held our breath. The echo died. We both stayed silent and waited a little more. Gord likely had the revolver out of his jacket and in his hand, sweeping the darkness for a target, hoping he hit it before it hit him.

A breeze blew my hair as I looked at the dark terrain around me, sniffed the pine air. My feet still hadn't relaxed from each of their securing hooks, my whole body tense as I lay on the ground.

Then I felt something cold and hard worm its way under the hair at the back of my neck. Thought it was a mosquito or a bug until, trying to bat it away, I felt steel.

Heard the click of a gun.

"*Hola*, fucker. That's a funny way of taking a shit in my outhouse."

«««—»»»

I needed to pee, but couldn't move. The muscles at the back of my neck were tight and my fingertips dug into the earthen lip of the hole.

"Gord," I called down an echo. "Paco's up here."

The owner of the gun kept it pressed against the base of my skull as he stepped to straddle either side of my prone body, leaning over to look into the dark.

"Gordy?" Paco called down. "What the fuck are you doing in my basement?"

"Hey…Paco," Gord said, trying to sound nonchalant, but his tone was unconvincing. I hoped Gord was thinking faster than I was, coming up with an excuse to get the gun off my head.

"Dude," Gord tried again, though I thought he was talking to me. "We got a fuck-up with the shipment. Some fuckers stole part of it, then came after us looking for more or something. We wasted them."

"Who the fuck were they?"

"We don't know. Most of it was unloaded when we got back, but I kept a few bags for personal use. Had them in the truck—some goddamn good ole boys I've never seen before thought they'd try their luck. We left them for dead back near the highway. Check out my truck—its shot for shit—we're lucky we're alive."

I felt Paco's looming body move away from me, the gun barrel gone, his feet crunching dirt.

"You stay put, Gordy. I'm taking your boy, checking your story. If it's bullshit, I blow his head off. Deal?"

"Deal."

I was sandwiched, face pressed to the ground, between two guys who couldn't see each other in the dark, but who had just made a deal for my life. What a great vacation.

"Get on your feet," Paco instructed.

I stood, hands held palms-up as I walked—stumbled, tripped, kicked scraps of loose metal—to the truck with Paco at my back, a rifle barrel leaning into my spine. Not an ancient, backwoods rifle one inherits from grandpappy, but one of the shiny modern ones which Paco had in his arsenal.

When we got to the front of the truck, he said, "Stay there, don't fucking move, keep your hands up—good bitch."

I stayed where I was and watched him move around to the driver's side. He pointed the rifle barrel into the bed of the truck as he looked in, but there was nothing to see. His coke was gone. A flashlight would've helped him, but maybe he could see in the dark. The interior of the truck cab was too dark, and I wondered what proof he would need to not shoot me in the head. Could he make out bullet holes in the doors? The smashed glass should've tipped him off that we'd really been shot at.

Then he did something weird. I thought he saw a ghost and wanted to shoot it. He raised the rifle up to his eyeline and aimed into the cab.

# THE BRIDE STRIPPED BARE

But he didn't shoot. Instead, he roved the barrel from the seats to the floorboard to the dash, and kept the rifle raised as he walked around to the back of the truck.

And then it hit me. He was looking through a scope on the rifle, and it probably had infrared night vision. Paco wouldn't be the type to use a flashlight to see in the dark. Let your rifle see for you—and shoot the enemy who skulked around your property.

He was a smart fucker. I hated him more.

On the passenger side, he looked through his rifle scope again, then looked at me—barrel first. Tilting the rifle up, he reached into the truck and grabbed something, then lifted a full hand to the rifle scope to get a better look. Looked at me while he dropped whatever was in his hand into his shirt pocket. Popped the glove compartment open, slammed the passenger door closed, did the same beneath and in the narrow space behind the seat.

Not looking happy (as usual), he slammed the passenger door closed, held the gun at me from a low angle.

"Where's the gun?" he asked me.

"What gun?"

He dipped fingers into his pocket and threw bullets at me. The box which was left on the seat. "Open your fucking jacket."

I did. I took it off, let it hang from an upheld hand like a deflated balloon.

"Lift up your shirt," he commanded. All this time, he was inspecting me through the rifle scope—which meant, of course, that the rifle was always aimed at me. So, I obeyed all his commands, hoping to God the rifle's safety was on. If it had one. "Lift up your pant legs one at a time. Kick your shoes off—don't touch them—kick them. Drop your pants—below the fucking knee, fucker. Pull your underwear down and lift your balls. Scratch your fingers through your hair. Okay, now get dressed—*ándele*! Head back to the shithouse."

I had never been strip-searched before, so it made me feel incredibly violated. Thank God it was dark so I couldn't see myself. How in the hell could I stash a gun under my balls? And if I had, how could I have walked? Especially in the dark?

Ultimately, it didn't matter. Paco had searched people by rifle scope before, obviously. He knew what he was doing—he had to, since he shipped a ton of drugs to and from two countries.

I tried to tell myself not to panic. Didn't say a word as I got dressed and continued following instructions back to the outhouse tunnel.

"You got bullets in your truck, *ese*," Paco called down the hole.

"No shit," Gord called back. "Bullet holes all over the place."

"I didn't say bullet *holes*—I said bullets. A box of them on the seat. Where's the gun?"

Gord may have paused too long. Paco was getting antsy, shuffling around the lip of the hole, barrel pointed down to see through the dark. I hoped Gord had the revolver hidden.

"I dunno—did you check the truck?" he finally said.

"It's not in there."

"It must've bounced out, I dunno. We were off-roading to get here. The windows got blown out—I'm amazed the bullets didn't bounce out too."

"Fuck that shit—get up here—keep your hands where I can see them."

I heard Gord's boots stomping on the wooden base, then he must've found the control for the elevator. Its chain rattled and the motor hummed, but not for long. All hollow echoes stopped.

"Paco, someone's gotta be down here to work the controls. I got it in one hand, but if I go any higher it'll drop, and I'll be stuck in the shaft."

Paco muttered Spanish curse words under his breath, then pointed the rifle at me.

# THE BRIDE STRIPPED BARE

"Get in the hole. You bring him up."

I sat on the edge of the blackness, legs dangling, looking into the abyss. "Gord, I'm coming down. I can't see shit. Sorry if I land on you."

"Wait a minute," he called back up. "Let me go back down. I'll work the controls, bring the elevator to you."

I looked back at Paco. He was looking down the hole with the scope. "Okay, Gord, do that. But I can see you from here—I got a scope, and I'll riddle you with holes if you fucking try anything."

"Paco, dude, be cool about this. I just want to make up my loss. I'll pay you triple for it. You can dance with the bridesmaids—fuck all three if you want."

The elevator lowered, setting Gord on the floor of the tunnel, then rose up to ground level. I stepped on and called to Gord to bring me down. Was Paco buying this? In a matter of seconds, Gord and I would both be in the tunnel, where we wanted to be in the first place. Was Paco stupider than I thought? He kept his gun trained on my head the whole way. I couldn't see a thing and didn't know I was underground except for a shiver of cold and echoes off rock. The platform abruptly halted. With hands held out in front of me, I felt only stone wall. Then Gord spoke and I turned toward the sound of his voice. I stepped off the platform. Gord grabbed my hand and pulled me away from the elevator shaft.

Paco bought it. Then he smartened up quickly. He swore a blue streak, telling us to get back into view. A storm of bullets crashed down the elevator hole, then Paco told us what he was going to do to our bellies, nice and slow.

I was being pulled into the darkness, stumbling, heard Gord's voice tell me to get up. I followed him, feeling the cold air around me with my free hand until I felt a tower of sandbags.

His voice was close beside my ear, muted by the rock wall behind me and the sandbags in front. "Stay here," he whispered. "Paco's going to head down. I can't believe he sent you down—he gets stupid when he's really paranoid. But now we need him to open doors, to the gun room at least. I'm going under the stairs, try to get a lucky shot. You try to distract him if you can."

I hissed out a whisper, "How? He can see in the dark! He's gonna fucking kill us down here, Gordy! It's a turkey shoot for him!"

"I don't know…throw some bags of coke at him. I know this room well enough in the dark. Wait—I've got an idea."

He put the gun in my hand, tore open the plastic covering the sandbags, grabbed a few from the top. His steps shuffled away, then I heard something soft hit steel, then another soft thud clang on metal stairs. He returned to get more.

"What are you doing?"

"I'm making a trail of cheese for the rat," Gord giggled as he took down more coke bags. "He's going to be so pissed when he sees his shipment scattered all over the place." I heard a tear in one of the bags, then Gord's nose snorted. "Help yourself. Better to die high."

His steps shuffled off again and I heard more thuds. Then the muted voice of the demon, Paco, sounded from behind the door at the top of the steps. Gord rushed back to me, took the gun out of my shaking hands, rushed away. I pressed my back against the stone wall and sweated.

Steps up the metal stairs rang, a shot from the rifle hit stone and ricocheted, steps clattered down the stairs again.

Then I heard beeps, a click, then the door opened.

"You're both fucking dead! No lights, eh? No problem. I spend every day down here, Gordy, it's the back of my hand! My coke! You pieces of shit!"

The rifle blasted a stream of bullets into the pallets, sending up clouds of cocaine. You couldn't help getting stoned just by inhaling the air. I figured Paco really hated us if he was okay with destroying his shipment.

# THE BRIDE STRIPPED BARE

Thinking of Gord—hopefully under the stairs, pointing his gun up, taking aim at Paco, waiting for the asshole to get in line for a good shot—I knew I had to help. I dug out a sandbag and lobbed it high over the pallet. Paco sprayed bullets, and maybe the bag burst but I couldn't see.

"Hiding behind the coke like a fucking pussy?" Paco said, then laughed. "You're trapped, bitches! You're blind. Throw me another one—I'll blow it out of the sky!"

I did as ordered. Paco must have felt the coke in his system, too. A coked-up psychopath was not a good beast with whom to go to war. But I dug another bag out and lobbed it over the pallets, braced my ears for the blast. Bullets ricocheted off the rock walls. Paco's boots started forward, clanging on the staircase. Exactly what I was hoping for. I kept up the distraction, throwing more and more bags for the fool to shoot until his steps clanged down every stair and he was fully underground with us. Cursing me and Gord for making him shoot his coke.

Gord screamed.

Three bullets blasted and echoed, a spurt of rifle fire shot up into the cavern ceiling, a body thudded to the ground like the heaviest sandbag of all. Silence. I held up my next bag like a kid with a stuffed bear. Hugged it to my chest as I listened.

"He's dead," said a voice.

Took me a while to click in that it was Gord's voice, not Paco's.

"Chris, you can come out."

Still holding the coke bag, I felt my way around the pallet into the open. The air smelled like a shitload of cocaine. I was getting higher with every breath.

"He's dead?" my whisper asked.

"Yeah. His rifle fell at my feet. So did he. Looking through the scope now. Fuck, I made a mess of his head."

"Where are you? I can't see shit."

"I see you. Just walk forward, a little to your right, almost there. Hi."

Felt Gord's hand grab my shoulder. Then he put a long gun into my hands. "Have a look."

I felt the contours of the rifle, found the scope, held it up to my eye. Greenish-white clouds of dust roiled in the air. The sandbags on the pallets were eviscerated, spilling powder in streams. I revolved the rifle in a circle, caught a glimpse of Gord, the barrel hitting him in the side of the head.

"Easy with that, buddy. Look down."

Paco lay face-down on the cavern floor. Well, not really—he didn't have a face. Barely even a head. Chunks of, I guessed, skull and flesh and hair lay in scattered clumps around the stump of his neck, a pool of dark green pouring out across dirt and powder.

The scope fell from my eye.

"That's fucked up," I whispered.

"You distracted him good—he never looked under the stairs," Gord said, slapping me on the shoulder and taking the rifle from my hands. My arms relaxed and I tried to get the image of the headless man out of my head.

"Follow behind me, hold onto my jacket, I'll take it slow," Gord instructed.

I clutched a fist of Gord's jacket as he held the scope up to his eye and led us both up the stairs and through the door. Eventually, we made it into the gun room. Gord found a light and we squinted at the glare until our eyes adjusted.

The arsenal was impressive. Like a kid in a gun store, I looked at everything, wanting to play with it all. Then I asked a niggling question.

"Are we gonna need any of this?"

"Never know," Gord said, taking down a machine gun, a rifle called an M-16 with a carrying strap attached to it, plus a few clips,

# THE BRIDE STRIPPED BARE

stuffing them into his pockets. I'd seen most of the guns in movies, so they weren't completely foreign to me. Then Gord took what looked like grenades, jammed them in pockets where they could fit. I copied him. Had no idea how to fire the gun and felt a little uncomfortable having explosives in my pockets.

He handed me a machete about three feet long in its own sheath, which had a strap that tightened around my waist. Took one himself. "Just in case of close combat."

"Close combat with who?"

"Whom."

"*I'm* the English geek, remember?"

"Never know who might be in the tunnel."

Ah yes, and I had thought it would be just a walk in the park…or, in the tunnel. Silly me.

Gord handed me a pair of ugly goggles that had two lenses which tapered outward as cones. "Paco should've used these instead of having his eye trained through a scope. He's lived in the woods too long."

He told me they were infrared goggles. I strapped them onto my head. He showed me how the lenses hinged upward, and how to change the sight from night vision to regular vision.

"Won't get too far into the tunnel without them."

We were heavily armed. I felt like a soldier—me, a professor of literature. Living a new life. No one back at the college would ever believe this—if I even got back there. I'd go out with a bang, that was for sure.

With goggles on, we went back down the steel staircase and into the green darkness. Stood facing the tunnel, cold air wafting over us.

"How far is it to Canada?" I asked.

"Not sure. But we probably have a bit of a walk ahead of us. Remember, though, it's a walk to freedom."

I looked at the gun in my hands. "You're going to have to show me how to use this thing."

Gord chuckled. But before he said a word, we both froze, thinking we heard something in the distance. Not down the tunnel but coming from the elevator shaft. He put a glowing green finger to his lips, and I followed him to the shaft. We stood and listened. Voices. A vehicle door closing. More doors. Laughter.

"Shit," Gord whispered. "The family caught up to us. I'll go upstairs to make sure. You stay down here, locked and loaded. Just aim and squeeze the trigger, the gun'll do the rest."

I felt cold from head to foot as I watched Gord be as quiet as possible climbing the stairs and vanishing through the door. I looked up the elevator shaft, listened. Could make out four distinct voices, but there could've been more. Wondered if any of them knew Paco's place as well as Gord did, and if so, were they about to peer down into the dark shaft? Could they see in the dark?

Stones and dirt clattered down into the shaft and hit me. I bit my tongue and stepped off the elevator platform.

"I think there's someone down there," a voice said, then called down an echo, "Hello?"

I edged my goggles back up the shaft to see two faces looking down at me. Tightening my finger on the trigger, I raised the rifle barrel upward.

"Can't see nothin'," another voice said. "How far down is it?"

"Hell I know, I never do a pick-up. Can't be far, I reckon'."

"How you figure that?"

"I dunno. It's hidden by this here shitter. Someone knocked it over, so I figure someone's down there. Hey, Paco—you there? Gord with ya?"

The voices paused, listening. My throat was as thick as a tree trunk. Dirt and a good-sized rock fell down the shaft, clattering on the elevator.

"See? It don't sound far down," one voice said. "Drop yourself down there."

"You drop down there; I'll break my legs."

# THE BRIDE STRIPPED BARE

"That's 'cuz you're so fat."

"Fuck you. I'll go down the other way, through the front door."

"You shittin' me? They ain't gettin' in that way. Paco's always got it locked up tighter than a nun's ginnie, with a ton of booby traps. Why'd you think he's got this secret entrance? This is the only way in—I'll put a pound of weed on it."

"B.C. Gold—not your homegrown shit."

"Fuck you, my shit's good. But you're on. Get your ass down there."

Legs dangled into the shaft and I watched as one of them twisted his body, trying to get a good hold of the earthen ledge, his boot toes kicking more dirt down. I had to do something, or I'd have company. Aiming the rifle at the man, feeling the rifle stock against my shoulder, I breathed slowly. And pulled the trigger.

Nothing happened. Pulled again. Cursed Gord in my head for not giving me a quick lesson. I figured the safety was on, but where on the damn gun was the safety?

While quickly scanning the gun with my goggles, I saw the controls of the elevator in my lenses. A light bulb went on in my head, then exploded. The man was dangling full-bodied down the shaft, his friend holding his wrists. They cursed each other. The dangling man was grunting and swearing, afraid to drop, but he knew he had to. Not knowing how far you have to fall makes the drop infinite.

The man dropped and landed on his ass, his head whipping backwards, smacking the wooden platform. An "Oof!" burst out of him. Moaning and swearing, he held his head and tried to get to his knees but was too dizzy. The other man called down to see if his friend was hurt, but the fallen man couldn't talk coherently at first.

I took my chance. Grabbed the elevator controls and pushed the button that started the platform rising. The man glanced around in the dark, holding on all fours as he felt the wood shift under him.

"Yeah that's it, bring the elevator up to me," the voice above called.

"I ain't doin' it. I told you—someone's down here!"

Before the platform could rise high enough into the shaft, the man rolled off the platform—whether by intent or accident, I didn't know. He hit the earth hard, wind knocked out of him once again, but still tried to get his hands and knees under himself. He reminded me of a wounded spider.

I kept my thumb on the elevator button as I stared at the man. I knew I had to kill him. I told myself to bury my civilized morality and just find the safety on the gun. It was hard with only one hand holding and trying to inspect the details of the rifle. I figured it had to be close to the trigger guard.

Eyes between the man and the elevator, I felt my heart hammer. Sweat and salt wormed around my eyes. The man got to his feet, coughed and farted a few times, feet shuffling backwards until his back leaned against the rock wall. Breath heaving in and out, he held a hand to his sternum. Maybe a heart attack would kill him for me.

If not, he made a perfect target.

The elevator reached the top and stopped, sealing the tunnel. I heard gunfire distantly above me, up the shaft, someone in the trees. Then I heard screams in the other direction, up the stairs and into the house. Guns blasted and more people screamed.

With two hands on the rifle, my fingers searching for the safety, I heard a click.

"What the fuck?" the hyperventilating man said, peering into the dark. At me, but he didn't know it.

At once, I raised the barrel and squeezed the trigger. The gun kicked me backwards onto my ass as bullets swept upward in a ragged line from the man's crotch to his forehead. He fell onto his face at my feet. My arms shook and the universe stopped to catch its breath.

I had killed a man. For sure this time—not just a drug-induced dream.

# THE BRIDE STRIPPED BARE

I was in horrified awe and numb at the same time. I stared at the corpse for a long time until the sound of a banging door brought me back to the real world.

Gord dropped down the steel stairs two or three at a time.

"I got a few of the fuckers, and booby traps got some more. Dumbasses. There's at least three more outside, but I locked up what I could, it'll buy us some time. Oh shit…you got one too."

He looked down at the dead man. I looked at him too, rifle relaxed in my hands.

"He dropped down," I said in a cracking voice. "There's another one up there, but I lifted the elevator, sealed him out."

Gord glanced up the shaft, then at the dead man again. He smiled in the green light of the night vision.

"Good thinking. That's the first man you ever killed, isn't it?" I nodded. He patted my shoulder. "Good work. Semper Fi. Now let's get the fuck out of here."

I followed him out at a jog as we headed down the tunnel, trying to keep from thinking about the man I had killed—what this made me now—a killer, a murderer. Or, a soldier in a strange war, maybe? I ran for what seemed like a long time, not feeling any pain in my legs, running on stilts, the goggles bouncing on my face, the machete slapping against my thigh and knee, cocaine in my veins to kill all pain.

I slowed to a walk as Gord did. We caught out breaths, looked behind us and in front, seeing nothing but a green-dark tunnel.

"Those motherfuckers," he heaved out between breaths. "The family doesn't give up when they're on the hunt." He glanced at me and chuckled. "I guess you figured out how the gun works."

"Took a while, but yeah."

He looped an arm around my shoulders. "Well, you might have to use it again. Cross your fingers that you don't. We got a head start so hopefully we can get to the end of the tunnel before they catch up.

They'll radio for reinforcements most likely, now that a few of theirs are dead."

I felt all the air go out of my lungs. I bent over at the waist and vomited a puddle of glowing green. Things were starting to hit me, adrenaline wearing off. I coughed and spat and puked a little more.

"You gonna be okay?" he asked. I nodded, unable to talk. "Take your time, but not too much. Can you walk and puke?"

I admitted to him, "I snorted a lot of coke while you were out of the truck...plus the air at the pallets was full of it."

"Good boy, that'll keep your head on straight."

"No, I mean, I think that's why I feel like shit."

"Nah, that's just from making your first kill. You still got the Black Betty in you."

"That horse pill?"

"Yeah, it lasts for about five years or so."

"Five *years!* What the hell is it?"

"Not sure. Secret family ingredients, they never told me. But you can snort tons of coke and just feel good and alert, not overdose."

"For *five* years?"

"Why'd you think it was so damn big?"

Shuffling forward a few steps, I spat out the bile taste in my mouth. Inhaled and stood back straight, sucked in cool breaths, cleared my head. Nodded once, and Gord and I maintained a walking pace for a while.

I asked him about the gun in my hands, so he gave me a quick tutorial. Showed me where the safety was, how to lock and load, how many rounds it fired per second. I commented on how he sure knew a lot about guns. He replied that he had learned a lot of things since moving out west, and since he'd met Venus. She was a world of knowledge—possibly now lost for good. We didn't talk about her much. I asked if he had ever killed another human being. His cryptic response was

# THE BRIDE STRIPPED BARE

"Who hasn't?" with a smile and a chuckle from the depths of his throat. He wouldn't say more, and I didn't ask for more details.

With rifle in hand and grenades swaying in my pockets, I felt like a soldier again. And it felt good. (Maybe it was partially to do with the coke, I had to admit.) Pushed away the professor side of me so that I could function, do what I had to do to survive. Must've gotten a second wave of coke to the brain, feeling blood speeding through my limbs, so I started jogging. Gord kept up. We didn't sprint, paced ourselves, shoes scraping soil and stone, getting further into the tunnel. I flipped up the goggles to rest on my forehead, two optical horns, preferring the joy of the cold darkness, no green vision bouncing my path ahead, making me a little dizzy. I followed Gord by the sound of his steps for a while before putting the goggles back down to give me clear vision.

Occasionally, we stopped, our shoes silent, only our breathing heavy. We listened back down the tunnel and, thankfully, heard nothing. No running steps, no voices, no gunfire. I relaxed a little more, feeling safe. Still cold, wondering how far beneath the Earth's surface we were. Down far enough so that someone on the surface wouldn't be able to hear us? If Paco was a professional drug smuggler, then the tunnel wall would have to be deep enough to stay hidden from any authority who may have suspected it existed. Ground-penetrating radar could probably find it, but if no one knew it existed, then no one would look for it.

I wanted to ask Gord how long Paco had been in operation. Did he know any details of the operation? When the tunnel was built, who built it, how was it dug without anyone taking notice, and did the entire family know it existed? Lots of question, still. But I doubted Gord knew (Paco being a very secretive man), or would tell me. Those details could maybe be answered at some later time. When we were safely finished our subterranean trek, our heads popping up like gophers into a new country.

I felt safer. More confident. Started thinking of Gord and me as the old friends we were when we were kids, on a hike into the unknown, enjoying the adventure. I caught myself smiling in the dark.

"What are you smiling at?" Gord asked, humor in his tone, goggles bulging his eyes.

"I don't know," I answered, my voice bouncing off the stone that surrounded us. "I feel good. This is kinda fun."

"Yeah," Gord said. "I guess it is."

Then we froze. Two small lights were far ahead in the tunnel, spaced apart, but wavering in and out of each other, moving, bouncing.

Accompanied by the sound of whining engines.

# Chapter 9

Gord told me to stand hard back against the wall on one side of the tunnel, stay low, keep my goggles on, keep the rifle barrel aimed at the target. And don't shoot him by accident. He'd be on the other side of the tunnel and a little behind me. We'd take whichever headlight—motorcycle, by the sound of the engines—was closest to us. Playing zones. Even if the targets crossed and switched sides, I was to stay on the one closest to me.

"Spray the bastard with bullets," he instructed. "But try not to shoot the wall too much. Ricochet. Don't throw a grenade—we're in close quarters and you'll kill us all. Don't fire until I do. They probably won't see us until they're close enough for us to shoot them."

"Who are they?"

"Duh, probably family. Canadian cousins who got the word by CB, text, satellite phone. Not good, but if there are only two of them squeezing us in, our chances are better than if we head back to fight the American branch of the family tree."

I obeyed orders, kept low, made sure the safety was off and the goggles on. It was as easy to see Gord or anything else through the gun scope with the goggles on, but I figured with a machine gun one didn't have to be too precise. Shoot a shitload of rounds and hope that one of them hit the target. I had my back half turned to press against the wall to buttress me to the rifle's kickback. Didn't want to be knocked on my ass again, especially if this time the enemy had guns too.

The guttural whine of their engines increased in echo as they approached. Headlights grew from pinpricks to klieg lights. Which didn't help to see them through the goggles, on either night or normal visions. I wanted to aim for the light to knock it out and give Gord and me an advantage of seeing them but not being seen, but I knew I had to go for a kill shot. Just above the light, hoping the rider wasn't too hunkered low for my bullets to pass over.

I was thinking too much. I had a machine gun, not a sniper rifle, with a full clip and a few more in my pockets.

Spray the fucker. The best strategy.

I jolted and the rifle almost slipped from my hands when I heard a gun close to my ear. Looked over—it was just Gord, the cave echo increasing the sound of the bullet's blast. I clicked in—he had started shooting—that was my cue to shoot too.

Stiffened my shoulder against the rifle butt and hooked my finger around the trigger. Squeezed it and didn't let go. Bullets poured out of the barrel—a star of fire perpetually bloomed around the muzzle—and I tried my best to keep my aim on the approaching headlight. Quickly forgot about aiming just above it. The gun sprayed. I had no idea if bullets were shot from the motorcycle to me—didn't hear or feel a thing—and I wasn't dead.

The motorcycle on my side went down, skidding to a scraping halt on the rock, the light bursting. Puffs of soil burst around the downed bike. I saw a boot punctured through the sole, torn to shreds, a wheel popped, the small tank pouring out gasoline.

I let go of the trigger only after I realized the gun was clicking empty.

I stayed crouched by the wall for a few minutes, then heard a howl behind me. Spun the rifle at the sound and clicked the trigger. Good thing the clip was empty, or I would've killed Gord.

# THE BRIDE STRIPPED BARE

"Holy fuck, buddy!" he said, stomping over to my side of the tunnel. "That's some good panic shooting! You kept *most* of the bullets on target." He stood over the motorcycle and rider, his goggle lenses swaying over the body. "Goddamn! You fucking made mincemeat out of this guy! And his bike! You wanna look?"

I sagged against the wall and caught my breath, face greased by sweat, hands tingling from the vibrations of the rifle. Flicked the goggles up to feel cool cave air on my burning face. I didn't want to look at my second (or third) dead man. I had just survived my first firefight, and I was glad it was over. Didn't want a repeat and didn't want to see the gory results. Flashes of Paco's head played in my mind.

Gord wandered over to the other motorcycle—his kill. Slung his rifle across his back, tipped the bike onto its wheels and rolled it over to me. He sat on the machine, kicked it to life, twisted the throttle to rev it up and spit green smoke out of its exhaust. Its headlight was smashed, but who cared when you could drive blind and still see?

"Killed the rider but missed the bike. Lots of practice sharpshooting since I moved out here. Hop on," he said.

I did, slinging the strap of the M-16 around my shoulder, the rifle barrel jutting up just behind my right ear, and adjusted the machete against my hip and leg.

With the engine revving he yelled over his shoulder to me, "This should make our trip to Canada a lot faster!"

I held onto his shoulders as Gord resisted doing a wheelie and sped us through the darkness. I flicked the goggles back down over my eyes to peer over his shoulder.

We raced down the tunnel and it seemed endless. It turned in a slow arc at one point, then straightened up. I kept wondering how in the hell did Paco—or a crew of Mexican druglords—build such a thing? A feat of modern engineering, especially since the whole thing would have to be clandestine. Where there's a will—and the promise of millions, or billions, of greenbacks—there's a way.

The tunnel snaked in an opposite arc and, once it straightened up again, we found our way was blocked.

By people.

A crowd of—we assumed—family stretched across the width of the tunnel. Some of them were in wheelchairs. They walked, hobbled, crawled, rolled. Most of them old and somewhat deformed—a wall of hideous, decrepit, malformed flesh crept toward us.

None of them fired a gun—all of them were unarmed. Gord did a one-eighty to get us away from them, but since no bullets had followed our retreat, he stopped. Let the motorcycle chug, idling, as we stared into the distance at the refuse of humanity.

"Is there something strange about them?" he asked over his shoulder.

"They're inbred freaks?"

"That's a given. But something else?"

I looked through the green haze, not able to see too much detail unless we got closer to them. They moved slowly, some members cutting off others—those pushing the wheelchairs of the others frequently squeezed against those on either side of the chairs, running over toes with the wheels, veering toward the rock walls. I focused on those closest to the walls, and every one of them had a hand on the stone, using it to guide themselves. Then I noticed that some of them were holding hands, leading one another.

The blind leading the blind.

I told Gord. He nodded. "Fuck yeah. The family must've sent them down as fodder, knowing we were armed. Hoping their numbers would swarm us. Unless, of course, this is where they live."

"Shit," I gasped. "Inbreeders…that makes sense. Genetically, an old, old family that keeps reproducing with itself must have a ton of members with genetic mistakes. Maybe instead of taking care of them, they put them down here to die?"

# THE BRIDE STRIPPED BARE

"Fuck," Gord gasped in return. "Venus never told me about *this*. Then again, why would she? Every family's got skeletons...and this one has a shitload and they're all right here."

We stared through the green darkness at the shuffling mob far ahead, their numbers clogging the tunnel.

"They might not be able to see," I said, "but if they grab us, we're screwed."

"I wanna try something," Gord said.

I held on as he revved the bike and headed closer to the mob. They reacted to the sound of the bike, angling their bodies and laggered strolls in the direction of the engine. Gord stopped the bike maybe fifty feet from their shuffling walk, got off the motorcycle, told me to get off, then snapped down the kickstand. I watched as he lifted his rifle and fired a burst into the people nearest the left side of the shaft.

They screamed and went down, blood shooting dark black-green through the night vision. Those not hit staggered away in the opposite direction, almost stampeding each other to find escape. Some tried to retreat the way they came but were blocked by those coming up behind them.

Gord fired another burst, this time at those crowding at the right wall. More went down in heaps, injured or instantly dead, wailing in some strange language. Gord giggled, fired more rounds into the crowd—in the center, then to either wing—bodies piling onto bodies, most still alive and writhing. Those still upright were desperately trying to get away from us.

"Fish in a barrel! Come on, Chris, you need practice with the gun, don't ya? Remember—they're family. Fuck 'em!"

It was cruel. Putrid. Like a sick, violent video game. Something out of Nazi Germany—but *we* were the Nazis. Another way to look at it: *we* had become the threat, not the mob. I felt nauseous, as usual, but I told myself that it was either them or us. I raised my rifle, closed my eyes, and squeezed off a burst.

Screams and moans, warbling and phlegmy cries rose up out of the crowd each time either Gord or I shot. Their mouths gaped in agony, which gave us a better view of…how all of their tongues had been cut out. Blood drooled out of their mouths, down their ragged, soiled clothes—burned stumps of blackened tongues. Tongues cut and cauterized. So, too, their eyes. That was the real reason why they were blind. Some of them had eyes drawn onto their eyelids, which were then sewn shut. The family took care of its own.

The terrible thing for me…it got easier to kill. Something had snapped in my brain when I killed the man at the elevator, and it kept snapping with each kill—either mine or Gord's. He didn't even seem to have the slightest problem with any of it. Who the hell (once again, I asked) was my best friend?

It was like we were at a carnival, shooting plastic ducks with BB guns. We could move the standing crowd to the left or right as we chose. Bodies piled up, blocking the paths of those behind—who were themselves being pushed forward by more of the living. We sprayed a fan of fire and watched one after one fall.

My second clip was empty. I had to get Gord to remind me how to change the clip. I reloaded, but then he told me to hold my fire.

"I think I get it now," he said as the crowd in front of us wailed and wept. "The family *wants* us to kill these deformed fuckers. They're the dregs. They want us to use up our ammo until we're unarmed, or these corpses fully clog the tunnel and we have no choice but go back to Paco's house. Fuck that—we've only got so much ammo, and we *are* reaching Canada. We gotta get on the bike and rush through them. You got your machete?" I slung the rifle across my back, pulled the blade of sharpened steel from its sheath, gripped it tightly. Gord continued, "I need my right hand for the throttle, so I'll hold my knife in my left. You put yours in your right. We'll scythe the crowd. Let's try not to slash each other."

# THE BRIDE STRIPPED BARE

"Brian Lumley would love this!" I yelled with a blood-lust laugh, which Gord echoed. "Well, if they were all vampires."

We both slung our rifles across our backs as we returned to the motorcycle. Gord snapped off the kickstand, and I was about to straddle the back when he held up a finger, wanting me to wait for a second, to hold the bike while he did something.

He stood in front of the bike, pulled a grenade out of a pocket, pulled the ring. I swallowed, then plugged my ears. A fastball pitch threw it over the heads of the first row of those still standing. The grenade burst and roared in the cramped cave like the engine of a 747. Shitloads of bodies exploded in all directions—those closest to ground zero were blown into spinning limbs and starbursts of blood. Those deeper in were dropped by shrapnel and shock and exploding eardrums.

But there were more bodies passed them. We couldn't see an end to the writhing, hunkering mass of crippled flesh. Thought for a second, as Gord straddled the bike and kicked it to life—that is one big-ass family! And the ones who confronted us were the *refuse*!

"Hold on—we're going corpse off-roading!" Gord yelled.

I looped my left arm across his chest and held the machete in my right—did a few practice swings to get the feel of the new weapon.

Gord revved the bike and shot forward, letting the front wheel pop off the ground in a wheelie so that we could get up onto the entwined mass of corpses and ride across it like a macabre flesh road to Hell.

I glanced down to see faces twisted, mouths gaping with severed worms of tongues (which also explained the 'language' of the mass: if the family rejects couldn't talk, then, if they ever escaped their tunnel prison, they could never tell of their horror; if they couldn't see, then they would never find their way out). Eyes were glazed over with thick white webs or burned in their sockets, weeping tears.

The knobby tires of the motorcycle hammered across the flesh, broke noses, tore the loose, wrinkled flesh of foreheads and necks, burned rubber streaks across spines and between breasts. Occasionally, a tail looped around a part of the bike or our feet but wasn't strong enough to hold on. Or it was hacked off before we dragged its owner too far.

And we hadn't even reached those standing.

Once we did, though, Gord hit the throttle and I stiffened my machete arm. We didn't need to kill, just cut a path through the jungle of flesh. The living squeezed on either side of us and faces and necks, hands and chests bounced back from the blade. Gord did the same on his side. The ones who couldn't get away from the noise of the motorcycle and the sting of our steel were pushed towards us by others, some falling beneath our wheels.

The bike itself, of course, did its damage. As much of a weapon as anything else. Running into whomever was ahead of us, toppling them, pressing them to the earth, tearing their bodies as we passed over. Some tried to reach for us with arm or tail (one even with some appendage that looked like a tentacle), but our legs shot out to kick them away as the machetes went to work.

At one point, I felt too many hands on my body, tearing at my jacket, trying to pull me off the bike. But my arm stayed around Gord's chest. Somehow, one of the hands was able to reach into my jacket, grabbing what it could.

A grenade rolled out.

I saw it drop into a nest of living limbs, fingers clawing at anything while in pain, and knew it was only a matter of time before enough of the hands and fingers pulled the ring, releasing the lever, and detonating the little metal egg.

I yelled into Gord's ear. "A grenade dropped! Get us out of here!"

The motorcycle kicked its front tire high as it battered against bodies. Gord slashed with his machete with his left hand as he twisted the throttle with the right. I hacked. Gord had to drop his feet off the motorcycle pegs to keep us upright. Blood and strips of flesh and shards of

# THE BRIDE STRIPPED BARE

bone showered us from behind. The shockwave of the grenade pushed us forward as it levelled bodies around and behind us, and we could finally see through the mass, an empty tunnel behind, their numbers thinned.

When we finally broke through, Gord skidded to a halt and we both got off the bike. Wiped blood and gristle off our blades, then sheathed them. Unslung our rifles, and we each spent a full clip on those who still walked or limped upright, and those who could still crawl with enough energy to be a threat to us.

Now I liked to kill. Sport of kings.

We left the dying to join the dead, hopped back on the bike after changing to a fresh clip each (I could do it myself now—I was getting to be a big boy!), and sped down the endless green darkness of the tunnel.

# Chapter 10

We stopped at a wall of stone. A stone ceiling and stone walls surrounded us, no sign of an opening or a tunnel to the surface. Our best guess was that, in all the mayhem of fighting through the blind, tongueless dregs of the family, we must have missed where the tunnel branched off, leading to a way out. We had only assumed that the tunnel went in a straight line, but it could've easily have been a labyrinth. Heading back across the terrain of corpses was not our ideal plan, but it looked like the only one we had.

I was exhausted, my slashing arm killing me. I sat back against the deadend wall and Gord joined me. Catching our breaths, re-living the hell we had just been through, glad that we were still alive.

Rubbing hands down my face, goggles perched on my head, I thought about something that didn't quite make sense.

"Where did those people come from?" I asked Gord, and myself.

"Like you said, they must've been in another tunnel linking to this one, the main one."

"But they were all blind. They should've been walking in all directions—down any branch—they'd even be right here."

He threw up his hands. "I don't know. The blind leading the blind? They all head in the same direction so none of them get lost? Your guess is as good as mine. We're alive, that's all I know."

# THE BRIDE STRIPPED BARE

But the problem still nagged me. I stood and strolled around the deadend, putting my goggles back on to see if there was even the tiniest gap in the stone. I tapped a knuckle against the rock as I paced from one wall to another, looking at the ceiling as well, hoping to see a crack in the rock and a sliver of sky. Was it still night? Even a waft of fresh air from the exterior blowing down through a crack would've been a shred of hope. I didn't want to head back the way we came.

The family, eventually, would come.

While knocking against the wall which Gord was leaning against, I noticed a change in the pitch. A hollow echo, not solid stone. Gord froze and looked at me.

"You hear that?" I whispered.

Then the entire wall moved.

Gord and I leapt back, watching the stone slide sideways, its base scraping on earth and stone, but also the grinding of rollers on ball bearings.

Two massive men, six feet tall minimum, muscles bulging out wife-beater t-shirts and sleeveless lumber jackets pushed the wall open to expose a gap that led outside. Dark pines and a full moon, fresh mountain air.

And about fifty men and women, none of them elderly or disfigured. All holding guns trained on Gord and me.

We stood still, hearts stopped, staring through green glows to see clearly the force of arms we faced.

Poppy stepped from around the tunnel gap and smiled, standing between the two giant men, his round blue lenses each dotted with little moons.

"Evening, boys," he said. "Welcome to Canada."

One of the men turned to ask Poppy, "Which one's the groom?"

Poppy chuckled. Pointed at me.

One of the men punched Gord in the face, sent his goggles flying, dropped him unconscious to the ground.

Poppy put something into the hand of the second man, who held the object sideways in his thick palm. He grabbed my throat, lifting my chin, and jabbed the object into the side of my neck.

The moon waned down to a green dot in my goggles.

# PART
- 2 -

# Chapter 11

I awoke strapped to a St. Stephen's cross, dressed in the costume—uniform—I had tried on at the tailor. I had pants on this time, but they weren't tights. Two thick brown animal skins, like bear fur, covered me from the waist down. My hands and feet were tied with dried animal sinews and I wore strange shoes or boots made of black metal, the toes each shaped into a cloven hoof.

That's what I saw when my head cleared. Whatever poison the massive man had injected into my neck still swam in my veins and made my vision somewhat blurry. I was indoors somewhere, the cross high above wooden floorboards, a black curtain stretching in front of me, spotlights shining down.

I felt as if I was backstage at a theatre. Which meant, I assumed, that I was about to be put on display. To reinforce this feeling, I heard the collective rumbling voice of a vast audience filter through the curtain.

Two men eventually arrived, both the size of the men who had rolled back the tunnel wall. It may have been them, but I couldn't tell. Each was draped from head to foot in thick black animal furs, with the heads of bears covering their identities. Each wore boots made of bear claws.

The lights dimmed to a subdued crimson and the curtain rose. The bear men on either side of me pushed the cross, which was on rollers,

# THE BRIDE STRIPPED BARE

to the edge of the stage. The audience was invisible without lights shining on them, but I could hear them. They gasped and murmured to themselves at my appearance. Children screamed with delight.

To my left was a cut log table with the circumference of a Douglas Fir. As broad as King Arthur's Round Table, I thought, with too many rings to count, ancient. It stood, perhaps, four feet high off the stage. The wood was highly polished, and I could see a thousand crisscrossed knife gouges across its shining surface.

I hated to think what it was used for. Probably not dining.

The two men stepped away behind me, giving me center stage. Then from my right came three smaller, thinner figures, each cloaked in furs with bear's heads hiding their faces. They stood only a few feet away from me, lined up to face the audience.

They simultaneously pulled off the bear heads and let their cloaks fall to hang just off their shoulders, revealing their naked bodies. They were beautiful. I knew them. They were the three women I had had an orgy with…in my dream. Or was it in my drug-enhanced reality? The white girl, the black girl, the Asian girl. Their bodies perfect, luscious, lustful. Painted with designs of gold that matched those on the ornate vest and jacket I wore.

Except, in this reality, there was a difference. Their bodies were those of young women, but their faces were of crones. The three old women I had seen in the gazebo. Elderly women painted with cosmetics to look like hideous whores. Their hair stylized—thick locks and curls woven with jewels and ornamental pins. Their mouths, topped by wispy moustaches, were toothless orifices haloed by wrinkles, deep lines cutting across every inch of skin like the rings of a tree.

Each turned her smile to me—old women shooting me looks of lust.

But it didn't last long. A rumbling of wheels on wood thundered to my left. Gord, dressed in his tailored uniform, was rolled out on a cross similar to mine, only smaller and lower. Later, I would see that his eyes had been punched black and purple, ligature marks bruised his neck. His eyes opened and closed as his head rolled from side to side, dazed. I doubted he knew where he was. His tied hands jutted over the posts of the X and he was pushed close to the edge of the stage. Which made me realize how much further raised I was on my cross.

He who was raised on the biggest cross becomes the main sacrifice? Was I the lucky one?

It was Poppy who pushed Gord out on the cross. The small man dressed in a similar vest and jacket, but the thread was green not gold, and the animal fur he wore on his legs was white. His cloven hoof shoes were dyed—or stained—red. Round blue glasses, as usual. I wondered if he even had eyes. He stepped to the opposite side of the stage from the three women.

The crimson light gave way to a stark white light.

Venus entered onto the stage.

She towered over those on the stage not pinned to crosses. Her cloven-hoofed, high-heeled shoes made of gold hammered the boards. She was nude, but her entire body was tattooed with rust-red henna in designs more intricate than those on our vests. It was difficult to distinguish everything her body displayed, but just at a glance I could see mosaics and chessboard patterns, limbs without bodies, faces in torment, mathematical symbols vomited by insects, letters from unknown languages, scenes of war and depictions of obscene lust between humans and animals, gods and devils. Hieronymus Bosch on a naked goddess.

Over the henna was a dusting of gold. Gold painted her nipples and lips and eyelashes. Poppy stepped to her, carrying a long white bear fur which he helped her put on. Attached to the cloak was the head of the beast looming high above the woven tower of her platinum blonde hair. Some form of wooden cradle kept the ursine head at least two feet above her hairline. She turned on a heel to smile at me, stepping heel-to-toe

# THE BRIDE STRIPPED BARE

toward me, stood at my side. Then she faced the audience so that they could bask in her majesty and beauty.

"Venus!" a voice cried, sobbing, desperate. "I'm sorry! It was a mistake—for the love of God, have mercy!"

Gord, his face leaning on his quivering bicep, blackened eyes weeping, stared across me to his bride. Former bride, perhaps. The audience hissed at him. Venus' eyes shot fury across the stage as Gord pleaded for his life. Her beautiful jaw roiled with snakes beneath the skin and her nostrils flared into skull pits.

My best friend yelled a wet burbling cry as Poppy leapt on him with a knife he pulled from his sleeve, and slowly drew a thick line of blood across Gord's forehead. The audience cheered as Poppy licked the knife clean and slipped it back up his sleeve. Venus smiled smugly.

The audience calmed when Gorman exited from upstage, wearing an animal's fur painted half black and half red, the colors split down the middle, with a beast's head hanging down his back. He passed between Venus and I to stand at the round table of wood, head bowed, mumbling in some language I couldn't understand. He passed his hand over the wood, then stooped to retrieve two golden goblets and a black wooden bowl from a hollow in the table.

Whatever prayer he intoned continued as he raised each cup separately to the spotlights, then rested them back on the stump; next, he raised the black bowl to the lights as the prayer went on.

Then Gorman—the priest of the marriage, I assumed—pulled a long dagger with a pearl handle from his sleeve, held it high as he mumbled his words, stood in front of Venus. She had to stoop to compensate for their height differences. Gorman held the dagger in two hands, raised it to Venus as she leaned over and opened her mouth. She closed her eyes and stuck out her tongue.

A thick, unhealed scar already sliced the center of her tongue. Gorman drew the blade down the scar and the flesh split open like rising dough, the end of her tongue cleft in two like the tongue of a snake. Blood swelled along the crease of her tongue and Gorman quickly put the dagger on the table, took up the goblet, and caught enough blood to fill the cup halfway.

He put the goblet on the table, picked up the dagger again, approached me.

"Oh, fuck no!" I yelped, then clamped my lips tight.

The audience laughed, and Venus smiled with her bloody mouth. A red V was smeared down her chin, dripping between her breasts. Gorman held the knife up to my face as he had with Venus, but there was no way in hell I was going to let him slice any part of my anatomy.

The massive men re-appeared from either wing of the stage and stood beside my cross. One of them held a strange metal mask like a face-shaped cage with a long flat piece of thin metal jutting from where the mouth of the cage-face was located. It had leather straps that could tie the cage to the wearer, but the man didn't need to use them since his hands were tied, and the mask was only needed for a temporary reason, not as a long-term torture device.

Then I remembered what this implement reminded me of, a torture device from Merry Olde Medieval Britain. A scold's bridle, or brank's bridle. To punish women who spoke too much. Or, in this case, to punish me.

He slipped the thin metal tongue between my lips and clenched teeth, ramming it in with the heel of his palm until it hit my uvula and I gagged. Then he jammed the metal mouth—a circular ring—between my teeth, wedging my mouth open.

I coughed and choked—my breath heaved—and I would've vomited but I had nothing in my stomach. The cocaine I had ingested made me feel no hunger, and the couple of times I had puked right after seeing a dead body—one of *my* kills—had emptied me out.

While my mouth was wedged open, the second massive man reached between my teeth with a pair of iron tongs and grabbed my

# THE BRIDE STRIPPED BARE

tongue. He pulled and I instinctively pulled back. The constant gagging, the threads of drool hanging out of the mask mouth, didn't make it easy for me to keep up the fight.

At one point, Poppy approached me, slipping the knife out of his sleeve, ready to drag the blade across my forehead to encourage me to stick my tongue out and keep it out. But Venus stopped him. With a glance, her eyes sharper than any knife. Poppy backed away and resumed his place on the stage.

It doesn't take long for your tongue to get tired. It may be the strongest muscle in the body, but human beings aren't accustomed to having it pulled and wrenched in a tug of war. I was exhausted and my tongue relaxed. The man with the tongs pulled my tongue out and held it jutting through the ring of the mask as Gorman uttered his prayer again. Then he used the dagger to carve a line down the center of the muscle.

My neck tightened, eyes squeezed shut and sweat beads bled down my forehead. Breath heaved in my burning lungs as I gargled out a scream. I tasted blood, swallowed it, coughed as it slipped down my throat half-inhaled.

One of the men tilted my head forward as Gorman put down the dagger and held the empty goblet under my chin. Like maple syrup from a tapped tree, blood ran down the crevice of my tongue to fill the goblet half-way. Then the tongs let go, the mask was removed, and I was left to suck my tongue, drinking my blood, soothing my wound.

I felt like what I was: a crucified man. Under constant and varied torture. I didn't pay any more attention to Gorman's mumbling and chants, my mind reeling, sweat in my eyes, the muscles of my entire body burning with exhaustion. They were trying to break me, and I was breaking.

Mouth open, I pulled in breath. Venus had the two goblets in either hand. I didn't see her until I felt the metal of the cup tip over my bottom lip and blood wash down my throat. I coughed, but my head was still tilted backwards, so I swallowed all the blood that hit the back of my mouth. I saw Venus drink the blood of the second goblet, smiling after with her perfect teeth, stained dark rust. I realized that we had drank each other's blood. To continue this communion, she tilted her face over mine, and slipped her bleeding tongue into my mouth. We tasted the iron of each other's mouth as the audience cheered and stomped their feet and pounded fists on tables.

Gorman stood between Venus and I, one hand clasped with mine bound to the cross, the other with Venus' long fingers and sharp nails folded into her father's withered palm.

He triumphantly spoke to the audience.

"The bride and groom are now joined to each other, but they still have yet to join as one to the family. The procession may begin."

More lights came on, showing the vast audience in the immense room. Severed bear heads with gaping jaws hung from the ceiling. The room was entirely made of split logs, but the walls were covered with overlapping bear skins of black, brown and white. The circular tables and high-backed chairs were wooden, with immense silver candelabras on each table. The men, women and children (as young as, perhaps, eight years old) who made up the audience all wore bear skins without heads, and it wasn't until they all reached the stage that I could see glimpses of their nudity beneath the skins.

The crowd lined up to either wing of the stage and ascended the stairs to walk to the round stump table at center stage. Gorman used the dagger to flick a quick slit in the fingertips of each person, and then squeezed out a drop of blood per finger, draining it into the black bowl. Each person then descended the stairs and returned to their table. This part of the ceremony took a long time to complete. I looked over at Gordy, whose face was raked with lines of blood that had poured down from his forehead. He couldn't open his eyes without blinding himself.

# THE BRIDE STRIPPED BARE

Instead, he hung his head to one side like a Christ and let tears flow when they could come.

The family proceeded past the stump table, and I watched them all. Men and women, boys and girls, all happily submitted to the bloodletting, sucking their fingers as they returned to become the audience again. Venus joyfully watched them too, and once or twice she met my eyes. She smiled and caressed my cheek with a knuckle. Flicked out her split tongue at me and licked up the blood it left on her bottom lip.

A new shock hit me when I saw the people next in line whom I recognized. They stopped at Gord and wept but were pushed ahead to the stump by Poppy. Gord's mother, father, brother and sister gazed up at me with fresh tears. All of them were dressed in bear skins, naked beneath. They had been like my second family so much that I called Gord's mother and father Ma and Pa. I couldn't find my voice, but I painfully mouthed their monikers to them, and they smiled through tears.

Gorman was about to cut Pa's finger, held over the bowl, but Venus stopped him. Her eyes pierced through the stare of the priest.

"No. They are not family. They come from the lineage of the *best man*," she hissed while snapping her glare over to Gord, who leaned an ear towards her. "Neither he, nor they, deserve to be bonded to our lineage."

Gorman looked at her, his dagger point held up, away from the bowl. "So...they are expendable?"

Venus raised an eyebrow while she glanced across the four members of Gord's family. (I wondered if they had been brought to the wedding only; had any been at the bachelor party as well?)

"Let them enjoy the feast," Venus said. "Perhaps they will fall in love with one of ours...and there will be a marriage in the future." She looked devil eyes down at Gorman. "The family can never be too big or have too many genetic strains in its make-up."

He smiled his lipless mouth at her, used the dagger to wave Gord's family off the stage. They left, Ma shaking and crying, Gord's sister, Elizabeth, looking into my eyes with sorrow and desperation. I hadn't seen her in years, and she was beautiful. I felt embarrassed for her when her bearskin cloak fell open and I saw a flash of her breasts. I looked away and she headed back into the audience.

The procession continued for at least an hour, maybe more. (The family could never be too big!)

When they were done, returned to their seats, Gorman lifted the now full black bowl to Venus for her to drink. He then lifted it to my mouth, one of the massive men squeezing my mouth to open my lips, and the blood was poured in. Gorman walked the bowl passed Gord, smirking as he did, then headed to Poppy. The three girls—or old women—to Venus' right were next. They drank greedily. The remainder of the blood was for Gorman, the priest. He drank and intentionally spilled much of the crimson to stain his cloak. A splashed bib sent trails of red down either color of bear fur to his shoes. The empty bowl took its place between the goblets on the stump table.

Gorman raised his arms to the standing crowd.

"The family renews its pledge to itself through the bride and groom, through the priest of the Great God Ursa, and through its many generations. The family is strong and unending and shall last from eternity to eternity. None shall break its bonds. Let Ursa receive you—"

"—and you," the crowd echoed as one.

"—and keep you protected with her hide and fang and claw." Gorman put the bear head that hung over his back onto his bowed head. "Ursa forever."

"The family forever," solemnly spoke the room.

Gorman lifted the bear head off again and let it hang down his back. Then he stretched his arms out toward Poppy and the three women—the bridesmaids, I finally understood. Poppy and the white

# THE BRIDE STRIPPED BARE

woman strode to the stump table. They kissed. Poppy took the cloak off the woman's shoulders, let it fall, revealing her full youthful nudity. Then he reached down and tore open an oval patch on the front of his fur pants. His erect penis sprang out. The woman lay on the table, smiling, and spread her legs. Poppy fucked her hard and fast—a rape of fury and madness—his grunts joining her moans and cries. Before they each climaxed, Poppy slipped his knife from his sleeve and slit the woman's throat. Her moans gurgled as her rapist thrust harder, then bellowed his orgasm to echo around the immense hall.

He got off her, semen dripping, leering his fangs down at her. Slipping the knife back up his sleeve, he tucked his penis back into the fur pants, pasted the flap back over his exposed flesh. Then returned to his place on the stage.

The woman bled across the wood, the rings stained red, her head sunken sideways to face the audience. But she wasn't dead. Her hands came up and pulled off her wrinkled face. Revealing the young skin, I remembered from the party. She smiled and sat up on the table, threw the flesh bag of her shed face triumphantly to the audience.

They scrambled after it as though it was a thrown garter belt.

The woman picked up her bear cloak and resumed her place beside her sister bridesmaids.

The two massive men appeared with knives, stood at either side of Gord's cross, and slit the bonds that tied his wrists and ankles. He fell to the floor, wrists limp and numb, wiping the blood out of his eyes with a sleeve. Blinked in the harsh light, stood slowly and painfully, needing to be helped to his feet by the men. They helped him to walk to the stump, told him to stand like a man not a hunchbacked dog. He wobbled on his feet slightly as the black bridesmaid joined him at the table and let her cloak fall.

She sneered at him with disgust, then turned her gaze to Venus.

"Must I fuck the fallen one?"

Venus kissed the air and winked. "The family will thank you."

She turned her sneer back to Gord, ripped open the flap in his pants, pushed him onto his back on the table. The audience laughed and cheered and shouted encouraging obscenities.

Gord was hard, even though he seemed too dazed to know where he was. The woman got on top of him and rode. Her hips buckled and pounded against him. As she approached orgasm, she pulled a knife from Gord's sleeve and stuck it into his hand.

"Cut my throat!" she cried. "Cut my goddamn throat!"

Gord's hands reached up blindly. She bent her head low for him to grab her hair with one hand and position the blade at her throat with the other. He couldn't muster enough strength, and her hammering pelvis made the blade slip off.

She held his knife hand against her throat.

"Cut my fucking throat, asshole!" cried the old hag.

With a flex of his bicep, Gord sliced a quick gash across the wrinkled and loose neck skin. The woman smiled as she bled, a scarf of blood pouring down between her breasts, dripping onto Gord's vest. She orgasmed and her cries echoed around the hall, across the hushed audience.

The life went out of her and she dropped onto her dazed lover. The knife fell from his hand and clattered onto the stage. Gord's chest heaved, pushed against the weight of the dead body on top of him. But only for a few moments, before she sat up, pulled her old face off and threw the scrap of flesh to the crowd. Again, they scrambled and fought for the prize—men, women and children.

A child of ten gleefully held up her reward. Then she plastered the flesh mask onto her own face and danced for applause. She took it off and gave it to her mother, who then folded it up and put it in her purse for safe-keeping. Then the mother used a napkin to wipe blood off her child's youthful, smiling face.

# THE BRIDE STRIPPED BARE

The two men dragged Gord's exhausted body off the table and returned him to his place, in front of the cross, but no longer strapped to it. He used his remaining strength to stand as upright as possible, his body sore, trying to coax blood back into his limbs. Gord leaned heavily against the cross, and looked like a very tired, old man.

It was my turn.

The men cut my bonds and needed to help me to the front of the table. That was the first time that I saw the backdrop of the stage. A sky of stars, and the constellation Ursa Major outlined on it, with a depiction of a bear drawn over the linked stars. Was this some form of bear cult? There had been such things all over the world, going back to paleolithic times and Ancient Greece. But in modern times, there were bear cults amongst the indigenous peoples of Northern Japan, Siberia, Finland…and in the American and Canadian Pacific coast! (How old was this family?)

The Asian hag bridesmaid joined me, her nudity exquisite beneath her cloak, her face hideous.

Venus leaned into both of us, speaking to me. "Fuck her, my husband, like you'll fuck me. Your pleasure is my pleasure, mine is yours. We are one. Welcome to the family."

The hag smiled ragged and blackened teeth at me and slowly eased down the flap of my pants. Though I hadn't felt it, I was fully erect, incredibly hard. She touched me, her fingertips lightly tracing lines up and down the shaft, nails circling the head.

She looked into my eyes. "Should I mount you? Or will you be a man and *take* what is rightfully yours?"

I turned to look at Venus, glared at her. "Why are you doing this? I'm not your husband. Who are you fucking people?"

Venus snapped her fingers, and the woman laid down on the table, legs spread, knees up, framing my thighs. The crone grabbed my wrists and pulled me down on top of her, leaned in close to show me every tooth and missing gap in her blood-stained smile. "We're your family now. For life." Eyelashes winked. "Or until death." She squeezed my jaw and drove her tongue into my mouth. "Now fuck this aged whore and make me happy."

I couldn't look at her face. I couldn't think of it as sex or love or even lust—it was just a physical act. My penis—which was still as hard as iron—wouldn't go down, no matter how hard I tried to think it away. I knew it would only deflate when it finished in the woman's vagina. I looked down between my legs—*our* legs—and focused on aim and thrust.

She guided me in, then held onto my shoulders. Too many times I glanced up at her face or over to the audience; shocked by it all, I wanted to leave my body. I was putting on a live sex show for a huge room of people, most of whom were egging me on, throwing their fists in the air as they cheered. Glancing ahead, along the stage, I saw Gord wobbling on his feet, his face cut and beaten and bruised, a picture of dejection—a shell of a man. I couldn't let myself think about how he got himself to this place—or how he got me here. So much hell had arrived into my life since my plane landed.

For a second, I glanced down at the woman under me, the sagging mask of age she wore, though the light in her eyes was still young.

"Fuck me, that's it, fuck me hard! Fuck me to death!" she grunted; her obscene mantra broken between syllables every time my hips thrust.

I hated her. Felt rage rise inside me. Looked at the crowd as they yelled profanities, gestured with their hands and arms and mouths—and I hated them all. The woman was one of them—the family—and I wasn't just fucking her, I was fucking them all. I wanted to rip her in half with my cock—for what she and her family did to Gord, to me, to who knew how many other victims.

I thought about Venus' tongue—the scar that cleft it in two before the dagger blade had drawn blood. It had been cut before, multiple times, so much so that she didn't flinch with each new slice.

# THE BRIDE STRIPPED BARE

She had been married before, I realized. But how many times? Did Gord know? There were still too many secrets in this freakshow of a family, and I had only been exposed to a few of them.

I was getting a chance to kill one of them, as I fucked the bitch, but I wasn't going to give her what she wanted. She only wanted a slit throat, to peel off her decrepit face and to join her youthful sisters. But I wanted more. If the family killed me, fine (what happened to Venus' other husbands?), but I was taking one with me.

I hammered into her and her cries of ecstasy rose, as did the cheers and taunts of the mob. She clutched fingernails into my biceps, scratching my vest, as my cock speared her.

After seeing Poppy and Gorman both take knives out of their sleeves, I reached into my sleeve as well. Blades must have come with the jackets. A strange accessory for a groom, but what wasn't strange concerning the wedding ceremony?

I reared up off my victim and slipped the knife from my sleeve. The hag smiled with ecstatic joy, stretching her neck. I looked back at Venus, whose eyes were those of an animal, as she urged me on to slash the blade across my victim's throat.

As I orgasmed, I plunged the dagger into the crone's heart and leaned on it, driving it deeper, two hands on the handle, twisting. Her claws scratched my head and face as she wailed, but I felt no pain. Only exhilaration. The dagger wiggled in my two-handed grip with all my weight on it, deeper into the wailing hag. Blood poured from her wrinkled gash of a mouth as her wail waned into a gurgle, and her clawing arms slowed to droop off either side of the table.

I pulled out my cock as I pulled out my dagger. Got off the table, strolled to my victim's head, slit her throat. Dug my fingers into the open maw across her throat and pulled her face off—her skin crackling as it tore free from muscle, like tape peeled off a roll. I lifted the wrinkled mask to the audience, scrunched it in my hand as I showed it to Venus, then threw it off the stage, onto the floor.

The hag had not undergone her metamorphosis. She was not beautiful. She wore a mask of bloody exposed muscle, her dead eyes gazing up at me before they were coated in her seeping blood. I held the bloody dagger loose in my hand as I glared defiantly at Venus. She still had a blood-lust craving in her eyes. She liked what I had done, desired me even more. Fucking psycho bitch.

"I'm not your fucking husband!" I yelled at her and at the mass of family watching me. "This shit is over! You let me go—you let Gord go—you let his family go! Now!"

Venus stepped up to me, her golden hoofs clattering on the wooden boards of the stage, her bear's head towering over me by at least three feet.

"Oh yes, you *are* my husband," she cooed. "Better than I could've expected!" She stabbed a fingernail in Gord's direction. "That other… waste of skin…did whatever I asked without question, with merely all the coke he could snort and all the pussy he could fuck. He called it love." She gripped my face in her hands, stronger than I had assumed, my gaze lifted to aim through the valley of her breasts. I could feel an intense heat emanating from her naked skin. "But you…you've shown true blood-lust. Fucking is not as important as killing. To kill *is* to fuck. A true family member knows this. You *are* my husband. I feel it. And so do you."

I smiled up at her, planted a kiss on each of her golden nipples, to her delight. "Then we must consummate our marriage, my dear."

I gripped the dagger in two hands and speared it deep into her stomach, wrenching it up to tear muscle in a ragged, bloody line, slicing sinew and scraping against her rib bones.

She stepped a hoof away from me, looked down at the jutting blade, and a wave of ecstasy washed over her body. She shivered as she bled, eyes rolling back to their whites. Venus slowly pulled the sticking knife from her belly, releasing a gout of blood down her abdomen to cover

# THE BRIDE STRIPPED BARE

her pudendum and to drip onto the floor between her cloven gold hoofs. She moaned and shuddered as the blade slipped free.

Looking at me through heavily-lidded eyes, a satiated calm on her face, she whispered, "Oh, baby...that felt good."

The dagger dropped from her hand to the stage. I watched as the gaping wound I had just tore up from her stomach to the underside of her breasts began stitching itself together. Bubbles of blood rose to the surface of her skin and congealed, hardened to form a row of blood buttons. More blood seeped from her body between the buttons to seal them into a long thick crust.

She tilted her smile down at me and delicately peeled off the scab. Flung it offstage where it was immediately scrambled after by young men, ripping it into pieces so each could get a bit of it, then they jammed their morsel into their mouths. Venus smoothed a fingertip down the healed pink scar. The only trace left of the mortal wound which I had given her. Which wasn't mortal at all.

"I'm always hungry after a good blood-fuck," she said, stepping to me again, planting a kiss on my lips. Then she turned to her family and raised her arms in celebration. "Let the feast begin!"

# Chapter 12

I had been strapped back onto my cross, Gord onto his, and both of us were kept in a wooden prison somewhere backstage, no windows, no furniture in the room, a heavy wooden door banded by iron strips, locked.

Gord's face looked like shit, one eye swollen shut, lips fat and deformed, and, of course, the fresh slash across his forehead. But he was alive. And, sometimes, awake.

"Gordy," I called to him, his head lolling from side to side as he slipped in and out of consciousness. "Can you hear me? Are you awake? You gotta tell me everything you know about these fucking psychopaths."

He chuckled and coughed, blood-pink saliva slipping threads down his chin. "Congrats, buddy," he said weakly. "You got the best girl in the world. And fuck—you killed that old bitch real nice! I think Venus really liked that. You're golden, my friend, golden."

"Gord—snap out of it!"

He stopped talking, mumbling nonsense under his breath until he began sobbing. I pulled once again against my restraints, but they were too tight. All I could think of was escape, for myself and Gord and his family. But where were *they*? And even if we could get out of here, how could we get out of this town? The whole area was controlled by them. Even Canada wasn't freedom.

# THE BRIDE STRIPPED BARE

"Gord, talk to me. Tell me something I can use to get us out of here. I stabbed Venus—and she liked it! I saw the wound heal in seconds! Who is she? *What* is she?"

He sniffled and coughed, spun his head to look at me with his one open eye. "She's like no one I've ever met. You see what I mean now? I wanted her so bad...but I fucked up."

I latched onto something, an old secret he wouldn't divulge. He had to tell me now—what did he have to lose?

"What did you fuck up? You said something about the *Swamp Hotel* back at the tailors."

He nodded. "I shouldn't have said anything. I'm sorry," he mumbled, not to me but to himself, to the family.

"What is this hotel?"

"Here. This is. The Royal Order of Ursa."

"Ursa? The bear? You mean all of those bear skins people are wearing, the fucking bear heads hanging from the ceiling—is this a bear cult? Gord! Wake up and talk to me!"

His head lolled from side to side, his words moving in and out of volume, but I pieced together what he was saying as best I could. "I didn't know if we were getting fitted for the pants here or at the tailors." He laughed and bloody saliva spilled from his swollen lips. "You see how small it was? That's nothing. But it was something to them. Something big. I wasn't supposed to say anything about it—couldn't even make the tiniest reference to it while you were within earshot. That's part of their code of secrecy. It's very strict. 'Swamp Hotel' is also kind of a password, for family only. But they think that if I spill a small secret, then I'm apt to spill big ones. And secrecy is what's kept them going for centuries. You would only find out about the Royal Order of Ursa at the wedding. But then, you wouldn't be allowed to leave. Same with my folks and kid sister and big brother."

The more pieces he gave me, the more questions I had. Something didn't sound right. But I finally understood that Gorman wasn't just Venus' father, but also some kind of high priest for the whole family. Slipping up in front of him would've been the worst.

"Are they a cult of some kind?"

Gord's fists clenched, pulling against the bindings, but he only made them tighter. His hands were turning purple, like mine.

"Cults are small, the family is huge. They'll kill me for saying all this, Chris. Maybe you too. But you're married to her now, so maybe not. But I'm definitely dead. I don't care anymore."

"No you're not and neither am I. And I sure as hell aren't married to that freak!"

He shook his head. "You don't understand. They've probably already got a legit marriage license for you and her. This was just the Baer wedding, the family ceremony. It means more to them than getting married in a church or at City Hall or wherever. And the family is *everywhere*. If they know you're married to Venus, hell buddy, the world's your oyster." He laughed through his tears. "You're set. You won't have to go back to that shitty college anymore. Name an Ivy League school and they'll put you there. Or you could quit your job and just be Venus' husband, live in the lap of luxury. Set for life. Don't we all work in order to hopefully retire rich and live lazy? Do you think I wanted to be a blue-collar slob my whole life?"

I had heard of secret societies and strange cults and cabals involving people who, unofficially, ruled the world. Conspiracy theories, which sane or insane people spent their whole lives obsessed with, but most of us didn't pay much attention to. If we weren't in the cabal... but no, we were now. Or maybe just I was. Why did Gord say I would only find out about the Royal Order of Ursa at the wedding, and then not be allowed to leave? Did he know what would happen to me—and to his folks and siblings? Did he set us up? (Doing what some girl told

# THE BRIDE STRIPPED BARE

him to do because he was in love, or lust, with her? Old diseases were hard to cure.)

I didn't want to go down that line of questioning, not at the time. Regardless if he had set me up, we were both screwed at that point. My priority had to be to get us out of there. We could discuss details on the plane home.

Maybe I could use my privileged position in the family to escape from it. After all, Venus and her brood could've killed Gord and me when we made it to Canada. Why go on with a wedding when the groom had adamantly tried to run from the bride? And if they were in Canada, were they also in other countries?

I asked Gord the last question. "Everywhere, they're everywhere," he answered between groans of pain. "Safe to assume they're across this country and probably through Canada too. Europe's a good bet, Russia too, maybe parts of Asia. That Asian woman you killed was originally from Japan, and the black woman, I think, came from Cameroon. I've met a few family members with foreign accents. They come from around the world...for Venus."

"Who is she in the family? The Queen Bear or something? And do you know if she's been married before?"

"She said she was divorced once and a widow once...gave me some names...Greg or Brian or something, but she didn't talk about it much. Said she didn't wanna relive the past...that I was her future." A feeble laugh escaped his throat.

A widow? I could see her being a black widow. But why would she kill a guy she married? For money, an insurance policy? The family was apparently stinking rich. I kicked myself for not having asked these questions of Gord about Venus before. Then again, it seemed like he was too smitten since all he could repeat was how great she was. I didn't want to criticize his new fiancée, wanted him to be happily in love. Hell is paved with good intentions.

God, that seemed like so long ago. Time was strange in this place. I recalled the clock in Gord's truck, showing the wrong time so I thought it was broken. Should've been my first clue that things were not as they seemed.

"Do you know if she's got kids?" I asked, needing more background information on Venus if I was going to get Gord and I away from her and the family. "If Gorman's her father, is her mother here? And if Gorman's a priest, is Venus some kind of priestess? Will every member of this cult bow down to her?"

Gord sighed, leaned his head back against the cross, smiled. "You always were the smart one, Chris. I never asked half those questions. I just assumed some stuff. What did I care—I was going to be set for life. I think she's big in the family—very big. But maybe not at the top. And Gorman scares the shit out of me. He might be her father—*might*. But, for all I know, he could also be one of her old husbands. Hell, the whole family could be married to one another."

The blood from hundreds of fingertips dribbled into the black bowl. If not a marriage—some profane form of cult marriage—then at least the whole audience participated in a type of communion. Mingling of the blood. More pieces were falling into place.

Before I could ask any more questions, the two massive men—who I overheard Venus calling Gitch and Skood—entered and sliced our bonds. Walked us out through a cellar of wood and stone, up a flight of stairs, and back onto stage.

A long table with high-backed chairs had been set up on the stage. Similar long tables were lined up in the immense room, where the guests sat, each chair meeting with place settings of pristine china and crystal wine glasses. Candelabra dotted a line down the center of each endless table. And between candelabra were elongated silver meat domes on thick platters. Presumably, the meal of the evening.

# THE BRIDE STRIPPED BARE

Positioned in the center of the stage table were two chairs which were taller than the others.

Gitch (I assumed) forced me into one of the two tall chairs, where I could see and be seen over the main course. My convex face reflected back to me in the polished silver dome. The stench of cooked meat made my stomach churn—to say the least, I was not hungry.

(Strange: the domes covering all the platters were not a foot or, at most, two-feet long, which would be normal. They were closer to five or six feet long. I wondered: *what in the hell is for dinner?*)

Gord was forced into a smaller chair to my left, and next to him was Poppy, sharpening knife on fork, hungry. The two remaining bridesmaids sat patiently at the other end of the table, one chair empty since the third girl was dead. The white and black bridesmaids smiled at me with their youthful, beautiful mouths, licking their fingertips, opening their bear cloaks to expose bare breasts, circling painted nails around erect nipples. I had never sat at a dinner table with partially nude people before. I ignored them.

Venus made her entrance, strode out onto stage, her shoes booming on the wooden floor, and took the tall chair beside me, pulled out by Gorman. The priest sat at Poppy's end of the table, a chair procured by Skood, placed so that the priest faced along the length of the table. He wasn't on display for the audience, as were the rest of us; his position seemed to have him watching the wedding party, to oversee the dining.

Once all were seated, Gorman stood and raised a golden goblet, ushering the attention of the family to himself. They all stood, as did everyone at the head table except for Venus and myself.

"To the bride and her groom, under the Great God Ursa, for the perpetuation of the family...may we all give thanks and praise and wish the new couple long life and many bloodlines."

Voices in the audience said, "here here!" and offered their toasts to us. Everyone drank but me and my bride (or, as Gorman had said, I was "*her* groom." I belonged to her). It was partially the heights of our different chairs and partially because Venus continued to wear her immense bear costume—uniform—as she dined, but I felt incredibly small. Like the male spider spouse of the black widow.

I gazed up at her and felt her cold hand caress my jaw. Glancing across the room, I tried to see where the doors were located, and what were the chances of escape. A mob of family, of course, would've stopped me. Maybe killed me, but then the bride would just get herself another husband. I had to appease my bride somehow, to learn more about her and her lineage, hopefully finding a weakness.

I plastered a fake smile on my face as I returned my bride's loving gaze.

"So…now that we're married, I guess we should get to know each other."

She tittered demurely behind a hand as though she was Marie Antionette. If she had been holding a fan, she would've fluttered it coyly. Fake bitch. I hated her even more. But if she was all about putting on an act, I would re-act to play off her.

"There will be time, my husband," she answered condescendingly. "I'm sure you have many questions, but they can all be answered on our honeymoon."

I perked up. I hadn't considered that this whole event—this farce—to be played out to include a honeymoon. "Oh? Where will we be going?"

She answered matter-of-factly, as though it was obvious. "To our family castle in the Carpathian Mountains, naturally. Your education will be continued there. You still have much to learn, old habits still to be broken. It's better to learn by doing than by telling, don't you think?"

I played her game of verbal poker, not expecting necessarily to win, but simply to learn the rules. If I could've picked up the steak knife (the knife up my sleeve was gone) sitting beside my plate and

# THE BRIDE STRIPPED BARE

plunged it into her breast, I would've. But then again, I'd already tried that.

"And what will I be learning?"

"If I tell you, it would spoil the surprise. I'll give you a hint because so far you are proving to be an excellent specimen." She pinched my chin. "You have excellent genes, much better than those of..." she sneered a glance over at Gord; he kept his eyes off her, delicately touching his wounded forehead, but he must've heard her. "The family has been very impressed with your performance so far. In the tunnel was lovely. But when you took it upon yourself to defy convention and kill Annabelle, my bridesmaid—especially *while* you fucked her—and then ejaculated into her...mmm. We later siphoned it out of her, and it was presented to me in a beautiful crystal sherry glass. It was delicious! But I digress. It showed that you had a true killing spirit, which is what the family looks for." She leaned passed me to glance again at Gord. "Your friend—that dog—followed orders to the letter. Showing no initiation, no intelligence, no passion. He relished what I gave him, not faithful to his soul. He had a weak soul, and meagre genetics. Your soul is black. And, as my husband, it will become blacker."

I nodded, not afraid of anything she was telling me, letting her feel confident about her powers over men.

"So, getting to know each other a bit more," I continued, "have you ever been married before? Got kids? Your mom and dad here? I'd love to meet my inlaws."

She smiled and her eyes flashed as she reached a hand down to my leg, but I could barely feel her fingernails through the thick fur covering me from the waist down. I reminded myself to ask about the bear motif, just to get confirmation on what I suspected.

"I've been married several times. Some of my husbands are dead, some absorbed into the family."

"Absorbed?"

"They fuck other family members, become entranced, and I let them go. I'm very…open-minded, to put it mildly. I own who I want to own until I get tired of them. But no one owns me."

"Is that right? So, you own me right now?"

She nodded. "More than you know."

I chuckled into my fist, elbows on the table, trying to block out the smell of the dinner in front of me. It was half repulsive but became half tempting. I thought I wasn't hungry, but with all that had happened in the past twenty-four hours, my body craved food, no matter what it smelled like. My nausea on the wane.

Skood began filling wine glasses. In the audience, other servants in bear skins and cloaks poured wine as well.

"Okay, whatever you say," I said to Venus with a sigh of false boredom. "Got kids?"

"I have several children," she admitted freely.

"Really? Three, four?"

She tilted her head to one side, needing a little time to consider the number she gave me. "Two hundred, three hundred… I've lost count."

I laughed out loud, couldn't hold it in. "Wow. You look great after so much…motherhood. Your parents must be very happy—or exhausted—to be grandparents many times over."

"My father is the priest at the end of the table. He's also the father of twenty-seven of my children. I had the first when I was twelve, as soon as I got my period. My brother, Poppy, has given me forty-two children. From conception to birth takes only a few hours, sometimes minutes, depending on how well the mother takes to…motherhood. That is how our family grows so large so quickly. There are genetic mistakes, of course. You saw some of those in the tunnel." She took a sip of wine as my heart stopped and I forgot to breathe. Then she added, "My mother's dead. Her name was Callisto. I ate her."

# THE BRIDE STRIPPED BARE

I couldn't retain my humor anymore. Whether it was a well-rehearsed lie, or the truth, she didn't flinch as she told me everything. After all, her dagger wound had healed in seconds, so I knew for a fact that there was some strange magic going on inside her. With such a large backwoods family, I easily suspected incest. Clichés are sometimes correct. But not incest to such a gross and grotesque extent. It was difficult to digest all she had confessed, so I stopped asking her about her past.

Then Gitch arrived on the opposite side of the table, grabbed the silver dome covering the cooked meat by its silver handles, and revealed what had been prepared for dinner.

Arms and legs cut off but displayed with fruit ornamentation alongside the torso. No head, just the neck. Cooked and glazed, surrounded by greens and small bowls of various dipping sauces. I gawked at the beast, my mind at first trying to match up what kind of animal or bird it was, what strange venison. But it was only when, in shocked curiosity, I stood to see the length of it from a heightened viewpoint, that I saw the tattoos on the neck. A rooster and a flying serpent.

Paco.

I stumbled backwards, kicking back my chair, staring at the *thing*. Bile rose up my throat and my legs shook, hands numb. The audience hushed. I scanned the room as silver domes were lifted off platters on each table. One table was centered with a platter of hands, another of feet; one bore a bald, barbecued head; others had pieces of carved torso—a chest with wrinkled breasts jutting upwards, nipples severed but replaced with cherries, toothpicks sticking from each; livers and coils of intestines, decorated with pineapple chunks; a platter of penises. The crowd watched my reactions before digging in.

Venus met my stare. "He wasn't family, so he's dinner," she said with a glance down at the cooked Paco. "Thank you—and your best man—for killing so many of the weak members of our family whom we transported down the tunnel to meet you. We had a feeling you'd provide the wedding feast, if properly motivated." She stretched out a hand to present the room and its many cannibal meals. "As you can see, we take care of our own. They won't miss the wedding," she said with a wink and a laugh.

My mouth felt like rubber. I vomited between my feet, stomach acid splashing across the shoes and matted into the fur of the pants. My gaze shot to Poppy, who was laughing, a large three-tined fork and a long steak knife in his hands, as he squeezed between my seat and where Gord sat.

He sawed off a hunk of Paco, held it out for me.

"Eat up, brother. The coke in his veins makes him extra spicy!"

I tried to run but could only get to the end of the table. The shoes practically welded to my feet were heavy and it was difficult to balance while walking in them. Gorman stood, snapped his fingers, and Skood rushed to me, slipped a thick arm around my neck. Walked me back to my seat, pushed me into it. Poppy's molars tore off the meat on his fork and chewed, mouth open, bits of meat clumps and flesh strings hanging between his teeth.

Gord was in another world. I think he didn't even know what the meat was. Salivating, he cut off a large steak from Paco's shoulder and pectoral muscle, dropped it onto his plate, then sawed off bite-sized pieces, stuffing them greedily into his mouth. Ravenous—as hungry as I once was. He washed down each mouthful with gulps of wine, his goblet instantly refilled by an attentive Gitch.

Poppy sat down and Gitch exchanged his wine bottle for a carving knife and fork, began cutting from the opposite side of the table, piling chunks of the dead man's torso and belly on the empty part of the platter up by Paco's neck stump. He then carried one steak at a time, dripping blood and juices, across the table to fill each plate. Gorman and Poppy and the two bridesmaids began feasting immediately.

# THE BRIDE STRIPPED BARE

"Just a little one for me," Venus instructed the behemoth waiter. "I'm watching my figure. But something extra rare."

Gitch pushed the knife into the belly, sawed up, split open the flesh at the sternum.

"Excuse my hands, mistress," he said to the bride.

"You're excused" she said, giving a look of lust to him as she licked a fang. "I know where they've been." Then she leaned over to me, still held in my chair by Skood's hands on my shoulders. "He's the father of nine of my kids," she whispered with a wink.

Gitch returned the wink as he rolled up his sleeves and sank his arm up to the elbow under Paco's ribs. A wet sluicing sound echoed in my ears as I watched, bubbles popping out from the meat that swallowed the waiter's arm.

By the look on Gitch's face, he was reaching around inside the dead man, breaking something off with his powerful fingers. Then he grabbed hold of some interior meat and pulled it out, his arm exiting with a churning, watery suction.

Venus passed her plate to his clean hand. He dropped Paco's heart onto it, then passed it back to her. She cooed to herself as she took up cutlery and sliced off a small morsel, slid it delicately between her teeth, tongue slipping out then in, chewed demurely.

Her eyelashes fluttered at me. "I love breaking a man's heart…and then eating it," she giggled. Some juice escaped her lips, which she wiped up with a finger, sucked her nail clean.

I felt dizzy. A pulse began in my temples and my muscles suddenly drained of all energy. I couldn't leave the chair under my own power even if Skood had let me. I was numb to all feeling, to emotion—couldn't feel hatred or humor or the need to run for my life anymore. Even if I could've saved my life, my body wouldn't respond. I looked over again at Gord and he continued to stuff food into his mouth, even picking up pieces that had fallen into his lap and sucking them in between his juice-stained lips. Face bent over his plate, only looking up to cut off another piece from the beast on the table and dragging it to his plate. Or not even: often he cut it off the body and put it directly into his mouth. He had carved a hole through the side of Paco large enough to see a few exposed ribs. His knife scraped meat off the bone, sounding like nails on a chalkboard.

Venus made a motion to Gitch, telling him what his next slice should be. My head was twitching as though I had just inhaled a pound of coke. I couldn't control my body, started scratching the jacket arms and fur pant legs, trying to free whatever black worms were crawling beneath my skin. I couldn't hold my head still long enough to see where Gitch was slicing. Not until he put it on my plate, did I see the flying serpent tattoo, its ink eye looking up at me.

"The skin is most delicious—crispy," Venus whispered into my ear. "There's a tradition in our family, dating back eons. We gain strength over our enemy by consuming his body." She wove fingers through the hair at the back of my skull. "Become stronger, Chris, by eating your enemy and his symbol of power. This is all a part of your ongoing training. There are many meals like this in your future."

Skood removed his grip from me, picked up my knife and fork, stuck them into my hands, wrapped my fingers around them. The cutlery shook as it hovered over the piece of inked meat. Venus wrapped an arm around my shoulders and covered my hands with her own. Like a mother to her young son, she helped me cut off a piece of skin and lift it to my mouth.

"Eat for mama, baby," she cooed. "Grow big and strong. That's a good boy."

The flap of skin sat on my tongue. Venus giggled as she closed my lower jaw, then lifted my wine glass to my lips, washed the meat down my numb throat. Then she helped my puppet hands cut another piece and wash that down too.

# THE BRIDE STRIPPED BARE

"Just think of it as a kind of pork," she said, cutting a piece of the serpent's body, slipping it to the back of my mouth. My gag reflex spasmed and I coughed out the morsel onto my plate. "You like pork, don't you?" She put it back into my mouth with her own fork, feeding me like a baby. The cutlery dropped and clattered onto the plate, though my hands hung in the air and trembled. "Eat pork Paco. A Paco taco! Devour your enemy. Cannibalism is not wrong—it's the banquet we give to ourselves. It is the forbidden fruit of Eden. The food of the gods is Mankind. The family feeds with the sustenance of itself. And its enemies, of course."

She continued to feed me until no skin was left. I swallowed it all. My stomach roiled with the forbidden meat inside me, but it didn't feel nauseous. It was as though my stomach—my body—had finally eaten something it had always desired. As Venus had said—the food of the gods. I craved more.

My wine goblet was filled, so I drained it in one swallow, then it was filled again. Venus showed me an immense ring on her finger: a blue jewel in a gold setting bearing intricate designs and symbols. Like the one I had seen on Poppy's finger. She popped open the jewel to reveal a cupped recess filled with red powder.

"This will help, sweetie," she said as she raised the ring to my nose. "There's some in all the wine, of course, but there's nothing like undiluted red cocaine."

She put a finger against one of my nostrils and coaxed me to snort. I did, wanting to be drugged up, drunk, gorging myself on any kind of meat in order to forget where I was and what was happening around me. A rush hit hard into my sinuses, crashing a pink light against the back of my skull. I felt awake and alive, the lights in the immense room bright, details vivid—designs on the handles of knives and forks, the flow of the wood grain on the table, the pinprick particles of gold dust on Venus' nipples.

I was hungry for many things all at once, including her. I plunged my face into her cleavage, sucked her nipple deep between into my mouth, scraped my teeth across the nubbin of flesh, bit into it.

"Yes, baby," she moaned. "Suckle mommy…feed off my body."

She held my head against her chest, shivers racing across her hot skin, shooting up the length of her tight neck tendons, her eyelids fluttering. I felt myself grow quickly hard and ripped open the flap on my pants. She must've heard the sound because her hand found my cock and began stroking it.

"Oh yes, baby, just a little pleasure," she sighed. "There will be time for more later, not to worry. The bedroom will be months of training all by itself." She took her hand from under the table and pushed my head off her breast. Her eyes were liquid fire. "Feast on your enemy now…then later you can feast on me."

So I did. My nerves calm, hands steady with feeling returned as they took up the knife and fork and attacked the beast—my enemy, fucking shithead Paco—in front of me. I couldn't satiate my hunger enough, and soon dropped the cutlery to tear pieces off the cooked corpse with my hands. Ripping strips of flesh with my teeth, plunging an arm through the cavity made by Gitch to root around for hidden delicacies. I wanted to eat all of him, to eat his bones, his soul. Much of my face was covered with Venus' cleavage henna and Paco's sticky juice. I craved the sweet reek of barbecued human flesh in my nostrils.

"Good baby," Venus whispered, scooting closer to me, wrapping an arm around my waist. "There's no such thing as excess. Not in this family." She took my hand and saw that something was missing. She glanced over at Gord. "Hey, fuckhead—give my groom your ring!" Gord instantly obeyed without looking at her. I hadn't seen that Gord sported a similar ring to that of Venus and Poppy. He slipped the coke ring off and passed it to Venus' reaching hand. She put it on my finger as though right there, at the dinner table in front of a barbecued human corpse, we

# THE BRIDE STRIPPED BARE

were fully married. She flipped open the blue jewel to show me white cocaine. "That's the weak stuff, for day-to-day use." Puffing her cheeks, she blew the white cocaine into the air, then snapped her fingers and Gitch handed her a small platter of red coke. She manipulated my hand to scoop the ring into the powder and fill it full. Snapped it closed. The excess, which had fallen to the table and on the sleeve of my jacket, she snorted. Her eyes smiled into mine. "We do nothing normal. Normal is for the outside world. We're inside the heart of the *real* world."

She scooped more red coke into her ring, lifted it to my nostril for me to snort, then refilled it again from Gitch's tiny platter. My head felt like glass which had shattered into crystal shards of cocaine. I was scrambled.

My lips felt numb, as though they were hanging off my chin, but I managed to ask, "Why's it red?"

"Blood, my dear. The family's genetically-pure blood." She winked and kissed the air at me. "Gives it that extra kick, doesn't it?"

Then the world stopped for a small pause. Movement slowed down as time warped. The blood in the coke must've had the opposite effect of an upper. Everything still moved—Gord still fed his face, Poppy still sat with his feet propped up on the table drinking from an endless goblet of wine, Gorman still stared down the length of the table, chewing slowly like a cow with its cud, and the bridesmaids still picked at their food, wiping their mouths with slow napkins, watching me lustfully. Venus still stroked my back like a mother proud of her son…

…and I saw what it was all about.

I saw what Gord had seen, the thing that had tempted him into this family, acting without reason or fear of consequence. Originally, I thought he had been thinking with his dick, hypnotized by Venus' beauty and sexuality. But that was only a part of the whole.

Addiction. The freedom to become addicted to everything, to indulge beyond your limits…there was no such thing as excess in this family, as my bride mentioned. Venus must have triggered my epiphany. There was no law to prevent any of them from doing everything—including killing. I had killed a bridesmaid in front of a room full of people—and they cheered. I was doing on stage what the family were also doing in the vast room. Eating human meat, snorting shitloads of coke (or drinking coke-laced wine). I recalled the Black Betty pill which Gord had given me back at his place…so long ago…that enabled me to do all the coke and pot and drink all the booze I wanted without being crippled by the after-effects. The high remained, but the consequences were erased. The party went on, and I didn't have to worry about paying for my excess. And, apparently, this pill would last for five years! That would be a long time to stay high and not pay for one's pleasure.

Wasn't that what Venus said about why I was chosen to be her husband instead of Gord? He hadn't proven himself to be evil enough. Had I won? Was I naturally evil enough for this evil family? (What the hell kind of monster was I?)

There was no law because the family was the law. I understood them instinctively, down to my bones, to my soul. They had spread themselves across the world, not in order to control the world, but to allow themselves ultimate freedom without repression—protected by their own kind in every corner of the globe.

They lived in a bubble, but it was a bubble like the Garden of Eden. Who would want to exchange it for the real world and all its misery and pain? The family was bulletproof. Like any cult, cabal, secret society, mafia—once in, it was damn hard to get out. But sometimes inside kept you alive longer than if you existed on your own.

Gord was alone when he had met Venus.

So was I.

Prey for the black widow.

# Chapter 13

I didn't want to escape anymore, even after realizing the purpose and essence of the family. If anything, I wanted to stay. For life. I was happy that I had been chosen to be Venus' groom over Gord, glad that he had spoiled his chances with such a small, stupid error. A true prospective member would've never comprised the family in such a way. (A new member of the mafia doesn't go around saying, "Hi, I'm a member of the mafia," and expect to stay alive much longer. No wonder Gord had shit his pants when he mentioned the Swamp Hotel.) The family was all; the individual was nothing. Gord was a fool. The strongest survive, and I was strong, made so in part by Venus and the promises of absolute freedom which the family gave me.

And I understood why Gord had tried to screw me and his family over, by handing us over to the family for whatever purpose. It was his *attempt* at evil. To betray his birth family and a best friend for the sake of his bride. Even if that meant death for his loved ones. Evil, but not evil enough. Passive evil—Gord would just get us to the West Coast, but it would be Venus who would do all the hard work of transforming us into family members. Once Venus saw a truly evil person—me—she took her advantage. Out with the old, weak-willed husband, and in with the new.

Pure evil was pure freedom.

I asked myself: wasn't that what I had always wanted? What everyone wants? Pure freedom. I didn't think there was such a thing. All the literature I had read, all the philosophy, was about the search for that freedom…and the perpetual failure of Mankind to find it. There was no such place as the Garden of Eden. So the family created their own paradise instead of wasting time and life searching for it. Create what you cannot find, and then protect it with your life.

I hated Gord a little bit, not for trying to betray me, but for giving up such a gift. But I could understand why he would change himself, transform his life, become almost unrecognizable from the friend I once had in order to obtain paradise on the West Coast.

It was my paradise now, and he was in hell. I loved Venus and would do anything for her.

When dinner was over, all of us moved into another room, a vast hall of wood, tall windows looking out to a surrounding forest. Huge chandeliers made of stag's antlers, with a bear's head centering each, hanging from the ceiling. Tall iron candlesticks with three-foot-tall tapers helped light the hall. A broad dance floor of dark and light wooden planks in a chessboard pattern took up most of the hall. Thick leather sofas and plush chairs lined three of the four walls. The fourth was taken up by a table as long as the room—a bar holding every type of alcohol, with many punch bowls of red cocaine. Smaller dishes were filled with pills of every color, easily mistaken for candy, their effects unknown (at least by me) until one popped a pill to feel its effects. I finally understood the need for Gord's truck filled with sandbags. I wondered if it would be enough for the crowd. No such thing as excess, after all.

Children were not allowed at the reception. They were taken home, put to bed, a grandparent babysitting. If it took a village to raise a child, then the family was a city. No shortage of babysitters, to say the least.

# THE BRIDE STRIPPED BARE

The guests aimed for the bar first, naturally. Venus handed me a flute of champagne and we toasted and kissed. I told her I loved her, that I submitted fully to her.

"Ah, that's sweet," she said with a condescending smile and a sip of champagne.

I felt a jolt of panic. She didn't say she loved me back. And perhaps I had just done what she hated Gord for—submitting easily to her.

I backtracked. "What I meant was...I'm glad to be a part of this family. I want this. Thank you for choosing me."

She giggled and kissed the tip of my nose. "Don't be afraid. We're married now. I won't kill you so soon."

I forced a laugh as she walked away, went behind the bar, had Skood help her remove the back brace that held the bear head high over her own head. I approached to watch. The bear skin had to be removed first, leaving the wooden brace. She turned and I saw her back. It appeared as though the main dowel support of the brace was stuck into her back. The wooden dowels were sharpened and pierced her flesh, under the muscle. No blood. She had been *literally* wearing the brace—sunken into her body. And she felt no pain.

The magic that swam through her body was still a mystery to me. An incestuous, psychotic cabal that stretched around the world was one thing. Within the realm of possibility—human, in fact, though mad. But how could such a people command magic? I did and did not want to find out.

Once people had their choice of poison, they mingled, took up places on sofas and chairs, came up to me and Venus to congratulate us on our marriage. Faces smiled at me when, before, they had growled and threatened. I recognized some of the Canadian cousins and a few people I had seen on main street when I was strolling for a breath of fresh air. All of them said "Welcome to the family" as though it was a password into an exclusive club.

Gord's family came up to congratulate me. Smiling, but I could see fear and confusion in their eyes.

"It's good to see you again, son," Pa said. "This sure is some wedding. Never been to one like it before. I guess these folks are big hunters." He gazed up at the chandeliers, the bear heads and stag horns.

"Yeah, looks like it," I replied, my emotions as contained as his were.

Ma hugged me and stayed close, keeping her voice low. "Honestly, Chris, I just don't understand these people." She tightened the bear cloak around her, a shiver shaking her nude body. "They dressed us up in these things, said we had to—it was their custom. What custom is this? And they flew us out here, put us up in this house. A creepy mansion, if you ask me. They said we wouldn't need to bring anything; all would be provided. I bought a new dress for this—they told me not to wear it. I said it was for my son's wedding. But then he didn't get married—you did. What's happening?" she asked in whisper of panic.

I looked down at the tears floating along the rims of her eyes, felt a pang of sorrow for her, but not as much as perhaps I should have. Just told myself that she was confused. We were a long way from home.

I rubbed her shoulder. "It's nothing to worry about. Gord and I have shared girlfriends before, you remember? It didn't work out between him and Venus, that's all it is. You got a free wedding out of it. I say just relax and enjoy yourself." I smiled like a used car salesman, only half believing my own lies.

She stepped away from me, wrapping the bear cloak tighter, retreating into her husband's arm. Gord's brother, Kevin, shook my hand and had an authentic beaming smile on his face. He let his bear cloak hang open proudly.

"This is some fucked-up party, buddy! I love it!" He sniffed, so I could tell that he had already been to a punchbowl. "There's a lot of gorgeous girls here—I think I fell in love about twenty times since I've

# THE BRIDE STRIPPED BARE

been here. I just might stay and be in the next wedding!"

He laughed and I laughed with him.

"Congrats, Kev, sounds great. I hope you do marry into the family. We'll be brothers-in-law."

He hugged me with one arm. "Wouldn't that be weird? After all these years, we join families. Hell, I always thought you were going to marry my sister." He and I smiled at Elizabeth, who gave a weak smile back, brushed off the remark and turned away.

Kevin leaned into my ear to whisper, "I wouldn't mind getting a piece of those bridesmaids. Both of them. Even the one you killed looked good dead! If she's still warm, I say she's still good to go."

He wheezed a smoker's laugh and coughed as he slapped me hard on the back. He was getting into the swing of things, obviously. Considering necrophilia. A future family member, easily. He wandered off back to the bar to freshen his nose and get a drink.

Elizabeth stared at me, arms hugging the cloak tightly around her body. She stepped up to me as her parents withdrew. They went searching for a vacant sofa, to wait until the party was over. I could imagine they simply wanted to get back to their room, Ma to pack her unworn dress, Pa to scratch his head and tell himself to ignore all that he had witnessed, both ready to get on the next flight out of town. Could they leave if they wanted to? Not just from the town and state, but simply from the wooden hall? Where was the exit?

"I don't know who you are anymore," Elizabeth said, her jaw tight. I couldn't see her eyes very well as she was standing in the shadow made by the chandelier bear's head above us. I recalled that her eyes were an astounding blue. Ultramarine. It was one of the first things I had noticed about her years ago when we first met in our teen years. I fell in love with her, obsessed over her to a pathetic degree, but she thought it was quaint and flattering to have an older guy like her. She liked the attention at first, but then it became too much, and she withdrew. Each date she went on with some random guy broke my heart again and again. She was the first girl I ever loved, and because it was never reciprocated, I hated her a little bit. Had she ever really known who I was?

"It's good to see you again, Elizabeth," I responded, deflecting her accusation. "I'm sorry to hear about your divorce. At least there weren't any kids to get caught up in the stress."

Her Adam's apple jumped, and she didn't blink for a long time. "Do you even know what's happening? Can you see yourself? You killed a girl on that stage—like it was a snuff show for everyone's entertainment."

"It wasn't real," I said, to my surprise. "She's okay—you'll probably see her wandering around here."

Elizabeth's eyebrows twisted. "What do you mean? You fucked her and plunged a knife into her. Those other two had their goddamn throats cut and their faces peeled off!"

I put a hand on her arm to soothe her, but she snapped it back. "These people have a morbid sense of humor," I continued my bullshit. "I mean, look at all of this. They're rich. Rich people are weird, eccentric. All that you saw was just some weird magic show. They wanted to make the wedding memorable, instead of the same old boring wedding. It was entertainment."

She blinked, looked away from me, taking in the room. Battling with the dilemma.

"Then why the fuck are we dressed in these bear costumes? Naked underneath! Your…your *wife* is naked! You can see everything. My brothers, my parents, the bridesmaids—everyone! And what's with that fucking priest slicing people's fingers to drip blood into that bowl? And that freak with the blue glasses who sliced Gord's forehead? This is *not* a magic show!"

A few heads turned our way since Elizabeth wasn't whispering anymore. I threw up my hands and shrugged. "I don't know what you want me to tell you. It's not a traditional wedding."

# THE BRIDE STRIPPED BARE

She scoffed a laugh. "That's an understatement."

"Your brother was going to get married to her. You would've been here anyway."

"Well, look at him!"

I looked over at the bar. Gord and Kevin were chatting, stuffing coke into their noses. The ugly red cut across Gord's head had stopped bleeding. The coke probably killed his pain, got him to normal again instead of being a basketcase begging for mercy from Venus. A woman approached the brothers, putting her hands on her hips to open her cloak. They both scanned her body and Kevin put his arm around her, all of them laughing. Then Kevin left with her, first filling a champagne flute with coke, the two of them disappearing into the shadows of the room. Gord wandered along the bar, inspecting the bottles on display.

"He's so fucking drugged up," Elizabeth continued, "he doesn't know what's going on or even where he is." She jabbed a finger into my chest as she glared at me. "As soon as I can find a way out of this freak farm, I am leaving with my mother and father. If my brothers want to stay and think with their dicks, fine. I'm not a part of this deranged family, and I never will be." She turned, stomping away to find her parents, but then came back and growled into my face. "They served us a fucking platter of what looked like brains! I threw up under the table. Was that magic? A joke? These people are sick and depraved, and now you're sick and depraved too!"

She sped away. I didn't know what to do with my hands, feeling nervous and ashamed from her words. Took deep breaths and glanced around the room, feeling lost.

Venus came up to me, now wearing just the white bear fur, no longer towering as she had before. The gold and henna were washed off her body, and she smelled like papaya and mango.

She waved the cloak to cool her skin. "Oo, that's much better. I can move again. Time for our first dance, sweetie."

# Chapter 14

She led me by the hand to the center of the dance floor where a ring of candles on their tall iron poles had been arranged. Music played from the ceiling and from every corner, something classical sounding like a romantic dirge, a suicide love song, words sung in whispers by a woman's and a man's voices overlapped, saying words in and out of time in a foreign language. Behind the violins and cellos, there was a lone flute and a balalaika, even the odd fade in and out of a samisen. A song of strange dark love full of ghosts.

It was beautiful, as was my bride. She moved lightly in my arms, like a paper doll, and her face moved in and out of the candlelight. I would see a flash of her cheekbone, then it would be swallowed by shadow and her lips would appear. A trick of the light, she was revealed to me piece by piece in a soft glow. Perhaps the light illuminated me in such a way to her. The guests crowded in to circle our candles, and their faces too seemed to float in the mutual yellow light, heads severed, bodies made invisible under the dark fur of the bears they wore.

Venus kissed me and pressed me close, wrapped her arms and cloak to envelope me, drawing me hard against her nude body. My fingertips felt the soft buttons of her spine and the two raised arch patterns beneath either shoulderblade where the sharpened dowels of the lattice backbrace had pierced her. Her skin was as smooth as talc, and incredibly

# THE BRIDE STRIPPED BARE

warm, almost hot to the touch. I inhaled her breath and tasted mint and cinnamon and champagne. I was hungry again, and she felt it.

Peeling away the flap on my pants, she took me out and caressed my shaft. I easily forgot that there were hundreds of eyes watching us. She rubbed the swollen head of my cock against the slit of her vaginal mound, leaving a cool, wet trail that slipped between her legs. My thumb and forefinger pinched and twisted one of her nipples.

"Fuck me," she moaned.

"Here? Are you sure?" I asked out of some modern propriety, forgetting the fucking and murder the guests had witnessed during the marriage. The cocaine erased all, made life new again by the second.

"We fuck for ourselves *and* for them," she echoed my feelings.

She leapt and wrapped her legs around my waist, sank her full weight down onto my cock. Either the cocaine or the lust gave me strength in my legs and arms and hips to hold and penetrate her body, to piston myself deep inside her, two flesh bodies joined as one. Her moans and grunts echoed across the room, adding our voices to the music. Her cloak hung down to cover our sex so we weren't appeasing the more perverse voyeurs. But we didn't hold back our cries and our eruptions into orgasm. I held her pressed hard against me as her body quivered. My legs shook. I could feel my hot semen pouring from her, down my shaft and inner thighs, peppering drops on the cool floor.

We held onto each other until the music ended, then she slipped her feet to the floor, and the audience burst into applause. We smiled. Venus blew them kisses, then saw me still jutting from the open flap. She tucked me up and sealed me in. Everyone else began to dance outside the candle circle as we left it. The music changed into something modern, metallic, speed-driven. I wouldn't know it at the time, but it was forbidden for everyone to dance or step foot inside the candle circle. It belonged only to us. My ejaculant stayed on the floor, marking our territory.

We freshened our drinks behind the bar where two high-backed, padded chairs had been placed. Similar to the ones we had sat in during the vows and feast, but less ornate, more worn, though each bore a bear's head perched on the tall back. We sat and twined our fingers as the adrenaline left our veins. My cock still throbbed, and I felt like I could fuck her again. Or fuck anyone, to be honest. I wanted to rape every woman in the room (and—my God—perhaps even some of the men!).

She squeezed my fingers and captured my eye.

"Then why don't you?"

My eyes narrowed to slits. "Did you…did I say something out loud?"

"You don't have to. You're my husband now. I know what you think and feel…and desire." She glanced down at the crotch of my pants, the flap visibly bulging. "It is your right as my husband to have all your appetites satisfied—at all times."

Slightly embarrased, I chuckled and folded a leg over a knee, leaned forward cupping myself, trying to make it go down. She pulled my hands away.

"Never be shy about your manhood. Our family believes in many ancient traditions. Just because something is of the past does not make it invalid. Stand for me."

I did and she angled me to face the audience, with only the bar and its towers of alcohol bottles partially blocking the view of my waist. She stood and lifted her arms in a V. The music stopped.

"Attention, guests. As you know my husband is somewhat new to the intricacies of family life. He must be taught one lesson at a time, but I'm sure they are lessons he will enjoy." The room laughed, wolf whistles pierced the air, a few obscenities could be heard. Venus reached down and ripped off the flap covering me—completely off. My penis swung free and began rising. My bride slapped my hands away when I

# THE BRIDE STRIPPED BARE

tried to cover myself. "This is my husband's beautiful cock. I worship it—as a woman should. And so can you. Anyone who wishes to taste it may come up here and test your skills at pleasing him."

Screams of joy erupted across the candle-lit faces, and women (and some men) scrambled up either side of the bar stage. I protested, but Venus pushed me back into my chair. I covered my eyes as the line formed, muttered "fuck fuck fuck" as I tried not to look at any of the people, or my penis which was hard and curved up my belly like a longbow.

I glanced between my fingers at it. My God—it had gotten bigger! I had been six inches (every guy measures and always knows this private knowledge about his anatomy), but this monster with its purple head half-tucked under the bottom of the vest had to be at least ten inches, maybe more. I didn't have a ruler handy.

My hands fell away from my eyes as I stared at it, jaw dropped. Venus pulled it away from the vest and held it up straight.

"Family secret," she whispered. "A wedding present for you, my love."

The breath rushed out of my lungs. "*You* did this?"

She nodded, a glint in her eyes. "A little potion in your wine. Old recipe. It grows when its hard—and it stays hard whenever you need it to. You might not even notice it after a while. Unless, of course, it grows even bigger!" She winked.

My eyes glazed over at all she was telling me. Bigger? My God—what man *wouldn't* want to join this family? The whole thing was a male fantasy come true. It couldn't be real. If it wasn't, then I didn't want to know what real was. Reality was boring. No life in the real world; an amazing life in this wonderfully unreal world. Maybe I was losing my mind; if so, I loved my insanity. God bless madness!

An old woman was smiling down at me. Grey hair, a wart above her left eyebrow, long breasts sagging out of her bear cloak, false teeth rattling behind her smile. With a shaky hand, she took out her teeth, held onto them as she struggled to get down to her knees.

"Fuck grandma's mouth, sonny," she said with a witch's rusty vocal cords. "I like my men sick and depraved."

I was in complete denial about what she was trying to do. Then reality intruded as she got to her knees and picked my sagging penis up with shaking, crooked fingers and guided it toward her opened gums.

Reality suddenly intruded. Madness didn't last long enough.

"Jesus Christ!" I yelled, instantly on my feet, tucking myself back in, trying to push my dick under the leg of the pants to hide it since the flap was gone. I knocked over a few bottles and almost tipped over a punch bowl when I backed into the table.

I walked backwards from the chair but forgot there was a line waiting for me. They swarmed, pawed at me, dug their fingers through the gap in my crotch, grabbed anything and everything they could, before I broke through their ranks. Gitch stood in front of me as a barrier with his arms crossed, but I saw Venus shake her head at him, so he stepped aside.

I found a small doorway in the back of the stage and it led me out of the room into an alcove with a small bear's head pinned to the wall. I didn't want to see another goddamn bear head!

Part of me was snapping out of the intoxication of sex, drugs and permissible murder. I had felt like a king, put on a pedestal by my new wife, but in a way she—and her family—were absorbing my personality. My soul.

The old, toothless woman about to go down snapped me out of a psychosexual dream. Freud would have had something to say about my reaction to the woman, holding her teeth in hand, mouth of gums and an arrow-point tongue. Castration anxiety? Who knew—I just needed to get out of there and compose myself, get my head together,

# THE BRIDE STRIPPED BARE

think seriously about what was happening. Or it could have had something to do with Elizabeth's condemnation. My old love and the new crone who had squatted down between my legs had called me the same thing: sick and depraved. Shame at a life poorly-spent...was that what had started to wake me up?

I sat on a wooden stool tucked away in a wooden room lined with painted portraits of ugly, inbred ancestors. Thinking about what I had gotten myself into. The coke didn't help me, or anyone, maintain perspective concerning their environment or actions. Elizabeth had a point: the family-controlled people by keeping the flow of drugs going. Hadn't I said the same thing to Gord when he was still the happy groom-to-be? I had too much powder in my veins to be sober any time soon.

A scream echoed down the hallway that branched off from the room where I sat. I rushed through wooden hallways, down dead ends, turned and waited to hear the scream again—next time it had less volume to it, was more distant. I sped through rooms, banged open heavy oak doors banded with metal, sped down small flights of stairs, then back up more stairs. Trying to locate the scream. A woman's cry.

I was in a narrow room, one wall wood, one wall stone. Medieval torture instruments hung on the wall or were shoved into corners. An iron maiden, a rack, pincers to pull out fingernails, branding irons, metal impaling shafts with corkscrews, lead masks inset with spikes, stocks and benches where a victim had their necks slowly crushed as a screw tightened. I had read enough medieval literature to know the uses for most of the implements, though I had rarely seen the real things beyond museums.

An immense oil painting hung in a gilded frame, taking up most of the stone wall. It depicted three grotesque figures, half human and half demon, faces distorted by pox and poorly healed bones, stirring a cauldron on which floated human body parts. The landscape behind the black-robed figures was pure Hieronymus Bosch, naked figures tortured in an endless Hell by demons bearing mismatched bodies of man and beast.

The scream pierced this room, louder than ever from behind the painting.

I pried open the frame and the painting swung open like a heavy door.

Two blonde men, twins, had the flaps of their pants open, their erect penises hooked upward like scimitars, one at the head and the other between the legs of a naked woman strapped to a wide wooden table. They stopped what they were doing and turned to me. The man at the woman's head shuffled to one side to show me that his victim was Elizabeth. Tears streaked her face and she pulled against her restraints. The man between her legs continued to lightly stroke himself despite my presence.

"Hey, Chris," said the one at Elizabeth's head. "My brother and I were just having a little fun with one of the guests. Is she related to you? Hope you don't mind."

Both brothers were tall and skinny, with faces cut from blocks of wood, angular cheekbones, sharp chins, eyes like dark brown knots sunken below their brows. The one between Elizabeth's legs smiled and smoothed his hands up her thighs. She tried to snap her legs closed, knees folding inward, but her feet were pinned solid.

"Yeah, we were gonna make her a part of the family. Maybe put a baby in her to make it official. Sometimes we need new flesh to keep the bloodline strong."

"Get away from her!" I growled between gritted teeth.

"Ah, come on, Chris," said the first brother, his belly bulging over the beltline of the bear pants, softly stroking Elizabeth's sweat-soaked hair. "You can join in. You're the groom—you get anything you want." He pointed at my crotch. "You're ready to go—can't deny what the body wants."

# THE BRIDE STRIPPED BARE

Too often I couldn't feel how my body had betrayed me. I was fully erect again, and since the flap on my pants was gone, my penis found its freedom.

"If the groom gets what he wants," I said, ignoring the thing between my legs, "then I want you two to get the fuck out of here. No one touches her. Undo the manacles—now!"

They sighed, disappointed, but they did what I commanded. Freed, Elizabeth sat up, curled her knees to her chest, caressed her wrists where the iron shackles had bit in. The twins tucked themselves back into their pants, about to leave.

"You," I said to the brother who had been between Elizabeth's legs. "Take off your pants."

He stopped, smiled, flicked his tongue out. "Hey, all right, now you're talking! Getting a piece of the groom works for me—I was in line before Aunt Ethel scared you off. We should've never let her go first, but she's got seniority over most of us."

The other twin chuckled and looked at me. "Yeah, she's fun, but doesn't get as much as she used to. We shoulda put her in the tunnel, but she's still got too much pull with Venus."

I glared at the first brother, who had quickly dropped his pants to his knees. I pulled mine off. "Don't get your hopes up," I told his leering eyes. "We're just switching pants. You can wear the crotchless bear legs."

They laughed and I threw the pants at him. I held his pants in front of myself as they passed me and left the room.

"Are you all right?" I asked Elizabeth as I got dressed.

She nodded and wept. Then threw her eyes at me, full of hatred. "Now do you see? Was *that* fake? A goddamn *magic* show?" She got off the table and found her cloak balled up in a corner.

"I'm sorry, Elizabeth. You're right. I couldn't see it before—they *have* been using drugs to control me—to control your brothers too. One moment I hate Venus, the next I love her. Back and forth—I can't control it. You haven't taken anything, have you?"

"Of course I haven't fucking taken any fucking drugs, you asshole!" she screamed at me, wrapping the cloak around her cold body. "Am I the *only* one resisting these people? The only one who thinks they're sick and twisted and should all be killed? I'm getting out of here. I'm taking my parents and I'm going to try and pry my brothers away from this scum, and when we're home, I'm calling the FBI to fucking firebomb this place off the planet!"

I lightly clutched her arm as she passed me. "Let me help you. It's not going to be easy. There are shitloads of them, inside and outside. I don't know how we're going to get your folks and Gord and Kevin away from the dance hall. If we all leave at once, the family's going to be suspicious."

She tore her arm out of my grip. "Let them! I'll run. Get as far away from this hellhole as possible!"

"No, Elizabeth, listen to me. They'll stop us. Maybe even kill us. We gotta sneak out somehow. But I don't even know the way out. We gotta find an exit first before we try to get everyone out." We stared into each other's eyes. I was feeling more sober, now seeing what the family would do to someone I once loved…still did. To Gord too, of course. The drugs made the user selfish, only thinking about satisfying their carnal desires, no matter who got hurt in the process. "Let's think this through…okay?"

She wiped tears off her cheeks. Voice croaking as she said, "Okay. But if you fucking betray me, I will kill you. Even if they kill me right after."

"I won't. I promise."

I followed her from the room, closed the painting behind us, and was about to try and figure our way through the labyrinth of the wooden hallways.

# THE BRIDE STRIPPED BARE

But Venus, the twin brothers, and Gitch barred the doorway out.

"Well, husband," Venus said, hands on hips, exposing her nude form. "I've never seen a man run from a line of free blowjobs. And now I see you've become interested in starting a new branch of the family tree. Well done, I congratulate you." She stepped up to Elizabeth, pried apart the thin arms keeping the cloak closed, took measure of the frightened girl's body. Venus sucked saliva off her teeth. "But why don't you bring this delicious little morsel to our bedchamber? I'd like to sample her myself."

Gitch moved behind Elizabeth, put his hands on her shoulders as Venus stepped away to whisper something to the twins. They hopped with glee where they stood and howled with delight, then rushed from the room.

Venus turned to face us, tracing fingers around one breast, asking Elizabeth, "I hope you like women…if not, you'll learn."

# Chapter 15

The bed chamber —belonging to Venus and myself, apparently— was a complete circle with small square windows held in thick wooden braces, like those on ancient tall ships, the wood black and weathered as though it had once been part of a ship. (The Mayflower?) Candles in sconces attached to the walls lit the room. A crescent moon shone through one window, but no trees or scenery except for the night sky could be seen. I assumed this bed chamber was on a top floor of the mansion, above the height of the surrounding forest. Boards creaked beneath our feet, even though red and black Persian carpets covered the floor, woven with scenes depicting torture and lust like those I saw in the background of the painting leading to the torture room. A kama sutra—if it took place in Dante's *Inferno*—covered the floor. On the walls hung paintings of nudes, men and women, fucking and sucking—a satyr raped a shepherdess, a minotaur mounted an obese woman who fellated an Irish wolfhound, an orgy of centaurs and medusas…the sexual mythology went on. Taking up much of the room was an immense four-poster bed covered in blue satin sheets with tasselled pillows, and three ornate mirrors stretched across the headboard.

"I'd like her pinned in place like a butterfly," Venus instructed Gitch.

# THE BRIDE STRIPPED BARE

The musculari servant grabbed Elizabeth and pinned her hands behind her back, dragged her to the bed as she screamed and fought, but her small fists bounced off Gitch's body and face, and he showed no pain.

"What are you going to do with her?" I yelled at Venus.

"Play with her, of course. Don't worry, you'll play too."

Venus folded back one side of her cloak to reveal the inner skin of the bear. With her arrow-point fingernails, she tore off a long strip of bear skin and handed it to Gitch. He took it, and the skin wound *itself* around Elizabeth's wrist. Gitch merely touched the strip of skin to the captive's wrists and it wound like a boa constrictor wrapping around its prey. He touched the free end of the skin to the bedpost, and it wrapped around the wood, pulling Elizabeth's arm with it, restraining her tightly.

Venus tore off three more strips of bear skin and Gitch touched them to the captive's other wrists and both ankles until she was spread-eagled on the bed. The skin strips cut into her flesh, made her hands and feet begin turning blue the more she resisted.

Gitch then moved behind me, kept a wide hand on my shoulder, letting me know that he would stop me if I tried to fight Venus.

Only able to raise her head, Elizabeth yelled at me. "You betrayed me! You fucking liar—you piece of shit! You're as doped up as my brothers and the rest of these freaks! All of you are thinking with your fucking dicks! I fucking hate you!"

Blood must've dropped from my face—my skin felt cold. I stared at the woman on the bed, unsure of what was really happening. A part of my brain was trying to convince me that it was all a show—just bizarre theater. Another part of me wanted to fuck her. Hate-fuck her for rejecting me when we were in our teens, when I shyly confessed that I loved her, and she shot me down.

Another part of me wished that I still had a knife up my sleeve. Had Venus disarmed me intentionally? Did she have a knife up the sleeve of her bear cloak? If I could get a blade, and if I could overpower Gitch (impossible) and Venus (beyond impossible), then I could cut Elizabeth free and we could continue our escape.

"She's a feisty one," Venus said, slipping off her cloak and sliding onto the bed, stretching her body beside her captive's, wiggling her toes with delight, tracing fingernails in circles around Elizabeth's abdomen.

"So, tell me, husband," she said without looking at me. "Why is this specimen so important to you?" She sucked Elizabeth's nipple.

"She's an old friend. Please leave her alone, Venus." I tried to make my voice sound hard and commanding, but Venus terrified me—of what she could do and how she could use magic against Elizabeth or me.

"Friends are nice to have," my wife said, planting a kiss between Elizabeth's breasts. "Not as nice as family, of course." A nail slipped along Elizabeth's jawline as Venus asked her captive, "Tell me, my dear, would you like to be a part of our family? I can make it happen."

"Go fuck yourself, you filthy pig!"

A finger tapped Elizabeth's lips. She tried to bite, but Venus pulled away and giggled. "Shh, shh, there's no reason for foul language. Confess something to me: are you unable to have a child?"

Elizabeth's fury was instantly erased, replaced by fear and embarrassment and confusion. Even I could see it in her eyes, standing away from the bed.

Venus smiled. "Ah, that's it, isn't it? You're barren. Such a shame when a woman can't perform the function she was put on Earth for. Tsk, tsk. And your brother told me you were divorced? Did your hubby leave you because you couldn't provide him with an heir?"

The fury returned. Elizabeth spat a stripe of thick fluid up Venus' face. Eyes closed, Venus wiped her face with Elizabeth's cloak, then reared up onto her knees to bring down hard an open palm.

# THE BRIDE STRIPPED BARE

I glanced at Venus' bear cloak, judging how possible it would be for me to grab it and search the sleeves for a knife. Then Gitch flexed his tightened grip on my shoulder, and the thoughts vanished.

Brushing away strands of hair fallen across her eyes, Venus said demurely, "Only my husband—or my father—may spit in my face when reclining on my marital bed. You haven't earned that privilege!"

She slipped off the bed and stepped to me (my gaze snapping away from the bear cloak), sliding a hand down my arm, kissing my shoulder, but still speaking to Elizabeth. "Never fear, my little morsel, the family has ways of making life sprout in desert sand." She kissed my earlobe and told me, loud enough for Elizabeth to hear, "Would you care to get your *old friend* pregnant? I won't be jealous. A womb is a womb—it is the continuance of the family that is most important."

I felt centipedes race under my skin as she touched me, spoke her breath into my ear, burrowing. I swallowed hard and said, "Just let her go." I turned to look at her at my shoulder. "Let us both go."

Venus' forehead wrinkled as she looked into my eyes, but I didn't know what she saw. I thought she may have been about to strike me for wanting out of the marriage.

"You love her, don't you? But you loved her long ago and she didn't love you. Ah, my poor baby." She leaned in, saw my inner core, my teenage secret. Kissing me lightly and giggling, she continued, "She's your old flame. Isn't that adorable?" Latching onto my arm, Venus looked at Elizabeth, as I did. "Now's your chance to make her love her. *Force* her to. She's tied to a bed. Isn't that what you always fantasized about? Rape her. Make your wife happy."

Gitch's hand left my shoulder, and I walked slowly to the bedpost to which Elizabeth's foot was tied, tried to find a way to loosen the bond. I forgot about the bear cloak and the knife, my mind feeling fogged by an outside source. Was that a result of Venus reading my thoughts? Neither Gitch nor Venus tried to stop me, maybe knowing that the magic imbued in the strips of bear skin wouldn't let them be loosened.

"I had a feeling your blood-lust was on the wane," she said, pacing to the side of the bed to gaze along the length of Elizabeth's body. "When you rushed like a coward from the dance, most likely attacked by your conscious." She leaned in to suck Elizabeth's nipple into her mouth and scrape her teeth along it. The captive convulsed, tried to shake my wife off of her. "I saw a man butchered for the first time when I was six," Venus said, then winked at me. "And look how I turned out." Elizabeth tried to twist her body away from Venus' mouth and hands, but she couldn't go far. I tried to pry fingernails beneath the strips, but the seam was tighter than mortar and brick. "I offer you the chance to take what you want, my husband, but you deny my gift."

She kissed her way down Elizabeth's ribs to her hipbones, fingers spidering over skin dotted in goosebumps, to trace the outlines of the bound woman's pubis mound, a finger sliding down her slit.

"I'll fuck her for you," I said sedately, staring into Venus' black eyes. "But not with a bodyguard watching, getting his jollies."

She giggled and clutched a fingernail between her teeth, then glanced at Gitch behind me. I turned to see him slip out of the room and close the door behind him. Venus returned to molest her bound victim.

"Come on in, Chris, the pussy's fine! I'll warm her up for you."

I ignored her words, kept one eye on her, making sure she didn't see what I was doing. While she was distracted, my mind cleared, and I shifted quietly to the bear cloak at a corner end of the bed. Wiggled a hand up each sleeve, found a knife. A purely golden blade with gems and ornate designs covering the handle. I hoped the knife had enough magic in it to cut Elizabeth's bonds.

Slowly sawing the blade against the bear skin strips, I watched the bond begin to split. Pressing harder, the blade cut deeper, and I felt elation

# THE BRIDE STRIPPED BARE

that I had discovered a secret of the family which had been staring me in the face the whole night.

The bear cloaks, the uniform worn by me and Gord and Poppy with their intricate designs and esoteric symbols, the knives that were a part of the uniform—there must have been magic in them all. And in what else? The bear heads? The cloven hoof shoes? The mansion itself? I couldn't know to what extent the magic existed or how it could manipulate or be manipulated. But at least I knew how prevalent it was.

The knife cut through the bear skin, and I saw Elizabeth glance at me, feeling the tightness around her ankle suddenly vanish. Blood flowed back into her foot and a smile tried to bloom on her mouth, but she held it in. Venus was digging into the sex of her captive, tongue swirling around Elizabeth's clitoris. I could tell that Elizabeth felt nothing but revulsion.

The magic golden knife.

I stared at it, held low, then glanced between the shoulder blades of Venus as she was bent over the bed. Elizabeth nodded to me, but I doubted the blade would kill my bride. It hadn't before. But if I plunged it in, would it give me enough time to cut the remaining bonds and free my teenage love?

Before I could try, however, Venus swept off the bed towards me, snatched the knife from my hand, broke the blade from its hilt, and threw both across the room.

"Really, Chris," she said, licking a line of blood off her palm where the blade had dug in before being so easily snapped. "I'm your wife now. I'll always know you better than you'll ever know yourself. Men are stereotypes of themselves. Yes, it has magic, but little boys shouldn't play with forces they don't fully understand."

Elizabeth and I were both in shock. I froze as Venus paced the room.

"You're not being very good family material anymore," she told me. "I don't mind wedding night jitters, but when I give you something,

I feel insulted when you don't accept it." She stopped to look at Elizabeth, still bound by three restraints to the bed. Venus tickled the captive's free foot, and Elizabeth kicked away her hand. "You, too, sweetheart. A woman of your age should have at least one baby. I'm offering. But it will mean you'll be an active part of our family. For life. Not just genetic fodder for experimentation…like your parents and brothers." She stepped to the door, hand on the crystal knob. "If Chris won't volunteer—his morality getting the best of him once again, as I knew it would—I have someone else who will."

Venus turned the knob and the door swung silently open.

Gord stood in the door, nostrils red with either coke or blood or both, eyes bulging, sweat slicking his skin. Gitch and the blonde twins loomed behind him.

Elizabeth's brother leered at the woman on the bed, licked his lips, and pulled open the flap on his pants.

# Chapter 16

She led Gord by the hand into the room, his penis growing as he ogled his sister and the woman on his arm escorting him to the forbidden. Venus glanced back to give a signal to the twin brothers, and I saw them leave, very disappointed. Gitch didn't go anywhere, however. He stood behind me, a hand again on my shoulder.

"The Patidean brothers said I get you again after this," Gord commented to Venus, desperation in his drugged gaze. "You'll take me back?"

"Of course, darling. One can always trust twins. They're proof that experimentation is natural and good. And we are a very natural family. That's what shocks so many outsiders. Homo sapiens are such a ridiculous species."

"All is forgiven?" Gord asked, pleading again.

"It was such a silly little error," she said soothingly, patting Gord's arm. "We won't let a minor thing like secrecy come between us. Wives and husbands shouldn't have secrets, should they?"

Gord looked at my shyly, tried to keep his voice low as he glanced at me and asked my wife. "And...*he's* not the husband anymore? I am?"

She raised an eyebrow my way. "Well, we'll have to have another marriage ceremony, of course." She cradled Gord's face. He glanced down at her body, then up to her gaze. "Do you think you'll be able to fuck and kill as he did? Maybe even come up with something more horrific? To stimulate the family's appetites before dinner?"

He smiled and nodded and began stroking himself. "I'll fuck and kill everyone in the wedding party—except you, of course."

She took his arm, stood with him at the foot of the bed, gazing over Elizabeth. "That's the spirit. Now, to prove your loyalty and to give me a good reason to take you back, all you have to do is rape your sister. Can you do that for me, my love?"

He fist sped up as he glared at his sister's nude body. "Should I fuck her to death?"

"Won't be necessary," Venus said as she pulled Gord's manhood to guide him over to the bed. A man following his cock, a woman in control of it. "We need her alive, to be bred, of course. You never made it to the family level, so I'll have to step in and assist."

Gord hop-stepped from foot to foot, excited. He was like a child, someone lobotomized, all Id with no Superego. The blonde twins must've filled his veins with red cocaine again, or a cocktail of drugs. His personality as I knew it was gone. "Okay. You and me and her? Sounds perfect. Let's fuck!"

He crawled up the bed between his sister's legs. Her free leg kicked at him as she screamed for him to wake up and realize what he was doing, but he batted her leg away and lined himself up. I tried to charge at him to pull him off but was stopped by a thick arm around my neck, Gitch dragging me away from the bed and holding me tightly, but not too tight to strangle me. I had to stay alive to witness the horror.

Gord aimed himself as Elizabeth screamed and twisted her body. He plunged into her and his hips pounded like a jungle cat mounting its mate. He grunted as his sister screamed and wept, then he mashed his mouth against her breasts.

"Gotta grow the family tree into a mighty Douglas Fir!" he laughed as he fucked. "I'll shoot a baby deep inside you and we'll start our own incest branch!"

# THE BRIDE STRIPPED BARE

Elizabeth wept, her body going limp, free leg tiring from vainly kicking the bed. She couldn't fight anymore.

"You won't have much of a branch without my help," Venus said as she knelt on the bed, Gord's bearfur ass in front of her. She looked back at me and winked, "Wanna see some magic?"

She wrenched down Gord's pants to bunch up at his knees, but he didn't notice, kept thrusting, his exposed ass cheeks clenching. Shock swept over me as I watched Venus' tailbone grow. Like an obscene snake, the flesh-covered bone grew longer and longer, slithered down the crack of Venus' ass and curled under, kept growing until it rose up like a cobra between her legs. She angled her hips to the side for me to see the tail phallus jutting out. She stroked it as she licked her lips and gazed at me. Walked on her knees until she could put a hand on Gord's ass cheek, aiming the tip of her tail.

"Hold still for a minute, sweetie," she said to Gord. "This may pinch a bit."

Guiding her appendage into Gord's rectum, Venus sighed as her lover arched upward and his arms shook. He grunted curses under his breath as he felt himself penetrated.

"Ah fuck, baby—goddamn!" he hissed between tight teeth.

"This must be done, my sweet. You enter her and I enter you. That way a magic family baby will form through your seed as it washes across her barren womb. Now fuck her—and fuck hard!"

Gord slowly pushed himself back into Elizabeth, and Venus matched his thrusts. They were like a locomotive picking up steam until they found a rhythm, and the force of two people rammed into Elizabeth's quaking body.

The victim wept and muttered "no no no no" under her tears, eyes closed, face turned away from the double-backed beast writhing on top of her. Bile rose up my throat, my tongue tasted stale, and my forehead burned as I looked away. The tenseness in my limbs lost, I was a puppet in Gitch's hands, and I wanted him to strangle me where I stood. He chuckled in a baritone beside my ear.

My head bowed as I sobbed, eyes blinking as tears fell. Through a watery gaze, I stared at the mosaic patterns of the vest and jacket I still wore. Wishing I still had a knife.

Then revelations came to me. Gord still wore his vest and jacket with, presumably, a knife up his sleeve. That was a small hope, but useless if I couldn't get out of Gitch's armlock. Yet the massive man didn't wear a vest and jacket. Was there something in the designs that held magic? I had assumed that only the three men in the wedding party had been given them because they were our wedding 'uniforms.' But maybe there was a greater reason. As I had experienced before, being the groom had its privileges. Did those extend to a privilege of magic as well?

I turned my eyes back to see Gitch looking down at me. "I am the groom," I said through a squeezed larynx.

He smiled his teeth, two of them gold, two silver, two copper along the top row. The bottom row of tiny teeth appeared to be made of black wood. Ebony.

"Yes, you are," he returned matter-of-factly.

"Let me go. Obey me."

Shook his head. "I obey the bride. We are a matriarchal family, in case you hadn't figured that out by now."

With both hands, I grabbed his arm and pulled. Moved my grip to his wrist and clenched a fist, used the increased leverage and managed to pry his arm from its choke hold. I coughed, able to breathe better. Fear was in his eyes. I had discovered something he had hoped I wouldn't—like using a magical knife to cut magical bonds. The jacket and vest gave me power over my captor—a lesser family member to the groom.

My grip slipped, so Gitch tightened his renewed armlock. But not for long. I folded both of my hands together to make a club, swung it over my shoulder to land on Gitch's nose, then jammed an elbow into his stomach. Weakened, his hold loosened. I grabbed his arm and twisted it, bending him over double. Kicked his face repeatedly with my cloven-hoofed boots.

A gold, two silvers and a copper fell to the floor. A stream of blood spat in stuttered lines from his mouth. I kicked his face again and all his teeth fell to the floor, the ebonies spilling like popcorn. I pushed him up to standing, to see the gore of his mouth and face. Half of his nose was ripped down to the cartilage, a split branching off his upper lip to halfway across his cheek.

The shoes did their damage better than I had hoped. And Venus was too preoccupied to hear a thing, her back to me and my victim.

I grabbed a twist of Gitch's shirt and threw him like a rag doll over my shoulder. His body somersaulted through the air and smashed through the wooden matrix of four windows and was gone. Cool night air blew into the room.

Venus heard the crash and felt the wind. She leapt off her lover, the thing between her legs spilling whitish-yellow fluid as she steadied herself on her feet then dove off the bed, claws open, flying at me.

I ducked out of the way as she smacked down onto the floor. Gord climaxed into his sister, fluid washing out of Elizabeth to soak the bed, his hard penis still inside her, his body collapsing to crush her. He shivered out the remainder of his orgasm. I had to ignore the profane sight and raced for his arm and sleeve.

Venus got to me before I could get to him. She flung me backwards by the hair, slamming my head to the floor. Flipping me onto my stomach, she straddled me, started trying to pull off the jacket.

"Discovered a little secret, did we, Chris?" she said, trying to pull my arms out one at a time. I kept hands tucked under my hips, holding the jacket tight across my chest. "It was a gift from the family. But I don't think you deserve it when you use it to turn on your own kind."

"You're not my kind, bitch," I growled.

# ROB BLISS

Got my knees under me and stood, reaching for the bedpost to hold myself up as Venus clenched her legs around my waist and rode me. We each had our magic, but was it a fair fight?

Hand over hand, I walked to the edge of the bed, Venus spun around to clutch onto my back, trying to wrench the jacket shoulders off me. She got one sleeve off. I dug into Gord's sleeve and pulled out his knife. He awoke from his orgasmic delirium and tried to get the knife. I stabbed his hands but didn't draw blood. May not have hurt him but shocked him enough to pull his hand away from the knife. He didn't know yet the magic he wore.

With Venus clawing my face, my eyes squeezed shut, I felt for the binding around Elizabeth's wrist. Leaned down hard on the knife to speed the sawing of the blade, quickly snapping the restraint.

Stumbling blindly along the bed, I felt Venus kicking her shoes into my stomach, but the wind wasn't knocked out of me. I grabbed one of her hands and plunged the knife in. She laughed and taunted me to stab the other hand. Felt my way to the post at the foot of the bed, hacked and slashed at the binding until I felt it snap back. Three of Elizabeth's limbs were free, though I didn't know how she could help me in my fight. She wasn't family, didn't wear magic.

A magic cloak. The white bear fur of Venus.

I followed the bed frame around to Elizabeth's last restrained hand. She called to me, pushed against her brother, fought him, but she couldn't heave off his bulk. He laughed as she screamed, gloated how he was still inside her, spilling sperm, drowning her womb with his seed. If she managed to fight him off, she would never fight what was just starting to grow inside her. She'd have to carry that for life.

"You can never get rid of the family you're born into—or that is born inside you," he laughed at her. Then he said to Venus, "Am I making you proud, baby? Can things go back the way they were? I'll do anything for you."

# THE BRIDE STRIPPED BARE

I hacked at the final bond as Venus raked fingernails across my eyes and face.

"Then fucking help me stop him, you piece of shit!" she yelled at Gord.

He slipped from his sister and dove at me. I fought his hands, felt for his face, jammed the knife into his eye. Then Elizabeth leapt on him and clawed at his face, pulling him away from me. Venus leapt on me from behind. I reached back and grabbed a fist of her hair, slashed the knife over my head at anything. Sliced off a strand of hair as she held on with her legs and still rode me. The hair dropped from my hand and I had an idea.

I jammed the knife into her stomach and twisted, but that just made her angrier. Her hands kept trying to rip off my face. I left the knife inside her in order to use both hands to pry her hands off my face. Held them away long enough to open my eyes and look around the room, see where I was, what I was facing. As I had hoped, a candle in one of sconces shined in my eyes. I ran with Venus on my back, then spun just before hitting the wall so that she took the slam. Grabbed the candle and pushed it over my head to where her head loomed.

Her hair caught fire. She screamed and I spun, trying to pull her legs from my waist. The pain of her burning head loosened her grip and she dropped to the floor. Rolled on the ground and smacked at her head trying to extinguish the fire, wailing with the voice of Hell.

I kicked the bitch in the tits.

Still with the candle in hand, I jumped on Gord, pulled him to the floor, lit his vest and jacket on fire. Mine was still hanging on by an arm. He screamed like a demon.

I grabbed Elizabeth, pulled her off the bed. Threw the candle onto the satin covers and prayed the thing would burn. As we sped for the door, I stooped down and grabbed the white bear cloak. We raced out the door and left the new groom and his bride burning in their bedchamber.

# PART
- 3 -

# Chapter 17

As Elizabeth and I ran down a flight of spiral stairs, a deep howl followed us—an earthquake from the throat of a beast that shook the walls and floor. Sparks cracked in the air and we felt electricity crawl across our faces, tingle the backs of our necks. We stopped on the stairs and looked back up from where we had come.

"Was that your wife bellowing?" Elizabeth asked as she took the bear cloak from my arm and wrapped it around her nude body.

"She's not my wife…anymore," I said, sticking my free arm through the vest arm hole and jacket sleeve, making sure they were both tight around me.

We headed down the stairs until it stopped at a landing. Hallways and doorways branched off in every direction. I could only assume we were on an upper level and needed at least to get to the ground floor to escape the house. Inch by inch we'd have to find our way out, hoping we didn't get more lost than we already were. And hopefully not meeting any family, all of them distracted by the party.

What sounded like a wall smashing, wood splintering, echoed from the top of the stairs. I picked a direction and Elizabeth and I raced away from the staircase landing, and whatever was coming down it.

We stepped around a corner that led down a narrow hallway out of view of the staircases. I stopped her and said we should take off our

# THE BRIDE STRIPPED BARE

shoes—the heavy metal clopping we made on the wooden floors echoed loudly enough to easily give away our retreat.

We stooped down to get a better look at what we carried on our feet this whole time. Strange characters, or runes, I'd never seen before were scratched into the black metal, a low heel and a split toe which neither of us could feel with our toes. They were practically vacuum-sealed to our legs, just above our ankles. Tried to pry them off for ourselves and for each other, but they wouldn't loosen without taking our feet with them.

We would have to keep our steps as light as possible, stay on carpet when we could, walk slowly and hide to let any danger pass. If we could wrap something around the shoes to deaden their horse-like clop, that may have helped.

We winced with every step as we ran down the hall, leaving a clatter in our wake like falling pots and pans, until the wooden floor ended in a circular room, coincidentally covered by a thick bear skin. From one of the largest, fattest bears I'd ever seen. Its head still attached, about the approximate size of the head of a great white shark.

Elizabeth and I scrambled away from the yellow fangs of the beast, its thick red tongue about the size of a man's arm lolled out of its mouth. The ceiling of the circular room was a terraced wooden cone with no windows, and there were no windows or doors in the room except for the one we had come through.

We started patting the walls, hoping for a hidden doorway. But we had taken too long to figure out the shoes.

A bellowing voice that was a cross between a woman's scream and a bear's growl howled at our backs. Through the open doorway we saw Venus stepping slowly to the door, her body filling it. Hair burned off, eyebrows gone, half of her scalp textured with bloated bubbles and charred skin, an ear melted like wax, the burn reaching down one side of her neck, exposing tight tendons, to end as a scorch that twisted the flesh of her left breast.

Still sticking out of her belly was the knife I had taken out of Gord's jacket sleeve.

Through her legs we could see a man cowering on the floor. A bloody black hole where one of his eyes used to be. Naked but for a few patches of vest material welded to his skin, hair burned off with an eyebrow melted and raised into a permanent inquisitive expression, his entire head baked sunburn red, legs as black as tar, the bear fur gone, the metal shoes still encasing his feet but also melted up his shins. Venus must've let Gord burn a little longer. Astounding he wasn't dead. But my mind tabulated quickly what I saw. The shoes couldn't be burned off—fire only increased their melt up the leg. But the vest and jacket could be eroded by flame.

And Venus *could* be hurt!

"The cloak looks good on you," she said to Elizabeth, words wheezing out with her smoky breath. "You better keep it on…you're going to need it where you're going."

I edged over to Elizabeth, wrapped my hand around her arm to make contact, to go with her wherever Venus was going to send her.

"Oh, don't worry, hubby," Venus said, glancing at where my hand rested, "you're going too. You picked the right room. But don't ever say I didn't give you a fighting chance. Prove your worth, and I may still be merciful. Your genes still have worth, even if your conscience doesn't."

She pulled the knife slowly out of her stomach, a pencil of blood flowing out with it, and threw it into the room. "Enjoy hell, you two."

The door slammed shut, locking Venus and Gord out, locking Elizabeth and I in. I tried the door, but it wouldn't budge. Scanned the walls and ceiling, waiting for what was coming next. I clasped my arm around Elizabeth's waist.

The floor shuddered and trembled as the back of the bear rug raised up in a great hump. Its head lifted off the floor, mouth gaping twice

# THE BRIDE STRIPPED BARE

what it had when lying on the floor. It was just skin and fur, but it came alive. Its claws distended and curved, arms wide to touch almost from wall to wall.

Elizabeth screamed and tucked into me, but a swipe of the bear's claw sent her flying. Hopefully the bear cloak protected her from injury. I swept a hand down and picked up the knife Venus had left. One knife for me, but the claws of the beast were like ten knives. I held the blade in hand like a sword and ran it into the bear's body, slashed the skin, jabbed in the point, then pulled down with all of my weight. But the skin was too tough for me to get more than a couple of inches tear through it. Then the beast fell on me, its body ballooning over me like a tent, then sucking in, squeezing me into a cocoon of leather and fur.

I could still hear Elizabeth's screams and the clatter of her shoes as they circled behind the bear. Knife still wedged through its skin, I sawed the slit and used my hands to pry the gap wider as the knife sliced. I was able to open the hole in the skin enough to wedge my head through. Only to see the bear's claws hook into the cloak Elizabeth wore and pull her into its jaws. She couldn't get the coat off her arms before the jaws closed over her, the beast's head sinking down the length of her body, swallowing her whole.

I sliced and tore enough of a gap to squeeze through the skin, clenched the knife in my teeth as I climbed the fur up to the back of the bear's neck, slashed at its face and neck. As I did with Gord, I stabbed one of the bear's eyes. I figured when attacked by an immense beast, the only chance I had at survival was to go for its eyes. It reared up, pinning me to the ceiling, wedging my arm so that I couldn't get too good of a stab or slash. But I had hurt it. Its roar rattled the ceiling, breaking off plaster, exposing wooden tiles which then rained down on me and it. The thing spun away from the tiles, ducking low, back on all fours, and I kept my grip on its fur to ride it down.

The knife hammered into its face and neck at random as it bellowed in pain and tried to throw me off its back. Before it smashed its back against the wall, and me with it, I managed to swing my body off the nape of its neck, but still held onto its fur with one hand.

But I fell to the floor when it crashed into the wall. The beast swung its maw in the direction of where it must've heard my shoes, but I got to my feet and raced behind it. It couldn't turn its massive body in the cramped space quickly enough. With its back facing me, I jumped back through the hole I had torn through it and kept hacking the knife through its body from the inside.

Its claw swept at me, tore four gashes across the back of my jacket, but it didn't reach my flesh. I figured being outside the beast was better than being inside it. Wedged a foot on the tear and swung myself through the hole, put the knife in my teeth again as I climbed up its back. But its skin was looser now with the gaping split. It shook me like a flea crawling up its back, rammed its flank against the wall again and again. The back of my head knocked hard against the wall, punching an indent in the plaster. It didn't hurt as much as it should have. I shook away stars and dizziness, and the knife flew out of my mouth and rattled across the floor. My fingers pried loose from the fur and I slipped to the floor as well.

The jaws opened like the mouth of an anaconda, yellow saliva dripping from wet fangs, and lowered toward me. I saw the glint of the knife, reached for it, got it in my hand.

Did what damage I could during the few seconds I was in its mouth before it swallowed me whole.

# Chapter 18

I fell through a tunnel of flesh that narrowed enough for me to touch the wet sides, feel mucus on my hands, smell the iron of blood and an acidic tang that burned my nostrils and stung my eyes as I slipped like a morsel of food swallowed by degrees.

I spread my legs and arms wide to slow my descent, knife in hand, trying to slice a line down the flesh tunnel, but it was too rubbery and covered by a gluey slime for the knife to have any effect. Eventually, the knife and my entire hand and arm up to my elbow was covered in slime. So too my shoes and legs up to my knees, so that even with them spread and pushing against the elastic walls, I slipped down the throat.

Until I sank through entirely and freefall dropped into a pool of acid. The aquatic muted noise of my splash echoed in my ears as I stopped sinking into the liquid, gaining buoyancy, and popped my head through the surface.

"Don't open your eyes!" Elizabeth's voice said.

I kept them closed, my arms treading water, spitting acid from my lips. I felt it tingle and burn on my skin and my hair felt like worms roiling on my head.

"Where are you?" I called, the echo of my voice bouncing off close walls.

"Follow my voice," she said, though it was still hard to direct myself given the echo. "I'm here, I'm here, I'm here," she continued as my arms splashed through the liquid, legs kicking.

Her arms grabbed mine and held on tightly, pulling me toward her. My feet felt something solid to stand on and I pushed my torso out of the liquid.

"Don't wipe your eyes, I'll do it."

I felt bear fur smear across my eyelids and felt like a little boy having his face washed by his mother.

"Okay, you can open them."

I did and saw only half of her face in a dull blue shadow. A pinprick light shone from far down a flesh tunnel ahead of us. Elizabeth's cheekbone and one side of her jaw was hazily lit by the light.

"I guess we're in the belly of the beast," I said.

In shadow, I couldn't tell if she was smiling or not. "Thank God I have this cloak. It protected me, but I got some of the acid on my hands and parts of my face. Burns a little, but tingles more. Doesn't hurt, though. You okay?"

I nodded in the low light. "I think so. I guess my vest and jacket are keeping me safe too, but the bear got its claws into my back. Don't know how long our magic clothing will survive." Held my hand up out of the liquid. The steel caught a blue shine. "But I still got the knife. Cut that fucker up pretty good before it swallowed me." I tucked the blade back up my sleeve and into the empty sheath. I noticed that the blue-gem ring Venus had taken from Gord and given to me was gone. Eroded by acid? Did it mean that, finally, Venus and I were no longer married? Who cared? A ring was a ring…it had always meant nothing…just like my marriage.

I heard the smile in her voice. "We might need more than a broken knife to get us out of this." She looked at the light at the end of the towering tunnel. "Shall we venture into Hell?"

# THE BRIDE STRIPPED BARE

I smiled. "Ladies first."

On hands and knees, we crawled, the tunnel high enough for us to raise our heads as we edged toward the blue. It stank like marsh gas and rot, decomposed flesh, shit and piss and bile. We choked and coughed as we crawled, tried to avoid breathing through our noses, thinking only that this was a prison attached to a prison, yet whatever path looked like an escape had to be tried. The blue light could be guiding us into a worse torment, but the tunnel of flesh was not an oasis.

We crawled and sweat poured into our eyes from the heat of the confined space. I wiped my sleeve across my face, now dry, the acid having evaporated, the slime burned off by the acid. The blue light grew brighter until it shone like a star, and Elizabeth and I had to stop and shade our eyes from it. She flipped the bear's head of the cloak to cover her face and shield her eyes as she kept her head bowed and crawled looking at her hands. I slipped my jacket off, inspected the claw marks shredding the back, saw that the slices had begun stitching themselves back together. I draped the jacket over my head, likewise, crawling with my head bowed, not looking up.

We came to the end of the tunnel, which dropped off into a depression illuminated by a ring of blue lights. We couldn't see below the haze of light from our elevated position. Elizabeth turned to hang her legs down over the slight incline, footholds of what looked like flesh-covered bone. A rib staircase that we had to climb down on all fours. I followed her until the stairs leveled out horizontally, and we stood. A plane of smoky blue light hovered a few feet over our heads.

Putting jacket and cloak back on, I gazed across this latest room. We stood amongst what looked like a forest of shoulder-high mushroom stalks made of thickly-veined flesh—half-animal, half-vegetable—with caps that inverted into wide oval bowls. We peered into the nearest bowl to see what looked like an infant, but one not entirely human.

Its tiny limbs flailed, grasping and kicking at heavy smoke that filled and flowed over the bowl like dry ice vapor. The cradle. A flesh tendril that was a series of red and blue twisted veins attached to the infant's forehead by a sucker. Another tendril attached itself to the infant's navel. Its flesh was covered with a bluish-white film, eyes and mouth closed, a paste of dark hair covering its head. A thin tail curled out from between its legs and flapped against the sides of the cradle. It breathed through flexing gills.

Elizabeth held a hand over her mouth. "That can't be…oh God…"

I put an arm around her, pulled her in, had a feeling about what was going through her mind. "It's not human."

Horror etched her face. She whispered in terror, "That's what's inside me…"

"No. We don't know that."

She pushed my arm away and paced through the mushroom stalks, peering into each cradle, her revulsion growing. "These *things*…what the fuck are they? What is that woman? Your wife! Is she even a woman?"

"Elizabeth, please. Don't jump to conclu—"

She spun on me, fury in her eyes. "I was just raped by my fucking brother! While he was getting it up the ass by some freak *thing* with a tail between her legs!"

The noise woke one baby, which began crying, wailing out a wet gurgle, which started the other infants heaving out their screams, the gills on either side of their jaws pumping like blacksmith's bellows. The walls echoed with deafening noise.

Elizabeth wept, her maternal instinct overcoming any revulsion, hands dipping into the nearest cradle, picking up the infant inside. But she couldn't lift it completely from its bed seeing it was still attached to the tendrils that, possibly, sustained its life. She trembled and tears poured from her eyes as the infant wailed out its pain.

# THE BRIDE STRIPPED BARE

I weaved through the mushroom stalks to help get her under control, took the baby from her hands and set it back down in its cradle. Coaxed her away and led her through the mushroom forest. I tried to peer through the blue-tinged darkness and roiling mist for an exit.

As I did, a tendril shot out from one of the cribs and attached itself to Elizabeth's neck. She screamed, her cloak falling open. Another tendril shot out and sealed its sucker to her nipple. Tendrils speared from the mushroom cradles beside and in front of us, most of them adhering to Elizabeth's body, wrenching off her cloak, sticking to her back, her ass, down either leg. They covered her from head to toe, front and back, her face almost completely covered. Some of them tried to latch onto me, but they fell away, retracted back into their cradles when they encountered my clothing. I easily pulled the ones off my face and neck. But Elizabeth couldn't pull them from herself as readily.

I guessed why. She was female, and possibly pregnant, and the infants saw her as a mother, a source of milk.

I grabbed her cloak, threw it over my shoulder, and started to wrench a few tendrils off Elizabeth. They left round pock-marks on her skin. Like leeches, the suckers pierced skin-deep enough to draw blood, and the blood flowed, unable to coagulate. There were too many to pull off, so she began to weaken at the blood loss. I ripped at them, but they didn't tear—merely pulled off, retracted back to their cradles, then shot back out again, aimed perfectly wherever Elizabeth was in the forest of mushrooms.

I pulled the knife from my sleeve and slashed at the tendrils. They severed easily and the hacked-off length of twisted flesh spewed out red and blue blood. The babies wailed louder, beyond a mere scream of hunger, into voices laced with metal—felt as though steel needles were rammed into my eardrums.

Adrenaline made my heart feel about to burst as I held onto Elizabeth and, with my knife hand, swept the space in front and around her, hacking through the thousand flesh ropes that suckered to her body. The metal screeching of the infants pierced through our skulls like skewers, forcing me to squeeze my eyes shut, but I tried to keep them open as I slashed and hacked.

I managed to cut away enough of the tendrils to push Elizabeth quickly through the forest. The tendrils kept coming. I felt the bear fur against my cheek, and it gave me an idea. Slashing away the tendrils on Elizabeth's back, I quickly put the bear skin on to cover her. The tendrils continued to shoot out, but they couldn't take hold of the fur as they could her skin. Cutting more flesh cables allowed me to cover her with more of the bear fur. Eventually, I had freed her entirely so that she and I were able to run through the remainder of the mushroom forest.

I stopped and held her steady as I looked back, told her not to get out from under the bear cloak. In our wake were severed tendrils with flexing sucker mouths lying bleeding and twitching across the flesh floor. Both of our shoes were splashed with blood, and blue mist blew across the forest of mushroom stalks. The screaming of the babies began to wane, but I could see them in their cradles, gills pumping in agony, pink mouths wide—too wide for normal, human babies, their jaws unhinging—tiny fingers clawing mist, tails snapping against either side of the cradles. The tendril umbilicals which were suckered to their navels had retracted back into the cradles, flicking blood while spasming, painting the nestling infants in their own red and blue life fluids.

At the far end of the forest, we came to a slit in the muscle wall tall enough for us to squeeze through, the slit sealing itself behind us. Elizabeth and I sat propped back against the closed wall, huddled into each other. We could still hear the residual wailing of the infants, but once the wall had sealed, all noise from the other room broke off.

# Chapter 19

"Are you okay?" I asked her while picking off a few remaining suckers, dead and drying up, from her bloody, exposed skin.

Elizabeth wrapped the cloak around her body as she shivered. Looked up at me with eyes wet and glassy from fresh tears. "I better not have one of *those* growing inside me. I will kill it…and if I can't kill it, I'll kill myself."

I combed sweat-soaked hair away from her eyes. "Don't say that. Don't let this place—these people—win. They'll try to destroy us if they can't assimilate us."

She sniffed and wiped her eyes, tried to blink away the images we had both just seen.

Nodding, she said, "You're right. We have to survive this goddamn family. Send the fuckers to Hell, if they're not already there."

I wiped blood off her collarbone. The pock-marked blood spots seemed to have halted their flow since the bear cloak went back on her body.

"They seem to carry their hell with them," I said, trying to lighten the mood. "Why wait until you're dead to enjoy damnation?"

She smiled and I smiled with her, felt exhaustion move through my muscles, making me want to sleep for a thousand years.

"Are the children all right, Mistress Venus?" a tinny, radio-like voice asked.

We craned our heads to see a figure stooping over our prone bodies. A hand extended to feel the fur of Elizabeth's cloak—how the person must've mistaken one woman for another. The female figure was blind. Copper wire sewed her eyes shut. Half of a gas mask stretched over her mouth and nose, the round filter also acting as a speaker for her voice.

She wore a nurse's uniform from the 1950s—white shoes and leggings and skirt—down to the origami crane nurse's cap perched on her head, hair tied at the back of her head into a bun.

Elizabeth and I must've stared at her in shock for too long.

The nurse repeated through her gas mask, fingertips brushing the cloak fur. "Mistress Venus? Do the infants have need of me? The mothers are busy making more milk."

Elizabeth stuttered out a response. "No, the…ah…infants are fine." She and I got to our feet.

"Your voice sounds different, Mistress."

"Oh…yes…I've, uh, had a bit too much to drink. It's been a busy night."

The nurse reached out, touched my sleeve. "I'm sure your wedding was quite grand. Is this your groom?"

"Yes, thank you—this is Chris."

I clasped the nurse's hand. "Hello. The wedding was lovely. You must join the festivities."

If a mask could smile…the nurse seemed happy. The eye muscles behind the sewn wire convulsed. "Thank you for the offer, but the babies need constant care, of course. The other nurses and I wouldn't think of being relieved of our duties. Would you care to inspect the maternity operations?"

Elizabeth and I looked at each other, shrugged.

"Thank you, that would be nice," Elizabeth said.

We followed the nurse, who stepped confidently as though she could see, leading us through a flesh hall that branched in an L shape,

# THE BRIDE STRIPPED BARE

until we emerged into a vast room shaped like an immense square tower that stretched high overhead. Bright white light shone from every wall, the ceiling, the floor. We couldn't see detail as we squinted, waiting for our eyes to adjust to the brightness. Once they did, however, it was still difficult to tell details since every direction was a uniform whiteness.

Nurses dressed in the same uniform as our guide, hair twisted into buns behind their caps, mouths covered by gas mask respirators, eyes sewn shut, were scattered throughout the room. Each one to a station. The mushroom cradles we had seen in the previous room rose out of the floor. A baby was put into it and tendrils grew out of the inner bowl of the cradle, attached themselves to the infant's forehead and navel, then a fluid—possibly a thin red blood, transparent—filled the bowl, covering the baby completely. The wings of the inverted mushroom cap folded over the submerged baby, then the entire cradle and mushroom stalk sunk back into the floor, disappeared. When it rose up again, the baby was gone, mushroom cap unfolding to form a cradle to receive the next infant.

We looked up to see where the babies came from. High, high above our heads, women of various shapes and sizes hung down from the ceiling in woven flesh hammocks, their splayed legs sticking through holes. They held onto the supporting ropes of the hammocks as they wailed out their birth pangs, pushing.

We saw the head of a baby emerge from the mother and easily slip out. A rain of fluid fell as the woman pushed, followed by the baby who fell out tethered by its long umbilical cord. Like a bungee cord that wasn't elastic enough to rebound, the cord unraveled to let the infant down into the nurse's waiting hands. She cut the cord with a pair of thick silver shears which she had holstered to her hip, then put the baby in its cradle. The mushroom filled with liquid, folded its wings, and descended into the floor.

# ROB BLISS

The nurse knew where to stand to avoid being hit by too much of the fluid or flesh that fell from the mother. (Perhaps this was the reason for the gas masks and the sewn eyes, I wondered.) The mess of filth beaded like water on rubber and was sucked down, the floor cleaned instantly. The entire white room stayed clean, as did the nurses. Once the baby had been freed of its lifeline, given over to its incubator, the long length of umbilical fell with the afterbirth. Elizabeth and I jumped out of its way. It coiled down and slapped wetly on the floor before a hole opened up and sucked it away. We couldn't tell whether the floor was an organism or a machine, but it operated efficiently every time.

No mother was finished giving birth after just one child. Each pushed and groaned and wept, the hammock swinging slightly with her convulsions, until another baby crowned. It too somersaulted through the air, its umbilical spooling out behind it, becoming gradually stiffer as the infant fell closer to the nurse's waiting arms. Between births, the nurse occasionally took a small facecloth from a pocket and dabbed the dew off her face. Readjusted where she stood beneath the mother, not always able to compensate for the hammock swing.

"How do you know where the baby is in the air?" I asked.

The nurse who was giving us the tour chuckled with the nurse doing the work. "Your husband is very curious about the process, Mistress. Unlike some of the others. We take it as a compliment."

"Yes," Elizabeth said, patting my arm and winking at me, playing the part of Venus to maintain our camouflage. "I've got a good one this time."

The nurses hummed with content, then the tour guide said to me, "We have excellent hearing, Master. We hear the baby emerge from the mother and we hear the umbilical unravel. We step out of the way for the effluvia to fall and be sucked into the floor, then we return to our places beneath the mother. We can also feel a change in the air pressure as the infant's body falls toward us. Not to worry, no delivery nurse would dare move from her post while a mother is in birth suspension."

# THE BRIDE STRIPPED BARE

Again, an umbilical rope and afterbirth fell and was absorbed by the floor. This happened across the entire room, mothers hanging from hammocks like flies in spider webs. Elizabeth and I watched in fascination and revulsion as the woman high above us delivered five babies. Then she sagged exhausted into the swaying hammock before it rose on its flesh ropes. A hole opened in the ceiling and she vanished. A few moments later, the hole reopened in the vast flat ceiling, and another pregnant mother in a hammock was lowered, screaming as the first baby pushed out of her, a nurse far below with open arms and shears waiting.

"Fascinating," I said under my breath.

With excellent hearing, the nurse responded to me. "We're glad you admire the process."

"Can I ask you something?"

"Of course," the nurse said, enjoying the attention.

"Why do you wear respirators?" I didn't want to say 'gas masks.'

"Prolonged exposure to the birthing fluids becomes toxic. One of the reasons why the mother is suspended far above the effluvia. Same reason for our eyes being sewn shut—I'm sure that was your next question. We also have no sense of smell—you're third question, perhaps?"

I chuckled mildly, as did the nurse. "How many babies on average does a woman have?"

"Seven."

My eyes darted to Elizabeth, who squeezed a hand over her mouth as blood drained from her face.

"Is anything wrong?" the nurse asked.

Elizabeth coughed into her fist. "No, thank you, I'm fine. Too much champagne I'm afraid."

"I understand," said the nurse. "Perhaps you'd care to leave—I wouldn't want you over-exposed to toxicity without the proper safety apparatus. But on behalf of all the delivery nurses, I sincerely thank you, Mistress Venus and Master Chris, for blessing these births with your presence. Another branch of the family will grow quite strong, I'm sure."

Elizabeth cleared her throat, wiped a finger beneath her eyes to smear away tears as she replied, "Yes, I'm sure it will. Thank you for the tour…for my husband. Can you show us the way out? I'm a little lost, feeling dizzy."

"Of course. Right this way to the Conception Room. A more inspiring sight to see, especially on your wedding night."

I had a feeling of what was going through Elizabeth's mind. Same as in the previous room, but where she assumed—*if* she was pregnant—she may have given birth to one bizarre baby, she now probably thought she'd give birth to a litter. Seven was the *average!* We saw five from one mother. Did others give birth to ten, fifteen, twenty? Animals had litters, not human beings. Even triplets were rare.

The nurse escorted us through the rows of nurse attendants and the mushroom cradles appearing and disappearing, of babies dropping from the sky, mothers howling out their pain as they dangled in mid-air, until we came to another slit in the wall, enough to squeeze through. We thanked the nurse—I did, Elizabeth could barely speak, bile stirring in her throat—and stepped through the wall into the Conception Room. Whatever the hell that was.

# Chapter 20

Once again, our eyes had to adjust from the bright light of the Birthing Room to the darkness of the next room we entered. But Elizabeth wasn't worried too much about what we were inside, but what was inside her.

"They just kept coming out of those women," she whispered to me in the darkness. "I'm not a goddamn dog! What the fuck is inside me, Chris?" A few more tears and sniffles came, so I tried to assure her, but wasn't sure how.

My vision was returning so that I could see outlines and shadows. I cradled her face in my hands and lifted her eyes to mine. "Look, when we get the fuck out of this shit, we'll take you to a doctor. Get the goddamn morning-after pill or something. Just to make sure, okay? We'll say you were raped—not by Gord, of course—but you didn't get a good look at the rapist, it all happened too fast—"

"*If* we get out of here—*if!*"

After a few more seconds, I could see her better in the dark, wiped a tear off her cheek with my thumb. "*When*, not if. Let's just get through this room, find an exit, try to get back to the house, or, even better, outside. There must be tons of cars for all of the people who came to the wedding. We steal one, drive all night—hell, drive for a week straight—we'll be in fucking Panama, they'll never find us."

She hiccoughed out a laugh, sniffled, wiped the tears off her face. Patted her abdomen. "Okay. I won't worry about this shit, not right now."

I put an arm around her, and we walked deeper into the room. Our eyes had adjusted enough so that we weren't totally blinded. Stripes of diffused orange light glowed in bands circling the walls. A geodesic dome formed the ceiling that stretched high above us, the inner cone of the dome glowing the brightest orange. The floor was spongey black and orange swirled flesh, except there was a layer of something semi-transparent over it. I looked at where Elizabeth and I had walked and could see the treads of our shoes imprinted in the floor. I bent down to feel that our soles had sunken into semi-soft wax. It even smelled like beeswax. Though that wasn't the predominant smell in the room.

It smelled like sweat and semen and vaginal juices.

Yet there was no one in the room but us.

We had strolled to the center of the room, no sign of any exit, though the walls closest to the floor were too dark to see anything. We kept our eyes on the stripes of orange light, broken by hazy bands of blackness, always looking up since that was where the light came from.

Wheels spun in my mind and I put together the shape of the room, the color of the light, the floor of wax. We were inside a hive. I whispered the revelation to Elizabeth, who spun where she stood to take in the room with a different perspective in mind.

"If that's true," she whispered, "then where are the bees?"

"I don't know," I replied, hearing my heart, tasting dried sweat on my lips. The room was hot. I put a hand on the elbow of Elizabeth's cloak. "Keep the bear fur tight around your body, no matter the heat—it has some kind of magic, I'll explain later. Let's check out the walls."

Our shoe heels slipped a little as they dug into the wax floor, like walking—not on ice—but on slush. The closer we got to the nearest wall, the easier it was to distinguish a sound other than our own foot-

# THE BRIDE STRIPPED BARE

steps. We stopped to listen, holding our breath, trying to peer through the darkness to the source of the sound.

I thought it was humming or buzzing at first, but that may have been because my thoughts were on bees and a hive. But both of those types of sound are usually constant in tone and pitch, and even if there's a change, they still sound like humming or buzzing. The constant tone wasn't broken by moans or cries or grunts. Those sounds came from people.

"Sex?" Elizabeth asked, mouthing the word.

I nodded, put a finger to my lips as I pulled her along to tiptoe closer to the wall. We stood within the dark shadow of where floor met wall, the first band of orange light just out of reach of my upstretched arm.

But the sounds were clearer. Unmistakable. Only muted behind a thick barrier. I touched the wall and it was the same wax as the floor. My fingertips left indents, the smell of beeswax on my skin. But the various stenches of human bodies were still thicker.

Shadows moved deep inside the orange light. Thin shadows, ghosts, more orange than black, difficult to make out from my close perspective. Shapes that moved and vanished. We stared at the light, seeing shadows the odd time, but then they would vanish in the light. We moved across the band as it stretched around the wall, stopping to see and hear the same things across the light.

I whispered in Elizabeth's ear. "I got an idea. I'm gonna get a closer look."

She stopped me from approaching the wall, whispered back, "Let's just get the fuck out of here. Find an exit. We'll search the room."

My male pride was struck down—I knew she was right. This seemed like the kind of place where curiosity would definitely kill the cat. I'd seen enough horror movies and read enough books to know that being curious *never* saved anyone's life. When the house is haunted—get the fuck out! Don't go opening doors and peering down staircases into the basement.

She went one way and I went the other. Hands patted the wax walls, feet tapped and slipped a little on the floor, as we moved through the shadows at the base of the striped hive. Smells of wax and sex stayed in my nostrils, waning only when I put some distance between myself and the walls. Perfectly smooth, not the slightest indent or slit or bulge—only where I pressed my fingertips was the wall minutely flawed. And the floor gave us nothing new but our cloven treads. We met back up after we had each inspected our halves of the hive…and found the same lack of escape.

My male pride returned.

I whispered, "Let me try my idea." She shrugged, spread her arms out to ask what the idea was, but I mouthed the words, "Just watch."

I stepped to the wall and pressed all ten fingers into the wax. They sank in, but it took some strength to get my two strongest fingers in as deep as the second knuckle. Pushed them in, pulled them out easily. Used my index finger to push in five holes where my four fingers and thumb could go in. I gripped the holes as though the wall was a bowling ball. Tried to pull out the wax between the holes, but it held too strongly. I only managed to warp the holes, stretch them out so that my fingers were too small inside them and they slipped out.

Plan B. Always handy to keep a knife up your sleeve.

I stabbed it into the wall, sawed and pushed the blade through the wax, carved out a small rectangle. The tip of the knife pried and hacked away wax until the rectangle was hollowed out enough to act as a ledge for my hands. Took a bit of work, but I was eventually able to carve out four staggered handholds, making a short ladder up the wall, far enough to get my head closer to the band of orange light, to see the moving shadows inside, hear the sexual cries, piece together my idea that the 'bees' in this hive resided—and fucked—behind thick wax

# THE BRIDE STRIPPED BARE

walls. Stretching along the bands of light all the way up the walls to the tapered peak of the cone.

The cloven toes of the shoes were perfect for climbing wax walls. They stabbed in easily and stayed wedged for me to put my weight on them. Being made of metal helped them slip out of the wax easily, as my hand reached for the next handhold and I pulled myself up to the light.

My face was bathed in sweat, reflecting orange light. Nose pressed to the wax, breath held, I saw the shadows tumble over each other deep inside the wall. Flattened an ear against the orange glow to hear moans and groans much easier. The buzzing we heard on the floor must've been the sound of muted ecstasy from a thousand throats blending together into a strangled hum.

I was able to hold myself up on the wall easily enough to become bored. To give in to curiosity. Took the knife out of my sleeve again and began twisting the blade to wear away the wax, hoping to form a peephole. To see how thick the wax was too, of course, not to just be a voyeur watching people fuck. If that was what was even inside the walls.

The knife bored a hole through at least a foot of solid wax before the tip released confined air. The human smells were thicker and made me gag, but I remained quiet. Held my breath as I peered in, but the hole was still too small to see anything but a pin of orange light pouring out. Still, the sounds of orgasm were louder with the wall pierced. I looked down at Elizabeth and she gestured that she could easily hear what was behind the wall.

I put the knife back into the pinhole and corkscrewed the blade back and forth, peeling off thin layers of wax with each twist, scraping them out of the hole like wood shavings. Jabbed the knife into the hole, gouged out more wax, stabbed it in deeper, but I could only get so much power with a single arm free, the other hand gripped hard on the handhold.

The knife finally stabbed through. A howl of pain burst out with the enlarged hole. Someone inside the recess grabbed the knife out of my hand—then grabbed my hand!

I yelled and tried to wrench my hand back, but it was pulled in harder, until my entire arm up to the shoulder was inside the wall. My other hand and both feet slipped off the wall and my full weight hung from the captured arm. I didn't budge from where I dangled. Something stabbed into my arm at the bicep and I yelled. Glanced for a second down at Elizabeth, who was screaming up at me, asking me what was going on. But pain burned my muscles too much for me to catch enough breath to speak.

I felt warm blood slip down the skin of my arm, then the sleeve of my jacket tugged.

Whatever held my arm was attached around my wrist and was cold metal. I thought: a handcuff? It was tight, cutting the circulation, and had no give when I wrenched back. I feared my body weight pulling against my pinned arm would eventually separate my shoulder—or wrist or elbow—or my whole fucking arm would rip off! Was that what the person inside the wall was trying to do? Sawing into my bicep?

Fear imagines everything—none of it good.

My arm wasn't ripped off, just my coat sleeve. Though my arm was still pinned and locked at the wrist.

Elizabeth screamed again, but for a different reason.

I looked down to see two fists punch through the floor on either side of where she stood and grab her ankles. The black and orange wax slush floor spun and sank in a swirl beneath her, and she plunged into the floor, her screams sliced off. The wax swirled back over her to close the hole and become relatively solid ground again.

A second fist, wrapped in the sleeve of my jacket, punched through the wax beside my head. It jackhammered from inside the wall until chunks of wax broke off, knocking into the hive to scatter across the

# THE BRIDE STRIPPED BARE

floor. Enough of the wall was punched out for a figure to stretch half of their body through the orange light to face me.

A bald man with some lost language tattooed across half his body and head, old thick scars and branding welts patterned his bare arms and chest.

He laughed in my face, tongue lolling out of his mouth. The tips of his tongue split to form two points.

He yowled, "Welcome to the fuck party!"

Then his tongue spooled out of his mouth and the two points split further until two tongues spun in either direction around my neck, tightening a flesh noose around me, pulling me through the wax wall and into the bright orange light.

# Chapter 21

I dreamt of a man with an octopus mouth full of tongues who jabbed a steal skewer repeatedly into my forehead. I tried to move my arms to stop his hand, but his tongues reached down and wrapped themselves around my wrists. Three more tongues tied my ankles and spiraled up my legs to pin them together. Tongues tightened around my neck, pushing up my chin so that I couldn't see his face, only the hand coming down with the skewer. Streams of blood trickled to wash down my face, smearing across my eyes. My vision saw through a red tint, the hand and the metal rod glinting in a harsh red light hacking away at my forehead. Chunks of bone peeled off and tumbled down my face, clogging my mouth to mute my screams. I tasted my own flesh, swallowed, choked on scraps of flesh and bone.

The dream lasted hours and I couldn't wake up. Didn't wake up until the man had cracked my head like an egg, pieces falling across my chest, only my face from my eyes down remaining, covered in blood, wedges of bone and scraps of skin pasted to my cheeks and chin. He held up a mirror.

I was Venus.

My eyes snapped open and reality was similar to the dream. In a room half stone, half wood, the fog of my breath puffing in the air, a white light shone down onto my face. The bare-chested bald man

# THE BRIDE STRIPPED BARE

covered in tattooed words and symbols hung over me, blue latex gloves on his hands. He held a tattooist's needle in one hand, a moist, blood-peppered cloth over the other. Imprinting something onto my forehead, then dabbing away the blood. The split twin points of his tongue slipped in and out from between his lips as he concentrated.

Some kind of brace was around my neck, raising up my chin so that I was unable to move my head in any direction. Flexing my hands and feet, I felt them tied. I think I sat in a chair covered in fur, could feel it soft under my entire body. Assumed I was naked, but too much of my body was numb. But I knew for sure that I was no longer wearing the vest and jacket. And the knife was gone.

I heard bare feet slap on stone and Venus soon lowered her burned face over mine. She had begun to heal, her skin now solidified wax, red and raw with only faint char marks remaining.

She clucked her tongue. "Why you don't want to be my husband, I'll never know. I'll let you have a mistress—or two or five or fifty—in fact, I'll insist on it. Is it love that makes you choose just one woman over many? Love rarely has had anything to do with procreation. In fact, having babies is hindered by love. What if the woman you're with is barren? As is—was—your chosen mistress? The species would die out if everyone only chose love. Fucking is much more important, and natural. Fuck anyone and everyone, I say. The species demands that every womb is filled with as many babies as possible." She smiled and slapped my cheek. The needle continued to buzz over my eyes, pinpricks stabbing my head. "Well, the family has developed quite revolutionary methods of *making* wombs where none exist." She squeezed my mouth. The tattoo needle stopped. She glared into my eyes, the scars of fire crisscrossing her face and neck, frozen red bubbles. "You owe me. You and your fucking girlfriend killed almost half a nursery of family young who were just trying to feed off her flesh! So now both of you have to replace what you've stolen from me."

She looked at the tattooist, snapped her fingers. He took his hands and the cloth from my head, put his needle down, and popped a few clasps on the brace around my neck. Removed it in two pieces. I let gravity slowly drop my chin to my chest, neck stiff. Before the light was clicked off, I saw that, yes, I was fully nude, sitting in a fur-covered chair, my arms and legs pinned by thick flesh straps, dried and as solid as cables.

I let dizziness pass as my head throbbed, drew in breath slow and cool. Coughed and heard my voice echo against stone. The tattooist swung the white light away from my eyes so that I could clearly see a closed wooden door with a small window in the wall opposite me. Hazy light glowed through the window. Above the door was a television sitting on a wooden ledge.

The screen flickered lines of electric rainbow until it settled on a view of Elizabeth, in a similar room and in a similar position as I was in. Naked, she was strapped to a fur-covered wooden chair, tilted back, her legs raised by wooden extensions projecting from the chair, a wide light shining down to illuminate her body and most of the room.

Her belly protruded at least two feet out from her waist and ribs. I could see movement beneath the taut skin; hands and feet pressed their imprints, then vanished.

Two nurses like the ones we had encountered in the Birthing Room were attending to her. One between her legs with a pair of metal shears glinting in the light, the other standing beside a mushroom stalk and cradle.

Elizabeth groaned and cried, veins like ropes on her red forehead as she pushed. A baby slipped out and the nurse with the shears cut the umbilical cord, passed the infant to the other nurse, who put it in the cradle. Tendrils extended to suckle to the baby's forehead and navel, then the cradle filled with fluid—a barrier that seemed to become a thick gel which the grasping hands and tiny feet couldn't poke through.

# THE BRIDE STRIPPED BARE

Then the cradle descended on its stalk, sank through the floor, gone. A new mushroom cradle grew in its place.

The infant had gills and a tail. None were boys. Unlike the infants we saw in the nursery, the ones coming out of Elizabeth all had sagging, developed breasts with nipples the size of corks hanging down either side of their tiny chests, and their teeth were needles.

"Genetic flaws," Venus spoke in the darkness. "Not from the family, of course, but from your barren, imperfect mistress. Her tadpoles will be at the bottom of the family barrel, naturally. Once grown to maturity, they'll possibly be used as slaves, or breeding cows—depending on the quality of milk they can provide. If they're no good for anything, though, they'll make adequate food. Of course, I wouldn't eat anything that came out of that cunt's cunt. But some family members have less discriminating tastes."

I watched the television and saw Elizabeth give birth again and again, the same procedure repeated, the infants resembling each other in their strange genetic attributes. I felt sick. And sad for what Elizabeth was going through. I prayed that she didn't think I had betrayed her again.

I counted seven babies, but Venus said that Elizabeth had begun giving birth before I had awoken. The average gestation period for a family birth was only a few hours. By the time she was done, umbilical ropes and blue masses of afterbirth were stacked in a pyramid wedged into a corner of the room. Liquids seeped out of the stack and pooled on the floor, running beneath the chair. Elizabeth fell unconscious, exhausted, and the nurses hooked up an IV to her arm, shot something from a syringe into her vein. Then turned out the light.

Venus said that there was a total of seventeen infants born from Elizabeth's drained body. She would sleep, painlessly and without nightmares, for hours. I wasn't to worry—mother and babies were doing fine.

The television clicked off.

The overhead white light swung back to shine on my face. Venus held up a hand mirror for me to see myself. My hair had been shaved off completely. The strange letters and symbols I had seen on the tattooist, on Venus, on the jackets and vests, were now in ink across my head above the line of my eyebrows. Only two letters were left as outlines, still needing to be filled in.

"We've made our mark on you now," Venus said. "Wherever you go, family members will see that you're one of us. Not to worry, the marks are made with special ink which disappears in a matter of minutes. Normal people—that scum—won't be able to see them. But family members will. And you'll be able to see the tattoos of other family members. The ink gives you special sight. It's how we all confirm each other as family members. Do you like it?"

I squinted against the light and the pain that seared my skull. "What does it say?"

"Many things. You'll learn in time. It marks you as a member of the Royal Order of Ursa. It also mentions that you are one of my husbands. A great privilege. You'll go far with that mark. You'll thank me one day." She took away the mirror, smiled down into my stinging eyes. "I may play with my husbands, but I don't get rid of them too easily. And they don't get rid of me either. Ever."

"What about Gord?"

"He was never officially my husband. I can change my mind up to the last minute. A bride's privilege. Though I'll be inside his soul for life. No separation, no divorce—I will always own him. Whether I want to play with him or not…well, my moods come and go."

That was putting it mildly.

Leaning in, she kissed my lips. When she slipped her tongue into mine, I bit it. She chirped and giggled, not in pain, but happy. She opened her mouth with her tongue pinned by my teeth, then used her

# THE BRIDE STRIPPED BARE

teeth to bite my lips. I felt pain. Yelled and released her tongue. She sucked the blood off it, licked a red stain around her lips. Then held my mouth squeezed and licked the blood off my lips.

She wore her white bear fur once again, taken from Elizabeth, returning full power and protection to herself.

"Still feisty," she cooed. "You're learning how to make me horny. But, alas, I can't fuck you just yet. I must first put someone between us. Not to worry, you know the routine. You saw it once before. But like I said, you owe me. Your mistress has provided her share. For now. She'll have to be gang-raped once she wakes up, of course. Would hate for her to sleep through the fun. Seventeen doesn't even come close to what you and her owe me." She leaned in and smoothed a finger over my head tattoo, looked lustfully into my eyes. "Ever taken it up the ass?"

She stood away and the chair tilted back, facing me at the ceiling, my legs thrown up by projecting extensions in the chair, straps spinning themselves around my shins, wedging my legs wide apart, raising them like an astronaut sitting in a space capsule. My ass cheeks spread.

Venus vanished into the shadows for a moment. I tried to gaze around the room, but the white light in my eyes prevented me from seeing how large or small it was. I could only see stone and wood and feel the cold. Felt like I was in a castle dungeon. The tattooist sat at an old-fashioned student's desk with arms as broad as canoe paddles. A collection of bottles and vials and various tools were arranged on a small rolling stainless steel tray, like the kind surgeons used, and between his feet sat an antique black leather doctor's bag. He picked through vials on the tray, reading labels, then stuck them back down into the doctor's bag. I had a feeling that the bottles weren't all filled with tattoo ink.

Venus reappeared in the light, Gord's arm in hers, leading him to the side of the chair where I could see him. He looked even worse than before—his burned, melted skin clearly defined in the harsh light. The gash across his forehead had been cauterized and washed of blood. One eye was still a blood-caked wound, rags of the vest and jacket sealed to his skin by fire, but the exposed parts of his chest were burned and bubbled. He wore fur pants again, his blackened legs covered, and the shoes were still melted up his shins, almost to his knees.

His remaining eye stared blankly with hollow dejection, as though he had been through a thousand wars—looking at me and through me at the same time. Was he even the same person I had once known, grown up with?

Venus kissed his cheek, but he didn't seem to notice. Only kept staring down at me, but I couldn't read his vacant gaze. Did he want to kill me? Did he still hate me for being chosen as Venus' husband? For wounding him with blade and fire?

She caressed a hand down his chest and cooed into his melted ear, "Baby, mama wants you to do a big family favor for her, okay? If you do it, I'll love you forever."

He swallowed and turned his eye to her, asked in a monotone, "Will you make me your husband?"

She pouted. "I'm sorry, sweetie, I can't do that. Only one husband at a time, those are the rules," she lied. "A queen can only have one king at her side. Multiple husbands would lessen the stature and position of the king's throne."

"What about many kings and many queens?" Gord asked in a voice cracked by fire and smoke.

She chuckled. "Well now that would degrade the positions of both king and queen, wouldn't it, silly?"

"How about no kings or queens?" he asked, his face concrete, eyes sunken into pits of shadow.

This question made me think that there was still some fight left in him. It gave me hope that he could still return from whatever madness he was locked inside of.

# THE BRIDE STRIPPED BARE

Venus was mildly insulted. She deflected the question and pulled Gord to stand between my legs. "Let's not talk about such silliness—we have a job to do." She pulled open the flap of his pants and withdrew his flaccid, blackened penis. He stood like a robot, staring down at me, as Venus caressed him. With little girl eyes, she asked, "Don't I turn you on anymore, baby? Come on, get nice and hard for mama. You got your sister pregnant—now you just gotta put some babies in your best friend too. I'll help, of course. In our family, both women and men can get pregnant."

Gord and I glanced down to see Venus' tail rising between her legs, the cobra twitching and ready. She put his hand on the tail for him to stroke as she stroked him. But he wasn't coming to life, dead from the waist down if not also from the neck down.

Venus looked up to flip her chin at the tattooist. He scanned his tray, then fiddled through his doctor's bag, lifting out vials to read their labels, until he settled on one labelled with only the letter V. Viagra? I wondered. Or was it blood from Venus herself? The tattooist dug around and pulled out a long steel syringe, poked it into the vial, filled it. He patted one arm of his schoolhouse desk for Venus to walk Gord over to him.

She angled the chair arm between Gord's legs, pushed on his shoulders to make him squat low. Stretching out his penis, she held it pinned to the scratched and stained wood of the chair arm, whispered into his ear. "This'll just pinch a little. Stinger here is a skilled technician. Tattooist, doctor, dentist—a jack of all needles. Not to worry, his hands are relatively steady."

I watched the needle push into a bulging black vein. Gord didn't flinch. Stinger lived up to his name.

All of the liquid was out of the syringe and into Gord's bloodstream. The steel was pulled from the flesh and the tattooist absorbed a spot of blood with a cotton ball, told Gord to keep the cotton pressed on the injection site.

Gord held his cock in a fist, staring at nothing until the sagging meat between his legs began to grow. I watched his face and more life came into it. But not necessarily in a good way. The melted muscles of his face twitched and his one eye blinked compulsively. Letting go of his penis, he flexed his hands into fists, rubbed his fingers together, cracked his neck and back and every bone in his warped body. He couldn't stand still.

As he paced a horseshoe path around my chair, Venus tried to corral him back between my upraised legs.

"Baby, you gotta fuck…come here, put it right in here, mama'll help you, okay?"

He glanced at her, at me, wouldn't stop pacing. Reached up and smacked the television, making it wobble, then clenched his hands together as though he was cold.

I chanced asking a question as Venus tried to hold Gord still. "What'd you shoot into his dick, bitch?"

"Just a little something to help him rape you. Now shut the fuck up and lie back—bitch!"

Frustrated, she tried to hold Gord's hands still, but he kept pacing away from her. He didn't seem to know what to do with a hard dick. Strolled around my chair and his penis swung like a bat—at least twelve inches, though I was sure he was never that size before (he would've bragged for sure when we were teens)—knocking it against my legs and the chair, against the wall when he wandered into a corner. Maybe looking for an escape as the erection serum raced through his body, maybe further dementing his already demented mind.

Venus tried a new tactic. Her tail had lost its vigor while she was trying to reign in Gord, the piece of flesh dangling from the base of her tailbone, along the crack of her ass and down to the backs of her knees. It flicked and swung, occasionally curling up on itself, like a cow's tail batting away flies. I wonder to what extent she controlled it,

# THE BRIDE STRIPPED BARE

or did it somewhat move by automatic reflex? And did only the females of the family have such an appendage?

She made the thing rise between her legs where she stroked it, curving up and out from her navel. Trying to get Gord's attention with it, inciting him to lust. He would pass by her, glance down at it, touch it lightly, pet it, then keep pacing. He disappeared in and out of shadows, his steps clopping on the stone floor. I could take a guess at how big the room was from listening to him.

Stinger held a hand to his mouth, trying to stifle a laugh.

Venus erupted at him. "How much did you fucking give him? He's a goddamn basketcase!"

"Sorry, Mistress," he said after clearing his throat, but the smile still formed on his mouth and his split tongue jutted through his lips.

"Well, do you have anything to fucking bring him down? Keep his cock up but bring his useless mind back down to Earth! Just enough for the braindead fuck to obey me!"

Stinger turned to inspect the vials he had, then lifted small metal trays inside the depths of the bag, searching. He pulled out everything, it seemed—a dentist's drill and tools, more vials of chemicals and jars of tattoo ink, replacement needles, scalpels, forceps, surgical needles and hooks, retractors, drills, bone chisels, a speculum, a rubber ball gag. I wondered how many people had been strapped to the chair before me, and had they been cured or killed under Stinger's care?

I glanced at the vials he was sorting through, saw a small black bottle with the letters "L.O.V.E." painted on it in red. A homemade elixir? Maybe it was all homemade. The "V" may not have been for Viagra or Venus. But Stinger didn't inject a needle into the bottle of "L.O.V.E."; he placed it delicately down into its own side pocket, kept searching for something else.

I glanced away to see that Gord was finally standing still. Just beside my right leg. Venus watched his face, stepped slowly to him, the tail prodding out ahead of her. Trying to assess what was going through Gord's fucked-up mind.

No longer with penis in hand, he instead held a hand mirror. In awe and horror, he gazed at his burned face and missing eye, probably for the first time since being injured. His facial muscles still twitched, but that must have only increased the shock of seeing his reflection. Glancing down at his penis, his eye turned to glass, but no tear fell.

Venus approached from over his shoulder. "You're beautiful, baby. You don't have to worry about a thing. The family has lots of experimental medicine and doctors all over the world—California, Switzerland, Brazil, China. They're all miracle workers, I swear. They'll take good care of you. We have castles in Europe you can live in, islands in the Pacific and Caribbean—anywhere you want to go, we'll set you up for life. But, baby, right now I need you to fuck."

Gord snapped out his arm and the mirror shattered against the wall. His head and body were a mass of twisted scarlet; only his single eye and his teeth beamed phosphorus white.

"Fuck your fucking, bitch! I'm not going to fuck ever again—and neither are you!"

He pulled a piece of metal from the back waistband of his fur pants. I recognized it as the blade of the golden knife that Venus had snapped from its hilt and thrown into a corner of her bedroom just before I burned it to cinders. There was still hope. Still a part of the real Gord deep inside his outer traumatized self. He had secreted a weapon, kept his mind blank so that Venus couldn't read his thoughts, kept the blade to use at the appropriate time.

Gord was a fucking genius! I laughed out loud, which distracted my bride, drew her glare to me.

Gord grabbed the tail where it curled up between Venus' vaginal slit, flexed his melted wax biceps, and wrenched the blade under the flailing muscle. It spat blood, red and black, across his hands and the

# THE BRIDE STRIPPED BARE

fur of his pants. The tail roiled in his hand like a headless snake and threw blood across his face as he held it up to Venus' horrified eyes. Crimson spat from her twitching tail stump, spattered the walls and chair, ran down the inside of her legs to pool on the stone and wood.

She screamed—not from pain, but from rage.

Gord took a bite of the tail's tip and smiled bloody teeth at Venus before he began to chew.

Then she began to change.

Her body stiffened as muscles beneath her skin bulged and molded her shape out of its feminine form. Bladders beneath the skin pushed her forehead high and swelled her cheekbones—the bridge of her nose extended, and her mouth gaped and split to expose two long rows of teeth jutting from black gums like a yellowed mountain range. Her arms and legs extended so that she had to duck her head to keep it from scraping the ceiling. Hands and feet elongated and grew six-inch claws. The white fur cloak became her hide, expanding to cover her entirely, sealing to her face.

She roared her bear howl through the mid-sized room, like the crashing waves of a storm-battered ocean.

Gord rushed to Stinger, plunging the golden blade into his neck, toppling the tattooist surgeon off his chair, butchering his face as he lay on the ground. The rolling tray, bottles and vials, steel implements splashed and clattered across the stone floor. Gord's hand flashed upward, a tongue split into a Y writhing in his hand, a living thing, quickly dying, before he threw it into shadows. Then kept hacking at the corpse of the tattooist on the floor.

I kicked and pulled hard against my restraints, the bear Venus between my legs, her maw gaping and roaring a breeze of putrid breath against my face.

"Jesus, Gordy—get me out of this thing!" I yelled.

My eyes were locked on my bride, so I didn't see at first as Gord rose off the floor with the doctor's bag in one hand and a filled syringe in the other. The bag dropped to the floor as he hunched over, looking for a way to attack the bear.

Venus roared into my face. I wondered if she would kill me—her husband. As her bear self, did she still know me? Her paws didn't swat at me, only gouged claws across the stone floor.

From the corner of my eye I saw Gord circle around her and leap onto her back. He drove the syringe hard into her hide. Hopefully it went in, able to pierce the thick bear flesh. And hopefully he was able to depress the plunger before she spun and batted him away. He flew into shadow and sounded like he had hit a wall.

The bear—my bride—roared until my eardrums felt about to burst. Her paws slapped at her shoulders and ribs, trying to find the syringe. Sticks of metal littered the floor, but I couldn't see the steel syringe. I held my breath and felt my heart pound as I watched Venus' movements slow down. She swayed drunkenly as her massive arms swung at walls. But she wasn't going down. Instead, her sway was broken by twitches and convulsions. Her paws shot out, seemingly beyond her control, to smash against walls, to crack wall timbers in two, to swat the television and its ledge off the wall, to buckle the door outward and let in light.

Then a deep lull paused her body, head rolling, tongue lolling out of her mouth, snot drooling from her black nostrils. I could only wonder what Gord had shot her up with. He came out of the shadows. In his hand was the bloody golden blade, crimson splashed up his arm. He kept his eye on the bear as he slipped to my side, tucking the blade under the restraint pinning one of my wrists to the chair. The steel sawed through the binding, but both of us were more intent on keeping our attention on the bride.

Gord was still a little dazed from whatever poison or panacea had been injected into his penis. I took the blade out of his hand and told him, "You watch her, keep out of her way—get another syringe if you can and shoot her up again! Drug the bitch until she's dead!"

# THE BRIDE STRIPPED BARE

One of my hands was free. Venus, still dazed, lazily swung a paw through the air, but even a slow bear paw had force to it. She smashed thick claws against the left leg extension of the chair, snapping it. The chair shook from her blow, but it must've been bolted to the floor because it stayed upright even with a leg missing. And I still had the fur-covered wood extension strapped to my leg. I managed to pull my foot away from the beast's next arm swing. Her other arm swatted the right extension, snapping that too, the wooden extension still strapped to my leg. The chair was propped up only from the back, laying me out on display facing the ursine bitch.

I flexed my arms to pull myself up the chair, pulling my legs higher toward my chest, but the wood bound to my ankles was like carrying around a pair of broken skis that wouldn't come off.

My chest was tight as I held myself higher up the chair's back. I watched Venus sway and stumble, slump back against a wall, her jaws snapping at air. Feeble moans came from the depths of her throat; she attempted to roar, but it faded out before gaining any volume or ferocity. I put my feet on the floor and kept sawing at the binding pinning my other hand.

I glanced at Gord who was back beside the body of Stinger, rifling through his doctor's bag.

My hands were free. Eyes on the bear, I hoisted one foot as best I could with the piece of wood attached to it and began to saw.

Venus got on all fours, blinking eyes gazing from light to shadow, and began lumbering toward me.

"Jesus, Gord! Shoot her with anything!" I glanced down and saw that Gord was shooting something into his arm vein. "Aw, fuck, Gord—not now!"

"Fuck you, Chris! He's got liquid cocaine in here! I need to coke up to stay alive! Have you seen my face? I'm burned to shit and missing an eye! My dick is a lump of coal! I'm a freak because of *you*! What do I have to live for except cocaine?"

"Holy shit, Gord, you want to play the blame game? Why'd you bring me and your family to this house? You *knew* what the family were going to do to us!"

"So? Is your life better than mine? You hate who you are and what you do for a living too. I figured we could all benefit from this family. I was actually *thinking* of you and my folks, trying to *help* all of you. I didn't know it was going to go this way!"

The liquid coke went into his veins and the syringe slipped out, fell back into the bag. His face twitched and his tongue swam around his gums. This was really no time for he and I to be having an argument, I reasoned with myself.

"Fine—you got your coke—now stab some poison into Venus while she's fucked."

I shot my eyes to her, saw that she was changing again. Turning back little by little by convulsions into a human being. A bear's jaw and nose hung beneath her human eyes and the top of her burned head; slender human arms, one of them still weighted down by a heavy bear paw; one leg was ursine, the other human.

It was the perfect chance to knock her down, hopefully for good.

Gord was flying high on coke and rage. I had to yell repeatedly at him to focus, get his hands back into Stinger's doctor bag, find the syringe and *any* kind of drug. His hands rubbed his face compulsively and his nostrils flared, but he looked at the bag on the floor and headed back for it. I hoped to hell it wasn't for another fix.

Thankfully, he returned to do battle with Venus with the syringe in hand, its needle piercing the black bottle stenciled "L.O.V.E." Hoped he knew what it was and what it would do.

"Go for the eyes! The weakest part!" I yelled.

He pulled the filled syringe out of the bottle, yellowish-red drops tipping the needle's point. But he wanted to get in a quick cheap shot first. Kicked her in the face, but her fangs caught his leg and tightened.

# THE BRIDE STRIPPED BARE

Gord screamed every name at her, pounding a fist against her head—she swung her powerful bear neck muscles and Gord slammed back hard against a wall. The syringe flew into a shadow.

I sawed the golden blade faster until both feet were free of the wooden extensions. My legs were asleep, but I could still hobble. Venus was trying to crush her jaws through Gord's leg. Stumbling and slipping towards her, I held the blade like a spear in front of me. I lunged and the gold penetrated her belly. Tried to wrench it sideways to open a wide gash, but she backhanded me with her remaining bear paw. I was naked except for the cloven boots that wouldn't come off, unprotected by any magic, and felt every ounce of pain.

Touch of concussion, knees and ribs and elbows throbbing and burning, but I had to ignore it all. Wouldn't have minded a sip of liquid coke myself, just to keep me on my feet as long as possible.

Taking my own advice, I rushed for the doctor's bag and grabbed the whole thing. Kept it pried open as I rushed again at Venus. She saw me coming, let Gord's leg drop from her mouth as she roared at me. Perfect. I smashed the opened bag into her mouth, punched the base of the bag so that as many vials of chemicals, ink, whatever, slammed into her maw, hit her uvula, dropped down her throat.

I was no surgeon; no time for precise injections.

She bit the bag and I stumbled away, backed into the chair. The white fur covering the chair fell and draped over my head. I wore it around my neck like a scarf, hoping it had magic, that it wasn't just a piece of surgical/tattooing theatre decoration. Gord shook his dizzy head, but his leg was fine. The fur pants and metal boots that had melted up his shins protected him from any wound, plus the coke would've killed any pain. I crab-crawled to him and pulled him into shadow, keeping our distance as we watched if the mouthful of chemicals had any effect on the bride.

Shards of glass fell from her fangs, liquids spilled down between her breasts, human again, but hairy. Her head swung from side to side, eyes blinking slowly, out of sync, as though she was looking for us, couldn't see into shadow. Her excellent bear night vision could've been waning into mediocre human vision. The drugs were doing something. Gord and I didn't really want to stick around to find out what. But she was still blocking the only exit from the room.

"We gotta distract her," I said, wrapping the white fur around my shoulders, about to take a step out of the shadow and into the light, needing all the protection I could get.

Gord held me back. "No, dude, I got the fur pants and still some scraps of the vest and jacket stuck to my skin. I've still gotta have a little protection left."

Sound reasoning in an insane situation. I let him go. He took a first step, and accidently kicked the syringe of yellowish-red fluid out of shadow and into the light. He and I smiled at each other. I picked up the poison.

"You distract her—I'll stick the bitch," I said.

Venus pissed down her human leg. She charged for the smashed chair I had been strapped to, possibly thinking it was an enemy. Crunched it in her jaws and smacked it into smaller pieces with her heavy paw. I slipped with long strides along the wall toward the door as Gord stepped bodily out of shadow and faced her.

"Hi, honey, I'm home," he sang.

Her breath roared out and ruffled the hair of his pants. I stood between Venus and the battered-open door. Held the syringe like a stabbing knife, leapt on her back, reached around and jammed the entire thing into one of her human eyes. Pushed all of the poison into her skull.

My bride bucked me off and I sailed through the doorway. She bellowed like thunder and Hell. Gord sped to me, grabbed my arm and rushed me with him down the hallway. We ran through flickering candlelight, zigzagging down wooden halls until we couldn't hear Venus anymore.

# THE BRIDE STRIPPED BARE

Exhausted, chests heaving, we sat down against a wall. Gord was still twitching, hands rubbing his face and neck, as we glanced down both ends of the hallway, trying to figure out which way to go.

"What was in the syringe?" I asked.

"Love," he said, spitting sweat off his lips, pupils as wide as dimes.

"Yeah, I read the letters too. You know what they stand for?"

Gord inhaled deeply through his nostrils and sweat reflected yellow light against his face. I could see in his eyes that the coke was in control. Maybe for the best at the moment. "Uh, yeah, Venus once told me about how the family made their own medicines and drugs and poisons, from plants and chemicals in a laboratory—they made everything for themselves."

"Okay, so what is L.O.V.E.?"

"'Lysergic' is the first one, uh…" He rubbed his wrinkled forehead, trying to settle his chaotic mind and memory.

"'Lysergic'?" I asked. "As in L.S.D.?"

"Uh, yeah, that's it." He sniffed some more, licked his gums, scratched his neck. "The O is for opium, V for valium and, uh, the E is…uh…"

I took a guess. "Ecstasy?"

"Yeah. That one. The "four-in-one," Venus called it. No, Poppy told me about it. Yeah, he does it all the time."

The revelations were hitting me hard and fast. "Um, Gord, was that what I was on during the bachelor party?"

His eyebrows twitched and he blinked rapidly for a few seconds. "Oh yeah, hell yeah, we were all on it. Makes for a fun night, don't it?"

No comment. I saw something that he was holding in his hand, slapping against his fur knee. Looked like a bloody piece of rope.

"Is that what I think it is?" I asked.

He held it up, laughed at it, waggled it in front of his face. "Caught a tiger by its tail!"

# Chapter 22

We raced down a twisting hallway, popping open doors at random, some already open but going nowhere, others padlocked. We banged our fists on the locked doors, pressed ears to the wood, but we couldn't find Elizabeth. I could only guess that she was still unconscious from giving birth. (There but for the Grace of God…) Hopefully it hadn't drained her to the point of death.

I found a door that should've been secured, but the ancient iron padlock fell to pieces when I wrenched down on it. A small window in the door showed only blackness in the room. I called to Gord, voice echoing against stone through the narrow halls. We had to keep up a call-and-response so that we didn't get lost in the tight labyrinth of branching hallways and cul-de-sacs.

Lights sat in rusted, cobwebbed cages high up on the walls, some of them working. Too many shadows in the dungeon. Gord joined me as I opened the creaking wooden door.

When it opened fully, fluorescent lights sputtered to life. A long narrow stone room faced us, walls lined with long wooden beds. More lights flickered to life down the room, showing us a doorway at the end of the room which was open.

We stepped in, smelling death and the dust of centuries. The ceiling and walls were wet and overlaid with thick green and brown moss. The

# THE BRIDE STRIPPED BARE

bars of light flickered, a couple of them buzzed before popping, but we were still able to see what lay on the beds.

Skeletons with bones a yellowish-brown, dressed in uniforms. The dead wore the fur pants and ornate vests and jackets. Rings with blue jewels were loose on their bone fingers. Nine beds against either wall, then we came to the end of the room, and the doorway into the next. Burned into the doorway's wooden frame were the words, "Room for one more..." A macabre signboard for where Venus had buried her ex-husbands.

"Exactly how many times has she been married?" I asked Gord as we inspected the dead.

"Helluva lot more than I ever thought," he replied.

I saw him slip off a ring from the skeleton, a piece of fingerbone coming with it. He tried the ring on for size and I saw a touch of sorrow in his eyes. There was still a part of him that wanted to be married to Venus. Old brides die hard. But knowing Gord, it wasn't that he wanted her specifically—he just wanted a wife. Not to be alone as he got older. Something most people wanted, a very basic and natural desire. When he saw himself in the hand mirror, his sorrow would've become more profound, wondering what woman would every want to marry him?

I could only hope (terrible it was to think) that Gord's ruined face and body, his despair, would prevent him from going back to Venus. The other option, suicide, was no option. What could I do for him?

Simple answer: escape.

One room led into another and another, fluorescent lights flickering to life, some popping dead, and the corpses lay on their eternal beds lining every wall. I was still naked, minus the chair's bear fur, which I had wrapped around my waist and held it there, but cold shivers kept moving through my body, seeping from the walls and the stone floor. I stopped at a corpse, told Gord I didn't want to show him my bits and pieces anymore.

"Good idea," he agreed, feeling how clotted with blood his fur pants were.

We stripped skeletons of their clothing and dressed ourselves. I wondered if the vests and jackets worn by the dead still had any magical properties left. If not, no matter, they would keep us warm. I kept the white fur wrapped around myself like a cloak.

"How do I look?" Gord asked, putting vest and jacket over the scraps that were fused to his chest.

"Like a million and a half."

"You look weird bald."

I smoothed a hand over my dome. "Feels cool."

His smile dropped. "My face is shit, ain't it?" Then he pulled open the waistband of the fur pants. "And I got a black dick! How in the hell do I explain that to anyone I wanna fuck?"

Took me a while to look at him, and he noticed the pause. I felt like hell and needed to confess something that maybe he had forgotten. "Sorry I started the fire. I caused your wounds. Best friends forever?"

He swallowed hard, voice cracking, sniffing from his coke high. "I don't blame you. I was out of my mind—Venus and the coke." He shrugged and twitched involuntarily. "Now it's just the coke. Who would've thought *that* would save my life?" He stepped up to me, gripped my shoulder. "You were saving yourself and my kid sister from that fucking demon. I was stupid enough to obey her. But the fire kinda woke me up. Knocked me into shock, and a part of me finally saw that she was the enemy. That's why I grabbed the knife blade."

I felt my new sleeve by habit, found that there was an intact knife that came with the skeleton's jacket. Pulled it out and held it up. Gord found one up his sleeve, pulled it out, toasted his blade to mine with a metal clang.

"You did what you had to do," he said solemnly. "Thank you."

Before I could respond, a wooden boom echoed through the rooms. Gord and I slipped the knives back up our sleeves and raced passed the

# THE BRIDE STRIPPED BARE

corpses back to the first room, saw the door closed, Venus' face in the window. Fully returned to her human self, the syringe gone, but her eyelid closed, blood washed down her cheek. She laughed as we pressed against the door, rammed our shoulders against it.

"You're home, boys," she called through the thick glass. "Have a chat with my past loves. They were all wonderful, served their purposes, as have you. I guess I'll be getting re-married again soon. Back to the hunt."

Laughing, she vanished from the window, clicked off the lights. Gord and I breathed against the glass. He tried to punch it, but only hurt his hand. If there was magic in our clothing, it didn't allow us to break the barrier of the crypt.

We swore and cursed her, smelled the dead all around us, our metal shoes echoing on stone. Then I noticed a glow emanating from Gord's sleeve. He reached in and pulled out the knife. Its blade shone with a white-blue light which eerily lit his deformed face. If he wasn't a friend, I would've taken him for a monster, locked with me in a catacomb.

I pulled the knife from my sleeve and it shone as well. I commented, "Even in Hell, there's a little hope."

We headed back through the rooms—the catacombs, as I had started thinking of them as, reminded me of the labyrinths under Paris and Rome and other old cities. Where people fled to escape persecution of whatever empire was in charge, where they worshipped their unpopular gods, where they buried their dead. But no catacomb had only one exit and entrance—they were more like warrens that stretched far below the surface world with multiple exits and entrances arising in unlikely locations.

Or maybe this was just a mausoleum. Following the light of our knives, we passed through the first two rooms again and into a third that branched off in an L. Here, some of the dead still had skin and thin muscle and sinews. But their skin was rust-red and leather-black, vacuum-sealed to bone, eyes lost, mouths stretched back to expose every tooth in the corpses' heads. Like mummies or sacrificial victims thrown into bogs. Their uniforms were, however, immaculate. The smell of decay was stronger here in this relatively confined space, the moss that covered the walls and ceiling acting as insulation and moisture absorption and muting the sound of our steps.

No doors, only doorways, closed one room from another. The next room branched off at an angle, sloping down deeper into the earth, the air cooler, smelling more like marsh gas. The moss on the walls was thicker, now covering the floor in mounds, green sponge that still seeped rank water when you stepped on it. Our metal hoofs left a trail of cloven imprints.

It was impossible to judge how far down the room led underground, but the dead who lay in their beds had even more flesh on their bones. Some were even plump. You could see how they had died—killed by their own hand or that of someone else. A white rope the width of my middle finger dug deeply into a neck, part of the flesh having grown over and swallowed the rope. Not a suicide because the corpse also had its wrists and ankles bound.

(It bore a tattoo similar to mine on its forehead. Several of the flesh corpses did, though not all. Though my forehead still pulsed, I had forgotten the Mark of Cain I bore until I saw it reflected on the corpses. I stopped Gord, lifted the shining knife to my forehead, and asked how the tattoo looked, was it bloody? Gord wrinkled his eyebrows and asked, "What tattoo?")

Another corpse didn't have any tattoos because it was missing skin from the eyebrows up. The eyebrows were still attached, but it appeared as though the person had been scalped, the dome of their cranium exposed. Another corpse still had the railroad spike that kill him driven through his forehead. Another was missing a belly and abdomen, his internal organs preserved in Mason jars, the jars stacked back into

# THE BRIDE STRIPPED BARE

his body cavity. Others weren't full bodies, legs missing, arms missing—or worse, the limb still attached but by only a thin and rotting ligament. I peered closer at one of these legs with the knife light shining against the rotted flesh, and I could see the marks of tiny teeth all around the stumps of the legs and the hips. Many teeth had chewed their way almost entirely through the limb from the outside in. Excruciatingly slow torture until they hit the femoral artery, and then the victim mercifully hemorrhaged out his life's blood.

So not all—if any—of Venus' husbands died of natural causes, to put it mildly. Nor would they have died quickly. I mentioned this to Gord, which stunned him and made him think about his desire to be one of the 'chosen.' Like me.

His brow furrowed, which twisted his bubbled skin, making him appear even more horrific in the blade's light. But I kept my comments to myself.

"Why does she do it?" he asked me—or himself, ultimately. "Gets married in order to kill? And not for any insurance money since she's rich and powerful. Just the thrill of murder drives her?"

I shrugged, trying to block out the stench of the dead around us. To some degree, the smell was masked by the ozone sulfur of the marsh gas. I wondered if we were beneath a lake of some sort.

"She mentioned genetics a few times," I replied. "Any family that *only* fucks family for, what, three or four generations—never mind a hundred or more—are going to start getting mutations. *Tails,* for Christ's sake, and *gills!*" I was just about to tell him about Elizabeth giving birth multiple times—all girls with tails—but I doubted if the father of her babies wanted to be reminded of just how fucked up his life was—even without the burn and the missing eye.

"Tails and gills," he repeated, scoffed. He had tucked Venus' tail, appropriately enough, into the waistband at the back of his pants. It didn't twitch anymore—just a lifeless piece of muscle. He pulled it out and snapped it like a whip against some moss growing out of the wall. "*This* is what I wanted to marry. And you *did* marry her. A fucking piece of tail!"

We began to chuckle, which soon grew into belly laughs.

"A fucking piece of tail!" I repeated. "And with her that's *not* just an expression!"

We laughed harder, buckling over, our foreheads burning and tears slipping down our cheeks.

"What the fuck were we thinking? She's a goddamn inbreeding mutant!" I shouted, which dropped Gord to the floor, feet kicking against a corpse bed, stomach muscles hurting. "And she's my *wife*!"

I sat down, laughing my ass off. Gord begged me to stop, the tail flipping in his hand—which didn't make it better. We howled and wheezed, pounded our fists and kicked our heels. After all, we had both been through hell, and we needed a good laugh to release some stress. It also helped make the corpses and the darkness less frightening.

And then a voice called weakly, "Hello?"

We heard it as our laughter subsided. Coming from the far end of the room we were in. We stood and shone our knife lights through the room and into another shorter room that had nine beds but only three of them filled. Two corpses…and one man still alive. Barely. Skin over bone, cheeks sunken, eyes mere pits, a tattoo on his forehead which I could see but which Gord could not. The man's fur pants and vest and jacket hung from his emaciated form like a false skin on a stick puppet of wood. The skin of his face and neck was stretched, showing only tendons and the shape of thin muscle, no fat to make him look less like a living cadaver. His chest rose and fell slowly, with long pauses in between each breath. The jeweled wedding band on his finger spun on bone, caught from falling off only by an arthritic knuckle.

"Are you the next generation?" he asked with a raspy voice, needing to draw in a deep breath after speaking.

# THE BRIDE STRIPPED BARE

"We don't know," I replied. "Maybe. Who are you? One of her husbands?"

He nodded. "The most recent. Still alive. Not for long, I hope. Bread and water…the torture of slow starvation." He tried to raise a bony finger, but it could only lift off the bed an inch or two. His eyes looked at Gord. "Tattoo?" he asked.

I glanced at Gord, who wouldn't understand. "He's not a husband, only me. He almost was, but then he was relegated to best man. I married her."

The man nodded slightly, understanding things I didn't need to say since he had probably been through it all himself. He closed his eyes and laid down his finger. Needing rest.

"What are these tattoos you keep mentioning?" Gord asked me in a whisper.

I explained what Venus had told me, and that he couldn't see the one on my forehead, nor any of the ones on the corpse grooms. Only family members could see them. Told him he should consider himself lucky. But then I wanted to take it back, knowing he would probably rather have a tattoo than a burn.

The man opened his eyes again, sucked in breath through his nostrils, tried to muster saliva to wet his tongue to talk. "You…locked in? To die?"

"She locked us in. Is there a way out?"

His sandpaper tongue protruded from his mouth as he licked dry lips, exhaled breath that already stank of rot. "Third room, lower bunk, middle of the room. Remove a stone behind. Tunnel. Each husband not dead, or dying, dug a little more each time. A little farther. Close." He knocked a light knuckle against his bedframe. "Echo on stone. I…too weak. No more."

The light of my dagger shone into the pits of his eyes, and I saw a weak glow of light shining on one of the man's palms. Reaching up his sleeve, I pulled out his knife. It dimmed in and out of a feeble glow. The shine of my knife, and Gord's, was bright and steady.

I told Gord my guess. "The knife shines brightly with life, but dims when the carrier approaches death? And dies completely with the corpse?"

Gord nodded and stared at the old man's knife.

"Kill me," the dying man whispered through a dry throat. "Please."

All the breath went out of me, my body sagging, feeling numb. Gord and I had both killed, but this was different. This man was *us*. A torture victim of Venus and the family. Gord had saved my life by battling the beast when I was hopelessly tied to a chair. But I knew I had to do this kill…this mercy killing, I told myself. Not murder. Salvation. Escape.

I laid the man's knife on his chest and looked at Gord. "Go find the tunnel. I'll meet you."

Gord turned and I saw the man's eyes glance at something, his forehead creased a washboard of wrinkles. His hand raised an inch as his voice whispered, "Wait."

"Gord—come back," I called.

We looked down at the man as his mouth moved, trying to find the words to communicate. But he didn't have the breath for too many of them.

"Tail?" he asked.

I turned Gord around, pulled the tail from his pants' waistband. Held it up for the man to see. I drooped over my palm like a dead snake, its chewed-off point hanging low enough to touch the man's jacket arm.

I explained, hoping to answer questions he couldn't ask. "Venus' tail. He cut it off."

"And took a bite. She was fucking pissed," Gord continued with a cocaine high smirk and sparkling eyes. "Changed into a bear, tried to rip both of us apart, but Chris stabbed some drugs into her fucking eye. I killed the tattoo guy too, cut out his tongue."

# THE BRIDE STRIPPED BARE

"Stinger," I filled in, seeing the smallest smile stretch the man's mouth, a sparkle of delight in his gaze. As though we were telling him an old story he knew too well, that we had been over the terrain he had walked long ago. He wanted to hear more. "But it didn't keep her down, I'm afraid."

"She came out of it, changed back into herself—but with one less eye," Gord chuckled, winked with his remaining eye. "That's when she locked us in."

I was serious, needed to know if the man could tell us something we could use, knew I should only ask questions which he could nod or shake his head to answer.

"That white bear cloak she wears, like this—" I lifted a corner of the fur around my shoulders to his gaze, "—is it magical? A source of power and protection to her?" He nodded and then glanced at the tail, desperately trying to lift his hand to it. I sheathed my knife, lifted his hand for him, put the tail across his palm. Gord held up his blade for the man to see. A smile tried to bloom on his pale thin lips. "Is this a source of her power too?" I asked.

He nodded. A laugh coughed up from his chest, replaced by a wheeze, tongue jutting out. He continued to cough for a while and needed to catch his breath afterwards. When he could speak again, he said, "Matriarchal family. Women have tails. Power." He felt the tail, stared at it.

I tried to fill in the blanks. "And the men? They don't have power?" The man shook his head, glanced at my jacket and his sleeve. "The clothes give us power? But just the husbands and the wedding party? Whomever gets to wear these jackets?"

The man nodded.

"So, if we've got her tail," Gord continued, "and if we can get her bear cloak…she's fucked? Just an average person? We stick a knife in her, and she bleeds, and the wound won't heal? She's as mortal as the rest of us?"

The man nodded and Gord whooped and cheered, punching the air.

I slipped out my knife to bring light back to the man's face, and so he could relish the sight of the queen's severed tail in his hand.

He glanced at me and Gord with eyes that would've wept for joy if he had had enough water in his body. We had made him happy. It was enough inspiration to keep us going, to keep fighting until we escaped the family, or destroyed them, or both.

"Gorman," the man said, then inhaled deeply again to say, "Daughter's tail."

I looked into his eyes to understand his message. "Gorman's her father, we know. Daughter's tail?" I tapped my lips as I connected the pieces. "Her power's lost...so...her father will try to usurp her power?" The man nodded. I continued, "Will Gorman try to take over the family? Make it into a patriarchy?" He kept nodding. I looked at Gord. "Maybe we can work the father against the daughter—let them destroy each other."

"If we get out of here," Gord said.

The man's grip fell away from the tail and I helped put his hand back onto the bed.

"Thank you," he uttered to Gord and I. "Now please...kill me."

Joy left our faces, though the man's joy was still written on his face. I handed the tail back to Gord, who tucked it into his waistband, nodded once to me, and left the man's bedside.

I watched his light grow dim in the darkness as he headed through the rooms. Looking back at the man, I felt terrible for him, but didn't feel I could kill him. I couldn't muster the savagery in me to stab him or choke him or do anything to take his life. Even though my rational mind said he didn't have much life left, and that it would be completely drained slowly from him by time.

"Can you come with us?"

# THE BRIDE STRIPPED BARE

He shook his head as best he could, blinked slowly with heavy eyelids. "Can't move. Pain."

Ironically, if I had tried to bring him with us, the jolt of movement would probably have killed him. But I couldn't give him more pain in his last moments on this earth. If only I had kept the tattooist's syringe, find a vial filled with something to help him sleep, to drift slowly into death. All I had were my two hands and a knife.

I needed to ask him first who he was to know something about the man I needed to kill. And, if he wanted to say, how he had met Venus, how she had gotten him in her clutches.

"Malcolm Miller."

The name was familiar, but I couldn't quite place it. It was impossible to tell who he was just by his appearance, since so few people looked like themselves on their death beds. He saw me puzzling over his name.

"Film. Horror."

My eyes bulged as my thoughts raced into realization. I told him a quick version of his biography, and he nodded, joy in his eyes. I thought I had detected an English accent in his feeble voice.

He was an English horror film director. Not big films, straight to video back in the '80s, but he had a large cult following. I had been a fan, and Gord was a huge fan. People were upset when he retired from directing after getting married. Now I realized to whom he had gotten married. Venus took over his life and convinced him to abandon his career. He was older, his films losing popularity, and she was young and rich. Had she always been young? Did she never age? If she had no magic, would she turn instantly into an old crone?

"How did you meet her?"

"Actress."

Venus had been an actress? It made sense. She played a beauty queen but was actually a psycho bitch in real life. With acting, she could easily lure men into her web. Never trust an actress, or actor. I mentioned how Gord had met her at a horror convention. Seemed as though she followed the horror crowd.

He nodded. "Horror attracts horror."

A simple aphorism that said so much, now that I knew much more about my wife. Gord must've mentioned the email I sent telling how I had begun writing horror. If Venus was a "horror whore," then the email could've perked up her attention. Hadn't he said something back at his apartment when I first met his bride-to-be? "You're in, buddy!" In the family. But even he probably didn't know to what extent. Was it at that moment, in Gord's shitty little apartment, when Venus had chosen me over him? The Venus Club! She knew she would leave Gord or relegate him to best man or boyfriend or sucker. Knew she would break his heart, but, to her, a man's broken heart was a tool of manipulation. He kowtowed to her too much, so she needed a man—a fan of all things horror—who had a little more backbone.

How much backbone did I really have? I caved in to her seduction too. Gord and I had been friends for so long because we were *exactly alike*.

But, of course, no husband would be allowed to have more backbone than she had. The matriarch didn't allow for a patriarch.

"Please...," Malcom Miller repeated, and I knew too well what he was begging for me to do. I was trying to stall.

I couldn't find the words, my hands shaking, the light of the blade flickering across his deathly features. I stuttered out, "I can't... Malcolm, you're a great man, we can get you out of here. I don't know how...I don't hate you enough to kill you."

His eyes closed and his breath exhaled in a sigh. I saw his finger move, tap his wrist. Eyes opened again. "Bleed me."

I looked at his hand. Frail bones, thin veins, he couldn't have much blood in him. He would die relatively quickly. My God, I thought, he doesn't even have the strength to pull the knife from his sleeve and slit his own wrist. A man should be allowed at least that. He had probably spent the last of his energy on furthering the dig of the tunnel, his last hope before he grew too weak.

I wouldn't be stabbing him, nor choking the life out of him—I would be a surgeon, opening a vein, just not stitching it closed. It wasn't murder, I had to tell myself. It would be an operation, cutting away a dying life for the health of the soul.

"Please," he repeated.

Tears slipped down my cheeks as I picked up his wrist, pressed the blade against his skin. He turned his head away from the light of the blade, kept his face in shadow. I curled his hand in mine, held it tightly, closed my eyes, and snapped the steel across his veins.

Not a sound came from him, not a movement, not a breath.

I looked at the wrist and a thread of blood slipped out of the open wound. I was afraid for him—not that he would die, but that he wouldn't. That some terrible miracle would happen while he lay in the darkness and the blood coagulated and stopped. I had to slice either up his forearm or cut the other wrist. If he lived, he would hate me, and I would hate myself.

I pushed up the sleeve of his jacket enough to expose more of his wrist. The jacket was stiff so I couldn't get to his entire forearm without moving him and pulling the jacket off his arms. Too much pain for him to endure.

Pressing the edge of my blade hard between the tiny wrist bones, I lined up my cut. Couldn't keep my eyes closed in case the knife slipped. Couldn't slash. I needed my backbone in place more than ever. Had to keep the cut slow and press hard for depth. A little pain, but of the type he asked for. Then he would go to sleep, at long last.

I felt his arm twitch and a low moan escape from his chest as I drew the blade up his forearm. Blood pooled out, slipped down either side of his papery skin, collected on the bed. Enough. I stopped cutting. He would, mercifully, not live.

I held the bloody knife and its red-tinted light up to see his face. A singe tear had collected in the deep corner of his eye. My throat thickened as I wept silently.

"Sleep, Malcolm."

He blinked a few times, then closed his eyes. I left his bedside to join Gord.

# Chapter 23

In the third room, the bottom bed in the middle row, right side, was pulled off two wooden dowels that had held its weight and the weight of its eternal sleeper. Bed and corpse rested on the floor, cutting across the walkway of the room. A stone about three feet high had been pulled from the wall and I could see a greenish-white light shining out from the depths of the hole.

On hands and knees, I peered into the tight tunnel, saw a tail hanging from a pair of fur pants. Gord was shuffling backwards towards me, so I waited for him to emerge.

Sweat poured off his face.

"Goddamn tight in there. They must've been digging for decades, maybe longer." He held up his knife. "I guess knives were the only digging tools of all the dead husbands."

I nodded. "Then they'll be ours too. How far does it go?"

"Pretty deep. It starts slanting at a forty-five-degree angle, but it's not too steep to crawl up. Only one of us can fit—if you were behind me, I'd just be throwing dirt and stones back in your face—and you'd be staring at my ass the whole time!"

"Okay. One at a time. I can go first if you want—we'll take turns. Little hot in there?"

"Boiling, yeah. I tapped the handle of my knife against the stone at the end and it didn't sound as solid as the walls. So maybe that guy was right—he was so fucking close to escape before he got too weak. But who knows what's on the other side—could be another locked room. How is the old guy?"

I confessed to killing Malcolm, and told Gord who he was, the famous director. Gord's jaw hung down, said he wished he had gotten an autograph…or was that too cruel to ask of a dying man? I waved away his concern, and suggested he forget Malcolm and concentrate on digging.

I squatted down to the hole, shining my dagger in, but the light could only penetrate the darkness a few feet. Left the white bear fur with Gord as I squeezed myself in and began to crawl, but the tunnel didn't stay perfectly horizontal for long. A gradual slope began to rise, so I used my feet to press against either wall to push myself up. The air stale and musty, my body heat quickly drawing sweat to my forehead, I was inhaling my own breath, which sent a wave of dizziness behind my eyes. I was like a cork in a bottle. My elbows pulled in, sleeves scraping on stone, feet pushing as I jammed my body inch by inch further into the tunnel. It would've been a horrible place and method in which to die. I tried not to think about it.

Reaching the end, a barrier of stone faced me, scratch marks from knives crisscrossing its face. I knocked a knuckle against the wall but couldn't distinguish if it was hollow or not. My knife handle was more dense and solid. But tapping the stone across its surface, then tapping the walls on either side of me, I could hear a difference. A little hope. But how long would it take to chip through stone with a knife? Weeks, months, years? Would Gord and I also degrade into weak skeletons before we could break through the rock?

Difficult to get good leverage with my elbows and shoulders squeezed in, I changed my grip on the knife and could only poke the

# THE BRIDE STRIPPED BARE

blade against the rock. Jammed it as hard as I could, scratching the stone, only grains coming loose. I was soon breathing as though I had just run a marathon, perspiration blinding me, but I didn't need to see in order to dig. Sweat beads felt like flies walking down my face, but I ignored their tickle and sting, just kept my hand hammering the knife against the wall.

I was getting frustrated, having no patience to hack away at a solid wall for an eternity in the hopes that the mere tip of the blade would eventually poke through. No wonder the diggers before me grew exhausted and wore away to nothing quickly. Thank God I wasn't claustrophobic. Gord and I, I feared, would soon be lying on grave beds, happy to bequeath the secret tunnel to the next uniformed grooms and best men who had been trapped by Venus.

I stopped my hand, thinking about something that had happened earlier. The uniform. The hand inside the wall of the hive that had grabbed my hand, cut off my sleeve, then punched through the wax wall to grab and pull in the rest of me. A hand wrapped in the scrap of my uniform. Wrapped in magic. Hadn't I picked up Gitch as though he was a rag doll and thrown him out the bedroom window? If the uniform was trying to strengthen my arm, it could only do so much with my arms squeezed in by the walls. Poking weakly with the knife point traced scratches and loosened grains of rock, but even those should've been impossible without the jacket assisting my arm.

I tucked the knife back up my sleeve and flattened my hands against the ground to push myself backwards out of the tunnel. Once back in the room, I didn't mind inhaling a deep breath of musty, corpse-scented air. It was like sucking in a mountain breeze.

"That wasn't long," Gord chuckled, watching me wipe a sleeve across my face. "It's a little slice of hell in there, ain't it?"

I smiled and nodded as I caught my breath, forced the dizziness from my head. "I got an idea. Might speed things up, I don't know for sure, but we gotta try something." I pulled out my knife and shone it down at the corpse on the floor. Gord watched, asked what I had in mind. "Long story short—I think these vests and jacket are kinda...I know this sound kinda weird, but this whole place is kinda weird... kinda magical." I sliced the sleeve off the corpse's jacket from the elbow down, pulled it off the skeletal arm, stood and held the fabric up to Gord's light. "If this doesn't work, don't laugh."

He chuckled. "Okay?"

I tucked the knife back up my sleeve, then stuck my hand down the torn tube of cloth, scrunched the cuff into my fist, held it like a boxing glove. I stayed in Gord's light as I stepped to the stone archway that led from one room to the next. Called myself crazy and prepared for intense pain shooting up my arm as I got into a stance and pulled back my wrapped hand.

The first punch didn't have all the strength behind it because I was afraid of pain. But there was none when my wrapped fist hit rock. And a chunk of stone the size of a baseball broke off and clattered to the floor. I lurched my arm back and followed through with the second punch. The blow chipped a grapefruit from the line of the doorway. I felt nothing—my hand went through stone like butter (if only I had a jacket when fighting Venus the bear; no wonder I had been stripped naked, and why Gord had been left to burn a little longer than the bride had).

Encouraged, I smashed my fist up the side of the doorway, punched chips out of the wall, sending them rattling down the incline into the fourth room, until the doorway was about a foot wider than originally.

Gord and I laughed and cheered. I slipped my hand out of the sleeve, checked for blood and bruising under Gord's light, saw not even a scratch on my knuckles. And only a little bit of stone dust was on the sleeve itself.

"Fuck yes!" he cheered, then waved the knife at the beds attached to the walls. "And none of these other fuckers ever figured it out!"

# THE BRIDE STRIPPED BARE

I clicked my tongue, slipped the sleeve back over my hand, bunched around my wrist. "Now, now, let's not speak ill of the dead. They tried 'til they died. Sometimes the answer is right in front of you—hidden in plain sight, impossible to see."

Gord shrugged. "Yeah, to tell the truth, I probably never would've figured it out either. I'd be scratching and scraping and only getting closer to lying on my death bed." He shone the knife light around the corpses. "Sorry, guys, no disrespect." Held the light to his chest as he opened the corpse's jacket he wore, scratched a fingernail against the pieces of jacket and vest fused to him. "Think these are magic? Or did the fire burn the fun out of them?"

"Doesn't matter. You've got new clothes, emperor. Now let's get the fuck out of here."

He smiled and closed his jacket. "Care to do the honors?"

I pulled out my knife and held it up. "Stay close and stay quiet. We still don't know what's on the other side." I winked and smirked. "I'll try to punch quietly."

I took the bear fur with me, still hoping that it held some kind of protection. If Venus came after us again—if she shook off the drugs, the L.O.V.E.—then we'd need all the protection we could get.

I hunkered down to the hole, Gord right behind me. Crawled and pushed my way through the tunnel as fast as I could before dizziness from a lack of oxygen hit my head, and before the space turned into an oven—now with two of us in it at the same time, heating it up. At the rock wall, I laid the bear fur in front of me to cushion my elbows as I put the knife in its sheath and stretched the torn sleeve along my right arm. Curled the loose end of my fist, then figured out how to angle my body for a blow with the most force. Had to lay on my side, arm extended, but even that would only allow for my arm to punch from the elbow not from the shoulder. Not a full reach, but it would have to do.

I started out knocking on the stone as though I was knocking on a door. Small chips fell away with dust. I closed my eyes and turned my head away from the target, my body instinctively twisting, but my shoulder still pinned to the floor.

A different tactic. I turned over onto my left side, giving my right arm more space to maneuver, not pressed against the tunnel ceiling. An awkward angle, but I punched with more force, snapping off more and more chunks of stone and dust. I coughed and heard Gord coughing behind me. Held my breath, eyes closed, punched like a jackhammer.

Felt a small coin of cool air press against my forehead. Opened my eyes but still only saw darkness ahead of me. Pushed my hand through the sleeve to feel the stone wall…and a hole in it through which I could stick three fingers.

"What's happening?" Gord's muffled voice asked.

"I broke through," I called back.

"Fuckin' A!"

"Hole's not wide enough yet, gotta do a bit more. You okay back there?"

"Holding in. Keep punching, Muhammad Ali!"

I smiled, but then tightened my lips. Made the sleeve again into a boxing glove, looked away from the target. My arm was getting tired from being held at an awkward angle, but I couldn't rest. Punching by feel alone, I broke my entire arm through the gap, then started punching the edges of the hole. It was like hammering through wax, the chunks of rock falling outward instead of toward me.

I scooted my body up to see if I could fit my head through. Needed more room for my shoulders. Tucked back down the tunnel and punched to widen the hole. Gord was bigger than me, so I punched more of a space than I needed to be free.

I crawled through and rolled on the ground away from the tunnel mouth. Gord had slipped his knife up his sleeve to use both elbows to

# THE BRIDE STRIPPED BARE

crawl. My knife lit his path. He pulled the bear fur out with him and we curled it up to use as a pillow as we rested on our backs.

Breathing pure air again that smelled of sweet water, we listened to our latest environment between breaths, the echo of water drops plunking into a pool. No light except that of our knives shone in the darkness. We sat up to inhale deeply and to let the sweat dry on our foreheads. I wrapped the fur around my back.

"We are some badass kung-fu motherfuckers," he said loudly, but I hushed him.

My ears pricked up. There was a sound—a bass baritone—distant, like radio static between the water drops.

We stood and raised our lights, approached the wall that our tunnel poked through. Wet moss clung to the wall, which looked more like coral than rock. Smelled of the sea. Our dagger lights couldn't reach too far into the darkness, but we could see a greater darkness beyond where it could reach. To the ceiling. Stalactites drooped their tips into the light of our knives.

We walked careful steps around the immediate vicinity until we bumped into a stalagmite. Then a small pool of still water that smelled a little of sulfur and a lot of salt. More stalactites and stalagmites squeezed in the space—the cave we had emerged into. Keeping our steps light and our ears tuned, we headed in the direction of the baritone static.

The sound came and went, grew in volume, and I could feel that it wasn't music—some chime or hum of the rock formation forest we walked through. It had the cadence of human speech. Sounds prolonged, then broken off, then emerged again in different tones, high register to low—a few words spoken, then a chant.

A yellow, flickering haze glowed against the roof in the distance. Gord and I stopped. Listened and watched, held our breath. I held my blade up to my face so that Gord could see the words I mouthed.

"Quiet. Slow."

He nodded and we stepped lightly and carefully, lights on the ground to see pits and water and broken pyramids of calcified rock which we didn't want to kick. (If only we could've pried the goddamn shoes off our feet, though maybe they had magic in them too. Hadn't I kicked in Gitch's face, torn the shit out of his jaw?)

The glow descended as we got closer to it, filling the vast cavern, shining against the cave's cathedral walls. We could easily tell that the baritone *was* a voice speaking, not just radio static, and was accompanied by other voices. Call-and-response, as in a church service. We tucked our knives back up our sleeves to keep our hands free. I still had the torn piece of sleeve around my wrist, and felt better with it on me, as though I had an alternate weapon.

We stayed low behind a stalagmite, peering around its pillar to see people gathered, about twenty of them sitting in chairs facing a man and a woman who held hands as another man in a black-and-red striped bear skin with its head perched on his intoned some strange language, a book in his hands.

Gorman was marrying an unknown woman to Kevin, Gord's brother.

# Chapter 24

Gord looked at me as though I had grown horns. I shrugged and put a finger to my lips to make sure he kept quiet. Instead, he leaned in to whisper, "The fucking family has brainwashed him, too. Are me and my brother that much alike?"

I rolled my eyes, cupped a hand around his ear to whisper back, "Try to see a way out of here." He pointed behind us into the dark cavern of stone, then shrugged. I shook my head, then cupped his ear again. "Those people entered somehow. There's probably an entrance behind them."

Gord peered back around the stone, then returned to my ear. "There's no way around them. We gotta go through. Do we just walk out and say hi and keep walking?"

I stayed squatted down low, peering around the pillar. Stalagmites dotted around the walls of the cave, the open floor space where the people sat cleared of stone pyramids. Our potential cover. We could take the chance and try to creep from pillar to pillar around the cave walls and not be seen. Doubtful.

Thinking of our options, I started liking Gord's suggestion. We were still wedding participants, and I was technically still family. What were the chances any of the people ahead of us—Gorman especially—knew what had happened between us and Venus? That was the only wrench that might destroy the plan forming in my head.

We had new uniforms, so we looked like normal members of the wedding. The only fault was Gord's wounds, but maybe we could blame them on excessive celebration. A missing eye, though? Stretching it a bit. My bald head and forehead tattoo, however, would likely be seen as a confirmation that I was one of them and wouldn't cause shock.

I told Gord that we'd go with his idea. We would walk out like we belonged there, just arriving late for the marriage vows. Gord could congratulate his brother, schmooze it up, make small talk, and I'd keep my eyes open for a way out. Once I saw one, he could follow my lead and we'd just walk out of the wedding and cave. He agreed. We stood up, still hidden but peering around the pillar of stone. I counted to three on my fingers, and we interrupted the subterranean wedding.

"Hey! How come you didn't invite us?" Gord said, arms wide as he strode toward his brother.

Gorman broke from whatever words he was intoning, shock on his face and on the faces of the guests. I realized that I may have misjudged how they would greet us.

"Hey! Gord! Chris!" said Kevin, digging hands out of the jacket he wore.

He also had the vest and the fur pants and the shoes. He was becoming family. His hands trembled as they reached out to Gord, shaking hands, slapping his brother on the back. Kevin's pupils were the size of dimes. I could easily see a thin crust of red dust rimming his nostrils. But I could've bet there was more than just coke in his veins.

"Where've you guys been—we were looking everywhere for you!"

"You're getting married?" Gord asked.

His wife was dressed in a bear cloak that was striped from collar to hem in orange and black. A small bear head was woven into her hair, not perched on scaffolding that was pierced into her shoulder blades. She was nude beneath, designs painted on her breasts and stomach and twisting down either leg. White, cloven-hoofed shoes, high heels,

# THE BRIDE STRIPPED BARE

looked to be made of leather. Swirls and letters and symbols were drawn across her cheeks—her family tattoo visible to me on her forehead. I wondered how many times she had been married before. She looked to be in her mid-sixties; Kevin was forty-two.

"Yeah I'm getting married," he said, swinging an arm around his wife, presenting her to us. "This is Danaë—ain't she gorgeous?"

Gord and I said our hellos, but Danaë wasn't happy—we were interrupting her wedding.

"Yes, thank you," she said sternly to us, then turned her glare and words to Kevin. "Can you please—just—I will handle this—can you shut your goddamn mouth for a second?" she said to her new husband, holding a jagged finger at him. Which she then swept over to Gord and me. "What the hell are you two doing here? This is a sacred service and you couldn't be found so you're not invited." She pointed specifically at me. "An exception can be made for you, perhaps—you're the groom of Venus, is that correct?" I nodded. Her anger calmed. "Then I'm sorry, forgive me, it's not my place to speak concerning your business…but this man—" Gord glared back at her, glanced at his brother, raised an eyebrow, but Kevin had his head bowed low, afraid to speak. "—this *outsider* has no right to intrude. I will allow him to be here—both of you—but, please, I'll ask you to take a seat until the service is concluded."

Gord and I had forgotten that our goal was to make an escape. We had gotten too caught up in the ceremony—a bitch of a bride and a scolded groom. We had both felt the bride's sting and actually intended to take seats and watch the rest of the wedding. But two things happened that changed how things played out.

Gord turned to head along the aisle of the audience and take a chair. Gorman saw him, told him to stop, asked what was dangling out of the back of his pants. Gord slowly approached the priest, holding the tail firmly in his fist.

"Recognize it?" Gord asked as Gorman stared at it in horror. "It's a tiger's tail." The priest raised his sunken watery eyes, his long fingers and fat knuckles inching forward to let the narrow end of the tail slip across his skin. "The bitch is dead," Gord said. "We killed her."

Gorman shot his eyes to me—I stared back, holding my face like stone, letting the priest believe what he wanted. Lies and truth meant nothing to these people—give them either one or both, they could assume what they wanted.

"Where is she?" Gorman hissed, lips opening a crack to expose his black teeth.

"She's lying in the room where I got this," I said, pointing at my forehead. Knowing he could see it, knowing I could see the tattoo scrawled across his head, also.

Gord added, "She turned into a fucking bear when I cut her ass-dick off!" He snapped the tail like a whip, the flesh cracking close to Gorman's nose.

Gorman's reflexes were quick. He snatched the tail from Gord's hand and held it as though it were a great treasure. The look of horror waned from his face and his eyes grew bright.

Something was going on in his mind, wheels turning. I tried to recall what Malcolm Miller had told me before he died. A malevolent smile of tiny black teeth formed Gorman's mouth.

He thrust his fist into the air, brandishing the tail at the guests.

"The bitch is dead!" he cried. "Now *I* hold the family power!"

Gord and I stepped back, spun toward the guests to see the men cheer and begin their attack. The women screamed as their cloaks were torn off, hair wrenched and twisted until they slipped to the floor. The men opened the flaps of their fur pants to release their erections. The rape of the wedding party began.

"Stop him, you fucking asshole!" Danaë screamed at Kevin.

# THE BRIDE STRIPPED BARE

But he stood impotently, not yet family, no tattoo on his forehead, the marriage rites not yet concluded. He was ignorant of the many curses beneath the apparent blessings of belonging to the brood of Venus. Now of Gorman.

Danaë snatched the tail from the priest's hand and pressed herself against Kevin, wagging the muscle in his face. "Kill this fucking usurper and I'll make you king by my side. We will rule the family!" Then she hissed at Gorman, "And we won't have to have a wedding in the goddamn bowels of the Earth! I'm as valid a family member as the others! I have wisdom and maturity—the young have fucked up this family for too long! You don't just throw away the old—gouge out their eyes and cut out their tongues to become bait for your traps!"

"That's enough!" Gorman bellowed as he closed in on Danaë. I saw him shake his arm, the sleeve of his cloak bulged out with something inside. As his free hand reached out for the tail, a knife dropped out of his sleeve, the handle into his palm. He spun it expertly to flip the six-inch blade down, ready to use.

"Give me the tail—the power's mine!"

"Go to Hell, old man," the old bride hissed. "She was your daughter. The power passes down to *her* daughter. Sons have no place in this family except as sperm donors."

"And what if I tell her daughter what you just promised your fool of a future husband? Look at him—that's the best you can do? You hag! You should've been in the tunnel to get trampled and slashed and run over by a motorcycle. You're worthless to the family. Barren. And what man or woman would want to breed you—wasting their magic on you?"

"I'm not barren!" Danaë screamed. "This marriage is blessed by the recent mother." She stabbed her finger to the ceiling. I looked up. Horror washed over me, chilling my skin and muscle and bone. "*She* will bring fruit back to my womb!"

Elizabeth was hanging from the ceiling of the cave, naked and bound to a St. Stephen's cross which was pinned to the stone, surrounded by stalactites, lit by an unseen source of yellow light. She didn't move, just hung, her wrists and hands tied to the cross, head hanging forward, hair masking much of her face.

But I knew her, because I loved her.

"She's merely basterdized family, you fool! A peripheral being—she will never have any power!"

Gorman slashed the knife in an arc, opening a mouth in Danaë's neck, severing veins and muscles, splitting her trachea—breath sucking from her lungs, bubbles bunching up and bursting off the top of her windpipe as blood vomited onto the priest's smiling face.

The body dropped and hemorrhaged. Kevin stared at it in horror. And people raped and were raped in turn, smashing chairs, using the splintered wood to choke and bludgeon and fuck. Heads were smashed against stalagmites, and the tips of smaller pyramids of stone were used to impale wounded and dazed women and men, in every orifice available, and a few made by blades.

I raced to Gorman, snapping the knife from my sleeve, digging its edge into his neck. His head craned back as he laughed, murder still in his eyes and the tail in his hand.

"Bring Elizabeth down," I hissed into his ear. He didn't hear me, but Gord did. I glanced to the ceiling.

"Gord," I said, bringing his horrified eyes to mine. "Undo the damage done. Save your sister."

Anger swarmed him. He snapped out his knife, grabbed Gorman's knife hand, stabbed his dagger through the old man's wrist and twisted. The priest's blade clattered to the stone. The tail fell as well, but Gord picked it up and wagged it in Gorman's face.

"Is this power to you people? To Venus?" He raised the point of his knife to aim an inch from the priest's eye. "Free my sister and you

# THE BRIDE STRIPPED BARE

don't die. And you can have the fucking tail—do anything you want with it. We're leaving!"

"How do you bring her down?" I asked.

The priest stared at the point of the knife, his vision flickering from it to the tail.

"Switch on the far wall," Gorman said, nudging his head to the left. "You can have the whore. Her young are useless." His ebony teeth smiled at Gord. "Did you like fucking your sister's useless cunt with your worthless seed…daddy?"

"Like father, like daughter," Gord snarled back before he drove the knife through Gorman's eye to the hilt. The priest laughed as blood and severed pieces of eyeball flowed from the cavity. The blood was black and oozed down Gord's knife, swam up the hilt to his arm, burned the sleeve of his jacket in a rush of acrid yellow smoke before Gord could drop the knife and rip off the jacket before the acid blood corroded his arm.

The priest continued to laugh, and I felt no weakness in his body as I continued to hold my knife at his neck.

"You degenerate *outsiders* are so goddamn stupid. Venus isn't dead, is she?" Gord and I glanced at each other. "Severing her tail doesn't kill her, though it *does* weaken her powers. You can't destroy this family; don't you realize that? We have survived wars and purges and the hatred of the masses for centuries. But while Venus' power is weak, I can take over. Make this a patriarchy. The men will rule—the men will choose wives instead of having wives choose them." He glanced at Kevin, who dropped his eyes again, squeezing his nostrils, sucking up the residual powder encrusted around his nose.

"You used to have a wife," I said, hoping sorrow would wound him. I released the pressure of the blade at his throat, knowing that if a knife in the eye didn't kill, then one severing his jugular wouldn't either.

He feigned sorrow. "So tragic...they all died. Killed by my daughter. Hadn't she told you? That's how I knew she was the strongest one. She's my true wife...my lover...my blood."

"I don't fucking care who rules this shit cult of yours," Gord said, picking up his knife again, but leaving the tail where it lay. "I'd like to see you all dead. Men or women, it doesn't matter—you're all fucked!"

Now that Gord had his knife in hand (though who knew how much it would protect against Gorman?), I released my hold on the priest and went to the far wall. Found the switch and lowered Elizabeth to the ground. I cut her bonds from the cross, tried to wake her but she was out cold. Wrapped the white bear fur around her and carried her over my shoulder back to Gord. As I approached, I saw the tail gone from the floor. Kevin was tucking something into the back of his pants. Tucked it deep, nothing hanging out. I knew he had a plan boiling in his brain. He had listened too closely to Gorman's speech, and surely felt hatred for the priest, killer of his wife.

"Gord, let's just go," I said, shifting Elizabeth on my shoulder.

He glanced at her, then at the priest.

"Take the family, it's yours. But we're leaving. Come on, Kevin."

Gord stepped away from Gorman, didn't see the smile on the priest's face aimed at Kevin.

"Kevin, you comin'?"

Eyes on the rock floor, Kevin muttered, "I'm staying."

Gord stepped back to look his brother in the eye. "What the fuck? We're getting out of here, going back home. We're your family—not these freaks."

Gorman interrupted, "He's a big boy, he knows what he wants."

"You shut the fuck up! Kevin, goddamn it—it's a trap, don't you get it?"

Kevin spun on Gord, eyes fierce with fury. "No, I don't get it, Gordy! I don't get nothing! What do I have? A wife, kids, a family? A

# THE BRIDE STRIPPED BARE

half decent job? I make shit money at a lousy job, live in a shitty bachelor apartment—I've been evicted from tons of shitty apartments because I can't make rent. I've been on welfare a ton of times, I've been homeless—yeah, you and mom and dad didn't know about that, did you? You don't know how shitty my life is—how shitty it's always been! I got nothing, Gordy. Fuck all!"

"What about mom and dad? Are they not your parents? You *do* have a family!"

"Kevin," Gorman said softly.

Gord pointed his knife at the priest. "I told you to shut up—this is between my brother and me!"

But Gorman held Kevin's eyes. "If you give me the tail, I can take power. You will be at my side…for eternity. You can marry anyone you want—have many wives, live as a king." He pointed down at the dead woman at his feet. "You won't have to settle for an old crone. Or, with my new patriarchal power, I can turn her young and beautiful again. No longer will Venus only have such power. All of your wives will be young and beautiful forever—as you too will be—and they will serve your every wish. With myself in power, the rules will change for men like you and me."

Gord stepped up to his brother, to speak close to his ear, get his words deep into Kevin's mind, trying to push out the propaganda. "He'll kill you, Kevin. He's a liar. First chance he gets, you're dead."

"You're close to becoming an official member of the family, Kevin, a privilege even your brother doesn't have" the priest said. "We'll go back to the main house and you can take your pick. I'll marry you to your woman of choice *tonight*. It only takes a wedding…" his pitted eyes roved over to Gord, then to Elizabeth, "…or a birth…and you're family forever."

Gord stepped up to Gorman, halted by the body at his feet. "And family can *kill* family—easily."

Fluttering a hand, he said, "She was mere proof that Venus' power is weakened." He raised his eyes to bore through Kevin. "Without the tail, Venus will grow a new one. Her healing powers are greater than those of the rest of the family. That is one way in which she retains power over the rest of us. We have to act fast."

Confusion etched all our faces, but it was Kevin who looked the most horrified. "A new tail?"

The priest nodded. "There's a way for her to do it. That only she and I know. Through the centuries, others have cut off her tail, but she kept it close so that no one could take it and usurp her power. I can stop her, which will disable her power for good. You could even marry her, Kevin. Would you like that? Would you like to be my son-in-law?"

Kevin was lost. The promise of Venus was too tempting, as it had been for us all. No one was immune to her power. Which was why Gorman wanted that power so badly.

"Kevin—goddammit—come on!" Gord yelled desperately.

But his brother didn't speak. Instead, his answer came in the form of stepping up to the priest and putting the tail in the old withered hands.

Kevin's eyes were dead as he said, "This is my family now."

Gord threw up his arms and stormed through the writhing, fucking, injured, dying and dead bodies on the cave floor, kicking them, stomping them with his cloven heels.

I carried Elizabeth around the orgy of rape and death and followed Gord out of the cavern.

# Chapter 25

We rose a worn and wet staircase of stone, rock walls like solidified wax, formed by a million slow drips over eons to erode and sculpt the cavern. The stairs ended at what looked to be the opening of a mine, an arch of old railroad ties framing the entrance. The stench of marsh gas was thick, almost suffocating, but we exited the stone alcove to feel the cool breeze of the night air against our faces, pushing away the thick stench of rotting vegetation.

A building lay before us, a wooden house that backed onto a marsh. A bridge of rope-tied logs wound through the still, dark water and deformed trees, pyramidal roots exposed above the water's surface, looking like multi-fingered hands grasping the bog.

I sat Elizabeth down at the mine entrance and called to her, patting her face, trying to bring her back to consciousness. Goosebumps peppered her skin, so I wrapped the bear fur tighter around her, even though the marsh air was warm with just a thread of cool breeze wafting through it.

She shivered herself awake, eyes blinking sleepily, head lolling from side to side as her vision adjusted to the darkness.

She looked up at Gord and I. "Where am I?"

"Long story," I said. "But you're safe. For now. What do you remember?"

Her face was like a stone as she reflected, then tears began as her memory returned. "I gave birth. To...to *things*. They weren't babies, were they? They couldn't have been real." She placed a hand against her chest, feeling bile rising. "Coming out of me..."

I held and comforted her as she wept, asked if she remembered anything else, but she said no. Then she asked what was on my forehead. I brought out my knife to shine and show her, told her that she had a tattoo as well, but Gord didn't and he couldn't see ours. She and I were family—me by marriage and she by giving birth. Her tears flowed again, but I tried to distract her from her sorrow. Asked if she felt strong enough to stand and walk. Gord and I helped her to her feet. She shivered and her teeth chattered as she tightened the bear fur around herself.

"We'll get you inside somewhere, find you some clothes, get you warm."

"What is that?" she asked, looking at the house.

I shook my head. "I don't know, but it *does* look familiar."

"Yeah," Gord agreed, "it does."

He stepped onto the bridge to see if it was sturdy, then I helped Elizabeth on and guided her steps. Black water lay on either side of us and steam evaporated from its surface, reeking of sulfur and rotted vegetation. I gazed at the house and the marsh that seemed to lead right to the door instead of stopping at dry ground. The house appeared to be three levels high, surrounded by swamp, if not built right on top of it. We may have faced the rear of the building, now with windows to show light inside, and we could only guess that there would be a door.

We made it halfway across the bridge when a voice behind Elizabeth and I stated, "You must still contend with the dead."

We stopped and turned to see a man covered in the same vines that hung down from the swamp trees around us and had patches of moss and mold dotting his nude body. A tattoo was on his forehead, a pencil-thin moustache above his top lip. I recognized him...from a dream.

# THE BRIDE STRIPPED BARE

The first person I had ever killed.

The dream (if that's what it was) of the three bridesmaids taking me to a forest, bringing me to a man tied to a tree and desperate to live. But I was drugged and would only obey my lust and blood-lust. They urged me to kill, so I did. This man died by my hand. So how could he stand before me?

"Who are you?" I asked, afraid to confess to Gord and Elizabeth that I was the murderer. I was afraid of their judgement concerning him, because he was no enemy of mine, nor was he a mercy-killing as with Malcolm.

"I usher the living to the judgement of the dead," he said. "It is my eternal task now, always a servant of the family. Death does not release one of their obligations to the Royal Order of Ursa. Ursa commands both the dead and the living." He raised an arm to point to the house. "Go into the House of Death to receive your judgement. To stay alive or to join the dead. Yet to remain forever in the family."

The definition of his features waned into darkness until he was gone, a shadow blended back into the night. Elizabeth held onto me as we turned our steps to continue along the log bridge through the swamp. But when we turned, we saw that the house was covered like the man, with vines and moss and mold eating away at its structure, softening its corners and angles, raising a steam of putrid gas high into the surrounding trees and dark sky. The house had been absorbed by the swamp.

And if I was correct, that the man had been the one I killed—a family member, someone's husband, possibly one of the bridesmaid's, grown tired of her companion, choosing me, testing me to see if I could kill and, therefore, become a husband for her, though I was usurped by Venus—if that was the true story behind the man and my killing of him, then I assumed that the house before us was the roadhouse of the bachelor party. Of the drugged and delusional night of excess, where killers and their ghosts resided.

The Swamp Hotel.

We walked the length of the bridge and came to a door with a wooden knob carved into a bear's claw. Swamp water lapped against the base of the door, seeped beneath it. The three of us exchanged a wary stare.

"You think what that…ghost…said was true?" Gord asked.

I cleared my throat, stared at the door. "Only one way to find out."

Elizabeth gripped my hand and I gripped the bear's claw.

The door didn't open, but we were inside. Standing in an alcove with a red velvet drape behind us, red paisley-patterned wallpaper, jeweled beads covering the doorway to our right, a flight of stairs with a thick wooden bannister rising to our left, a lamp with a stained-glass shade hanging over our heads. It was not just warm, but hot. The wallpaper sweated diamond beads.

Two coins rolled down the stairs, bounced, glittered silver in the light, and landed side-by-side four steps up from the landing. Gord stepped toward the stairs to reach the silver, tried to put his hand on the bannister, but he couldn't get a grip. His hand went through the wood. Looking at his hand, he couldn't see any transparency, but it still wasn't solid. He put one hand through the other, then put both hands through his sister and me and we did the same to him.

Elizabeth watched her hands as she tightened her fists, passing fingers through her arm, sweeping her arm through the velvet drape. She gazed up at me. "We're dead."

I tried to chew my lip, but my teeth sank through. Thinking about the man in the swamp. Shook my head. "No. We're still alive. But we've been made into ghosts. To interact with the dead, to receive their judgement." I let out a long breath as I looked at the staircase. "We're in their house now."

Gord glanced at the silver coins on the stair, one having landed heads-up, the other tails-up. He stepped not up, but through, the stairs

# THE BRIDE STRIPPED BARE

until the fourth stair was level with his thighs. With two fingers he reached down to see if he could pick up a coin. And to our surprise he did. He smiled, picked up the other coin, tucked both into a small inner pocket in the vest.

"If you could pick them up," I said, "then they can't be real."

He shrugged. "Money's money. They might pay for something."

With part of his body still in the staircase, he looked up to the step of the staircase, asked, "What the fuck is that?"

Swamp vines weaved themselves into a thick mat as they grew quickly, following the contours of each stair, speeding toward Gord. He jumped back before they reached him, though they continued to grow down the stairs and across the floor, weaving a thick carpet that slipped beneath the beads and through the doorway.

We were all able to walk on the vines, and Gord tried to pass his body through the stairs again but was stopped. Instead, he could climb the vine-covered steps one foot at a time.

I understood. "The vines were a surface we could move *across* instead of slipping *through,*" I explained. "The swamp is escorting us into the House of Death."

An unsettling thought. But like following the yellow brick road, we stepped over the carpet of vines and slipped lightly through the doorway of beads.

# Chapter 26

The vine path weaved itself down a narrow hallway, some tendrils growing up the walls, swarming over black-and-white and sepia photographs of, I assumed, ancient family members. A woman in a petticoat and bonnet pulled down to her eyebrows sat with her tail curling out from the back of her wide dress, being held in her folded hands. A man stood beside her ornate chair wearing a black suit, a long black beard stretching down to his breastbone, a stovepipe hat rising off his head from his eyes up. The couple didn't smile but stared with wide white eyes at the camera. Another photo showed a family of six: two girls in long dresses with large bows in their hair, two boys both in sailor suits, mother and father standing expressionless behind their children—all of them with tattoos on their foreheads. (The first couple had hats covering their tattoos, I guessed.) Another photo showed a man in a civil war uniform of the Confederacy, long curved sabre at his hip, white gloves, with a Van Dyke moustache and beard, staring away from the camera's lens. His uniform bore designs and letters which were similar to the ones on the wedding party jackets and vests.

Down another short stretch of hall lined with photographs, some in ancient wooden oval frames, more than a few with weathering marks tainting the photographic paper, of family from bygone eras. Family members with tattoos and sometimes tails exposed to view. But these photos

# THE BRIDE STRIPPED BARE

were a little more risqué—women wearing corsets but without dresses, bare-assed and bending over to show the length of their high-curving tails—men wearing bear pants, some with patches sewn onto the crotches, others with stitched laces, others with nothing but their penises exposed. We didn't linger too long to see the changing generations.

At the end of the hallway, the vines grew up one wall, barring our way. Our hands could not pass through the weave. A doorway opposite this was open, the twisted green vine carpet leading us in. Elizabeth had taken the lead, ushering us into a dining room of round tables of dark wood, blue wallpaper imprinted with the family's language, a bear's head over the bar. Brass rails lined the bar, glasses hung upside down, taps with pump handles advertising beer I'd never heard of, an ornate mirror behind the bar that didn't reflect the bartender nor the crowd of dead people sitting at the tables.

Smoke hazed the air. Not knowing what else to do, we followed the vine path that led to a table in a corner of the room, the vines growing to swarm it. We sat and gazed across the room, observing the dead.

A pretty woman with slit wrists talked to a thin man with smallpox scarring his face. Two men with cut nooses hanging down their backs played a game of darts. But the darts didn't stick into the dartboard—they vanished in mid-air from each man's hand once thrown, the board untouched, the darts perpetually returning to the thrower. Two women with faces deformed by assaulting fists, skin permanently dyed black and blue and yellow, with black eyes and swollen cut lips sat at one end of the bar, likely trading war stories. A man with a bullet hole in his forehead gave his dinner order to a waitress who had a gaping wound in her throat. A woman who was half naked, but only on the left side of her body, clothing corroded, the exposed skin burned and melted either by fire or acid, strolled around the room softly playing a concertina.

A waitress came to our table. She wore a crinoline dress and had black feathers woven into her hair which towered in tight coils off her head. Torn through her dress and skin was a charred hole, and clearly seen through the hole was her beating heart.

"Welcome to the Swamp Hotel. We move in time and space. We are everywhere and nowhere. We exist and are dead." She spoke it all by rote, bored, then she said, "Cover charge is two heads, no tails."

The three of us were confused. Gord reached into his pocket and brought out the two coins, inspected them, held them in a flat palm to show Elizabeth and I. On both sides of both coins were bear heads. He handed them to the waitress.

She took them, put them on her tongue, swallowed them. Then she reached into her chest cavity and pulled out a deck of ancient playing cards. Passing them to me, she ordered, "Shuffle and deal one card each."

A loud boom and crash burst through the room. The mirror behind the bartender shattered and shot out a million shards of spinning glass which stuck into the bodies of the people in the room, spearing into walls and furniture.

No one flinched, but all eyes turned to our table.

The bartender called out, "The living have arrived to decide their fate. Ursa's mercy upon us all!"

The mirror shrapnel hadn't reached us in our corner. We stared at the faces which stared at us and saw the bits of mirror melt and run down the faces and bodies of the dead like mercury, which then pooled on the floor and solidified. A worm's-eye view of the room reflected from the entire floor but superimposed over this was a constellation of stars and a full moon. I looked up and saw painted stars on the ceiling, with a bear's outline drawn to connect the stars. In the full moon was the face of a snarling bear.

"Shuffle and deal," the waitress repeated to me.

I let my shock pass as I concentrated on the deck of cards, each one depicting a method of death, mostly by medieval methods of torture. I

# THE BRIDE STRIPPED BARE

tried desperately to guess what I was doing, what was about to happen, but it was impossible to predict. Surely nothing good could come of it. The dead around the room kept their eyes on us…on me.

With the deck shuffled, I dealt out a single card for Gord, Elizabeth and myself. Face down.

The waitress tapped the table with her finger and said, "Deck down."

I sat the deck within her reach. She lifted the top card, set it beside the deck while announcing, "No more bets."

Her eyes roved slowly over the three of us, then across the three cards resting on the table.

"Card up," she said to Gord.

He flipped up his card. It showed a man being choked with wire as his tongue protruded and eyes bulged, blood slipping down his neck as the wire sliced as it cut.

The waitress smiled, lifted the card to show it around the room, called out, "Choker!"

The room laughed and howled, hammered fists on their tables and on the bar, stomped the floor mirror of mercury, making it flex and warp, though it didn't shatter. A man at a table with a bowler hat on his head and a blindfold of rusted barbwire across his eyes stood and brought his smile to our table. Stood beside Gord. Unwrapping the wire from around his eyes, tightening it around either fist, he held the length between his hands. He stuck out his scarred tongue to lick across the wire, cutting in freshly bleeding wounds, licking his lips at the taste of blood and rust.

His bloody mouth said, "Words can't express how happy I'll be to choke you to death."

"Card up," the waitress said to Elizabeth.

Her flipped-over card showed a figure lifted off their feet by a thick hook that entered the mouth and curved out of the eye, the eyeball stuck on the hook's barb.

The waitress leered at Elizabeth, a corner of her lip lifted to expose a fang as she showed the card to the room and announced, "Hooker!"

Cheers and cat calls flew up to make glasses hanging over the bar rattle and sing. Men hooked arms with women and twirled them in a dance—a man with a noose kissed the severed neck stump of a woman while digging his hand beneath her petticoat—one of the other waitresses climbed up onto a table and flashed her maggot-filled vagina at several tables—a man sitting alone took his steak knife and slit both wrists, phantom blood spraying from either arm like sputtering fountains.

A thin man with a multitude of small fishhooks piercing his lips and nose, eyebrows and ears, stood up from behind the bar. As he came closer, we saw that his eyelids were kept closed by tiny hooks lined up, their barbs jutting out from his bottom eyelashes. A hook-shaped scar was branded into his forehead, across which lay the family tattoo.

Our waitress stepped to one side to allow him to step a hobnail boot up onto the table, stretch a leg over Elizabeth's head to balance on the back of the booth. Legs on either side of her, he slipped down the cushioned back to sit behind her, her body cradled in his. Blind eyes edged around her jaw to gaze at her. His mouth unhinged like that of a snake, releasing a wide, long tongue on which rested a rusted iron hook. Dangled it between two fingers, rocking it back and forth.

"I like hooking women," he said, flicking his tongue back into his mouth.

The crowd yelled and laughed, kicking their legs against the unbreaking floor mirror. The man kept his hug clasped around Elizabeth's arms.

"Card up," the waitress commanded me.

My card showed a man from the neck up, anguish in his tightly-squeezed eyes, blood pouring in rivulets down his face and neck, a disembodied hand carving flaps of skin from his head with a straight razor.

# THE BRIDE STRIPPED BARE

The waitress drew a sharp fingernail along my jaw to my lips, uttered beneath her breath, "Lovely." Then she took up my card, spun on her heel, holding the card high for all to see. "Scalper!"

The crowd danced across the mirror, making it bend and waver and rattle, the singing glasses behind the bar bursting, bottles frothing alcohol, spraying the crowd who danced under the rain of spirits with their mouths open. Ghosts fucked ghosts. Ghosts tore wider the wounds of themselves and each other, black centipedes poured out like blood and crowded up the walls and swarmed the ceiling—rained down with rum and whiskey and gin into the hungry and thirsty mouths of the dead.

The waitress slapped the card face-up in front of me and smiled with lust and the desire to see me die. She reached down to pull up the hem of her dress, exposing her shaven pudendum. Two fingers slipped across the smooth mound and curled under. She pulled an opened straight razor out of her sex, slid its edge along the cleft, splitting her mound, leaving behind a trail of fresh crimson. Bending over the table to face me, she held the bloody razor between us, let a ruby drop slip down the silver blade, then licked the razor clean.

Her eyes reflected like those of a nocturnal animal, a spot of reflected silver deep in her pupils as she whispered to me, "I'll peel your skin if you peel mine."

The room erupted once more as the waitress held my stare, then stood back to loom over our booth. She tipped her chin to a shoulder to silence the rowdy room. "Dealer's card."

We all stared down at the remaining face-down card. Our executioners watched as well: Gord's tightening the barbwire around his bleeding palms, Elizabeth's cocooning her body with his, chin leaning on her shoulder…and mine smiling down at me, using the thin edge of the razor to flip the card over.

It showed a Valentine's heart violently split in half by an axe.

The faces of our executioners fell. The waitress's form flickered for a half second to transparency, and the dead look in her eye made her appear as though she were about to die again. Her heart stopped beating and she wavered dizzily on her feet. The razor dropped from her hand to clatter on the table. She picked up the card, reached an arm behind her without turning her gaze from me, and showed the card to the room.

"Love will tear us apart."

The mirror screamed as it shattered under the heels that rested on it. The floor sank into black marsh water, taking the crowd with it, hands reaching up a last time, hats and bonnets floating amongst the severed tree roots and marsh weeds before the bodies of every ghost sank below the mire.

Only our waitress stayed standing, as did we, all on a bridge of swamp vines leading through the still-standing doorway out of the sunken room. A silver platter on which sat three small crystal glasses with bell mouths floated to us. Each was filled with what appeared to be grey ashes.

The waitress raised the razor in one hand and sliced her thumb against its edge as though she were peeling an apple. Black blood wormed out. She held her thumb over each of the glasses to allow a few drops to bead on top of the ashes, then sink down to form black veins within the grey.

"Drink up, then get the hell out of here," she hissed as she lifted the tray up to us.

We drank. It tasted exactly like ashes and blood, of course. And everything—colors, shapes, sounds—were more vivid than ever before. We followed the vine path through the doorway.

The roar of a bear spun us to look back. Saw the waitress holding her heart in hand, squeezing it down into her fist, blood both red and black drained from between her fingers, down her forearms, into the swamp at her feet.

She tore her heart in half and dropped it into the bog.

# Chapter 27

I, and only I, arrived in a traditional Japanese room. Wood and rice paper décor, sliding doors, tatami mats covering the floor, a low black table in the center of the room, a bonsai tree sitting on a pedestal. A small room with a muted white light shining through the paper walls. The trail of vines ran along the border of the room and stopped at a wall on which hung a painting of a geisha serving tea to a samurai warlord.

I looked away from the painting to see a geisha kneeling at one side of the low table with a tea set in front of her. She sat on her heels and a large pillow sat across from her. Smiling, she gave me a low bow, palms flat on her thighs, waiting for me to be seated.

I looked at the painting. The geisha was gone; the samurai warlord drank tea alone.

I sat on the pillow cross-legged and watched as the geisha slowly poured from a porcelain teapot into small cups. She was beautiful: white powdered face, black hair stretching in a perfect waterfall down her back to the floor, her white kimono decorated with cranes and koi. Her eyebrows had been plucked and re-drawn as tattoos high on her forehead. But when I looked closer at them, I saw that they were composed of the usual family letters and symbols, only drawn small and squeezed together.

Her lips were painted white with a small fingerprint of red in the center of her top and bottom lips. She smiled as she handed me a filled teacup with both hands, head bowed, eyes averted from my gaze.

I took the cup delicately with a return bow and sipped lightly. She sipped after me, then held her cup, waiting for me to finish and put my cup down first. Once she did, her hands sank back up the wide sleeves of her kimono, then her right hand reemerged with a knife similiar to the one up my sleeve. But hers was smaller, thinner, the handle decorated with the letters and symbols of our tattoos.

Always smiling, she raised the point of the blade to her forehead, didn't flinch as the steel cut a line under the tattoo of her right eyebrow. Blood slipped and curled around her eyes, sped like a thick tear down her alabaster cheek and into her lips. She continued slicing around the tattoo until a thin red line framed the black ink.

She laid the knife on the small table between our cups, then wiggled a long thumbnail under the carved flap of skin. Like peeling off a Band-Aid, she pulled the tattoo off her head, exposing the pinkish-white bone of her skull beneath. She laid the flap of skin on the table beside my cup with the words facing me. Took up the knife again and cut out the other eyebrow tattoo, laying it beside the other patch of skin. The two cavities in her forehead bled, raking lines of blood down her face, but bypassing her eyes. Head bowed, she let the slow drip of crimson stain the lap of her silk kimono.

I stared at her and at the pieces of skin, not knowing what she expected of me. I took up my cup to sip again and she watched my hand. Put the cup down and waited. She smiled, but I could sense she was impatient. Knowing I was missing whatever it was she expected of me.

Her soft voice instructed, "Eat me."

She bowed her head again and I looked at the tattooed skin. She watched the movements of my hands, smiled when I reached out and took a flap of skin, raised it to my mouth. Her eyes raised higher to

# THE BRIDE STRIPPED BARE

watch as I stuck out my tongue and placed the skin on it. Held it, letting blood seep off it into the cup of my mouth. I pulled my tongue in and closed my lips over it. Tasted like copper and salt and felt like soft sponge. I sucked the cannibal morsel to the back of my tongue, swallowed it, felt it worm down my throat. Took up my tea cup to wash it down. She smiled, pleased.

I ate the second piece of skin, washed it down, then I watched her face and the blood dripping off her forehead, slowing down, solidifying like wax.

She bowed low after I swallowed the second piece, then stood, shuffled her small feet, enclosed in white silk socks split between her big toe and the other toes, over to a small panel high up on the wall. Slid it open and brought out a cylindrical pillow with tassels on either end as long as my forearm. Slid the panel closed and shuffled over to the painting. She laid the pillow down on the vine-carpeted floor beneath the painting.

She stood in front of me, gestured for me to stand. I did, and she began undressing me, each article of clothing vanishing as soon as she had removed it. My vest and jacket, my protection, was gone. Naked, I watched her undress. She let her kimono drop to the floor an arm's length away, where it, too, vanished. Kept her head bowed, fingers entwined in front of her sex, letting me inspect her. Then she lay down on the floor, head resting on the pillow, arms straight out at her sides, silk socks still on. Waiting for me.

I walked over to her, stood at her feet, gaze down at her beautiful body. My penis rose, jutted out and curved up, the head against my stomach above my navel. Still ten inches. Kneeling down and delicately separating her legs, I shuffled my knees across the tatami mat, bent her knees up, her feet off the floor, as I positioned myself.

Slowly I guided my penis between her labia and deep into her. Her eyes fluttered and she restrained herself from letting out a low moan.

Fingers clawed the paper mat as I moved in and out of her, watching her small breasts shift on her chest to match my thrusts. She turned her face to one side, shyly trying to keep her facial expressions contained, but her mouth opened to utter soft moans and squeals which escaped from deep in her throat.

I wanted her. Felt lust and rage burn inside me as I sped my thrusts and was soon pummeling into her. My face burned with the roiling of blood in my veins as I stared into her eyes, which never looked at me. I felt like an animal devouring its prey. My hand came up and gripped her slender white neck, thumb and fingers pressing into her soft skin, pushing down onto a small vein that pulsed beside her Adam's apple.

Her nails tore into the tatami as she cried and wept, blood renewing its flow down her forehead, the sight and smell of it driving me harder into her. I bent my head over hers and licked all of the blood I could, slipping my tongue across the two gaps in the flesh, tasting the sweetness of her skull.

I bit my incisor teeth into the peeled skin of her left eyebrow and tore it open wider like a dog trying to get its fangs deeper to taste the marrow inside the bone. I could smell the marrow inside her, and I wanted to eat my way through her skin and muscle to get at it. Her body shook like a small leaf in a hurricane, desperately hanging onto its tree limb, as she wept and cried out her orgasm.

My teeth tore off a strip of skin branching the two eyebrow gaps, and I chewed and sucked the meat into my mouth. A broad patch of bone faced me, pooling with fresh blood, as I rammed myself into her, wanting to split her body in half, cut her open to consume her with all of my appetites. I wanted to sip tea between bites from bowls filled with her flesh.

Her blood and the scraps of her body hung from my lips and were stuck between my teeth as my mind churned with thoughts of consuming her with my cock and mouth.

# THE BRIDE STRIPPED BARE

"Scalp her! Scalp her!" a voice called to me. I looked up to see the samurai in the painting urging me on, his red cock jutting out from a split in his kimono, clutched in his fist, a lecherous leer on his face. "Grab her hair and chew a line across the hairline. It'll come off easily—I promise you!"

I reached a hand to the back of her hair and gathered her hair into a fist. Leaned my teeth down to touch the top of her forehead.

The cries and moans of the woman changed to laughter. Blades of blood washed down her face. She raised a hand to her mouth to stifle the new, strange sounds emitting from her throat, but she couldn't hold them in. She opened her eyes wide to stare for the first time into mine. Her chest heaved beneath me and her neck stretched tight as laughter took over her body. I looked away from her face to scan down the length of her body. From the neck down she was no longer a young woman. Her torso and breasts were a loose wrinkled bag of skin dotted with brown patches of age, moles sprouting tufts of thin hair, white scars of ancient wounds.

I got off her, sat on my knees between her legs, blood and fluids dripping off my erect penis, gazing down in horror at the hideous skeleton of creased, reeking skin that sprawled in front of me. She continued to convulse with laughter while I stared down at her.

The metal, cloven-hoofed boots attached to my legs exploded into pewter dew. Shocked by the noise and feel of my feet free again, I leapt back from between the woman's legs, and inspected my legs and feet. Wiggled my toes. My skin rotted away, down to muscle and sinew, down to bone, until from my knees down I was skeleton. The woman's laughter increased.

"You are not a man!" the samurai yelled at me from the painting. I looked back at him and he was a frozen drawing again, semen shooting out of his penis, splashing across the rest of the painting, erasing it.

The woman wiped tears of blood away from her eyes and cheeks as she looked up at me, letting the laughter fade from her throat.

"You don't like me anymore, husband?" she asked in a sarcastically demure voice. "How about this way instead?"

She smoothed her hands down her face, smearing away her youth, the face of an ancient crone looking back up at me. Her hands swept across her chest and stomach, continued down either leg. Her body from the neck down was again that of a young woman, soft and without the slightest taint of age.

"Which part of my body would you like to eat now? I am still me, young or old, but your appetite comes and goes with age. You think you are a good man, but you are a liar and a cannibal. Yes, husband?"

My throat felt thick, hands cold on my thighs, toes of bone flexing without my control. I felt legless and too afraid to try and stand. I sat sprawled on the tatami, the woman wrapping herself back in her kimono, laughing, always laughing. She had emasculated me with sexual humiliation. She owned me. I was her slave and knew it.

"I'm not your husband," was all my feeble voice could say.

She giggled. "You fucked me before you fucked Venus. We are bound together for life. You chose the Asian girl amongst the three bridesmaids because you desire Asians more than any other race. You are a racist."

"No," I stuttered. "You chose me. What's wrong with liking a particular type of woman more than another type? Do you like white guys more than Asian guys?"

"Type? You can only see in types. Like all men." She giggled behind her hand. "I read your mind. We all did, Venus as well. We saw whom you preferred and gave you what you wanted. A woman controls a man not when she denies his desires but when she satiates them."

A lump wouldn't swallow, and my words could muster no volume. "I'm not a racist. Would I have been if I'd chosen either of the other two?"

# THE BRIDE STRIPPED BARE

She giggled and smeared blood around her mouth. "Of course. There's no escaping your lusts or your prejudices."

"Then why did I marry Venus?"

"Ah, Chris-san," she said, eyes wide and blinking from left to right, seeing me from two varied perspectives, mocking me. "Venus chose you. So many of us wanted you, especially after you killed at our bidding, but Venus saw you as her prize, so we could only fuck you, not own you. But still, you will always be my husband. Sometimes a woman can own a man only by releasing him to his bigotry and passions. You are owned and controlled by your addictions and hatreds. The samurai is correct: you are no man."

I shuffled back from her, and some of the bones of my feet fell off, tumbled away like dice. I panicked and shuffled back further to a paper wall as she laughed. Then her face turned old to match her body as she got to her feet. Bowed low to me, smiled.

"You honor me, husband. My death at your hands completes my life's meaning. If you wish to leave this room, you must be a man." She shuffled her socks over to the panel in the wall, slid it open, brought out a man's kimono and a long samurai sword. Proffered both to me with a low bow, the kimono draped over her forearm, the sword held horizontally in both hands. "Do a warrior's duty."

I glanced at the painting on the wall. The samurai and geisha were both back in the picture, their ink bodies frozen. But now the geisha was seated on her knees with her head bowed, smooth neck waiting for steel. The samurai stood over her with his sword raised, his face contorted into a mask of rage and death. The sword about to sever his victim's head.

Every bone that comprised my feet and shins dissolved into chalk, but as soon as pieces of my body had vanished, they began to congeal back into existence. My flesh legs returned, and they began to grow thick brown fur until they became the fur pants. My torso grew a vest and jacket, my protection returned. The cloven-hoofed shoes never returned. I swung onto my knees and used the paper wall to help brace myself as I unsteadily stood. The paper turned to flesh, and I felt a heartbeat beneath my palm. My legs gained strength and balance. I took the kimono and sword.

The woman knelt before me, head bowed, the nape of her neck exposed, two small bones of her spinal column my target.

"It is easier to kill an old and ugly woman than one who is young and beautiful. It is the way of the patriarchal world. Yes, husband?"

I hated her. Denied to myself every accusation she had thrown at me, knowing it was a trick—psychological warfare to break me, make me into one of the family members. Making me confess that I harbored the same thoughts and feelings as Gorman. Venus, too, hated the old and infirm members of her own family, as I had witnessed in Paco's tunnel. Father and daughter were twins, but of opposing genders.

I understood the trap.

I put on the kimono, raised the sword…stepped around the woman kneeling on the floor, and slashed the razor-sharp blade through the painting.

I leapt through the frame and was free of the room.

# Chapter 28

I awoke on a floor of thick brown bear fur, still dressed in the kimono, the sword loosely gripped in my hand. Gord and Elizabeth lay nearby, all of us waking from a strange sleep.

Floor, walls and ceiling were all covered with the thick bear fur, no windows or doors visible, a massive bear head roughly the size of an elephant's head hanging down from the ceiling over us on thick iron chains. Candles dotted the head, some stood upright in its jaws, one jutting from either eye, and others lined along its snout. Thin tapers and thick pillars all poured a crust of thick white wax down the bear's head, throwing enough light for us to see each other by, but not much of the rest of the room.

There was furniture, but it was buried beneath fur. What looked to be a bar stretched along one wall, shelves aligned behind it, even bar stools along the front. The stools were like pillars, immoveable, and plush with fur. A fur-covered rail stretched around the three edges of the bar.

In the shadows were booths with tables bolted solid to the floor, but without chairs hedging in the booth. There may have been paintings or signs on the walls, but we couldn't tell beneath the fur, only able to see the edges of the frames and rectangular contours of something pinned to the wall. All walls and furniture were soft, our hands sinking deep into the fur.

Groggily, we all sat up, facing each other in a circle, inspecting our changed appearances.

Added to Gord's clothing and his melted boots were two metal gloves on either hand, first and index fingers split like crab claws, his thumbs poking through holes. With his jacket and vest hanging open, I saw that the old pieces of cloth were no longer fused with his flesh. Though he still bore the scarring from his burns, the wrinkles and whorls of his skin were now shaped into the family's symbols and designs. And his missing eye had grown back!

Instead of the shortened white bear fur I had given her, Elizabeth now had a full-length white fur wrapping her shoulders and extending down to her bare feet. Her metal hoof shoes were also gone. And wrapped around one leg was a leather bullwhip, its handle pushed into her vagina.

Elizabeth turned her back to me and her brother as she spread her legs and sorely untwisted the bulbous bullwhip handle from inside her. Pushed what remained of the whip down off her leg and left it coiled on the floor, then wrapped the bear fur tightly around her body as she turned back to see me and Gord.

"Well, what the fuck happened to us?" Gord asked with a chuckle. He asked me, "Did you go to samurai land or something?"

"Close," I replied. "Let's not sit under that, please."

We all looked up at the bear head hanging over us. Like a strange Sword of Damocles. Then stood and gazed around the room, looking for a place to settle.

Elizabeth commented, "Looks like the bar in the Swamp Hotel again. Only covered in bear fur."

We sat down in a corner of the room.

"Keep on the lookout for anything about to pop out at us," I cautioned them, and myself.

One by one, we told our stories, eyes always on the fur furniture and every shadow the room held. I started. Told about the woman and

# THE BRIDE STRIPPED BARE

the scalping, the sex and the samurai in the painting, and then how it all changed from euphoria to degradation. My feeling and the physical manifestation of sexual emasculation.

"I totally understand that," Gord said, a dazed look in his eyes.

Elizabeth went next.

"I was in a bedroom. A boudoir let's call it. Four-poster bed, satin sheets, these tall paintings on the wall in rich golden frames showing weird animals—beasts having sex with women and men."

"Sounds like Venus' bedroom," I said offhand. But both Gord and Elizabeth were struck silent by my comment. Far away, sad looks in their eyes.

"Oh yeah," Elizabeth said in a whisper, her voice cracking. "Guess I'd forgotten about that."

"Sorry," I said.

"No, don't be," she inhaled, wrapped the thick fur around her shoulders. "Well, shit, now that you mention it, I guess it was history repeating. You were there," she said to Gord. "I thought we had lost Chris. But you—or the other version of you—was wearing this coat. I asked where you got it and you smiled all cocky and said you had ways of getting what you wanted."

She paused her narration, rested one hand in the other, eyes blinking rapidly as though she was trying to prevent herself from crying.

"Elizabeth?" I whispered. "You okay?"

She nodded and put a hand over her mouth, thinking, fighting with something terrible inside her. Gord shifted over to put his arm around his sister, but she pushed him away. "No, not now, okay? Just…no. No." She broke down and sobbed. Gord and I glanced at each other, not knowing what to do except wait and see if she could go on. But I had a feeling that history had repeated itself in that room. It was as though something terrifying from each of our experiences was repeating, but as a distorted version of reality. Something too hard for us to handle. The Asian woman I had killed, raped and murdered, told me more horrifying things about myself than when I had killed some lone man tied to a tree. I had blamed much or all of my killing and torment on drug hallucinations. Perhaps if you thought something real was actually a dream, then maybe it wouldn't affect you as much. But the Asian girl, I knew even while killing her, was real. I was possessed and out of my mind when I did it, but I eventually sobered up. And had secretly hated myself since.

Elizabeth didn't glance at Gord, kept her eyes always on the fur floor, but said to her brother, "You—or the man I thought was you—tried to rape me in that room. But I fought him off. He saw that I was cold. There was a fireplace. He lit a fire, took off his bear skin, laid it on the floor. Told me to sit and warm by the fire. The bear fur you gave me, Chris, had lengthened into this one. I went to the fire because, even with this fur on, I was shivering uncontrollably. The other Gord put his arm around me, told me that I was beautiful in the fire light, that there was nothing wrong with incest. That we should abandon Chris, maybe even kill you, and be husband and wife in the family. Then I could… I, ah, I could…" She couldn't speak; retched and looked about to vomit, trying to control her breath so that she didn't. A hand hovered over her mouth, and from behind her fingers, eyes on the floor, she said, "He said I could sell my body to other family members or non-members and make a *couple bucks*. That Venus wouldn't give him an allowance anymore since he wasn't her husband. We needed to get money any way we could so we wouldn't be poor anymore. He would steal drugs from the family and sell them to outsiders. And I could sell my body. I didn't have to worry about getting pregnant from a john because I was barren. Then he told me how he really wanted a new truck." She retched again and a little vomit spilled onto the floor, soaked the fur. Sweat beaded her forehead and she picked tears from the corners of her eyes. She needed time to compose herself, spat a few times onto

# THE BRIDE STRIPPED BARE

the floor. I looked for water, but, of course, the room was all bear fur. "He attacked me, tried to rape me, but I got out from under him. I leapt onto the bed, but it instantly vaporized into ash which filled the room. The ash from the bed and smoke from the fireplace stung my eyes and made me choke. I had collapsed into a corner. Gord—the double—walked out of the smoke, a leering smile on his face, his penis hanging out of his pants and this whip in his hands.

"'You're a feisty one, aren't you?' he said.

"I made myself small in the corner, wrapped the white fur tight around myself, tried to find a way out, or something I could use as a weapon. But I couldn't see through the smoke and ash, couldn't stop coughing. Which, of course, told him where I was in case he couldn't see me.

"He unraveled the whip, stretched back his arm, and cracked the leather lash above my head. I yelped and jumped where I sat.

"'You listen to your older brother, like it was in the olden days. Don't make me bride-burn you for disobeying,' he said. 'Either you get used to putting out for the customer by fucking me, or I cut you to shreds with the cat o' tiger tails, sis,' he said, and I saw the end of the whip split into nine whips made of flesh striped orange and black.

"I couldn't stay huddled in the corner, waiting to be killed. I got my feet under me, pulled the fur over my head and raced, stooping low under the cracking lash over my head, and tackled him to the ground. He only laughed and pawed me.

"He pinned his body on top of mine as the fire crackled and billowed out smoke. I thought the room had caught fire, that he would want to leave before we both choked to death, but all he could think of was to rape me.

"I punched my fists against his face, kicked my legs hoping they would connect with any part of his body. Tucked my elbows in and kept my face low to the ground, hoping to breathe purer air. I twisted the bear fur tighter around my body. His face arched over the back of my neck and he kissed me. I screamed and panicked and slammed back an elbow. It was a more powerful blow than I had expected. (I realize now that the bear cloak must've given me increased strength.) I pushed him off and stood. I kicked him in the face with my bare feet, wishing I had the weird shoes back. Blood poured from his nose, his teeth loose and bloody as he smiled. I glanced at the wall where a window dissolved into view, with vines circling it. Hadn't noticed it before; it just grew there. Sometimes a door is a window, I thought. I was prepared to dive through it and fall a thousand feet to the ground if it meant getting away from the smoke and the rapist.

"I ran. But not too far before my left leg was pulled out from under me, chin hitting the floor. I looked and saw the length of the whip coiled around my leg, the striped flesh ends sticking to my skin like suckers, trying to burrow in. He pinned me to the floor again, grabbed the handle of the whip and corkscrewed it into me, saying he had to rape me to teach me how to be a good bitch. I screamed and tried to fight him off, but the pain shooting through my entire body was too much. I beat my fists against his head, which slowed him down and pushed him low enough down my body that I was able to raise my legs, get my feet pressed against his chest, and push. He flew across the room and landed in the fireplace.

"While he burned, I ran—still with the coat on, still with the whip inside me—and dove through the window.

"Then I woke up on this floor."

Gord and I were in awe at Elizabeth's story. She wept quietly for a few moments and spat bile onto the floor. A thick silence held in the soft room for a long time. Eventually, I nodded to Gord to tell his story, hoping it would distract Elizabeth from her hellish memories.

"Well," Gord began, "I went back in time too. Right back into Gorman's tailor shop, the trail of vines leading through that curtain of

# THE BRIDE STRIPPED BARE

black beads covering his back shop, where all the clothes were kept. You were there," he said to me, "with your wedding uniform on, plus the pants. I was still naked, and Gorman was pulling out a jacket and vest from a wardrobe he had, which was never there before. I was as happy as hell getting dressed up because I thought I was still the groom. I *knew* that. And you were still the best man. So, Gorman was holding up the vest for me to put my arms through, checking how it fit me. Did the same with the jacket, and later gave me the pants and shoes to try on. Things were a little different this time for a few small reasons and one big reason. Instead of making a small slip of the tongue for Gorman to get pissed off about and then spread the word around to Venus and the rest of the family, I started bragging.

"Chris, the whole time you were just standing there in your suit, smiling and nodding at everything I said, saying nothing, not even moving. You looked like a bobble-head doll. I went on and on about how the family was this big cabal, some ancient tribe of people who worshipped some bear god named Ursa. And they all had weird magical powers.

"Gorman kept dressing me, not flinching at anything I said. I was kind of insulting them all, saying how they were incestuous inbreeders, the woman all had tails and they ruled the men. They were killers of outsiders and of their own kind, mass murderers. They had this guy, Paco, basically working for them, having his drug tunnel on their land, with tons of shipments which led into Canada, where there were more family. Tons of coke and pot and whatever else coming and going between the two countries and no one outside the family knew about it. No one knew about the true family, about how much they controlled in this region and around the world. I spilled *everything*.

"By this point, I'm dressed. Gorman smiles at me. Says, 'There's just one more part of your uniform, sir.' He brings out these gloves, which latched themselves onto my hands. I'm looking at them, can't feel my fingers inside them, and they're heavy, making my arms tired just holding them up.

"I ask him what they are, and Gorman says that they're to prevent me from every touching my bride. That I won't be able to feed myself, bathe myself, or even scratch my dick. Everything will have to be done for me by my wife, Venus. She will control every aspect of my existence; I'll be a baby in her hands.

"He said it was punishment for revealing family secrets.

"I get pissed off and tell him to take them off. He taps each one with his long, bony fingers and they start to get hot. Feels like there are a thousand needles piercing my hands—except my thumbs."

He wiggled his thumbs hanging down from the steel mold of the gloves.

"I screamed for him to take them off, they're burning my hands. He laughs and says he can't do that—orders from Venus and the family. I say I'll see what she has to say about that. The gloves burn hotter, dropping me to my knees. I try to pull one off with my feet, but the shoes are no good and the gloves are on solid.

"I staggered up to my feet to take a swipe at Gorman with the glove, but he easily ducks it. I scream at you, Chris, to help me, but you're just standing there, smiling and nodding, watching. I throw another punch at Gorman and he ducks out of the way. My arms feel like they're weighted with lead as they burn, I can't lift them. I'm just standing and screaming.

"Gorman then puts a flat hand on my chest and his palm burns me. Smoke rises up, smelling like burning flesh and hair. He chuckles as he moves his hand across my chest and stomach, scorching my melted skin, re-melting it, branding the designs of the jacket and vest onto my skin. The clothing burns off me completely, rising off my shoulders and ribs as black smoke. I can't lift my arms to push Gorman's hand away.

# THE BRIDE STRIPPED BARE

"I look down at the pants and shoes I still have on, see the vines again, watch them move into the wardrobe behind Gorman.

"He says, 'If you want the burning to stop, you must choke off the air supply.'

"Then he grabs both of my hands and delicately turns them to face me. The claws widen and clamp around my neck. I start to choke and wheeze until my air is too cut off for me to make a sound. Then Gorman brings that full-length mirror he has over to me, and I see myself again. My face is turning purple. My good eye bulges out like a cartoon, and my other eye re-emerges from its hollow socket and grows. Both of my eyes are completely red, and my face is fucking blue, almost black. I'm thinking: I'm gonna die, I'm gonna kill myself and I can't stop my hands. The gloves are in control. And Gorman's got a shit-eating grin getting bigger on his face.

"Then I remember where the vines led. I ram like a bull into Gorman, knock the prick down, and dive through the doorway of beads.

"And then I woke up on this floor."

He held up his hands, still encased in steel gloves, skin melted into designs and symbols. Skin color normal, eyes normal, both the same size.

"Do they still hurt?" I asked.

"No. No pain at all. And my chest feels fine, better than usual, in fact. It's kinda like having a really cool body tattoo. Guess they call it 'branding.' Don't know what the hell it says, but I kinda like it." He swallowed and shook his head to disperse the memories. "Fucking weird shit in this goddamn house."

"And it only gets weirder!" echoed a voice far above us.

We jumped and got to our feet, then moved across the floor to get a better vantage point of the top of the bear's head. Poppy sat astride it, gazing down at us through the blue glasses sealed to his face.

He applauded slowly. "Well done you three. You are survivors. Few make it this far. Those who don't, of course, become ghosts of themselves. But the house isn't done with you yet."

The great bear head opened its jaws and roared, the growl like the sound of a jet turbine engine—the wax coating its face and head shattering like glass, candles tumbling to the ground. They lit patches of fire on the floor bear fur, and the flames quickly grew and climbed every piece of fur-covered furniture and up the walls.

When the bear head roared, Poppy was thrown off, did a somersault backwards through the air as he fell, and landed straddling a bear that had risen from the floor. Or, I should say, a beast in the rough shape of a bear, covered by bear fur—no eyes or features that were not covered in fur. It could've been a sofa that had become bear-shaped. Poppy rode the beast as it slowly lumbered around the trees of fire toward us, shuddering light reflecting in his blue lenses as he laughed and threatened, "The house always wins!"

We scrambled in three directions, trying to stay away from both the bear and the fires. Poppy and his mount charged toward Elizabeth. She unraveled her whip, cocked back her arm, and snapped the flesh ends, but they went wide. She didn't have enough time to snap the whip again, having to rush away from the bear's charge.

I raced up behind the beast from one side as Gord raced to the other flank. I swiped the samurai sword at its hind leg, but the fur and flesh were too thick. The blade glanced off. Gord rammed a glove into the bear's leg on his side, but his fist bounced off, momentum throwing him back toward a patch of flame.

Elizabeth leapt through a tower of flame toward me, the white cloak wrapped around her, whip trailing behind. She fell into my arms. I saw Poppy's bear turn and race for us through the flames. I grabbed Elizabeth's arm and pulled her across the room, weaving between fires, trying to see Gord as smoke stung our eyes.

# THE BRIDE STRIPPED BARE

I looked behind us. The bear's snout sniffed the air, couldn't exactly smell us amongst the smoke and fire, flames clinging to patches of its fur, feathers of fire seeming to rise off of Poppy's head. Elizabeth began to spool her whip as we raced for the bar. We dove over it, sped over along its length as the bear caught our smells and crashed through fur and the wooden bar beneath, roaring louder than the roar of the flames.

Elizabeth saw Gord race from between fires toward us. The bear was coming. I jumped onto the bar and raced toward the beast as it smashed its shoulders down the narrow gap between the bar and the wall. As I leapt off the top of the bar to tackle Poppy, Elizabeth reared back the whip and struck. The flesh ends glued themselves to the bear's face, began burrowing through its fur, drilling holes of blindness where its eyes would've been had it been a real bear. The beast reared and threw Poppy and myself off its back.

The sword slipped from my grasp, so I locked both arms around Poppy's throat as we wrestled amongst fires. He rammed his fists into my face and stomach, brought a knee up against my nose. My body flung back, and I lay on the floor a few feet from a patch of burning fur. Gord jumped over my prone body and swung a steel glove into Poppy's mouth. Teeth and blood flew off with the punch, but the man still stood. And laughed a bloody smile.

"I like your vest," Poppy said to Gord. "I got one too."

He rammed a driving fist into Gord's stomach, doubling him over. I struggled to my feet and caught the next blow meant for Gord on the side of my head. My ear rang and the rush of flame around me sounded like water.

Another fist came my way, but Poppy's feet slipped out from under him. Gord had hooked his wrists around Poppy's legs and pulled. I dropped my knees onto Poppy's shoulders, pinning him, hammering my fists into his face as hard as I could, trying to smash his glasses. But they weren't glass. They were a part of his face, lenses as hard as bone.

He laughed, dripping red teeth at me and said, "You punch like a girl!"

Then he screamed in pain, my fist raised but not swung down. I looked behind me. Gord had punched a glove into Poppy's shin, snapping the bone, the man's foot wrenched sideways.

I looked over Gord's head to see Elizabeth running towards us, trailing the whip, the bear lurching blindly behind her, its black hole eyes spewing flames while its claws swiped at smoke.

Part of me hoped that the bear was Venus in shape-shifting disguise. But with 'L.O.V.E.' and a doctor's bag of other inks and poisons in her veins, it was unlikely.

I pulled Gord off Poppy and we stumbled through a wall of flames. My kimono had been burning the whole time, and I never noticed. The vest and jacket and pants protected me from the fire's burn. Still, the upper part of the kimono burned and wrapped my upper torso in a cocoon of flames. A wall of flames blinded me, so I couldn't see as Elizabeth dropped out of the fire, slipped her cloak off in mid-air, and slapped it down over me. The flames snapped off in an instant. Elizabeth pulled the bear fur off me and the last wispy hairs of soot puffed up across my face. My kimono was vapor.

I choked and coughed, fighting for air, as Elizabeth looped an arm under mine to help pull me away from the encroaching fires around us. I kicked myself to standing and made sure the white fur was around Elizabeth.

We saw Poppy hobbling and half-crawling away from us, slipping through screaming flames, trying to avoid the thrashing and rearing bear. But he yelled from the pain in his leg and coughed with smoke, and the blind bear followed the sounds.

Both bear and rider had wound their way around and through towers of flame to the center of the room. Elizabeth and I looked up to see the piece of fur-covered ceiling where the chains holding the bear's

# THE BRIDE STRIPPED BARE

head had burned through to the wood and the wood began to crack. Plaster and fire fell, and the bear's head roared a pillar of fire as it dropped.

Poppy and the bear were smashed into the floor beneath the bear's head. Flames swarmed the beast's stretched jaw and head and its howl soon died beneath the tidal roar of fire.

Elizabeth and I wrapped an arm around each other as we shuffled around the spreading patches of inferno, trying to find an oasis of air.

Gord appeared through a gap in the fire, the sound of his voice drowned by the roiling heated air, waving us toward him. We stepped over a low wall of flames, the hem of Elizabeth's cloak snuffling them into smoke, to meet Gord by the wall.

Fire had burned through the thick fur to expose a door which was also being eaten by a blue frame of fire. One at a time, the three of us tucked our respective vests or bear cloaks over our heads as we burst through the door.

We raced away from the Swamp Hotel, smoke rising off our backs. We fell to sit on dew-wet grass as we sucked the cool night air into our lungs and watched tongues of flame rise high through windows and doorways, brick and board burning and crumbling, wood exploding, the roof caving in and shooting up pillars of sparks.

The sign had the words 'Swamp Hotel' carved into it but had been painted over with 'Roadhouse.' Both eras were erased by fire. The signboard dropped and burst into smoke and smoldering coal on the burning porch.

We stared for what seemed like hours at the bonfire that was once the House of the Dead, heat thrown back to warm us, to bring smiles to our faces that the dead were finally dead.

And we were sill alive.

Dawn was rising.

# PART
# - 4 -

# Chapter 29

Before the light of the burned and sunken house waned to darkness, we searched where we sat and saw Poppy's jacked-up pickup truck parked beside a stand of trees. Keys under the floorboard mat. A shotgun and a hunting rifle on the gunrack across the back window, a .357 Magnum under the seat, boxes of ammo for all weapons in the glove compartment and under the seats. Gord laughed, remembering his old pickup truck. We got in and I drove since Gord's hands were still encased in the gloves. Elizabeth sat between us, her bullwhip left behind on the grass. It wasn't a souvenir she wanted to keep. My sword lay across her whip, also abandoned.

We pulled out of the driveway as the final sticks of the house burned, coals smoldering, the marsh gas returning to replace the scent of thick wood smoke. I kept under the speed limit, in no rush since I wasn't sure where we were going, following Gord's directions as we headed down the unlit night road.

So I asked, "Where're we going? Where *can* we go?"

He sighed and leaned his head against his side window. "The hell out of Dodge, I figure. We could try for the airport. Even if there are family members working there, hopefully either they'll all be at the wedding or there will be enough non-family members to act as a buffer and allow us on a plane."

# THE BRIDE STRIPPED BARE

I glanced down at his hands. "I don't know if they'll let you on with those gloves. Definitely set off the metal detectors."

He chuckled, held the gloves up to inspect them. "Wrap some bandages around them. Say they're protective coverings—new technology. If the airport doesn't work out, we can try for the border. Get you and Elizabeth back home through Canada. Fuck the family. If we have to battle them the whole way across the continent, so be it. But we should head to my place first. I think we should all get some half-decent clothes on."

I drove down the black highway for a little while before Elizabeth changed our plans. Worry in her eyes as she looked at Gord. "Mom and dad and Kevin…we gotta save them."

Gord tapped a glove against his knee and chewed his lip as he thought, mumbled a swear word under his breath.

"I think we can forget about Kevin," I muttered.

"What do you mean? He's our brother," Elizabeth said, feeling insulted that I would consider leaving an innocent man behind. But he wasn't innocent anymore. Who was? Elizabeth.

"He's gone over to the other side," Gord explained. "You were unconscious, hanging on a cross—long story. Gorman promised Kevin the world and he took it. He's as fucked up as Chris and I once were."

"All the more reason to save him," Elizabeth rebutted. "Whatever spell Gorman or Venus or whoever puts on people—shoving coke up their noses—it can be broken. Gord, goddamnit, we have to try!"

He let his head slip back against the seat, tapping his metal gloves together as they rested in his lap, sighing and considering what his sister had said. Elizabeth had proved herself a fighter several times over. Her brother wouldn't win over her, and he knew it.

"Chris, turn the truck around, head back to the mansion. This nightmare ain't over yet."

# ROB BLISS

<<<—>>>

I followed Gord's directions, since I had no idea where we were, and inched along the side of the road as we approached the mansion, tires crunching gravel, seeing lights through the trees, hearing people's voices—screams and laughter and moans. I stopped the truck when Gord told me to, sure as hell not pulling into the driveway as though all was well, and we were just party latecomers. We wanted to have the truck ready and not blocked in when we escaped—fire up the engine and hit the gas to speed down the highway, getting a headstart just in case some family members decided they were in the mood for a car chase.

Took the keys out of the ignition, slipped them under the floormat. We took the guns with us, but Gord was pissed that he couldn't fire, much less hold, any of them. Standing outside the truck, I tucked the Magnum down the back of Gord's pants.

"You'll be our holster then," I said with a wink. "Better to be armed than not, going into a place like this."

"True enough."

I took the rifle and Elizabeth carried the shotgun as our bare feet walked slowly, numbly, over the gravel of the driveway, hearing the mansion's interior sounds growing as we approached.

We saw cars and trucks and vans of every make and model, several motorcycles and ATVs—even a few police cruisers—parked haphazardly around the front grounds of the house, backed into trees, everyone blocking everyone else. A good sign—no one was intending to leave any time soon. The party looked to be going on all night and day, maybe even for a few days. A good sign and a bad one: the house would be packed with people.

We stayed low as we crept between cars. I saw the house's front façade for the first time. A gothic mansion that spread across our entire

# THE BRIDE STRIPPED BARE

perspective, the wings stretching into forest on either side so that we couldn't accurately determine the house's full sprawl. Spires towered off the roof like porcupine quills, windows high up around their circumference, gargoyles of stone and wood aiming their watchful eyes on anyone approaching. Stained glass beveled windows blocked a voyeur's view into the interior. A wraparound porch held up by thick columns sculpted like small totem poles showing the faces of people in anguish, squeezed in between animals of myth. A bear's head with opened jaws topping each pillar.

Cameras everywhere. But was anyone watching them?

The outside still belied the interior dimensions since we all knew that the house was like an iceberg—most of it residing under the surface of the ground. Would we have to go through it all again to find Gord and Elizabeth's mother and father? And even if we got them, would we have to race through the subterranean labyrinth anyway, back into the stalagmite cave to fine Kevin?

The party would never end, which wasn't a good thing for us. I was starting to feel as Gord must've felt before Elizabeth told us we had to go back. I just wanted the hell out of here. We had to save ourselves…we could pray later that nothing bad had happened to Ma and Pa. Fuck Kevin, I still thought.

Weaving through the vehicles toward one side of the house, sheltered by the thin trees of the forest edge, Gord told us to stop, stay low, as we gazed over the structure that loomed ahead. We all tried to think of the best way to get inside.

Gord glanced around at the vehicles nearby. In a small copse of trees nearby were two dead headlights hovering high off the ground. Gord slipped around cars to check them out, and we followed. A large 4x4 truck with massive tires, jacked up like Poppy's, the cab at least ten feet off the ground, sat with an unobstructed run out of the trees toward the house. The truck had twin tailpipes like chrome horns sticking up on either side of the cab, just behind the windows. No exhaust pipe under the vehicle to drag and get smashed. The truck was definitely built for off-roading.

Gord clicked his gloves together as he thought, until Elizabeth put her hands on his and whispered for him to be quiet. "Stealth or smash?" he asked no one in particular as he looked from the truck to the side of the house.

"What do you mean?" I asked.

He cleared his throat, pointed a glove at a pile of cut logs stacked against the house. A firewood ramp that extended up to the level of the porch. I began to see the blueprints of the plan forming in his mind.

He whispered, "We could either break in—circle the house to find an open door, quietly punch out a window—" he smiled and tapped his gloves together, "—to let ourselves in…or we could make a more memorable entrance."

"Think the keys are in the truck?" I asked.

He clicked his tongue. "These are small town folks and a loving family. Everybody trusts everybody. No one steals from his neighbor, especially if they're related."

We shuffled hunkered down, slipping between cars until we got to the driver's door of the truck. It was unlocked, keys dangling from the ignition on a bear's head keychain. Elizabeth was about to climb up, but Gord stopped her.

Said to both of us, "You two ready for this? We're gonna do some major fucking damage, right?" He held up his gloved hands. "Since I can't shoot worth a shit, maybe I should try driving?"

We nodded, and Elizabeth said to her brother, "Once we're inside, smash through everything, kill everyone—run the fuckers down—Chris and I will shoot anything that moves. Except for mom and dad, of course. And Kevin."

"Can I just wing Kev?"

# THE BRIDE STRIPPED BARE

"Gordy, concentrate, just kill every member of this family. Think of it as a video game, or a horror novel."

Gord laughed and said, as he turned around to show the gun sticking out of his waistband, "That's my sister! Crazy psycho bitch!"

She toasted her shotgun to his Magnum. I joined the toast with my rifle.

Elizabeth added, "Gotta be psycho to kill psychos."

"Then just call me Psycho!" Gord said proudly.

I smiled at Elizabeth, knew I loved her, wanted her to survive this even if I didn't. Gord climbed into the driver's seat, Elizabeth sat in the middle, then me.

Gord stared at the ramp of logs leading up to the porch, his exposed thumbs hooked under the steering wheel. "Keep your side window rolled down," he said to me. "They might shoot back, and Elizabeth needs a clear shot." He smiled at us as he pulled up a wing of his jacket to cover his face. "And I don't want a face full of glass."

Elizabeth and I turned away as Gord smashed a glove through the windshield. Kept punching it along its length to loosen the shattered shield from its frame, then pushed the whole thing out onto the hood. It slipped across the steel to the ground. He did the same thing to the back window.

"Might want to put your seatbelts on," Gord added, something we all had forgotten, a little distracted by adrenaline and fear.

My heart pounded and sweat slicked my forehead. "I think I'm shitting my pants."

Elizabeth helped her brother crank the keychain, and the engine roared. We three stared at the log ramp, hoped the wall of the house was thin, that we wouldn't be crashing into a steel vault on the other side. The r.p.ms shot up and the growling engine rocked the truck like a cradle. Gord jammed the stick in 'drive' and we were all thrown back against our seats.

Tires spun on grass, the truck lurching out of the copse, Gord turning the wheel to aim the massive tires at the firewood ramp. We hit it harder than we had expected—the front popped high, but the wheels still hung low enough that they smashed through the porch bannister. The front fender came down hard to hammer through the wall of the house, back wheels spinning to push us through, seatbelts digging into our waists and chests.

Wood and plumbing fell around the truck cab and we ripped through electrical wires. We hit a second wall soon after smashing through the exterior—into a pantry of some sort—jars and cans bursting off exploded shelves, some tumbling in through our open windows. Gord slammed the gear stick into reverse, wrenched the wheel hand-over-hand (or glove-over-glove), tore the shit out of more of the wall, then popped it in drive again and aimed the smashed and buckled steel of the hood through a doorway. Smoke from the whirring wheels grew into thick blue and grey clouds in the small room, making us cough and choke, but the truck easily burst through the door frame, the wrinkled hood flying off, and we sped into the vast reception room with partiers still going strong. They probably each had a Black Betty nestled in their bellies.

I glanced over at Elizabeth and Gord. She had stayed ducked within the cloak the whole time and was unscathed. Gord had one glove on the wheel, the other holding a wing of his jacket up to his face. I had my head tucked into my jacket and was half slipped down by the floorboard. I had been there before.

People screamed and some tried to get out of the way. Others cheered and laughed and punched fists into the air. Doped up, looking for any excitement, may have even thought we were rowdy guests looking to make the party more memorable. Some people ignored us completely, and continued fucking on the floor, locked in their ecstasy. A pair of them fucking doggie style were the first ones Gord bounced

# THE BRIDE STRIPPED BARE

the truck over. But they lived. I glanced behind us as we passed over them and the guy was still fucking the girl doggy style, both of their feet and shins crushed, the girl's head smacked hard and bloody. I had forgotten that the truck was jacked up pretty high. If Gord wanted to kill, he'd have to aim with the wheels, not the hood. I told him so.

"Hey, you try driving with crab claws!" he joked and whooped out a laugh.

The truck skidded on the polished wooden floor and slid sideways, sending candle tapers flying, slamming three people against a wall. Two of them began to die with smiles stretching their bloody mouths just outside my window. The engine revved and the side of the truck scraped the dead along with it until the bodies sagged and fell beneath the tires.

Gord cranked the smoking wheels, aiming for any fool who stayed still long enough when there was a monster truck barreling up behind them. He angled the left wheel toward the pair still fucking happily for all to see in the middle of the room. Wanting to correct a mistake.

The big truck wheel bounced over their bodies, crushed their bones into one another—probably made them cum. Gord was burning rubber tracks in curlicues across the floor, the fat tailpipes towering up from either end of the cab chugging smoke like a locomotive. Neither Elizabeth nor I had fired our weapons, but I figured the chance was coming.

The truck skidded to slam its side smashing through tables and a stack of chairs, making people run. Chased a woman who had her bear cloak wrenched off when someone stepped on it. Her arms hooked backwards following the cloak and her feet left the floor. Landed on her back, cracked her head, looked up at the ceiling only to see a tire tread smear the face off her skull.

Gord pulled a tight donut to rev after the man who had stepped on her coat. A chunky guy with small stubby legs, wearing no pants, pissing himself as he ran. He kept glancing back as the monster truck zoomed up behind him, stopped in his tracks, raised his hands to stop the behemoth—and bounced off the grill. He arched high and flew long like a football, backflipped in mid-air, legs flailing in two directions like a skier's broken skis and crashed into a huddle of people who were trying to hide behind an upturned table.

The truck's tire cracked the table into splinters—seatbelts wrenching us back—crushing the mass of clinging flesh against the wall. Gord jammed it into reverse and used the back bumper as a ram for a while, didn't want to kill the engine too quickly.

I put an arm behind Elizabeth as all three of us craned our heads around, gas to the floor, the rear bumper trying to nail a guy, but he dove out of the way. Gord cranked the wheel and the truck spun 360 degrees, halted just before smacking into a tall skinny guy with long greasy hair, bear cloak wedged open by his erect penis, his nose and upper lip powdered red.

He smiled, gave a peace sign with his fingers, and used the half second when Gord was clicking from reverse to drive to leap up onto the bed and race to the back window. I tried to cry out for Elizabeth, but I could only get out two syllables of her name before the long-haired bastard grabbed her hair and half wrenched her backwards through the glassless window.

She screamed and clawed at his hands, but he held on, pinned his steel shoes against the cab to get leverage, both hands twisted in her hair, wrenching her head back. The shotgun slipped from her hands to the floorboards.

Other people, now brave, rushed to the truck, hands reaching into Gord and me from either side, a man sprawled over the engine holding onto the windshield wipers. Gord kept a foot on the brake as he lifted up the shotgun and wedged a thumb against the trigger. Not good aim, but it was a shotgun. He levelled it up onto the dashboard and fired

# THE BRIDE STRIPPED BARE

both barrels, blew a cavern through the head of the man on the engine. I aimed the rifle across a gap in front of Gord, told him not to move, and quick-fired three shots to smack away the hands and bodies of people hanging onto his side mirror, clawing at him.

Then I aimed out the back window, but there was no way to get a clear shot at the greasy hippie holding onto Elizabeth, using her as a shield.

"Keep driving!" I yelled to Gord.

He stomped on the gas, spun the wheel, and swerved serpentine across the dance floor, trying to fling away anyone still clinging on.

I didn't have the time to reload the shotgun. And the rifle was too damn long for the inside of a truck. I dug a hand behind Gord's back as he drove and pulled out the Magnum.

"Hey, not too frisky now—we're just friends."

I was watching Elizabeth and her captor through the back window, the barrel of the Magnum held up just in case it went off and I hit the wrong person, waiting for a shot. The truck slammed into something and jerked away, scraping the bumper chrome along a wall by the sound of it. Screams erupted, became static, background noise, easily ignored. People ran in every direction, their hair on fire from the candles we smashed every time we moved.

Elizabeth had been right—it was *exactly* like a video game, or a horror novel.

The guy holding Elizabeth's hair swayed with the movement of the truck, twisting her head back and forth, in and out of my line of sight. I needed to increase my chances of hitting him and not her. Popped off my seat belt and crawled through the back windshield, the Magnum coming with me, of course.

The truck swayed left and right, bodies smacking off either side of the truck bed, tires hopping over flesh speed bumps, crashing through tables of half-eaten food and glasses of wine. So it took a while for me to get to the hippie. The long-haired fucker never stopped dope-smiling the whole time. Lips wide, teeth open, laughter at the back of his throat. Gord slammed on the brakes for whatever reason and Elizabeth and the hippie flew toward me. Passed me. Both of their heads through the back window. Gord glanced over, took a glove off the wheel, and punched a hole through the hippie's forehead. Gave him an instant lobotomy. Elizabeth pulled her hair out of the bastard's grip, slipped on a few glass jam jars over to me and took the Magnum from my hands. The hippie lay face-down, sliding, over the bed of the truck. She blasted a hole through the back of his head. What was left of it. Basically, he had a neck stump and half a chin left. The blood made the bed even more slippery.

I grabbed her around the waist and hoisted her back to the window so she could climb through and I could climb in after her.

"We got a headless hippie in the back," I shouted to Gord.

He laughed. "We could open the tailgate and let him out, but that might invite more in."

An older man popped up beside Gord, wagged his split tongue at him, pupils like pinpricks, smelled like piss. Gord pulled a glove off the wheel to punch, but his metal fist glanced off the man's ear. The old bastard wouldn't let go. The truck slewed, shattered a punch bowl of red dust, and someone fired a shot at the right front fender. Elizabeth took the steering wheel so that Gord could use both hands to hammer the teeth out of his visitor's mouth. The man still didn't let go. So Gord jammed the cone of his glove down grandpa's throat until his nostrils expanded and he began to choke. His hands finally slipped off and he dropped, the truck's back right tire bouncing over his corpse.

Elizabeth still had the Magnum in hand. I rifled through the glove compartment and ammo boxes, did what I could to reload the shotgun and rifle, checked to ensure that the Magnum was fully loaded, six rounds. Elizabeth scratched the back of her head, and a fist of hair detached. She watched it fall between her fingers.

# THE BRIDE STRIPPED BARE

"That fucker!" She grumbled and swore. Snatched the Magnum back, kept her body turned enough to be able to glance out the front and rear easily. Gun tight in her hand, she waited, wanting another person to jump into the cab—she was looking to kill. It was so easy after the first one, terrible to say.

But no potential victims took a chance anymore. There were few people left alive in the room. Many crushed against walls or mashed into smashed furniture, or pressed hard against the floor, bodies crisscrossed with tire marks, limbs severed and scattered…and blood smeared in abstract designs across the entire dance floor and up the walls. The truck was the better weapon than the guns could ever be.

A bear skin moved. A body rose up from under it, crawled on all fours along the floor, paws slipping on blood and a piece of scalp, a woman in her forties scratching out the last of her existence, trying to find safety from the elephant in the room. Us.

The truck idled as we watched her crawl. She stopped to cough up blood, vomit out a thin stream of yellow-brown bile, then she kept crawling. I aimed the rifle at her through my window.

"Too many goddamn bears in this house!" Gord said. "Time for Goldilocks to get payback!"

Elizabeth's eyes were slits, looking into mine. "I want her. She's mine."

Gord kept his foot on the brake as Elizabeth and I snapped off our seatbelts. I took the rifle with me as I joined Elizabeth in her hunt. Jars of jam and marmalade and pickled vegetables fell out of the truck with us.

Following Elizabeth, I gazed at the damage done to the truck. Crunched metal, the stink of oil smoke rising through the exposed engine, green coolant pissing to the floor, blood smeared across the paint job, gristle and brain wedged in tire treads. A pig-in-a-blanket sat in one cracked open headlight.

Elizabeth ignored the damage, stepped a slow march toward the crawling woman, gun barrel pointed down at the end of a rigid arm. Gunslinger eyes. Gord and I watched for anyone who may have come back to life to rush us, but we let Elizabeth enjoy her kill.

She stood over the woman, watching her crawl, leaving behind a trail of bloody hand prints, until the woman finally noticed someone looming over her. Stopped her slow trek and craned her bruised face and bloody teeth up to see Elizabeth looking down.

"Please," the woman begged in a soft voice. "Please don't...I don't want to die."

A thousand-yard stare gazed down as the Magnum angled towards the woman's forehead.

"You or me, bitch...somebody's always gotta die."

The woman closed her eyelids to wait for the bullet blast...but it never came.

"Elizabeth!" a male voice called.

"Gordy!" a female voice called.

Both echoing from high up by the darkened ceiling, but we couldn't see them until the voices screamed and the bodies dropped out of the darkness.

Ropes unraveled in the air, ankles bound by shackles, wrists tied behind their backs, ball gags slipped down to collar their necks, each wearing a noose. The drop was too quick—impossible for the mind to register what the eyes saw clearly.

Not until the ropes snapped taut, nooses jerked hard, heads popping off like dandelions, spinning end over end as the bodies crashed to the floor like stringless puppets, did we all know who the man and woman were. Gord rushed from the truck to inspect the dead with us. We all stepped to their upturned heads laying on the floor far from their bodies, eyes still open, horror frozen on their faces, blood forming pools around the ragged stumps of their necks still attached. Pieces of spinal column were still hanging by sinews from the heads.

# THE BRIDE STRIPPED BARE

Ma and Pa.

Why in the hell did we think we could've saved them from the family? I thought.

None of us could scream or weep or yell—the sight was too foreign; no part of us held a language that could decipher what we stared at. I'm sure it was even more horrific for Elizabeth and Gord to see the torn heads of their parents staring up at them from the floor. The body and mind of both of them diving down deep into shock.

I stepped away from the decapitations, tried to shake the images from my mind, trying to not let the shock settle too much over me. Gord and Elizabeth both stared down, the gun hanging loosely in Elizabeth's hand, her arm swinging slightly.

The woman who had begged for her life to be spared now had her mercy. And she took advantage of it.

I stood behind Elizabeth and Gord, the rifle held loosely, trying not to look at the heads on the floor. But in my peripheral vision I saw the crawling woman muster her last bit of strength to lunge for the gun in Elizabeth's hand. She easily grabbed it, rolled away, slipped and shuffled to her feet, body bent and pained from too many unseen injuries. But if she was going to die, she would take someone with her. The last person who had tried to kill her.

Well, second-to-last.

She raised the Magnum and Elizabeth just stood and looked at her, not comprehending what was real and what was fantasy. So she couldn't react, caught facing the barrel of a loaded, powerful weapon. Blood dripped from the woman's smile.

I raised the rifle like a hunter sighting his prey, eye aiming down the barrel, marking my target. Squeezed the trigger. The bullet entered the woman's left temple and brain and blood and bone sprayed out of her right temple. She craned over and fell like a Douglas Fir chainsawed at its base. The Magnum skittered across the floor, dragging blood behind it.

"Well done," a female voice announced.

We looked up at the stage where I had become a married man to see Venus and two other women applauding. Venus wore a new white bear fur, and the burns scarring her face had almost entirely healed. Her hair had grown back, reaching the length of a brushcut, back to its original color, red. None of the drugs that Gord and I had attacked her with seemed to have an effect. An addict rarely felt their customary poison, needing more and more. Venus' tolerance must have been beyond human, and her magic must've protected her from many methods of assault. Her missing eye was growing back in, smaller than the other, about the size of a dog's eye. The two women, white and black, on either side of her both wore brown bear furs, bear's heads dropped down their backs. They were the last remaining bridesmaids, neither with a scratch on them. They made me recall the maid I had killed.

"The three of you have survived the House of the Dead—I'm impressed," Venus said. She put hands on her hips, pushing her cloak open to expose her nude body, branded with the many family symbols. "Perhaps if mom and dad had been with you, they could've survived as well."

"You fucking cunt!" Elizabeth screamed with pure fury, snapping out of her shock, racing for the Magnum lying in blood.

The two bridesmaids formed a line, one behind the other, and Venus closed her cloak to wrap her body, then stepped in front of her maids. Elizabeth spun and fired all six rounds at Venus until the gun clicked empty. Only two of the bullets had hit Venus, but they didn't move her, merely appeared as small black starbursts staining the white fur. The gun wavered in Elizabeth's hand for a few moments until her arm sagged and her rage began to wane. Venus put hands on her hips again to expose her body, and the bridesmaids stepped out from behind her. Looped their arms with Venus', lightly kissed either of her cheeks, then both said, loud enough for all of us to hear, "Thank you, Mistress."

# THE BRIDE STRIPPED BARE

Venus smiled down at me. "Care to take a couple shots, husband?"

I let the rifle barrel sag to point at the floor, kept my eyes away from my wife, wondering if she would just let us all walk out of the house and take our chances heading home.

She paced the stage with the bridesmaids strolling arm-in-arm at her sides.

"I don't know how you managed to get through the dead and live to tell about it, but my father told me you were headed that way, so we let you go. I'll assume my brother failed to stop you as well."

"Poppy's fucking dead!" Gord said. "We barbecued him and his pet bear rug!"

Venus bowed her head and nodded at nothing as her stroll slowed. She shrugged, "Oh well, men are the weaker of the species, can't be helped." She looked at Elizabeth and smiled. "I like your cloak, Elizabeth. Queenhood becomes you. Perhaps you'd like to join me in ruling this family. Do you like to eat pussy?" She stopped and raised an eyebrow. "Kevin does."

Elizabeth grit her teeth and stepped to the front of the stage. I rushed after her, holding her arm, hoping to prevent her from climbing up to confront Venus. There were too many members of Elizabeth and Gord's family dead or lost to add herself to their numbers.

"You fucking piece of shit! You killed my parents! We burned that last shithole—the Swamp Hotel—to the ground—and we'll burn this one too! I'll wipe you and your psycho-fuck family off the face of the Earth!"

I held her from lunging onto the stage. Gord stood and looped his arm through hers. The three of us gazed up at Venus, who must've enjoyed looking down her nose at us.

"You set yourself an impossible task, but I do like your spunk." Venus winked. "I could use a girl like you. The family could use all of you—you've proven yourselves stronger, more powerful than ninety percent of the entire family. We need more like you in our gene pool."

She licked her lips and smiled down at Gord. "You even managed to slice off a piece of my tail. It's been done so rarely; I'm always impressed by those who manage it."

Gord sneered at her. "You lost your power, didn't you?"

"How so?"

"You can't change into a bear."

Venus stifled a chuckle, then glanced at her bridesmaids, giving them a signal. Venus turned to show her back to us as the maids lifted the fur cloak over their mistress's waist. The tail had grown back. Not as thick, about the diameter of a rat's tail, pink and raw like new growth. It was long enough to reach the bottom of her ass cheeks but would probably keep growing to reach the backs of her knees again.

The maids dropped the cloak and Venus turned to face us with a smug smile.

"That means nothing," Gord challenged. "Take away that cloak and you've got fuck all. Why'd your two slave bitches duck behind you when my sister shot you?"

Anger boiled inside Venus, her fists clenching, muscles writhing along her jawline. She threw off the arms of the bridesmaids, ripped open their cloaks to expose their breasts.

"Self-regeneration for this family is child's play! You are swooned by parlor tricks, Gordon! Would you like to see real power? The power that I hold over all of my 'slave bitches'?" she mocked. She raised two hands of ten long, sharp fingernails. "Here is true power!"

Turning to face the maids, Venus stabbed her spiked hands simultaneously into the bridesmaids' breastbones, cracked ribs and tore through ligaments, her hands twisting as they dug deep into the women's chests. Fingers curled inward and squeezed before Venus wrenched back her arms.

The faces of the maids swooned with ecstasy, wept tears of joy. Bloody beating hearts were cupped in each of Venus' hands as she

# THE BRIDE STRIPPED BARE

turned to face us again, the maids collapsing bodily on either side of her.

Venus bit into the pomegranates of her bridesmaids' hearts, red juice slipping into the deep valley of her cleavage. With a chin greased with shiny crimson, she swallowed the morsels, then said, "They were my sisters. Gordon, you should show your sister how much you love her by eating her heart. Why don't you do it for me right now? Such an act gives you power over your, or any, *psycho-fuck* family by making you the worst of them all. It is evil that keeps me alive, forever growing stronger. Something you will never have!"

She tossed the remaining chunks of heart off the stage at us, and again proudly displayed her nudity, letting her cloak slip entirely from her shoulders as she turned to show us her tail. It had grown thicker and longer in a matter of seconds, now waggling to tickle her upper thighs, no longer pink, but as red as a bleeding heart.

I swallowed a hard lump, knew none of us should let Venus have her moment on the stage, had to focus back to our only real goal.

"Just let us go," I pleaded. "This is over. We don't want any part of it. We'll go home and never say a word to anyone about you or your family."

She squatted down at the edge of the stage in front of me, holding her knees spread wide, the tail curling up, writhing along her pudendum slit. It grew, flexing like a worm.

"That sounds like a great offer, Chris, but I'll have to ask my daddy first." She called off. "Daddy, they don't like our party and want to go home."

We turned to see Gorman and Kevin enter from where the truck had crashed through the doorway into the room, stepping over bodies. With one eye socket gouged into a black hollow, Gorman carried the old piece of Venus' tail in one hand, slapping it against the other hand as he climbed the stairs at one end of the stage. Stopped to look down at his *other* daughters laying with dark and bloody holes in her chests.

Venus stood and a change came over her face, staring at the piece of tail her father held. She met his eyes, took a step back from him.

"Is it wrong for a father to eat his daughter?" he asked, taking a step toward Venus, who edged farther away from him.

She watched his eye as he raised the tail to his open mouth, Gord's bite marks still at its tapered end. "It won't work," she countered. "The matriarchal lineage of this family won't change if you eat it."

Gorman stepped on the white bear cloak, made a point of wiping his feet on it. Put the narrow end of the dead tail between his teeth and snipped off a morsel. Chewed and smiled with his cheeks bulging.

"Perhaps not, dear daughter." He swallowed the piece, snipped off another chunk and spoke with his words muted. "But I have a plan. You'll love it…wish you'd thought of it yourself." He swallowed, patted his stomach, then snapped his fingers over his shoulder.

Kevin stepped up behind him, took the shoulder of Gorman's red-and-black striped cloak, helped the priest remove his clothing while the old father continued taking bites of the tail. He turned around to show his back to Venus, smoothing a hand across the small of his naked back, pressing fingertips into muscle.

"Can you see anything yet?" he asked his daughter as she stared at her father's back. "I think I can feel a small bump, like a spinal bone, trying to push through. I'm giving birth from the top of my ass!" he laughed as he turned to face Venus, snipped off another bite of tail, chewed rapidly as his eyes stared deeply into hers. "What do you need to make gunpowder?" He ticked off ingredients with his fingers. "Sulfur, saltpeter, and charcoal…mix any *two* of these ingredients and you have nothing. Mix all three in the correct measurements…and you can blow up the world!" A bite, jaw muscles writhing under parchment skin, his molars grinding the flesh of his daughter. A single line of blood wept from his missing eye socket. He raised a finger. "I am an exulted member of this family. Male, yes, but that shouldn't hinder me anymore

# THE BRIDE STRIPPED BARE

in my purpose." A second finger joined the first as he smiled and held up the remaining length of tail. "Second ingredient...and it is delicious!"

He took another bite and stepped off the cloak toward his daughter. Venus stepped back, body tense, waiting for him to strike. Glancing over his shoulder, she saw that Kevin hadn't moved, still had the priest's cloak in hand, so it wasn't likely that he was part of whatever plan Gorman had for his daughter's destruction.

"So what's the third ingredient, you're wondering? And I wondered that too. For a long long time." He smiled, eyebrows raising in delight as he nodded. "Yes, my dear, your father—the man you are so much like—has been thinking about doing away with your power—if not you as well—since you were born. Shortly after I killed your mother and fed her to you, I entertained the idea of killing all of my family members. Taking power for myself. The males of this family know they will always be subjected to the will of the females. Because that's how it has always been. So they don't resist their lot in life, become complacent. So, too, do the females never question their right to rule." Another piece of tail went into his cheeks. "But I am old, have seen and done so much throughout many eras of Mankind, and I thought I could do one monumental act before I died. Create an earthquake that would shatter the foundation of tradition in this family and inspire every generation after me." His incisors snipped off another piece of dead flesh, had about three inches of tail left to devour. "A sea change from matriarchy to patriarchy. It would, of course, entail getting rid of the queen first." He motioned to Gord. "This wonderful *potential* husband of yours did me a favor by cutting off your tail. It had happened before, but you knew to protect the severed limb. I knew I would have to strike quickly because there would only be a small window of opportunity before you grew it back." Another inch went between his molars. I gazed at his tailbone. Difficult to see if anything had grown—it could've been a shadow, a play of the light, or it could've been a growing bump. "I just had to calculate my three ingredients before I took a chance at overthrowing you. And now I have them." A bite, and one-inch left.

"You have nothing, old man," Venus hissed, holding her ground. "Your mind is going—senility setting in. A disease of the outsiders will be your death. There are no ingredients that can give you the power of a woman. If there were, you would've tried something before now."

He popped the last tail piece into his mouth, smiled as he wiped his hands. "That's true, but we haven't made sweet incestuous love for so long. You've been so busy hunting down your grooms, turning them into your pie-eyed, lust-driven, breeding slaves that I've rarely had a moment alone with you, my precious one. You have protected your tail very well…with your cloak, your grooms, and every female of our lineage. So how can a father possibly get a piece of his daughter's sweet ass?"

Venus smiled, shook her head, let loose a half-hearted laugh as she put hands on her hips, proudly displaying herself to her father. "You're as stupid as a husband. You thought that if you had one more chance to enjoy this—" she fluttered hands down the length of her body "—that you'd have the opportunity to cut off my tail? To destroy me!" Her chest trembled as she laughed. "You're thinking too much with your ego. Like all men."

Gorman sucked his finger and winked. "You may be right. You always are, my love. But any man will tell you that the way to a woman's ass is through her heart." His body became rigid and a pause held on the stage. Then Gorman suddenly yelled, "Now!"

Gitch and Skood rushed out from behind the stage curtain. Gitch's skin showed burns and still bore the scars I had given him—his face mangled, jaw twisted to one side, tears in the flesh having been sewn together with copper wire—and he wasn't as stable on his feet as Skood

# THE BRIDE STRIPPED BARE

was. It was as though Gitch's legs were broken but he still ran on them, ignoring terrible pain, trying to overcome his many wounds. His face twitched; hands shaky as he held a knife.

Skood held Venus. Pinning her arms back, fighting against her writhing, watching Gitch attempt to wield the knife. Venus' new tail had lengthened more to lash against Gitch's hands, then tucked deep between her buttocks and lay flat against her abdomen. Gitch's hands shook and he didn't seem able to manipulate his fingers very well, thumbs frozen into a hooks, making his hands look like a monkey's paws. He tried to pull the tail out enough to slip the blade under, but it was impossible in the struggle.

Gorman stepped toward his daughter as he yelled at Gitch, "Just cut it at the goddamn root!"

Father then pressed a hand against his daughter's cleavage, pushing her breasts aside, using all of his weight to press his hand through her chest, trying to crack her ribs by sheer force, her heart as his goal.

Venus kicked out and landed a foot into her father's stomach, dropping him to the stage. Skood had pulled Venus back too late, trying to make room for Gitch to get a solid grip on the base of her tail. She kicked backwards, punching her heel into Gitch's face, sending a muted scream up his throat as he stumbled back, copper wire tearing his lips and cheeks.

Venus' tail snapped back to rise off her tailbone and shook like the tail of a rattlesnake. Her arms and legs lengthened, claws growing from her fingernails, face contorting into a bear's snout and jaws as thick hair grew rapidly across her bare skin.

Easily, she broke Skood's grip on her, spun on her heel and swiped a paw through the air. Skood's face flew across the room. A second swipe of a paw gouged a hollow out of his skull, taking with it three-quarters of his brain. The remaining piece of brain in the bowl of his skull sluiced down the length of his body and slapped wetly on the floor. Then his body crumpled after it.

Gord, Elizabeth and I started backing away from the stage. Gord headed back toward the truck, I headed toward the hole in the wall where we had come in, and Elizabeth was just backing away, pulling her cloak tighter around her body.

It didn't take long before we came to our senses, the other two following me out of the room, but we saw something happen on stage before we got the hell out of there.

After swatting off Skood's face like a piece of tissue paper, Venus cured the pain in Gitch's jaw by severing his head with a left hook. And she hadn't stopped growing. Paws the size of hubcaps, head ballooning to match the one that had hung from the ceiling in the House of the Dead, that Poppy straddled, standing on her hind legs until she reached halfway to the ceiling of the room.

Gorman backed away, tripped on the legs of his other bridesmaid daughters, sat down hard beside them. Saw the remaining pieces of their hearts on the floor where we had stood. He leapt off the stage and drove the heart chunks into his mouth like apples from Eden, taking huge bites, chewing and swallowing as fast as he could, feeling the small of his back as he kept an eye on Venus.

Consuming his third and final ingredient. But for what?

His spinal column grew…one inch, two inches, four, ten, fifteen inches—he crammed the last pieces of the two hearts into his mouth, cheeks bulging, molars grinding down muscle, swallowing as quickly as he could without choking, having to hold heart chunks into his mouth while he chewed, pieces pushed out but then shoved back in… twenty inches, twenty-five, thirty…

He swallowed the last bite, mouth smeared in blood, chest heaving as he pulled in air through his nostrils, eyes on his daughter as he backed away. He bumped into Kevin, who had followed his master off the stage, waiting to be commanded.

# THE BRIDE STRIPPED BARE

"Get out of my way, you fool!" Gorman growled at Kevin, pushing passed him.

Elizabeth yelled "Kevin!" and he looked at her, the spell momentarily broken, but to no use.

Venus fell back to all fours, shaking the room, her paws punching holes through the stage floor. Kevin turned his eyes to her. She growled a storm of noise into his face before crushing his head and half his torso between her jaws, swallowing his screams. Spat out his severed head and torn body with a twist of her neck, throwing it high and far to slap down at Elizabeth's feet.

I grabbed her and the three of us ran toward the crashed-through doorway in the wall, jumping over bodies sprawled across the floor, righting ourselves when we slipped in swathes of blood.

I glanced back before we raced through the doorway to see Gorman's body and face distorting, growing, his fur cloak expanding to cover his entire body, but the red and black of the priest cloak bleaching to white. Was it the color of royalty? The hollow of his eye socket remained black.

He moved out of the way of his daughter's swinging claws, staying far back from her until he too grew into an immense beast towering on his hind legs.

They were exactly alike in size and dimension and the color of the fur. Twins. Father and daughter taking on their true forms, fighting for supremecy in front of the stage.

We didn't stay to see which one emerged the victor.

# Chapter 30

The sun had risen higher in the clear sky as we raced to Poppy's truck, then sped down the highway back to town. A ghost town. Of all the inhabitants at the wedding, many dead, who knew what their true numbers were and when they would re-group to hunt us down? We didn't feel safe in town or outside it and didn't know how far we would have to go until we ever felt safe again.

I drove. Gord told me to head back to his apartment.

"What if someone's there?" I asked.

"Don't worry, they're all at the party. Besides, I wouldn't mind seeing more of them die, would you?"

"We gotta get out of here—who knows if they'll head after us," Elizabeth said, glancing back down the road.

"We *are* getting out of here," Gord responded, glancing in his passenger side mirror. "We'll go to the airport, take our chances there." He smiled and wrinkled his scarred forehead. "But we might need different clothes—and maybe some passports—before they let us on a plane."

I slowed the truck as we entered the town proper, every door locked, store signs flipped to *Closed*, no vehicles parked at meters along Main Street or down any side streets, not even a single dog barking. The sun was shining, and it was a beautiful day.

The town was dead, and we had, happily, killed it.

# THE BRIDE STRIPPED BARE

We hoped, anyway.

I pulled into the small parking spot behind Gord's building and left the keys in the ignition. Climbed the stairs to his apartment. He looked at his hands, then at us.

We all started laughing.

"Fuck me," he said.

"Lost your keys?" I asked.

"Lost my fucking hands!" He sighed and shook his head at the locked apartment door. "Stand back," he warned us.

Elizabeth and I stepped down a few steps as Gord swung a metal glove above the lock of his door. The vest still worked. The door crashed inward; the lock punched into the room.

"Who needs keys when you have claws?" he joked, and we followed him inside.

The sandbag of cocaine was still split open and spilled on the coffee table. I glanced around the room, felt like I hadn't been inside the apartment in years. A miracle that any of us had made it back.

"All my clothes are in the mansion," Elizabeth said, then stopped and stared at her brother, sighing disappointed. "Gordy, really? You still doing that shit after all we've been through?"

Gord pulled his face out of spilled coke, powder puffed in and around his nose. "I've had a bad night, sis, cut me some slack. I think I'm building a tolerance—not good. If you're not too picky, I've got some sweatpants—I think they belong to Venus—and tons of t-shirts. I'd rather not make too many stops before we hit the airport."

"My passport," Elizabeth said.

"Shit."

There was no way in hell we were going back to the mansion to grab Elizabeth's passport. There were two giant bears having a fight there, to put it mildly.

I asked, "Do you have your driver's license?"

She raised her arms and gave me a look that reflected my idiocy. "Where would I keep it?"

"Shit." I looked at Gord. "Got any ideas?"

He shrugged. "Fuck the airport—we drive. Keep driving until we get Elizabeth home, or we get somewhere safe. We'll deal with paperwork once we can breathe again."

Elizabeth used a pillow to wipe powder off Gord's nose. "You're not going to keep us safe if you keep your nose white."

Sorrow fell across Gord's face as he looked into his sister's eyes. He touched his gloves lightly to her arms, swallowed a few times as he mustered the strength to speak. "Look, Elizabeth...I'm sorry. Everything you said about Venus brainwashing me was true. But that's no excuse. I can't excuse what I did to you. You don't have to forgive me...but I couldn't forgive myself if I never said I was sorry."

Tears rose to her eyes as she nodded, then cleared her throat. "It'll take a while. Might need a therapist or two. But eventually, one day, I'll be able to put the past in the past and not let it haunt my present and future. I survived this night...I'm one tough cookie."

"You are," Gord whispered back.

They hugged and held onto one another for a while. I let them have their moment by searching Gord's room for clothing we could all wear. Throwing shirts and pants out of drawers and closets—no need to keep the place clean since we were never coming back. Pair of jeans and a t-shirt, socks, and a pair of dress shoes I found in Gord's closet, which he had probably only worn once, hated, thrown into the back of his closet. If they fit me, they were probably too small for him. If I knew him, he rarely kept receipts, and never returned anything.

I dug my passport and wallet out of my luggage but didn't want anything else. Travelling light in these circumstances was the right idea. No baggage check, get on the plane, get in the air as soon as possible. Within the country, we shouldn't need passports. But if an airport guard insisted, then maybe we could all take a train back East.

# THE BRIDE STRIPPED BARE

We all dressed as quickly as possible, Elizabeth having to help her brother on with everything due to his hands. Gord said he wanted to keep the jacket and vest on, for protection. We didn't argue with him, but Elizabeth and I didn't want any reminders of the family. We dressed like normal people, and it made us feel much better, cleaner, lighter. The bear fur cloak was left in front of Gord's bookshelf.

We still didn't know what we were going to tell any guard at the airport about Gord's hands. Disability. The gloves were a form of treatment. His scorched face should confirm the extent of his injuries. If the guards x-rayed the gloves, they'd only see Gord's hands beneath, no drugs or weapons. They might buy it.

Back in the truck, I pulled out onto Main Street, about to speed out of town forever. Thinking silently: so this is how a town becomes a ghost town? Will this place ever be populated again? Hopefully not.

I looked into the rearview mirror.

In the distance, where the town began, something lumbered on all fours down the middle of the street.

"Oh shit," I said in a hushed voice.

Elizabeth and Gord turned back to look at the town speeding away in my mirror.

"Get the fuck out of here, Chris," Elizabeth muttered, fear lacing her words. "Get the fuck away from here as fast as you can."

"No, turn around," Gord said, glancing from his sideview mirror to the road ahead, gloves tapping the door frame.

"Gordy!" Elizabeth snapped in panic. "She'll kill us."

He looked into his sister's frightened eyes without blinking. I saw sadness in his gaze. "Not if we kill her first. She'll never stop hunting us, especially if the family *really* is around the world." His eyes shot to me. "Chris, turn around. I'm serious."

I had a terrible feeling that I knew what he was thinking of doing. We had been friends for a long time—like a married couple, we could almost read each other's thoughts. I swallowed a lump in my throat and cranked the wheel, slowly headed back into town.

The bear wasn't running, possibly injured, its slow heavy steps pounding the road. Still a giant not to be trifled with. But a slow bear was still a hell of a threat.

We came to the main intersection of town, gas stations on either side of the road. "Stop here," Gord said.

"Gordy—what are you—" Elizabeth began, but her brother was already out of the truck, jogging towards the bear.

Elizabeth and I watched him, hearts pounding in our chests, skin cold. The bear wasn't moving any faster now that Gord was out of the truck. His jog veered off the center of the street to one of the gas stations. We watched him go up to the locked door of the store, smash a glove through the glass, batter the door, and let himself in.

We couldn't see what he was doing, but he was behind the counter. I wondered if he had ever worked in a gas station, knew his way around one. Possible, since we had lost track of each other for five years. Was that really what he was doing when he met Venus, instead of working in an auto shop? I reflected how he had never mentioned his job since I'd arrived, not in any email either. No wonder he got suckered in easily by the bride's charms and money.

A few seconds passed then he was outside, headed to the nearest pump, smashed both gloves down hard onto the hose where it connected to the pumps. Broke it off in one shot. Maybe that was why he kept the jacket and vest on, for strength as well as protection. Gas poured out. He did the same to the three other pumps, gasoline flooding the gas bay.

The bear neared. Blood stained its white fur. Gord jogged across the road to the other station, smashed four pumps, spilled gasoline. But this time when he broke his way into the store, he came out with a fat cigar in his mouth, thankfully unlit. Gord's melted metal boots splashed through liquid rainbows.

# THE BRIDE STRIPPED BARE

He headed back to the truck.

Stood at the driver's side open window and looked with sad eyes at Elizabeth and me. One thumb curled around the cigar to take it out of his mouth as he said, "Sis, I'm sorry. I've been a selfish shit my whole life. I want to be a good person for once, but I'm not sure I even know how. I don't know if this is the right thing to do, but I feel it's a *good* thing to do. I think this will help your wounds to heal. I got you and Chris, mom and dad and Kev, into this shit. I can at least get the two of you out of it. I love you, Liz."

Elizabeth wept, her whole body trembling.

Gord looked over at me and smiled. "I've never been good with women. Understatement of the century, I know. Sorry I got you into this shit, Chris. Take care of my baby sister."

I nodded, my eyes burning, throat filled with sand. "I will. I love you, Gordy."

"Love you too, buddy."

We hugged through the window as Elizabeth got out of the truck and ran around the hood to embrace her brother. Looked up at him with tear-stained eyes.

"We can all escape. Your wounds will heal. You don't have to do this."

He wedged the cigar into the corner of his mouth. "Yeah I do. You're the last of our family. You need to be free. This is freedom… for all of us."

He flipped a glove, palm up, and showed me the Zippo he had stolen from one of the gas station stores, clasped between his thumb and the rest of the glove. Winked at me.

"Light me up, would ya, buddy?"

I took the lighter and flicked up a flame. He puffed the stogie to life.

"Time to go bear hunting," he said between puffs.

He strolled away with a beaming smile. Elizabeth hung onto my door, so I got out to wrap my arm around her, held her close as we watched Gord walk down the middle of the street.

Two pools of gasoline had grown from either gas station bay to meet in the main intersection of town. Gord stopped his shoes in the pool.

Yelled at the bear, "Come on, bitch! Your old hubby needs some good lovin'!"

The bear sniffed the air, surrounded by the sweet stench of gasoline, distinguishing the smell of a human being—prey—within the fumes. Gord waited patiently.

Venus roared and reared up onto her hind legs, towering over Gord. We could see puffs of smoke rise off the crown of his head and sail away. The pool swelled to slip under the bear's paws. Gord took a few more puffs, then let the cigar drop off his lips.

Fire climbed the bear, swallowed her, plumes of flame bursting off both upraised arms. Her head burned blue and white, black smoke billowing from her mouth as she howled out the last of her rage.

Blue fire shot out like tracer bullets to either side of where Gord stood. Rushed into either gas station, erupted forests of flame framing the road.

Explosions from either side of the intersection burst across the street and wiped away two lives. Thick smoke rose from towering flames, fuel pouring and pouring from activated pumps which wouldn't be turned off until all of the gas was gone.

We drove away, Elizabeth shuddering as she wept, me with a blank stare seeing nothing but the unending road, a problem tickled at the back of my brain. But I was in too much shock and sorrow to contemplate it fully.

The bear had only one eye.

# Epilogue

We broke into the houses of the town and stole money. No one was home, of course. Stole credit cards and found the driver's license of a woman who looked close enough to Elizabeth. We headed East by train and weren't followed.

Elizabeth and I did what we could to repair the damage done, helping each other over months and years. We tried to forget, though that was impossible. The nightmares came, and we held onto each other until they faded. A ringing phone would make us jump. We couldn't watch television—all the sound and fury from the idiot box, the death and destruction that occurred around the world every day reminded us of how mad the whole world was. Not a corner of it was sane; there was madness everywhere. It would always exist, so we needed to escape from it for a long time.

We both left our jobs, saying we didn't feel right going back to a normal life. Normality felt like an insult after what we had been through. Plus, we still didn't feel entirely safe in our part of the world. If the family was everywhere, then we'd never feel safe staying anywhere. We could only lie low and hope that we could remain invisible.

We told no one about the family. Everyone everywhere was a potential family member. They had terrified us into silence.

# ROB BLISS

We pooled our money, packed a single bag each, and got on a plane for Fiji. I proposed to her, my true bride, and we had a small ceremony on the beach. Outdoors, watching the sunset, sipping champagne with the preacher who married us and the hotel concierge who acted as a witness. Then they left us alone and we enjoyed our honeymoon in paradise.

A wedding as far removed as the one we had witnessed (or been in) before. Perfect.

We stayed in Fiji. Found a small place to live. I worked teaching preschool kids. Elizabeth worked as a waitress in a bar. We didn't need, or want, much money. We were in Eden—money was useless.

Soon, Elizabeth was pregnant. We were having a baby boy. We named him Gordon.

He was a month and a half premature, a tiny red bundle clinging to life in an incubator. We adored him and knew he'd grow strong and be the center of our lives.

The hospital staff said that the tiny nubbin of a tail was just an evolutionary throwback and was nothing we should worry about. It would either fall off as the baby grew, or quick surgery could easily cut it off. Best to do such surgery when he was still a baby, since kids healed so quickly.

We watched the tail grow over the first few months of our son's life. And patiently waited for it to fall off.

ROB BLISS was born in Canada in 1969. He has lived an horrific comedy of a life.

He watched half of his family die before he reached the age of twenty, with the other half absent. He is very familiar with coffins and graves, funerals and unholy weddings. He has held dozens of mindless jobs such as eating-while-driving courier, chain-smoking catering delivery driver, oyster boy, burned burger flipper, sleepy grass cutter, accident-prone car parker, illiterate baker's assistant, idiot construction worker, truth-telling salesman, lazy security guard, acrophobic roof cleaner, and many others. He hates work (except for writing) and always will.

He has an honours degree in English and Writing from York University, Canada. He has 100 stories published in almost 30 magazines, plus three anthologies. He is the winner of *SNM Magazine's* Author of the Year for 2013. He has read thousands of books in all genres and is never without a book by his nightstand.

His favourite horror authors are Edgar Allan Poe, Ann Radcliffe, Brian Lumley, Bryan Smith and Edward Lee.

Website: robbliss.flazio.com

Facebook: https://www.facebook.com/rob.bliss.779

Twitter: https://twitter.com/BlissRob

*I AM A STAR. I'VE FINALLY FOUND THE YELLOW BRICK ROAD TO FAME. I COULD TEACH ANYONE. AS LONG AS THEY ARE WILLING TO DIE FOR IT.*
— SAM-I-AM

# CUT

## ROB BLISS

A bomb goes off in Buffalo, N.Y. That same day FBI agent, Daryll Peltier, receives the first of many correspondences from a serial killer calling themselves, Sam-I-Am.

The gruesome torture and murders of the killer's victims are filmed and broadcast on live television. Creating a puzzling masterpiece of blood and torture which the FBI can't unravel.

Daryll and her partner, Frank Zepano, began a hunt for the killer across the continental United States and into the Caribbean. The hunt involves cryptic messages, a strange and powerful cult, an unstoppable nano virus, the International Space Station, a trailer park psychic, a tabloid newspaper journalist, a computer hacker, the Oscars...and a body count of one victim per state.

## AVAILABLE IN
## TRADE PAPERBACK & EBOOK
### NECROPUBLICATIONS.COM

Made in the USA
Coppell, TX
26 October 2020